In Praise of Magdalene's Well

"This story of Mary Magdalene and Jeshua helps to reunite the feminine and masculine aspects of the Great Mystery, long recognized by indigenous people. We are inspired to reclaim the Divine Feminine in each of us as we seek to balance Mother Earth and ourselves. I believe the Magdalene tradition will usher in the Aquarian Age."

Rainbow Eagle, author of "The Universal Peace Shield of Truths: "Ancient American Indian Peace Shield Teachings" and "Native American Spirituality: A Walk in the Woods"

"This story is pure enchantment. I read it with wonder and emotional intensity. Yes, it contains much sadness but ultimately it is a story of love. And what else could one write about Jesus the Christ? As I read this, my relationship with Jesus grew even deeper along with my commitment to him and his teachings."

Linda Porter, author of "Angels, Beings of Light"

Magdalene's Well

By Saga-Rhose

This book is dedicated to every woman and man who have ever felt the pain of the wounded feminine. This negation is a result of the inability of humanity as a species to recognize the importance of the equality of both their feminine and masculine aspects, the negative and the positive, the yin and the yang. It is in the healing of this very phenomenon that we will finally find the illusive Peace.

Copyright © 2004 by Saga-Rhose

ISBN 0-7414-1980-7

Digital art by Saga-Rose after John William Waterhouse

Published by:

PUBLISHING.COM

1094 New Dehaven Street
Suite 100
West Conshohocken, PA 19428-2713
Info@buybooksontheweb.com
www.buybooksontheweb.com
Toll-free (877) BUY BOOK
Local Phone (610) 941-9999
Fax (610) 941-9959

Printed in the United States of America

Printed on Recycled Paper

Published May 2004

Acknowledgements

Our Guardians, the ten beings who work so closely with us on this mission, will always have our love and great appreciation. Thank you, Gs.

We offer sincere thanks to the numerous friends and readers of the Guardian material. They have trusted the voice that comes through us and their confirmations have helped us *stay with it* in this mission of balancing the masculine and the feminine energies. There have been many times of doubt and many more times of confirmation from these seekers. Without the authentications of those who have received the poetic or chronicle readings, we may never have continued until we ultimately listened to our beloved Mary of Magdalene, MiryAmah to us, tell her miraculous life story.

There are those who were especially helpful in their own unique way and we wish to give them special thanks.

Betty Ross, our cherished editor and a sincere fundamentalist Christian, put her religious beliefs aside and expertly edited the first draft out of love for her friend, Saga. We sincerely thank you. Your unconditional love is your greatest gift and we appreciate you so much.

Linda Porter, author of *Angels: Beings of Light • The Wisdom and Teachings of God's Messengers on Earth,* and heart-tied friend to Rhose, thank you for your never-ending encouragement. Linda has acted as therapist, friend and consultant in this dual effort. Such a shining example you are.

Hazel Crosbie, our friend and long time advocate of those seeking spiritual guidance and our connection to His Holiness, the Dalai Lama, read every word of the first raw draft of the book, typos and all. That was no easy task and we appreciate her support and encouragement as she looked past the technology and into the heart of the story. *Listening* as we do and typing to keep up with the words and the mental movie results in a very rough draft. Sometimes to have a friend *just believe in you* is what counts the most. Thanks for believing in our common mission and us.

We send a heartfelt thanks to Roger Miles and Suzanne Stallard, publishers of *Way of the Heart, Elohim Quarterly* and Tom Huber. Tom is a regular reader of Guardian Teachings and met Roger on a return flight from vacation. He did a great marketing presentation for us and earned an audience with Roger. Roger and Suzanne have included our material in the journal on a regular basis and given us the courage to move on with our work. From the beginning of our communication with Roger, he assured us that our messages rang true for him.

Thank you to La'a of The Awareness Press at Journey Into Soul for her continued support, including the promotion of our work in her own presentations. Her work and her encouragement are blessings beyond words.

Last but not least, many thanks to our families, who do not totally understand our work, but nevertheless did not create insurmountable roadblocks. The roadblocks they did create provided us with the learning opportunities and the discovery that we did, indeed, have the energy and dedication to finish this project. You have all been the proving ground that unconditional love works. Ken, thank you for your left-brained scrutinization of every business venture we consider. We love you all and cannot thank you enough.

Contents

Preface

This book is more magical than fiction. In 1997 Saga made an attempt to communicate with her angels via the keyboard. In no time she was peeling poetry-readings off her printer like the skins of an onion, multi-layered and capable of evoking great tears. I, Rhose, oddly enough, was incredibly excited at this phenomenon because there was a part of me that had been waiting for *something,* some magical element to fall into place that was to propel us into our *real work.* The poetry had the same rhythm and verbiage as the verses I spent hours transcribing, as a young girl in the sixties. I would only listen and the *musical words* were already there. Other than adjusting a word or two for the sake of the rhythm, the message and rhyme just flowed. The poems were always about Peace, or Utopia, or whatever message a child of the sixties might have. Saga's readings had the same messages, although in much greater detail and depth, and they came about the same way, but they were somehow encrypted for the reader, some secret bit of coding that told the reader that the message was truly real and from a place that could know the secrets of their hearts.

Saga had to be convinced and encouraged at times, since the material she brought through was heretofore unknown to us. The fear that it might be just imagination is always at the back of her mind. As for me, I have seen too many amazing confirmations to be concerned. I talk big when the material comes through Saga, but when it comes through me, the roles reverse in completeness and I become the one in need of proof and she becomes the convincer and encourager. Saga does most of the *bringing through* of the material, while I converse with our guides, who are known to us and our many loyal readers as the Guardians, and with Mary Magdalene, who oversees our Guardian group.

Thus far our work has taken us on a journey we longed for but only dreamed of until the day Saga first heard the voices. During my onslaught of questions, to a seemingly bottomless well of information, our Guardians began to send out an inspirational message for the day, via the Internet. In sharing that message we amassed quite the list of e-mail subscribers.

After a years worth of daily inspiration, we offered a monthly teaching. The topics varied but the messages of *Finding the Joy* and *Unconditional Love* always prevailed. After two years of Teachings, our monthly transmissions have taken on a new format. Readers are invited to ask the Guardians whatever is on their mind and some are answered publicly, in an Ann Landers-type layout. Since most issues are universal, we can all benefit from the experiences of others.

Saga does some of her best communication for us while driving, which can be a bit disconcerting for me. I imagine that is just proof that we *do* have those guardian friends watching out for us. On one such day, as we searched for the perfect name for a book shop and café that we hoped would manifest in our area, she announced with some mysterious conviction, *Magdalene's Well*. I *knew* when I head the words that this was no accidental title. Something was trying to come through. We were already familiar with the tinkling voice calling herself MiryAmah, and we knew well that she was the one known in *his-story* as Mary Magdalene. She then told us that she would like to tell us her story, a song of her life that comes from her heartstrings.

One of the most amazing things about the origins of this book is that this story unfolded in less than three months. At a rate of about three installments a week, and in a time frame of less than an hour each time, MM, as we came to call her, would pick up exactly where she left off the time previous, this time answering all the questions I bombarded her with regarding the last installment, and then carry on with the next portion of her soul song.

When this moving tale found its end, she instructed me to shape it so that it would be easily understood. As I would read the words she gave us, I could hear her read them to me. At times the information had become turned around or the timing was off, and I would feel as if someone put me on pause. Then, I would hear her try to explain the concept so that it could be more readily translated. One of the really amazing things about this story is that Saga not only heard it but she SAW it as it came through. Acting as a conduit for this story activated all her senses and some chapters were quite painful, so she would have to gather strength before we could move to the next step.

We did not incorporate into the story all the information gleaned from MM during my insatiable questioning but instead chose to stay with the original information. A couple chapters were included, however, from the additional information she supplied. I asked about the physical characteristics of she and Jesus and about the casting out of her seven demons. I included her answers in this narrative, but where to put them as far as a time frame is strictly a guess on my part.

Whether this version of her story is true or not, we will perhaps never know for sure. More importantly, does it matter? Hearing the story from the woman's point of view is long overdue. She offers concepts long forgotten that could unquestionably be of benefit to our modern day world. By mere suggestion of the word itself, History is indeed his story, and leaves half of the whole hiding somewhere in the ethers. The woman whose character and reputation have been smeared with mud by a male-dominated religion certainly deserves a chance to speak for herself. Ironically, after all is said and done, I, who have always been skeptical of organized religion, now see an institution worth saving.

Magdalene's Well of Remembrance

I begin at the well, for that was the real beginning, when I finally gazed upon the one I knew I would find. The moment when our eyes met was the beginning of the mission and the beginning of our joy and sorrow.

Once we saw and *knew* each other, we immediately fell into a routine of being together as much as possible. I still had the sisters to learn and work with, as he had the brothers to do likewise. Your tradition of calling men within the church brothers and the women of the fold sisters is an old custom, you see, and even we referred to our followers as such. We knew that we were destined to lead, but we also knew that we were not above or beyond anyone in importance and still had much to learn as well.

We didn't say much that first day, upon that first glimpse in that lifetime, but somehow we instinctively *knew* when the other would be at the well and we timed our coming and going so that we would see each other. I had heard of this man and felt compelled to meet him thusly. You have no idea how wonderful it felt just to look into his eyes. Words were not needed. We just left together that day and stayed together until the tragic end of the first phase of our mission.

The cross was a future *probability,* but not unchangeable. We wanted so badly to shift attitudinal concepts within consciousness so that the feminine and masculine could feel the joy of a loving, respectful balance. Even within the brotherhood there was an enormous tilting of the axis of balance as they pushed the sisters further and further away. We will talk further of this later in my story. For now we speak of the well and the place where recognition and reunion took place.

Once we left together, we naturally shared our time with our groups, the brothers and the sisters. The attitudes had long made a division and women usually grouped to do their womanly duties, while men, who were by now believing that they were the most important group, would not tolerate women attending their sessions.

Slowly we integrated each other within the groups, and eventually integrated the groups as well, so that when Jesus and I walked about and talked to the masses the crowd would mingle and not split according to gender.

The Apostles (the men) found this quite uncomfortable because the fear of the feminine was deeply ingrained. They would complain about this mixing, saying the women distracted them and they could not concentrate on the important issues up for discussion.

The Disciples (the women) had their own demons to conquer. Both Jesus and myself had an inner group of twelve, making us the thirteenth member. This was the perfect number for the inner group, but we both had many apostles and disciples among the masses. To be such just meant that you were working for the cause. In our case, the cause was to bring the balance of energy back through masculine and feminine expression.

The Divine Marriage was, of course, demonstrated between Jesus and myself. We were to be an example of how to merge (marry) the two integrating energies created by the Source, The Divine Creator, so that all creation could again integrate with this mighty Divinity. Growth is necessary in all physicality and in and of all places of experience. The merging of the divine energies (masculine and feminine) facilitates growth to the point that the brilliance of the light of experience grows and glows and rides the singing trail back to the Divine, where, when all have found their way home again, will one day go out on another great mission.

The love Jesus and I felt for each other was evident and not kept secret. We walked hand in hand and lightly touched each other in public, always in gentle, appropriate ways of demonstrating affection. For instance, Jesus would take a strand of my hair and tenderly move it back into place among the other strands and tell it that he loved it and every other fiber of my being. There were those who thought this was obscene. This was a jealous reaction, for Jesus was and still is quite compelling and charismatic, and everyone wanted to be his best friend. I had a little trouble with that because attitudes had deteriorated to the point that to be a best friend with a woman was seen as lowering oneself. Yet Jesus made no qualms about the fact that we were best friends, and he never once made me feel left out of his world as we worked upon our mission.

We soon realized that the greatest threat to our work would be the way we wanted to work side-by-side, openly loving and cooperating and with the same goal. Little by little the brothers pushed us apart as they constantly reminded Jesus that this was not acceptable and would, in their minds, compromise the mission. We may have had a common divine mission, as do all of you, but we were still fully human, as you are in this physical go around you now experience. We had moments of doubt and times of depression. That was the beauty of both of us working together, one could keep the other stable and rekindle the hope.

My training had been in intuition and connection to the unseen but known. Jesus was trained in sensitivity to physicality. We were to be as two pillars holding up the mission, both equally a part of the process. My unseen guides were more supportive than the Apostles that bombarded Jesus, and doubt and worry set in. Not that Jesus didn't hear and acknowledge his unseen guides in all of this, for he did. What I am saying is that he was more confused and concerned about those physical voices because they were coming from that which he had been trained to listen to.

The story of working through all of this will be long and it could conflict with your present recorded history, for as I have many times said, history is only half the past experience. It is *his* story and not *her* story.

My work actually began long before the time of Mary of Magdalene but the truth of that emergence and childhood may be of interest to you. My lifetime was full of meaningful events. Yes, I think I will begin with the story of my early childhood, yet this may seem too magical and mystical for many readers. Nevertheless I reminisce. I do remember quite vividly though, we met at the well and knew each other instantly!

Blessed be,

The Magical Mystical Emergence

My coming was expected, as was that of my beloved Jesus, but it was within the community of women, the followers of the Isis teachings, which the expectation and the planning for my emergence occurred. Every last detail was planned and it was imperative that this child emerge from a loving, free willed union. For that reason, until the last minute, no one knew exactly who my parents would be; but I knew. Just as there are things you need not know that would confuse your physical experience, (*life*) and your discovery journey, those awaiting and expecting my arrival had to discover the truth of my coming.

My mother's name was different for me, for I had a soul name that I used for myself from my first speaking, which came clearly and confidently at about three months of age. I only awaited the development of my vocal cords, for I knew from the beginning how to speak and understood language in any form.

I came to a temple priestess and her gardener lover. From these two there came great love and affection without judgment. That was the factor I needed in order to emerge, total love and balance of masculine and feminine. Our beginning was divinely intimate, within the emergence temple, yet the temple was already a focus of controversy and had to go *underground,* as you might say, to a secret location. Once my mother knew of my coming, as with all the priestesses, there was great celebration and preparation. My father was part of the entire process and the birthing procedure was much like your Lamaze procedure, with the father playing his part.

It was evident soon after the news of my growth within my beautiful mother, Rose, that when she and my father were together there beamed a brilliant glow around them. The *knowing* came to all who perceived the expectant couple and preparation for my birth and my great mission began. They too knew that I would suffer and all of my sisters prayed for me even before I moved from pure soul experience into the physical.

At my emergence from within the birthing temple, there was great expectation and beautiful music. Wonderful smells and loving hands received me into this world. I immediately became a beloved one to all within the temple and was protected to the point that no one outside was told of my existence.

I needed to have growing experience outside the secret safety of the temple though, and soon told my sisters, when I was not yet a year old, that I would need to live within the community of my mission. I voiced it as, "let me be where I need to be to do my work."

It was arranged that my gardener father would be granted a traditional marriage to my beloved mother, then we would move to a village called Magdalene, chosen for the vibrational coordinates. I grew and thrived in a loving home. I was beautifully dark and sensually aware of my effect on those who looked upon me. My father was darker of complexion than my mother, for he came from a region where this pigmentation was the norm and the way of survival. They loved my blend of pigment, for they said I had a *glow* that integrated all beauty of being.

I was schooled, unlike most little girls then, in the ways of the world. I was also told that the Great Goddess would bring a true love to me and that together we would change the world. I was told that this was an enormous attempt and that I might suffer much in this mission, but even then I knew that I had come to do so if necessary. As a reflective child I would visualize my beloved Jesus and I dreamed of him often, yet I knew not his name. As a child of the priestess community I was encouraged to move about within my dreams and explore the images and messages sent through them.

Later in this life experience, when I first saw my beloved at the well, I instantly knew him as he knew me. I knew that my love was deep and total beyond measure and I believe he felt the same. Our childhoods were very similar in that we had loving parents and much training. He had traveled to the land now called India for his training at about eight or nine years of age. I had been sent to a secret land deep within the mists, which I cannot translate nor really locate for you. It was part of the plan, you see, that Jesus would work with those masters in physicality that would sensitize him to the bridge between the ethereal and the physical, and I would work the opposite way so that I could balance the effort of the mission.

Neither Jesus, whose parents were humble and without privilege, nor myself, who did have parents of some wealth and circumstance, had any physical problems. We were beautiful children, but not too beautiful so as to attract undue attention. We did not have physical deformities or what some might term as unattractive physical make-up because we were supposed to have total attention on our mission with no problems of self-esteem. We were not full of ourselves, but we were not ashamed either. We were comfortable in our own skin, as you sometimes hear people say.

It might seem that we were lucky to have loving parents and a secure childhood, but when you think of what was yet to come, our burdens would be tremendous. Our early circumstances were such to give us strength of body and character for the mission.

I remember as a little girl when I lived in the land of the mists, the great priestesses and priests, the sagas and sages who amazed me constantly as they demonstrated my training as delightful fairy tale-like stories in which I was physically active and involved. I rescued many a lost elf or magical animal back then and felt the self-satisfaction of knowing I had solved the mystery correctly and played the game the way I was being led to do. I was learning to listen to my guides and guardians, you see. That is a major talent within the feminine, this reception or sensitivity to the other worlds unseen.

At the secret emergence temple, from my birth celebration to my confirmation, I was nurtured by all the priestesses and by my mother especially, of course. In the old days, I was told, the temple was at the center of the communities, but now, because of those who sought to stop the practice of training in love-mating and child-rearing, because it was counter productive to their agenda of control and fear, our temple was in a secret location.

It was located deep within a wooded area that would seem as an oasis in the desert-like dry region that was the usual fare. This wooded area was within a mountain valley and was shielded by an optical illusionary entrance that looked much like just more mountain terrain, but a passageway was there for those who knew the way.

This passageway, I would later learn, was very dangerous and only those who knew exactly which step to take could successfully go either inside to the temple environment in the woods or without into the dry arid area of the outer world. Our little paradise was the result of several natural mountain streams that mixed with hot springs originating from a volcanic source. The resulting steam, mixed with the arid air, created this hidden oasis. It is hidden to this day and still the temple lies therein.

The temple is only tended by keepers now and not the priestesses, as before. The keepers are women who see that the eternal flame remains alight. They cannot practice too much the old ways since there is no masculine counterpart willing to fulfill that role, thus the priestess cannot practice sacred sexuality and cannot bring the babes up within the compound as before.

Many of the keepers are well into the crone years, with a few over one hundred fifty years old, so childbearing is long past for them. Their energy is now directed to keeping the wisdom, the sacred duty of the crone. There are still those younger initiates who go without, as they call the outer world, to become impregnated, but not many, for fear of revealing the sacred temple. It is one of the few remaining, you see, and for now, until the time is right, they must be *kept* by the keepers and ready to be of use once again.

You might wonder where these women come from? They are rescued. Little girls abused or women battered who call forth to the Great Mother, if their lesson is done in their area of experience, may be selected by the wise ones who can monitor the grief of the feminine and hear the cry of those ready to move into sacred service. They sometimes bring their children, for as we said, children are sometimes rescued. For the most part girl babes, but if a boy is in danger because of his sensitivity to his feminine side, he may be rescued as well. We have brothers here too, but that is another story.

But I wander here. I was a happy little girl in this place of wonder and support. I was always told of my importance and beauty. I was not told my entire mission until I was about five years old, but because I was so aware from such an early age, the telling was just a confirmation. The Catholic practice of confirmation is similar to this event, I believe, in that I knew my purpose but needed it officially confirmed.

My confirmation was an enchanting event. The priestesses and the sisters (other young ones in training) celebrated much as in the

Hawaiian tradition, with dancing and feasting and even hanging flowers around my neck. The High Priestess spoke of my mission and how I was to be sent into the outer, the world beyond the secret temples, to bring awareness and respect back to the Great Mother. She told my sisters that I would suffer much, no doubt, because of the total disrespect and contempt for the feminine in the minds of so many. She warned that the mission might seem to fail but that it would be like the seed of a mighty and powerful flower that would bloom one day if the seed were planted in the proper place.

I was so proud to be chosen, yet so afraid, because I knew that this would be quite difficult. The one thing that kept me going was the reference to being pulled to my counterpart, my beloved, like a flower's essence pulls the bee. I knew I had this great event to look forward to and that I would not walk alone in this mission. When she blessed me with a kiss on my forehead, the priestess' way of blessing, I saw her cry for the first time. She had tears of sorrow and joy all mixed together. Each child had a day of confirmation, but I had never seen this look before in her eyes. I knew we were heart-tied in a strange and wonderful way, through many lifetimes of experience together. I cried too.

The next morning I awoke to a caravan of women who would serve with me. No one served another, as a slave would tend someone, instead, we served together with all knowing their part in the mission. No one was more revered than another. All were equally important to the mission. They would take me to the place of my teachers, within the mists.

We traveled through a tunnel that went deep underground. We were escorted by little beings that did not look physically like us. They had short legs and long bodies with large heads and they made me laugh because they were always clowning around and liked to play tricks on each other. They were the beings of the underground, of the middle place, and they guarded the inner passages.

We emerged in a forest area after days and days in the underground passages. A mysterious luminosity kept the tunnels alight. The little ones could somehow control this light source and even bring it to brilliance as we progressed further into hidden pathways of Mother Earth. They walked beside us and prepared food for us twice a day, at the beginning and at the end. I measured a day only by the stopping and the starting. It might not have been actual day or night, I could not tell since we were in underground tunnels.

The forest area where we surfaced was a much cooler environment, a place much like the oasis of our home. The exit was through a huge tree and the cave opening was located at the base of the tree that was interwoven into the mountainside so tightly that one could not see the secret entrance. The tree, alive and aware, controlled the portal and changed itself to open the doorway to the forest when the little ones told it to allow us to pass. It was so magical that I, as a child, was delighted and thanked the tree for its great service to those on the pathway.

We rode horses along a path that was concealed under fern-like plants, quite hidden from those not intended to see the trail. A white doe (deer) was sent to lead us. I did not know that some of those who would be my teachers could shape-shift, and this doe was one I would grow to love and learn much from.

The forest ended at a fog-covered lake. We dismounted our horses, thanked them for taking us to this place and gave them the choice of joining us on the misty island or having a time of freedom in the forest. Most chose to swim alongside the boats into which we loaded first our gear and then ourselves for this journey, but a couple told us that they would like to taste the freedom of the forest for now and gleefully romped off into the trees with our blessings. Your story of Dr. Doolittle is not so far-fetched and for those with a certain awareness, talking and listening to the animals is quite possible.

I will never forget how it felt to float quietly within that ornate boat to the shores of the misty island. The boat had no oars or visible means of propelling it, but it moved ahead as if magically pulled on an invisible cord. It looked somewhat like a Viking vessel but the symbols carved on the sides and the curvy points in front and back were definitely Goddess Images. They symbolized fertility and the circle of life as drawn in a never-ending cycle, much like your infinity sign, you see, one cycle ends and another begins. I remember the horses snorting water from their noses and paddling through the lake as they swam alongside the boat, with just their long necks and heads above the water. They reminded me of sea serpents and were my idea of what a sea horse must look like. Of course later in my lessons I would learn differently.

When we arrived upon the shore, the horses, one by one, emerged and shook off the water with great twists and much gyration. Then they rolled in the sand of the sacred beach in glee. As I was watching and reading their thoughts of joy, down a path came the most beautiful elder woman I had ever seen. She had long hair of purest white, a wrinkled face, and a smile that beamed kindness and wisdom. She was truly a striking vision to behold. She walked up to me and said, "We have been waiting for you, little one. Come join your sisters to prepare for service to the Divine Mother. You are beloved beyond measure by all that is good and sweet. Remember that, little one, every day of your life, no matter where you go or grow, because it is your truth."

Blessed be,

Entering the Mists

The mists of Avalon are the same place as my new home and school, so the similarity you sense is real. This place has manifested in several locations, two of which were in your European area, near the British Isles and off the coast of France. But that is not as important as what kind of places the misty isles were, for they were magical and spiritually charged, for certes.

As the Mother (High Priestess) led my companions and I through the winding paths leading from the water's edge, I felt the difference in this place of mists. It seemed super-charged with energy, but this energy was not of the type that would speed you up and create tension, rather the type that eased your being and soothed you. I noticed the trees seemed more alive and more colorful than any I had ever seen. The Mother, as she lead us through the pathways, would speak to some of the trees and I would see them shiver and leaves would rustle like a small wind had moved them, yet there was no breeze.

We walked in silence until we came to a cave opening that was covered with ferns. We entered there and walked through a natural cavern tunnel until we arrived at a massive wooden door with a crystal embedded in the middle, at eye level. The Mother-Priestess looked into this crystal and the door opened. Inside there was a beautiful court area open to the sky, and surrounding it were window openings in the natural rock. I could see women of all ages watching and waving. The silence ceased and the sisters waved and greeted us with "Welcome home, child." There were some young men and boys in attendance also, and they looked quite happy to be within the compound, but for the most part it was a place of women.

A pretty young girl of about ten years old came to meet me. I had no idea that she was really in her sixties and one of the *Eternal Children.* An eternal child never grows past the pre-puberty stage. They agree to accomplish their mission by being a child of wonder and vulnerability until they exit their physical experience. The tale of Peter Pan illustrates this concept in a story-telling way. Eternal children are rare now. It is just too difficult for them to stay child-like and in a child state when the parents are geared for their growth and maturity. If they do not grow properly they are taken to doctors who manipulate their natural state through drugs and even surgery. They were much more accepted in times past.

The Mother-Priestess introduced me to this eternal child, my life-long friend, Lieta. She was as light as I was dark, with soft blond hair and incredible blue eyes. She took my hand and led me to my new chamber-home. We would share an area since it was known that I would be lonely at first. Later I could choose to live alone if that suited me.

Within the chamber were two child-sized beds that were made of carved wood. The carvings were of animals, little people and what you would term fairy people (the little flying type) and many circular symbols. They were perfect for the imagination of a child. The beds were like little houses with curtains at the side that could be pulled for privacy.

Crystals were imbedded within the carvings, usually in the eyes of the creatures depicted or the centers of the circles. But one huge crystal was embedded within a circular table near the middle of this cave room, for all dwellings were inside the rock, with windows and balconies naturally carved in the side of the cliff. This table was child-sized and the crystal was so clear that one might think it a sphere of ice, for it was round and smooth and rose above the surface of the table like a jewel. It was at this table that I could visit my mother and keep the mother-daughter tie strong or visit any place I should desire. I would be trained to use this visionary tool wisely for to see too much is as dangerous as to see too little. We used the table much as anyone in a home would, as the heart of the home and a place to do many things. Lieta and I played fascinating games there and I studied my texts and *examples to learn* also there at the heart-table.

The purpose of the crystals was for communication in that those entering crystallized portals would have to have a blended vibration to open the door. They used their eyes to look at the crystal and they communicated, or emitted the proper frequency to activate the safety mechanism. Other crystals were used as *scrrying* devices, a reflective surface used as a gazing ball of sorts, to visualize other places and times.

There were several cats present and Lieta told me that they were friends who helped in the energy work. I loved animals and accepted their presence and loved to play with the kittens. I eventually learned to talk to them and they were a funny lot, sometimes wise and sometimes so *catty* in that they would quarrel and complain about each other to the point of slapping one another. I often wondered how they could be so aware and then be so nasty and moody. Lessons would come later and I would understand what they reflected in such behavior and also understand the way they transformed energy, lowering the vibration for those entering the outer.

Now all this seems unreal and magical, but remember, I entered such a world so that I would be grounded in the unseen, the power and the reality of what some would call *unreality*. There are so many more experiential opportunities than you can ever imagine. Your fairy tales, stories called fictional, are kept for your sake in the realm of this so-called *unreality* to keep from boggling your minds. This is necessary, for to know everything for sure means discovery loses its power. It also does not help you develop sensitivity and creativity for these are a discovery process. So my story may seem as a fairy tale and that is fine. It was such to me, the child full of imagination. Imagination is creation and developing this aspect of an individual is vitally important to evolvement.

I met everyone else at dinnertime. The sisters and the brothers there all helped in some manner or another, in total cooperation, in serving the meal. The meal usually consisted of fruits, vegetables, eggs, and sometimes meat if an animal met an accidental death. If this happened, the ritual of eating the meat of the animal would send its energy through us and into the Onement. We always blessed every bite we took, but silently and automatically, for even the cabbage had given itself and its energy to us and we acknowledged the merging and the offering. One makes an offering of self in true sacrifice. True sacrifice is never the taking of one through victimization.

Even though the meals were sacred, they were still fun and there was much laughter and merriment. There was also much serious talk of how we would integrate with the masses and bring about the balance of the Sacred Feminine and the Divine Masculine.

Soon I would meet my teachers.

Blessed be,

Preparation for School on the Misty Isle

After settling in my room Leita showed me around the places I would be visiting during my apprentice years on the Misty Island. We located the kitchen first, since every child wants to know where to find the cookie jar. We then visited classes already in session. The other students were always involved in some project or other. They were never sitting and taking notes or just listening. They were *doing* and totally absorbed.

I was then shown the living quarters of the High Priestess, who welcomed me like a long lost friend. She did not talk to me as an adult addressing a mere child. She spoke to me as if we had been friends for eons of time, and later I would realize that was truth. I visited the chambers of the other priestess instructors and the place of the men priests and the few young boy students. You could sense the shift in energy as you entered there. It was different, yet still comfortable and welcoming.

I was then given my leave to wander the island itself. A squawking raven swooped down and lit on my shoulder, and to my surprise announced that she would show me around, not to worry. I pretty much went where I pleased with Raven telling me to take caution when I headed toward a cliff drop-off or other such precarious places. The most important thing I remember was that *no one told me what I must do*.

The next day I would begin attending classes if I felt I was ready. Leita and I spent the evening in our quarters planning my next step. It was decided that I would begin with a class in imagination. "Everything begins with visualizing" Leita said, and that was imagination.

Blessed Be,

Imagination

Imagination was a good choice for a starting point, and Leita did well in advisement without pressuring me to conform to such advice. It was solely my own choosing, through my own intuition.

Leita would always go with me to my first day of classes since the other students would be involved already, having joined the class at various times. She would introduce me to the others, including the master teacher, and leave when she felt I was integrated within the group both to her and my own satisfaction. She was so very protective. It always amazed me that the teacher could conduct a learning session and have so many people at different levels of mastery.

My teacher was elfin-like in that she was small of stature, almost as small as Leita, but not an eternal child-soul. She was magical and just to be in her presence made us students happy. She seemed like a mystical playmate that only a child could imagine. She was a wise one, without a doubt. She wove important lessons within our play and we thoroughly enjoyed the experience.

We would learn that all creation, our very existence, was the result of imagination when the Great Source imagined all beings and created, in the beginning--the sparklers--and then the Great Mother Divine birthed us into experiencing and discovering who we were and from whence we came. We saw this lesson visually upon the ceiling of the cave room we occupied. I will never forget the beauty of the Source Light as it was portrayed; the colors were beyond my imagination. There we witnessed a panoramic view of the imaginative action and reaction, all those sparkling soul-lights dancing and vibrating within the void, which was suddenly full of life. All were different colors and no two were exactly alike, yet all were part of the Source. We all found our light immediately and saw how it all began for us, and we saw that we were all beautiful beyond words.

We enjoyed lessons in this class like no other. We practiced manifestation through imagination of the one, in which each one of us would bring something into our moment through imagining within our being. This was done by being aware of the energy centers you call chakras, but which we called *portals within*, for each portal was an energized spinning doorway. They are like the spinning doors you have on some of your business establishments. The imaginative thought would travel up through the physical body, spin within the portal, then move on until it shot off the top of our heads like a tornado and manifestation would occur depending on the strength of the intention. We had fun with this one, laughing and feeling the energy move through us. It felt wonderful to be alive and have that tingle move through our bodies.

The younger students, like myself, were content to manifest things that delighted us, such as bunny rabbits, flowers, sweet food and such. It took many weeks to accomplish this result, but the older students, who were thinking at a higher level and manifesting light, protection grids, and invisibility techniques, encouraged us. Of course our teacher, who never really had one name, (we had to imagine a perfect name for her from our own perspective, I called her *Firefly* because she glowed) would weave in lessons about how one must not manifest just to amuse or to amaze because it could do terrible harm to self and others within the experience. She taught us, ever so subtly, that imagination was, in fact, creation, and you are responsible for what you create. That was the first Universal Law I learned. We absorbed that lesson well, often by creating little monsters that we thought would be fun to play with. They were not so much fun, however, and Firefly would have to step in about the time we were terrorized to hysteria. That knowing of how far to let the lesson go before she ran interference showed her great wisdom, for often a child is denied the learning experience because someone protectively jumps in too soon for the lesson to be assimilated.

When we had learned how to create through imagination as individuals, then we were given the lesson of group consciousness, or group imaginative creation. The first time I entered that lesson I witnessed what you might call *a rude awakening* because I had thoughts of blue flowers in a crystal vase, for I loved blue flowers, but the majority had other images in mind. The prevailing image was a giant cauldron made of shiny bronze. As it manifested in our midst I felt like I had not contributed to the creation of this group, as though I was not one with them and I felt the first pangs of great disappointment. Then I raised myself up on my tiptoes and looked within the giant bowl and there, lying in the bottom, was a single blue flower. I knew then that individuals made a difference in a group, but I also learned that the group idea would manifest in the most powerful manner.

All this creation was wonderful. Next we began working on thoughts that would benefit the whole. We concentrated on what was good for everyone. Certainly, a giant bronze bowl was not good for everyone and not practically useful and a blue flower was a cheerful messenger, but having this ability, what could we do to benefit all those in physical experience, including the animal, vegetable, and mineral kingdoms and untold other beings experiencing in the same space and time? This was the essence of our lesson.

These imagination classes were great fun but also led us to deep thoughts about the responsibility of creation. When we were ready we would *know* that it was time to move on in our lessons to other classes. It was always emotional to leave what was familiar and comfortable, yet we knew we had to keep learning and growing in awareness, for we were those kind of souls especially chosen for the work. Another lesson; change is necessary for growth.

I left my beloved *Firefly* in my seventh year. Two of us graduated from that class the same day. I moved into a new phase of my training. Still my roommate and my closest friend, Leita and I discussed the next step that I would take in my priestess training.

The next class would be Divine Energy, the Life Force in Motion.

Blessed be,

Divine Energy

Graduating from a class was always a personal accomplishment in that students graduated when they were ready and not on a schedule. Some would stay longer to master the subject; some would stay only a short time. My stay in Imagination Class was about average, two years in your time cycles. I was given a wonderful send off to journey further into my priestess education. As I said before, it was a sweet-sad time for I had bonded with *Firefly* and the other students, as was always expected of classmates. Without such bonds the learning would never be complete.

As usual Leita took me to the first day of Energy Class. I had a Wizard teacher this time and he was truly an amazing sight. He seemed taller than anyone I had ever seen, certainly taller than my father and the men I knew from my early years. He stood about seven feet tall and had not one strand of hair on his head, not even eyebrows or eye lashes. His eyes sparkled as he shook my hand and I felt a pleasant tingle when his hand touched mine. Again, the student would name this master teacher, for his real name was a vibrational feeling, not a sound. Since our senses are limited in our physical bodies, the sound of his name was *unhearable* to us.

Also again, students were at various stages of learning and many were involved in experiments when I arrived. I remember seeing students standing in a circle, holding hands and their hair was standing up and waving in one direction then another as the students called the energy differently.

The most important aspect of this class I learned right away. Ra, as I came to call my teacher, gave me his undivided attention and told me how all beings are made of energy, which is the life force without which they would not exist. He told me that this life force was the reflection of the original Source and actually its echo, and thus part of it in an extended way. Then he talked of the dualities of this force as manifested in energy, the masculine and the feminine. At seven years of age I was already able to grasp such concepts, and realized that I had always felt the two energies within myself, but knew that I had chosen to express in the feminine just as my brothers had chosen to express in the masculine. Yet we always had both energies to draw upon, there within our beings pulsating and balancing our physical bodies, our thoughts and our actions. Ra emphasized that to be wholly present in any experience, both dualities must be balanced and active. He went on to tell us that the outer world, (life outside of the misty island we called the *outer*) was greatly out of balance because of the long held bias and jealousy between the genders. He tantalized us by telling us that we would learn more about the origin of this attitudinal corruption in our present/past/future class.

To illustrate how the energies must be equal to be at their *wholeness,* he had a student come forward and he chastised this girl to the point of tears. I was very concerned and aghast at this treatment because I had never seen such hatred in a man's eyes. He rebuked her by chastising, "Misty, come forward because I want the entire class to see what a sorry student you are. You just do not measure up. Possibly that is because you do not have the capacity to comprehend this material. You are not beautiful either, I might add. I can only imagine what kind of family you came from." Ra rolled his eyes and looked so mean. He went on to say, "I wish you were not in this class because you are not of the same quality as the other students." Misty was crushed.

Then he called me forward and complemented me on how wonderful and how naturally talented I was. The praise held no joy for me. He paired me with Misty (her nick name) and then he called forward two more students and praised them as well. All the time Misty stood quietly, looking defeated and beaten down. He then directed his assistant to take a giant beam and teamed us in twos to hold it up. The other team did well. The beam looked heavy but the two students were able to keep it horizontal by working together. When we were given the beam Misty collapsed. She had no energy, no strength. Then she got mad, either at herself or at Ra, I am not sure, and she rose with that beam from the floor and even held it higher than I was able, making it slant toward me. The assistant came to our rescue for I was beginning to feel the weight of this unbalanced object and was about to collapse myself.

Ra came to Misty in a flash and touched her on the top of her head and sent a light through her that was pinkish in color and said, "Forgive me, for this lesson was difficult and your pain has brought knowing to the entire class. I lied to you to provide you and the class the opportunity to see what happens when life force is negated. The energy becomes depleted and unable to meet its challenge. I will never lie to you again and I will never hurt you again but in the *outer* you will experience this again." He turned to the rest of us and said, "you all will, for that is the mission of those in this training, to bring the life-force energies back into balance through the heart center." When unbalanced, societies collapse. They lose hope and become corrupted to the point that they negate their own existence. The rise and fall of such groups will continue until the beam is balanced. The beam of the light of experience is like a giant lintel and it takes the duality to keep it level and in perfection. An unbalanced beam will always fall and destroy what breaks under its great burden."

Ra then came to each of us and laid his hand upon our heads and our auras became so bright that we looked like a room full of rainbows. "That is your life-force glowing," he said. "Respect it and love the light you reflect for that is your true gift to ALL THAT IS. Notice the differences in colors and vibration. See how each individual has a uniquely beautiful glow. Now I will touch you again and you will see the masculine and the feminine energies only this time with the masculine glowing blue and the feminine glowing red."

Each child had unique patterns but each had almost equal hues of color dancing and reflecting from their beings. We learned much about our selves as we observed our own glows, but we noticed that looking from the inside out was slightly different than from the outside in. The inversion was the reason that a being would know self from the heart out, where another being would perceive from the mind inward. The mind made up the outer layer of color, and the heart center, or the core of the essence was closest to the physical.

"When you go to the outer and enter your mission you will be able to attune to auras and to energy patterns once you have graduated from this class. You must keep this a secret or you will be persecuted due to fear, for those masses in the outer live and react out of fear and what they fear they destroy. You will notice darkness in some auras and some other affects, such as cracks, lightning-like flashes, and even holes with no color. This all has meaning and you will learn how to read such when you are among those with the effects. No one can tell you that a hole, for instance, means a wounded soul. It may and it may not. Each entity has a slightly different reaction to their outer experience. You will sense this. When you look at the duality you will see much blue, sometimes it will be a murky blue, but not much red, even in some women you will meet, will this be true. Blue without warming red is cold and lonely. It is your mission to bring more warmth into this outer place of experience. This mission may take many lifetimes to complete but it starts now for some of you, and for others this is your continued mission."

We also studied the energy vortexes within the body and the spinal pathway that directs the energy upward. There were small vortexes within the soles of our feet. We all stood barefoot upon a grassy meadow because this lesson connected to Mother Earth and to feeling the coolness and texture of the sweet wild grass. We moved about in all of our classes; we were never really confined to a classroom. We learned that there was another small vortex in the back of our knees. We also found similar vortexes in the palms of our hands and in the inside of our elbows. These energy-conducting places were connected to major portal energy vortexes that were doorways to other such places and guards of energy not yet ready for the next stage. These chakras were seven in the body and three beyond the physical. Energy would rise through Tara, the Mother Earth, and into our little feet (most were under age ten in this class.) We watched it rise in others and felt it ourselves. We were instructed to use our imaginations to see this energy at first but before long it was miraculously visible. The energy glowed and vibrated and just to think that Tara was responsible for all this life force movement was amazing to all of us. To amaze a student is to reach them in the most powerful way.

Ra explained that Tara blended her energy with all beings that shared her space and place, just as all beings exchange energy within this realm in constant merging and purging (for some energy is not compatible.) Energy could be corrupted however, Ra warned us, and we would have to recognize such negating vibrations and learn to block them and not let them merge with us. Evil, we learned, emitted anti-energy. This force of negation depletes the vibrancy and brilliancy of energy. The effect is different than darkness, which is the mystery waiting to be discovered. It is murky and stagnant and it is where corruption grows because there is no balance or brilliance to keep the purity. This murk of which I speak is not really a pure color, but itself a corruption of color. Darkness and whiteness are opposite ends of the color spectrum and pure in essence, one the mystery and the other the mastery.

In this class we learned about color and the wavelengths of each color vibration. We literally saw the long waves of the cool blue as Ra demonstrated how the color sounded and radiated. We likewise saw the short waves of red that were full of energy and warmth. We learned to hear the colors as well as feel and see them. We learned this out in the gardens and in the forest or along the sea. Our classroom was Mother Nature herself and we loved seeing, feeling and hearing color. What a symphony, what a visual delight this lesson, as we became more in tune with this aspect of existence. Seeing rainbows emit from Ra's crystal prism (he kept in the deep pockets of his long white robe) was astonishing. We all played with this prism and delighted in making rainbows and hearing the sounds of the colors blend. We learned that all colors of light merged became white, yet if we painted the colors, which we did by even making our own pigments, all colors merged and became murky and dark. Ra explained that this was because the painted colors were a reflection of light, not light in and of itself. Mixing the paint-pigment colors all together was to stop the reflection to the point that nothing reflected and the murkiness then became a total negation of color--thus murky and not a color at all, but a corruption of light.

I asked then why had I seen this very same color within the caves and in other areas upon Tara as I traveled. Was this a bad place, I wanted to know? Ra explained, "It is not a bad place but just a place where there has been an unproductive merging of energy. The natural mineral earth colors are rich brown, greens, reds and blacks. Stones are of various shades including all colors of the visual spectrum. If you were farming and you found soil of this color you would know that it needed something else to blend with it to become rich and productive. If you saw water like this you would know that it was fouled and unhealthy. You would not feel the vibration, nor hear the sound in this shade of murk. You would feel emptiness for it is lacking reflection of the Divine."

I spent another two years in this class and by the time I left it everyone glowed and hummed with a beautiful soul sound for I became aware of vibration and the essence it revealed. In the midst of these open, innocent and sweet beings, my classmates, and the other beings we experienced then, I felt energized and full of joy. I would graduate then to another class. The next would be about Compassion and Suffering.

Blessed Be,

COMPASSION AND SUFFERING

I was about nine years of age when I entered the compassion and suffering class. I knew when I met my teacher, a fragile looking elder woman with long white hair, that this class was not going to be as much fun as those previous. I was the youngest student, for this was a heavy subject and one that would be too disheartening for the very young ones. They needed to start out, as I did, with the magic and the fantastic aspects of life experience. This class was very subdued and serious, with not much child-like play. Our teacher had lived the subject and knew it well.

As with all the classes, I would name my teacher a name that suited our relationship and the spirit of the class. I drew a blank for some time for I could not bring my joy level down to the seriousness of this subject. Finally I realized that from my perspective, the name *Che* was best for this elder wise one for she was just that, *Che.* Che represented the feminine in her wisest years, she who stands back and watches, unnoticed, and quietly steps in when she is needed, thus *Che,* the invisible one.

Since most had already accomplished my previous lessons, we used our earlier class experience to visualize the outer. You might say we learned to astral travel, for we could imagine ourselves looking in on situations while not being there physically or noticed by those within the moment. This was never done for fun; this was a serious intrusion and only certain approved moments in time were allowed to be visualized in this way.

In using this technique, my first such trip to the outer was a visit to the home of a young girl. This young one was hollow-eyed, sad of face and very thin and pale. I could see that if she were happy and healthy she would glow in beauty. Her father was a tyrant, the first of which I had ever observed. He was far worse than Ra appeared during my previous class when we experienced the wounded feminine. At every meeting with this child the father belittled and aggressively hit the girl. Of course he made this her fault because she revolted him, as he should have had the son he desired. She somehow deprived him of that opportunity by emerging as a female child instead of that of a beloved son. She often wondered how she did that. Had she come to life by taking someone else's chances away? She, like most abused children, held the guilt and the blame, yet she was innocent.

As I watched her I felt her pain and disappointment. It was like a dark, heavy and murky rock within my chest. It was so undeserved and about the time I thought I would die myself in empathy for her, Che, my teacher, came to me and showed me the truth of this soul. This child, who was always referred to simply as *She* also (a non-name to those who would refuse to utter a personal identity) was a master soul who had agreed to suffer as example in this situation, for the entire community knew of the circumstances and felt remorse but did not intervene. She would offer opportunities for compassion as situations arose in which there could have been intervention, but it never came. She would be an example of suffering as she presented the results of such treatment. They felt sorrow but did nothing. She was a brave soul and her mission Divine, for she gave this father the opportunity to see his error and his selfishness and change. But he did not.

You might wonder, where was the mother in all of this? Well, she was in the same condition as the girl, beaten down and tired, and each month when she found that her moon time came once again, a time when she would normally have gone to the women's house, she stayed with her girl child for she feared more for the child than herself. He always knew when she had failed him, and she suffered when he discovered that she again missed her chance to bring him a son. It was all madness, literally, for anger controlled this tyrant. He had no compassion. He did not suffer, however; he claimed to be mistreated and suffered much without the son he desired to prove his worth to the community and himself. He had had a similar tyrant in a father who was sorely disappointed in him and had treated him much the way he now treated his own child and wife. He learned well. Families disappoint each other and cause the rage to come. Che held my hand as the visitation unfolded in front of my eyes like a dark drama on your television screen.

"This is a difficult case for you to witness, but it is reaching its apex and it will teach you much, child. Be patient and watch the way it plays out, for you will learn much from this example of life experience and this little girl's life will matter even more."

I looked back toward the scene. I saw the mother, again in her moon, again violated by her own husband, who had been so different when they wed. Then he had brought her gifts and said wonderful, tender things to win her love. It was his way of *winning* what he wanted, for he thought her beautiful then, an asset to own. She would make him feel more successful within their society; she would impress, for sure. But now she was no longer beautiful to him, for he had beaten her ugly, both mentally and physically. This day he gave her the worst beating ever then raped her again, all the while roaring, "you had better bring me my son or I will kill you and your little brat and start a new family!" The mother knew he meant this and that some other poor woman would suffer as she and her child had. She already felt sorry for this future one that would take her place one day, and so she began to plan.

The girl child cringed in the corner of the small living quarters. When he emerged from the beating and the rape of her mother he looked at her differently and said, "soon you will need to be prepared to serve a husband and I will make you ready. You will be better suited as a wife. I will make sure of that!"

The girl's mother heard the threat and knew that she must work fast. When he left she cleaned herself up as best she could and took the child to visit the old wise-woman. This frail old one had long white hair that she stubbornly left uncovered, which hung in waves to her waist. She specialized in herbs and natural medicines made from minerals and plants and such.

The wise one knew when she saw the beaten pair what the mission was. She prepared three teas, one for each family member. That evening at dinner the tea would be served, she instructed. The mother simply accepted the gift, for she had no money to pay, and gave the old one a slight smile of gratitude and quietly left with her child closely following. The wise one watched the pair walk away. She stood in the door of her lonely shack with tears running down her old and wrinkled cheeks. She whispered, "Soon your suffering will be finished." They walked away like two dead ones. They were dead, in their hearts, for all life had been beaten and stolen from them.

As she usually did after a terrible episode, the mother knew that she must prepare the best dinner possible to keep him from raging and repeating the madness. She borrowed food from her own mother, knowing that she could never repay her for all the food she had donated to this very same cause. Kissing her sweetly on the cheek she told her, "I love you, mom. Always remember that." She prepared a feast and heavily salted everything for the evening meal. It would make a great thirst.

The tea was served after the silent meal. There were no out bursts so the meal must have been acceptable. That was the extent of any gratitude that she had ever received from him since he changed into this monster, the day the daughter was born. The old one had made it very clear which tea should be given to each member of this sad family. To make sure he did not drink the child's or her tea, for he often took their food, she put a small floating bug in each. His was pure.

Upon drinking their tea the mother and the girl became very tired. The father began to feel terrible and bellowed his protest, "What is this you feed me, something poisonous, no doubt?" He was in so much pain he could not reach his wife to punish her yet again. She and the child just lightly fell to the floor, like tired, old rag dolls, and left their bodies, free at last. Hand in hand they left the suffering. He, on the other hand, suffered hours and hours, and finally when his spirit passed he had to review and relive the pain he caused. This was worse than the poisoning, for the pain was great. And there watching was the son who would have come if only the father had taken the kinder, more compassionate attitude toward his small family. This was the greatest pain of all, for this soul had waited long to reincarnate with this father but would not come to be abused.

I remember sobbing in sorrow for the entire episode. At my age I was on the edge of womanhood myself and to see such waste of feminine beauty and opportunity was an abomination to me, one who had been protected from this kind of madness. Che asked me to think about how the sorrow was overcome by the compassion.

Other such visits took place, over and over again. We visited governmental chambers, homes, temples and tribal councils from all over the face of Tara. Again and again we saw the effects of imbalance in the masculine and feminine energies. We learned that imbalance caused corruption in thinking and attitude and that the masculine energy is good in its state of perfection, but when corrupted it had no heart. We saw that patriarchy and matriarchy were imbalances and subject to this twisted thinking and attitude because the duality, the Divine Marriage within each of us, and within our relationships but outside of our selves, should be the example and the stability of all experiences. We also could see that corruption of energy was like a disease, for it could spread unseen and affect masses of beings in its wake, those beings that bought into the false ideology then strengthened it and passed it along. We watched, over and over, much suffering and acts of compassion and realized that compassion was there in the murk of darkness, like a little light spreading and trying to enlighten the experience and bring back the perfection. Compassion, the manifestation of love, never gives up.

My next class would be *The Divinity of Love.*

Blessed Be,

The Divinity of Love

Entering my next class was a delight. Upon seeing the class, in the first moments, there was a joyous red/pink aura that surrounded all students and their own auras blended into this beautiful light perfectly. There was also a distinct humming sound that sounded like a lullaby that I had heard and loved as a small child. My teacher was the most beautiful light of all, however, yet her face was grotesque and in a different circumstance one might have been revolted by her leprosy. The sheer love and devotion that the students gave to her as they surrounded her, transformed her into the most beautiful goddess. It was then that I learned that thoughts are ugly, not beings, no matter how they choose to manifest.

I called this teacher Sheila, because the *She* in its invisible aspect was there, but it was followed by the sound of beauty perfected through devoted love, the *la*. I found Sheila to be incredibly pleasant to look upon and never more saw a fault in her being.

The entire class just opened their circle around Sheila when I approached and said, "Welcome, sister," and took me into their hearts and their circle of love. I have never felt as included and accepted as I did with that class.

Sheila's instruction helped me understand that Divine love has no conditions or no end. Just as a parent will love a child who seems to the outside world as evil, even as they hate the deed but not the being, so too does the Source love all creation. Just as a parent experiences extreme pain and sorrow when a child takes the murky road of non-growth and negating choices, so too does the Source, only magnified beyond measure. So this Divine Source never stops loving but does suffer extreme sorrow caused by free will choices that lead to stagnation.

I learned that love, unconditional love of this type, could be manifested in so many ways that this very experiment of the Source, sending sparks of itself out as individual souls to find their way home again, is for the purpose of seeing how many ways this love can manifest. The reflection of the Source within each soul-light also reflects creativity and that aspect ensures a multitude of ways this love could emerge. A most exciting and perfect plan, I felt. From our life experience there is no way to build a formula for this special vibration of sound and light called Divine Love, for it is endless. The point is that at the depth of each choice is this never-ending and constant love, glowing and keeping watch.

Love is perhaps the most misunderstood of all the emotional choices, for it has become a bargaining commodity. "If you will do this, I will do that." Or worse yet, "If you do not become my slave, I will not love you." Then, in this corruption of the original divinity of love, there came the day that beings took the attitude that certain ones were more worthy of love than others, and they separated the beings into a hierarchy of those deemed deserving. Women, it is sad to remember, came in just above the poor beasts who served humanity so dearly. This was the real fall from grace, for grace is a feminine quality of the Source, just as justice is a masculine quality. As your artwork often shows the Goddess presenting the scales, these energies must be connected to the feminine, for she is the overseer of such. This might seem confusing to you. Let me try to clarify here. Justice is the work of the masculine, yet the feminine watches over to make sure that there is equal grace balancing this justice. Divinity manifests equally as feminine and masculine. Divinity has no real physical shape and is an ever present soul energy that is within all beings, yet can manifest its essence in selected moments. This manifestation then can be as Goddess or God, depending on the energy needed to bring a balance to the moment.

Early on in the history of this planet there were the humans who thought they were talking to this very same Being, this Source of ALL THAT IS, but were actually communicating with beings who were part of the creation project as it unfolded on this earth. These creator *gods* as they called themselves, were much as scientists and worked to develop (human) beings solely through focus on the physical bodies of such. Their understanding was limited in that they didn't realize that anything they created would attract a soul – a very fragment of God/Goddess, All That Is. The *creator gods* were aware on many levels but were still developing a balance in their own experience opportunities. They were learning also, but had not yet taken the course toward equality of the energies in totality. Some have moved into this balance and some have not. Because of this there are many who worship entities they consider to be God, but their deities have many personalities and priorities, depending on their awareness. Those that worship these creators of physical bodies reflect their attitudes of olde, which no longer echo the creator-deity's present state of knowing. The *creator gods* have progressed in awareness but the religions created in their names have not. Worshipers get stuck and are reluctant to be led, you see. That is why worshiping can be limiting in some aspects.

The practice of sacrificing to God is a corruption that unfolded because of this. The Source wants all beings to live a full and merging life. Killing animals and sacrificing beautiful young children or women was never received as a gift of love to this One. The greatest gift is to find love and respect within each relationship, including that with the animal, mineral and gaseous worlds, for experience merges and moves in a beautiful dance of give and take in this creation story. All beings are part of the plan and none more divine than the other.

The greatest challenge for all of us, according to Sheila, was to bring balance back to the forefront here upon this lovely planet, Tara, but to do so by merging, not purging. This would be the ultimate manifestation of Divine Love, the beautiful Goddess again merged with the equally beautiful God Source. Make no mistake; The Source has always been equally both energies, for that is the reflection of all of us. But so many have only acknowledged half of this Being of Purest Divine Love.

I spent another two years, until I was eleven, within this group. We constantly played out scenes, like actors and actresses upon a stage, in which we had to figure out how to resolve situations in a way that Divine Love would manifest or be recognized. We rarely visited the outer in this class because there was not much that reflected the truth of this Divine Balance at the time. Places hidden in secret temples still practiced the feminine but they were losing ground, as the prevailing attitude of patriarchy spread across the land like a dark disease. This was the time of judgment without grace.

We were seeds of love and sanity. If we could take root and grow in places of dimness, we hoped our small pure light would begin to make a difference. We knew that it might take eons of time, yet we hoped, for nothing is impossible in Divine Love or for the sake of Divine Love. We all left with our mission clear.

My lessons would involve one more class, Leita told me. It would be a class to integrate me into the outer. This class was simply called *merging*.

Blessed be,

Merging

On my eleventh birthday, my sister-students celebrated my merging into womanhood. My moon time also began that day, and the sisters of that age later took me to the moon lodge, a place of great honor. The teachers, men and women, and the students, including the brothers, all danced and celebrated my day of birth with much laughter and merriment, for they knew that every single soul that incarnated was a gift to this physicality, and my emergence was appreciated.

I spent five days in the moon lodge. I had always wondered what it looked like within this place since we did not enter until we came of age physically. Leita, my beloved friend and guardian, took me there about midnight, after my celebration. We walked the wooded path until we came to a lodge that was built of logs and stones; each blessed and consecrated. I entered through a heavy, carved double doorway. The carvings were circles and abstract figures of women in all stages, from birth into the physical until the transitional leaving. There was a giant carving of the moon and its phases at the top of the doorway and the solar sun was in the middle of the doorway. A crystal was imbedded at about eye level under the moon phase carvings. Lieta put her eye close to the crystal and the door opened.

There was a very old woman, long into her wise years, who administered to this lodge. She was well past a hundred years of age, I was told, and still looked healthy and able to carry on much longer. She greeted us with a warm hug and a welcome. The interior was quiet and incredibly beautiful. Velvet curtains, or a fabric similar to what you now call velvet, hung around bedchambers and on the walls. The middle of the room held a warm hearth and a pleasant fire burned brightly. Around the hearth were comfortable chairs, some with women lounging and reading. Some were quietly meditating or sleeping. I noticed a room off to the right, which had a golden doorway. I would later learn that this was the collection room in which each woman would go to offer her moon menses. This sacred substance would be used wisely for it was a precious gift from each *Moon-Maiden*. We were called that until we entered the wise woman stage.

Luna, I learned, had taken the task of overseer on her first day when she entered the moon temple, as I did this day, and the other guardian had known that she could leave and be done when she saw Luna. She was called *Moon-Maiden* too for a long time, until she became the wise one (those who kept the sacred blood and internalized their power.) Luna greeted me lovingly with "Welcome to womanhood, dear one. You will find this blessing twisted into a curse perhaps, but you must always remember that this blood of life is sacred because you are a sacred vessel, as all women are. Never forget that. Never let anyone convince you otherwise. You carry the blood of the Goddess within your being, as all women do. Without it no physicality is possible."

The others there instructed me in the care of this monthly time and I learned to collect the sacred blood as they did. The first blood was the most sacred, followed only by the last blood from a woman. This substance some refer to as *star fire,* was used in many ways, but mainly this substance was used in medicine in its powdered dry state, or in protective amulets or as the true blood offering to the Source.

My time in the moon lodge was pleasant. I listened to various musicians, for there were always a variety of talents present. I also learned to sing within this lodge since a gracious sister with a beautiful voice was usually there when I was. In fact, most of the women were on the same moon schedule. Luna knew many ways to make us feel wonderfully relaxed. She had teas, heated herbal wraps, incense, devices that emitted a mist of special aromas and even the music and song all kept us serenely comfortable. We tended each other by combing each other's hair, giving massages and practicing our energy balancing techniques, (similar to the Reiki practice.) This insured the power of the blood, for to bleed in shame or sorrow is to deplete the power. In this place we also read the books of our choice. Most already knew how to read and do figures because that was woven into our classes in appropriate ways. I chose to read old tales of the ancients of long, long ago. Fact or fiction, I could never get enough and I wondered where fact ended and fiction began.

After I left the lodge, Lieta took me to my merging class. In this class I would learn to take what I knew into the outer and merge with those there and attempt to bring the energy into balance. I learned from day one that I must keep my knowing private. I must keep it safely within myself for if I revealed the treasure of my being, there would be those who would steal that treasure. This, of course, would do no good because one must earn such knowing, but they would destroy it to keep such knowing from devolving their illusionary, controlled world of circumstance. Jealousy is a destructive attitude and the root of all imbalances.

We knew that once we left this place the memory of sanity and loving balance would be our secret key to moving through judgment, control, negation, and degradation. We knew we had our work cut out for us. Our teacher was an old sage man. He was just back from the outer where he switched places with an old saga woman. Both would live six years within and six years without to keep the pulse of the outer, into which we would be merged.

I simply referred to this wise one as *Sage* and he smiled so slightly that one would have to be quite aware to catch the rare glimpse of an upturned lip. For the most part his face reflected the sorrow he felt from the awareness of the imbalance in the outer. He had more lines and wrinkles than ever I had seen before, and each one seemed to enhance the mystery of him. What had he experienced out there?

I remember the first day when he told us that as women we would be considered the lowest of the low, as our animal friends would be considered also. We were astounded. How could that be? We were part of the plan and without us no human would have emerged into the physical. Also, the animals gave us their very lives for food and clothing and other important physical needs. Did they not willingly merge with us in so doing? How could you not love the lamb that gave you its body so tender? This, I think was the hardest class for us, since we knew that our balanced, beautiful life would soon tip drastically. We began to lose our sweet naivety.

One day Sage came to me and asked to take a private walk. He had other students in a meditative state, visiting some of the places in the outer where they would be sent. They would, of course, as I would, go to a temple first and merge slowly into the societies of their mission. Sage took my hand and walked into the misty forest down a winding path. Deer, birds and other forest animals were drawn to us. A raven swooped by, cawing its raven song and then flipped back and lit on Sage's head. The Raven turned out to be an old friend that always stayed near to Sage and they conversed for a while in a strange bird-talk like way. Then this black one turned to look at me, cocked its head and said in my language, "greetings, little one. You are beloved by the bird people and all of the animal kingdom. We will always be near to guide and guard your way. We wish you success on your journey." Then he flew off into the mist of the forest.

The wise one looked into my face after stopping to hold both my hands. "There is much that will be expected and asked of you. Your very heart could be torn out metaphorically and maybe even physically. Your courage will be tested and your beauty will probably be negated. But you will have the greatest opportunity known to any woman. You will represent the Divine Feminine and you will meet the Divine Masculine and merge with your counterpart. One moment of this Divine Mergence is worth a lifetime of suffering, you will learn. We do not know if this mergence will go full bloom, or be stopped in mid flower, for this is the flower of God, for sure, this Divine Mergence, but the gardeners are the judgmental ones. Will they recognize and honor this flower without twisted judgment or need to control its bloom? That is the opportunity. They may not. The flower will then go undeveloped, but it will be such a beautiful experience that no matter the outcome, the outer world will never be the same again. It will be changed for the better forever. The tide will turn because of total love and total integration of the masculine and the feminine as reflected in you, my child-woman, and your beloved."

It all seemed so unreal to me because my reality was not suffering or degradation, it was confirmation and appreciation. "Will I be sad all the time?" I innocently asked, yet I was ready to take the task because I new it was my mission.

"You will be the happiest woman ever to live in physicality, equaled only by the one who would mother your beloved on the day of his birth. You will also know sorrow like no other, for that love will come hard on a society that deems such love unworthy. Are you ready for such a task?"

At that moment, as if in slow motion, I noticed every single living being within the forest, the trees, the plants, the animals, the birds and even the insects. They all seemed to be focused on me and waited for my answer to the Sage. "Yes, of course, I would gladly be on this mission to bring back the joy."

"So be it," he said.

I knew my class was done. There was no celebration, yet there were farewells. One did not celebrate going into the murky masses. One just wished the other well and kept them in their vision of light. I left the misty isle the next morning. I thought this was the deepest sorrow I could ever know, but I looked forward to seeing my family once again. They had visited on occasion, but not nearly as much as I would have liked. I missed my darling mother and I longed to walk and talk with my wise father.

I would go to the temple near Magdalene. It was within a mountainous area and secret to the outer. I would merge from that location.

Blessed be,

The Merging Temple

The month spent with my family was the happiest memory of my childhood and I consider it my farewell to my little girl stage of experience. My parents visited often in the two years of my preparation for merging with the outer. I looked forward to their visits and developed a very close relationship with my little brother, Josephius, whom I lovingly referred to as *my little Joe.*

The merging temple was built, as are many hidden temples, within the rock of the mountainside. There were a myriad of chambers, all of which served a definite purpose. Exploring them was my greatest passion, for there was no place kept closed to any of us.

I was schooled in the divinity of the feminine and how it balanced and complimented the masculine. I learned about sacred sexuality and how this physical merging reflects the original intent of the Source, which is to have these two complimenting energies balancing each other to perfection. I learned how to care for my body and how to gather herbs and when to use them to keep good health and a balanced physical vehicle. These herb gathering times were the most pleasant to me because I liked being out in nature, for as they promised, the animal beings were always there watching over me.

One day a sister initiate and I were high on a mountain stoop attempting to harvest some herbs that tended to grow in places difficult to access. We somehow found ourselves on a ledge with no way down and a dangerous drop threatened our safety. We experienced our first fearful moment together and I must say I did not like that feeling of helplessness. A raven swooped down and did that familiar back flip I had seen in the forest long ago, then it spoke to me, not in a bird language, but in my own.

"So, we meet again, little one. It looks like you need some assistance here; you are out on this stone limb way too far." He dropped to the ledge and began to walk away, looking over his shoulder to make sure we had the idea to follow him. My sister and I looked at each other hopefully and followed. The Raven took the route that appeared to be the more difficult but we knew we must trust our rescuing friend. Raven suddenly disappeared around the corner of a rock, peeked back at us and cawed, then we realized that the path was hidden right there, very close to where we had been stranded, all along. Once on the path, we knew we were safe again. The Raven did another back flip, circled around our heads and flew off into the landscape.

Life experiences can be quite metaphoric and as we talked on our way back to the Merging Temple, we discussed how the answer we seek might lie hidden so close to us and yet go unnoticed. We decided to never again panic and feel hopeless, but instead to explore hopefully all options in any situation.

Perhaps the most difficult time at the Merging Place was learning how the imbalance had occurred and how far off balance society really was. It had affected the animal beings too, I would learn, and some of those beings had taken this idea of male dominance. Yet, I would learn, there were still others that preferred the female dominance. The ideal, even within the animal realm, was that there would be duality rather than dominance. Nothing, I would learn, could compare to the corruption of the masculine role, or energy, as it was unfolding in my time. The most difficult part of this lesson was to not separate ourselves or the mission of the feminine from that of the masculine. To hate is to separate and our mission was to merge, not separate.

The priests had created an organization that they named *Religion,* which dictated rules that were meant to keep the masses ignorant and controlled. Power struggles abounded and manifested in wars and destruction, as well as murder, time and again, and were justified by those who said they spoke for God. The power of the feminine was drained as she was lowered repeatedly to the status of an object to own instead of a co-partner in experience. They didn't realize, or didn't care, that to do this was to dishonor the duality of the Source, the very God they presumed to serve. That which is thought *owned as property* then becomes enslaved, and my sisters were all objectified even to the queens who would have to find a suitable male to rule, even as she would sit upon the throne. Those who violated such rules were persecuted and their story was banished from the record, thus *His-story* became the only record.

All this information and other lessons of the corruption were so depressing that we ended our day with a meditation time in a wonderful evening chamber to bring us out of deep sorrow. It was such a beautiful place, with light music, usually harp or some stringed instrument, the burning of incense, often Lavender, rubdowns, also in lavender oil or another appropriate herbal oil, and quiet meditation. I would later miss this wind-down time, for seldom in the outer would a mere woman enjoy such an arrangement.

I would go back to Magdalene soon. I would be known as Mary of Magdalene. I was glad that I would begin my mission there, close to where I began this life opportunity. I knew that my life's mission would begin soon. I was confident in my ability to move into this mission, while I was not sure how it would develop.

My last teaching was how to become invisible. Not as Harry Potter and his invisibility cloak, but how to blend into a crowd, or how to slip off to the side of social events and not be the focus of attention, for that was deemed the essence of disrespect. The acting Mother of this temple, another wise woman with long flowing hair streaked with white and gray, taught me this technique.

"When you are in your wise-woman years this will come automatically, for to not see the power of the wise one is to deflate it, they think, and they are right if the ignored wise one allows this attitude to degrade her self esteem." She taught me to keep the secrets of the feminine and how to metaphorically plant seeds of change and balance into my everyday conversation and actions. The greatest lesson, however, I believe, was that she taught me to love myself totally, in a non-egotistical way. She said, "You can only love and honor others as you do yourself." The greatest power of the feminine is the ability to love divinely and unconditionally. When the feminine loses respect for herself, she loses the ability to give this blessing to others. Then she feels empty and worthless. My beloved teacher urged, "Never stop loving and respecting yourself, Mary, no matter what anyone says of you, for you are beloved by all beings. You are the hope of the Mother Love. You will face one of the greatest challenges of this Divine Mission. You must hold your power of love high and bright always." This seemingly simple lesson proved to be not so simple.

Blessed be,

ENTERING THE OUTER

I was sent forth to begin my mission at age sixteen. That was the official age for entering the adult realm since the time of olde, but there were those, I would later learn, that would hurry the process, and cut short the precious childhood time.

My parents brought me an adequate wardrobe, which seemed to me heavy and confining. My beautiful black hair had to be completely covered at all times. I would join the household of my aunt, who lived in Magdalene, and I would be useful and help with the duties of the house and wait for my mission to begin. I was not told that I would be united with another, or that I would have a specific way that I would enter into my work. I was told that only the Divine Mother and myself would truly know how this would be accomplished. They said it would be an *awakening* that could not be mistaken. So I lived each day in expectation.

I had learned that each moment, each mega-second within each moment, was precious and a joy to behold and that I would not be able to bring the Feminine Factor into experience unless I loved every minute of every day. So, while I looked forward to tomorrow's opportunity, I also loved the eternal *now*. There were difficult times when I would wonder what there was that I could love about a particular moment. No one ever told me it would be easy. In fact, I had been warned otherwise.

One morning as I was making my daily trip to the well to bring water to the household, I saw one of my priestess sisters among a mob of angry men. I do not know why she was not camouflaged in the required dress of the outer, but she wore the usual priestess robe, light and beautiful, or at least it was before she was pelted with mud and filth. She must have wandered too close to the edge of our safety zone. The men who tormented her had such ugliness upon their faces, I noticed, for I had never seen the hideousness of ignorance so plainly before this time. I wanted to run to my sister and stop the madness but she looked at me and shook her head *no*.

They didn't even notice. All they cared about was spoiling something beautiful because they felt disconnected from it. They called her cruel names, including a whore, which I later learned meant that she enjoyed and shared sexuality. How had the most sacred of feminine gifts, the very essence of life itself, become defiled and degraded, I asked my sweet aunt.

"Jealousy," she said, "has invaded the minds and hearts of too many men and women and is now even taught to the children. It is the greatest of sins to see the merging of the masculine and the feminine as a sin of temptation. It puts a stain upon every emerging babe that comes through this attitude. It makes balance and sanity in society very difficult indeed."

I knew depression after this episode and forgot the advice of the Mother-Priestess from the Merging Temple. She had instructed me to focus on the emotion of joy. She said to acknowledge pain and sorrow, but to never lose sight of joy. After several days of doom within my heart, I again met my priestess friend at the well. This time she was properly garbed in the required cover-up clothing. She smiled at me and said, "That will teach me to test the limits of safety. I will not let them take my joy of being a woman from me. I have already healed myself and I will just keep private my joyful moments of gathering herbs and singing to the Mother Earth, for my love will flow no matter what they do to me."

I was amazed at how good she looked compared to the battered woman I saw just a few days previously. Her eyes still had the sparkle that was always evident in those priestess trained. She only came to the well, she told me, because she could feel my pain.

"Be compassionate, Mary, but do not let the pain of women bring you down, for we need your strength and your determination to the Divine Mother. We need your example to survive and move through the madness that has come over our brothers and broken so many of our sisters." And she assured me she would do likewise as she kissed my cheek and walked away.

"Who was that woman?" asked an old woman that usually collected water at the same time as I. "She looks so happy. I was like that once too, you know."

She looked at me with such sad eyes and noticed me for the first time, I think, for she usually just trudged to the well, with eyes downcast, not thinking or noticing her surroundings. Then she said, "You have that same glow, my child! Keep it!" With her eyes shining intensely, she pleaded, "Somehow keep it glowing, dear young one, for it is soothing and reassuring to one such as me, one long sad and invisible to this world of judgment." Then she too kissed my cheek and said, "I can go now in peace for I have known my time to leave this life was near and I had asked to meet just one sister of purest light and I have seen two today."

She walked away with her small pot of water balanced on her frail shoulder, a little less stooped and with eyes twinkling and looking about her noticing everything the morning had to offer. I never saw her again at the well.

I left that day with the return of joy to my heart. I felt awakened and blessed by my encounters with the old one and my sister. I recovered my determination to carry on with my soul mission. I began to notice the singing of the birds and the dust circles dancing again around my feet. A dog wagged his tail at me and a burro brayed in a soft loving way as he walked by on his lead, bearing his heavy load. I put my pot of water upon my head, following the burro's cheerful example, and bore my own slight burden. I sang the song of contented appreciation of life and moved on. A Raven dove down upon me and did a back flip, circled me twice and then flew off into the grove. This had to be my old friend, no doubt, checking in on me and reminding me that I was never alone in this quest.

Blessed be,

THE SECRET MEETINGS

There were secret meetings among the women of the old ways and my aunt was one who would hostess such meetings. We called our meetings sewing circles because we brought needlework with us. I remember well the first such meeting.

The sisters all came about the same time, from many directions. Upon entering the house, we all went down a narrow stairway into the wine cellar where my aunt pulled out a particular old bottle of wine. It was not the best wine; in fact it was a bottle no one would usually desire, being from the low end of the batch. As the bottle was pulled she reached into the space behind its cradle and tripped a lever and the entire wine rack pivoted and opened into an inviting interior room complete with a blazing fire in the center. I often wondered how that fire could be un-vented there in the depths of that cavern and later learned that there was indeed a channel for the smoke to travel. It tunneled through the baking oven-vent in the food preparation center.

We entered. There were twelve of us, plus my aunt, which made thirteen women in the chamber. This number was the norm for such gatherings. There were some small rooms off the interior circle where there were priestess robes of beautiful colors and fabrics. We were invited to find something more appropriate for a joyous sister meeting and we quickly and happily rushed to the dressing rooms and threw down our heavy garments and changed into the beautiful clothing there offered to us. We giggled and chatted like little girls even though some of us were of the wise woman age. We emerged more ourselves and with happy expectation for the meeting. We never knew what to expect but knew this gathering would be interesting, without a doubt. My Aunt, whom I have not yet named, to ensure that there not be a colossal controversy for her memory in history, for that is her story to tell, you see, was the high priestess within this group. She had a stunning aqua blue flowing robe draped over her ample body and she reminded me of the sky on a sunny day. She also had a headband around her head, worn like a crown, made of a silvery and gold substance that was twined beautifully and circled her head in perfection.

She later told us that this represented the two ways that life experience left its record, silver represented the light and gold the sound. There were more groups that met, of course, in other such places, but so secretive must the meetings be that I never knew of them. The secret sacred group members could be any woman I met in my everyday life in the outer. It was necessary for safety and for the cause to keep this so. I often saw a little dove embroidered upon the robes of other women I encountered at my daily well visits. I had wondered what this dove meant, but out of respect for the quiet well moments, for most women did not chat there as they were in fear of being chastised, I never asked.

Bringing my memory back to the first sister meeting, however, allow me to continue. In our lovely robes we came together in the heart of this chamber, this first day for me, and sang our soul songs together, all a different unique tune and all spinning and twirling in a great circle around the fire, all singing a unique harmony. When finished, we sat down on cushioned pillows for our ceremonial rite and our meeting.

My first meeting was a delight because I felt once again connected to the power and beauty of the feminine. My Aunt passed around a bottle of very good red wine, but not the trigger bottle, which was our secret key to this place. We were each handed a small gold cup, which represented us as a holy vessel of God, my aunt said. We filled it with red wine, one by one, and held it forth waiting for everyone's cup to be filled. I just followed the example of my sisters.

"This is wine, the fruit of the vine's essence," my aunt began, "and fills the small precious cup, which represents your womb, the divine cup of Father/Mother God. The wine represents the blood that fills this cup each moon-time, waiting to nourish life and love. You are the divine vessels of emerging souls. It is through your blood that life must come into physicality. This blood is a precious gift and a powerful substance. Protect and respect your gift, my sisters, for without it there would be no doorway to this opportunity in physicality."

Then she instructed us to drink the wine in our cups and refill the cups once again just as the womb is refilled each month. We began to feel the effects of the wine soon enough since we did not often partake. As we drank the wine she told us the secret of the wise woman.

"Notice, my sisters, that when you drink the wine it is no longer in the cup but within your bodies, affecting and warming you, is it not? Your cup then is empty for a time and then the day comes when it no longer fills upon the full moon. Know that the power is within you still then, and even more powerful than before, for the blood of your wombs is given to the children that emerge or it is given to Mother Earth when there is no need for such nourishment, but when the blood does not fill the womb cup, its essence fills the entire woman and she holds this power within her as wisdom. This is a great threat to those in the corrupted masculine mode who fear that they would have to deal with this power should they acknowledge it. They fear losing control and power. Thus the wise woman is seen with an empty womb, instead of with a full heart of wisdom. Every cup of wine is representative of the divine feminine womb and those who drink without respect take this substance while they disregard the sacred essence of it. They consume and consume with no regard for the grape or the symbolic feminine. This thoughtlessness is the tragedy we face, for it represents a disregard for the essence of life itself."

After this message we enjoyed each other's company, chatting and working on our sewing projects, for those with husbands and fathers in their household would have to show progress in this matter to avert suspicion. I noticed some women sewing little doves on their heavy outer garments. I approached my aunt and asked her about the significance of the number thirteen, as she had indicated that all such circles were thirteen in number. She told me that one of the elders of the group had withdrawn so that I could enter. She was close to her departure, my aunt said, and was happy to make way for one such as I.

I picked up my own needlework and as we sewed and chatted my Aunt casually said to me, "soon, Mary, soon you will have the sign you have been waiting for and you will begin your mission." I felt the flush of truth and expectation rush through my body; from my feet to the top of my head it warmed me. I could always tell the power of a statement by this feeling. I wondered how it would begin? I knew I was ready to move into this task and I was eager to start. I began to sew my own dove on the sleeve of my street garment.

Blessed be,

THE DIVINE DANCE OF DUALITY

I continued my daily routine, all the while wondering when I would have that confirmation that my true mission would begin. I reasoned that simply getting water each day from the well surely could not be the extent of my destiny. Yet, everyday as I went to the well I would see women in various stages of slavery and drudgery to the political and social system of our time, walking as if asleep, unconsciously completing their task and moving back to their slave holder's quarters.

I could tell the down trodden from the sisters, for the sisters held their heads higher and they often hummed a tune as they fetched their precious water. They perceived the immediate environment in totality. Nothing seemed to avert their quiet attention. It was so for myself as well, for a bird did not fly but that I did not notice and thank it for its presence and joy.

I began to have deep dreams when I rested at night. Of course I always dreamed and often it was of the priestess temples and the freedom therein, which I sorely missed. It was becoming harder to awaken from these dreams. They were intense and worrisome in that there were always some symbols of balance tilting dangerously out of alignment, and I was constantly trying to tilt the symbolic balance back to its rightful place of stability. I could never quite succeed and greatly desired some assistance.

I usually woke up exhausted from all of this dreaming and my aunt and friends noticed that I seemed more tired than usual. I could feel urgency of attention needed within the dream but it had yet to reveal itself to me in the light of day. I felt anxious during my day, like there was something ominously threatening there, just out of my reach.

One particular dreamtime was much more frightening than the others. I could not keep this balancing factor from tilting all the way over and spilling its precious contents, which were immediately consumed in a cavernous hole full of molten lava. I could hear screams and knew torment was upon the people and the beings that made up the substance of that spill. I cried to the Great Mother/Father God, "What would you have me do to help these poor tortured ones?" I thought no answer to my plea was forthcoming when I saw the kindest eyes looking at me through the mist, with a look of love I had never before known. Without words, or even thoughts, I knew that I would not be alone in this mission. The Divine Masculine was not lost, but waiting patiently and preparing to merge once again with his beloved.

I awoke that morning as if a great burden had been lifted, because I knew that I would be able to make a difference and that I would have a counterpart, a great helper in all of this.

I was not sure who this might be and even envisioned an old sage, a wise one, who would be as teacher to me, with myself as willing student. My aunt, whom I shared all my dreams with, said "you will be both student and teacher, as well as High Priestess and She who will lead forth."

"How, then?" I asked, "Would the masculine play into this plan." Because I knew that the eyes I saw were masculine, but I had never seen such gentleness and awareness in a man's eyes. She showed me an hourglass full of sand. She set it upon a table. With the sun streaming through the window, the sand within sparkled. She said, "For the sake of illustrating truth, imagine, child, one side is the feminine and one the masculine. Both sides are equally important in the measurement of time, do you not agree?" She said then as she turned her attention to the sand within, "The sand is as energy pouring downward, giving of itself to the other aspect."

She picked up the hourglass, which was beautifully carved, with one side ivory and the other ebony. Both sides had intricate carvings thereon, with the sun prominent on the ivory side and the moon prominent on the ebony side. She told me the end that was white was like the masculine in the light of day, aware and ready for action. This masculine consciously moved into experience, the grand landscape of opportunity. The other side, the dark side, was of the feminine and it controlled the night and the intuitional wisdom, the connection to the Source, for she, the feminine, looked within and could feel the presence of truth and love and she would take the energy and resolve it as such.

She then set the hour class on the table with the masculine globe full of sand above the empty feminine. "Notice," she said, "that the masculine fills the feminine and the sands change in shape and volume as poured forth through a spiral down into the feminine's awaiting and expectant cup. When all is given and it is empty, it stands ready to receive in like manner." She tilted the glass over then and said; "Now the feminine will fill the masculine in this continual "give and take," this duality dance of experience. Neither side will control the other when the channel is clear, each give and take equally.

She then showed me another hourglass, but the channel between the globes was blocked in this one and the ebony was tattered and the ivory was tarnished. There was no way for growth to manifest because when the hour glass was turned, up-righting the feminine half, there was nothing to give and no way to receive anything from her empty chambers.

"It would not matter which side held the sand," my wise old aunt said, "for the sand, as all energy, must stay in motion and be shared to stay alive and charged. Within this situation the energy (sand) then just swished back and forth within the masculine side, never experiencing the divine spiral of sharing with the duality counterpart. Eventually mold and rot would set in and the smell of stagnation. Each grain of sand then affected the other and ultimately, the sand therein would become putrid and solidified, unmoving and stuck like mud caked and baked on a desert with nothing growing thereof."

"This" she explained, "is much like the future of human experience for the channel is being blocked a grain at a time, each day that the feminine is choked off from her counterpart, her divine duality."

Since I still saw the world in wonder, just as a little child might, my aunt always called me this as an endearment. "You see, child, everything must move through this dance of life, the give and take, to stay fresh and pure and in evolution. This is the Sacred Duality, without which growth in any mode would not be possible. Your purpose, as is true for all of us in the society of priestesses, is to remove the blockage, a grain at a time. You will have those on the other side of this blockage working as well, and there is one who will touch your heart and soul and in whom you would literally move a mountain to unite with, for he is the duality of thee. You will see soon enough, for I sense the time is near for your mission to spring forth. You must soon begin the process of restoring the flow in this Divine Duality."

Blessed be,

IT BEGAN AT THE WELL

I constantly thought about my life as it unfolded day to day. All young women were expected to marry and fulfill their mission of mother and wifehood, which was seen as their only true contribution to society. I didn't feel that I needed this validation of my womanhood. I had been trained differently and my parents and siblings all held a completely different view. There was a multitude of ways a life could be offered in service. To voice that view was dangerous, we knew, for those in power were religious fanatics and they feared equality within duality greatly. Their entire structure was based on the "fear of God" and the dominance of the masculine, which kept the masses in line with their vision and control. They ritualized life down to the last mega-second to insure that there was no time for the feminine to discern. They also created the sin of learning. That was Eve's great sin, you see, that she wanted to *know*. To know was a way out of slavery and dominance, and would lead to a need for equitable treatment of all beings within the structure of freethinking, because to know meant that she would know then the measure of her worth. No being held in bondage is ever given this right, for in doing so the holder of this bond would have to face a truth he does not wish to see.

I knew how to read, which came quite naturally to me from early childhood, and I could also read the secret code of the feminine with ease, having always been around these symbols during my early years. I had to hide this ability now, however, because I was not born male and thus had, according to the elders who ruled, no capacity for processing knowledge.

I do not know of any woman who does not have extreme sorrow down deep within her being for this lie laid upon us, that we are so ignorant and shallow. I, too, felt the pain of the feminine degraded and negated in such a society. I knew not how I could change the trends, but I knew I would do anything to try. I knew also that I had been born to do so. One day on my daily trip to the well, I felt somehow *lighter* in my mood and in my pace as I seemed to walk on the very air itself. The birds and animals all gave me much attention, singing and talking lightheartedly in their own language, and I reasoned that the love they bestowed upon me was the reason for this blissful feeling I enjoyed.

I arrived at the well and found a young woman in tears. The depth of her sobbing came from a place deeper than the source of the water. Her heart pain was such that she could barely retrieve her bucket from the base of the well. She felt my presence and gazed at me with painfully sad eyes as I asked, "Why do you cry, child?"

She said, "today I have become a woman and no one cares. I am ordered to do my work and stay away from all others in my family because I am cursed for my great sin. Why does God curse women with this terrible thing each moon time? Is it the proof of my sin as a woman, as I am told?"

"No, child," I said, "it is, instead, proof that life is possible from within your sacred womb, your holy cup of creation. It is jealousy and ignorance that keeps your blossoming day unholy. You are a rose bud now moving into bloom. What gardener would wish the flower to never bloom but remain as an undeveloped bud? You are now the entryway for creation. Never forget that you are blessed this day and never cursed because of this."

I held her tear streaked, little face in my hands and kissed away her tears and she seemed to sigh and brighten, then she embraced me as well. As I looked up I saw a light surround her and I knew that this embrace had energized and blessed her, as well it did me. I felt that something had come through me but I sensed that something else was present in this blessing, something that was united with my own essence and blended into purest love.

Then I saw him, walking toward me and smiling. Those eyes, they were amazingly brilliant and exactly the same as in my dreamtime vision. He was of a muscular build, with powerful arms and a strong jaw line, but there was such gentleness upon his face that one did not feel his strength as a threat. His hair was long and flowing and his eyes a piercing deep blue, as were my own. This was an unusual color of eyes for this area. It was not preferable, only tolerated, as so many slight differences would be. I had learned to change my eye color to black through a technique taught to me by my Mother at my early school on the Misty Isle.

That was my shield but this day I did not even consider shielding my soul windows in such a way. I just noticed every detail of him as he noticed every detail of me.

His followers, mostly men, were talking to him and I noticed they called him "master." Still, he walked toward me, as if in trance, with our eyes locked in recognition. He seemed not to hear them call to him. It concerned them greatly and they looked back and forth to each other and murmured, "what has come over the master?" He did not take his loving eyes away from my own gaze. He walked up to me and said, "I have waited long for you, have you not expected me equally?" And then he embraced me gently. The feeling of that moment is impossible to describe, so I will let you imagine.

I said, "yes, master," with a lump in my chest and throat that was both pleasant and most obviously painful, for the knowing had never been so strong and the reunion had been so desired from within my very soul.

"Do not call me master, dear one," he said, "for if I am master to you then you are master to me and as you know, we have much work to do before we can openly call you such as you deserve, my beloved."

"What would you have me call you, dearest beloved one," for I found myself echoing his endearment. "I must certainly give you all due respect."

We were so caught up in each other that we did not notice the commotion around us. The followers had never seen the master behave in such a way and thought me an enchantress that had bewitched him. When we finally broke our trance we noticed the confusion. "Fear not," Jesus said. "I am still the Jesus you know and love, as you are ever my beloveds also, but this day I have finally united once again with the duality of my heart and I can but find joy and happiness in this reunion. Rejoice for me, for I am happier at this moment than ever before in my life."

He then took my hand and said, "Simply call me your beloved as I do you and I will be filled with joy," and we walked away together with the crowd of followers straggling along in wonder and confusion.

My little girl friend, who was no longer in tears, watched all of this in amazement. She asked politely, "Lady, may I be honored to take your full water jug back to the house of your aunt and give her the news?"

"Yes, please do so and please know that on the day you found your womanhood there was a miracle, for this woman, myself, has found that which my own sacred cup, my own sacred feminine soul has longed for forever. Let this miracle be a beacon of hope within your own heart but remember too, my child, I who have been happy and content even as I was, single upon my mission, you too, child, must realize the oneness of you."

The crowd began to stir but I continued, "Even though I have been blessed to have now found my hearts desire, my counterpart, who comes to meet me in this task, this would not be possible without this duality within our very selves first. This heart full of sacred respect for your very essence as it reflects in the feminine and the masculine is the *Knowing*, the knowing of your own worth and your own beauty, the treasure of yourself. To find a true love in another is a blessing, for certes, but the greatest love is within your own heart. No matter what you choose to do, let the Divine Duality manifest within you. You will then be sacredly blessed and finally free to live your life as you choose, you see."

Jesus smiled at me, understanding perfectly what I said, but those with him did not, for they felt that no one could be the equal of the one they called Master, much less give a woman permission to walk alone if she should choose.

He turned to the crowd and said "hear me, no son is more precious than a daughter. This is the message of my true Father and my true Mother and your true Divine Parents as well. Love and respect your wives and your daughters as they do you and watch your life become blessed as your beloved one's bloom before your very eyes and bring you great riches within your very soul, where the only true riches can manifest eternally. To be truly rich is to have a full heart, full with respect and compassion for all others, especially your feminine counterpart as she loves and honors you too. All other earthly riches are but temptations to stray from the truth and to hide within fear of lack. You lack nothing. You give away your wealth each time you do not recognize the divinity of your mother, your wife, your daughter or any other feminine being. Nothing is complete without its other half. Your hearts are not complete, my friends. Think on this while you wonder of my supposed insanity this day. Is it insane to be so touched by love?"

And we walked away. Some of Jesus' followers looked perplexed and confused. Some tried with all their hearts to understand. Jesus said, "Mary, you carry the Mary name of "she who loves and must sacrifice the most," can you continue in this mission knowing that you will be hated because of your great love?"

"How is it, my beloved?" I asked, "that because of love I will be hated"?

"I will also be hated because of love," he said. "We have important seeds to plant, my dearest one, and I do not know if we will see the harvest. It is the greatest sorrow that beings of choice would choose to hate and to fear love. We have a great task ahead of us. We must fight fear with love. Fear separates but love unites!"

Blessed be,

MOVING INTO MY MISSION

When I walked away from the well, hand in hand with my beloved, I knew that my water-bearing days to the household of my dear aunt were at an end. Now I would quench the thirst of those deprived of their femininity. I also had other small duties at the household but they would be taken over by the new novice, for I would now move out of the group of thirteen of which my aunt led, and create my own group when the time was ripe. I knew that my aunt's group would not meet until the new priestess arrived and entered her life in the outer.

To tell the story of myself and my beloved Jesus will be difficult, for I can only tell it from my heart's perspective. There has been much written of Jesus, and much is true but some is fabricated to reinforce the agenda of those who would mold the memory. I then will concentrate on our relationship only, the way I remember it in that all too brief sojourn.

We walked together for a few hours upon leaving the well, as Jesus headed to another community where he said he would spread the word of duality. We talked as we walked with his followers, keeping a polite distance because they knew that their master needed this time with me. They still had no clue as to why, however. They wanted to deify Jesus, and because Jesus had such a glow of the Christ Consciousness (the Divine Knowing) it was quite understandable and yet regretful since they all had the spark of that same light and could develop it as Jesus did.

That's what Jesus came to demonstrate, you see. The followers were long steeped in the idea that women were inferior and that sexuality was the sinful price to pay for wanting to *know,* as the symbolic Eve desired. This knowing, as I said before, would result in mankind's discovery of their own divinity and since the women already held the sacred womb of emergence, to know their worth could, according to those who feared this power, make them hard to control and uppity or thinking themselves superior. Since Jesus was in the *KNOW* already, he could not be controlled by the established status quo and thus he held no fear and only knew the truth of sexuality and how love moved through this doorway of emergence. Yet he knew that he could not just reach into men's hearts and change this concept in a moment, for it was deeply ingrained. Change is always resisted with a great force of fear and the more drastic the fears the more chaotic are those within the change. It was not the mission of Jesus to bring chaos but to begin peace.

Jesus asked of my priestess training. I questioned him, "How did you know I was of the sisterhood, dear one?"

He smiled that heart-warming smile that I would come to love more than life itself and said, "It is the way you walk, the look in your eyes, the glow on your face, the very way your garments drape over your body, my dearest, how could I miss it?"

That worried me because the safety of the sisterhood depended on our invisibility. I frowned as he spoke to me these things, wrinkling my brows into a concerned expression. Jesus laughed that wonderful laugh, he bellowed out with glee, and gave me a side-ways hug as we walked along and said, "Do not worry so, my love, for only those in the *know* would pick up on such obvious manners and mode. Those who are blinded by duality's imbalance just feel a twinge of something they can't quite comprehend. Will you tell me of your early years and your training and allow me to share my childhood and training too, for we have much to learn of each other, do we not?"

My smile was his answer. Often we would answer each other with a simple smile or a look of concern, depending on the question. We would share these things in private for our schooling and our early training were not for general knowledge.

We came to a small village and Jesus asked the followers to come forth and gather around him in preparation for meeting the townspeople. The women followers allowed the men to step forward as usual. Jesus said, "hear me once again, for I have said this many times and in many ways, no one is more worthy than another and when I see you women stepping back when I ask that all of you come forward, I see you judge yourselves unworthy. Come forward and stand in a circle, all of you, so that we are not leader and followers but one in purpose, all equal to the other."

The women then joined the men in a great circle with Jesus and myself also part of this arrangement. Jesus smiled sweetly and looked deeply into each person's eyes, one by one and said; "Now, that is better. Now we are one circle of energy surrounding the heart of our mission and the purpose of our Father God." To each person he said, "Bless you, for you are beloved."

When his eyes finally completed the circle and rested once again upon my own he said, "I know that you wonder of whom this lovely woman is that has joined us at the well and who has me walking so lightly and smiling so brightly. Some of the followers laughed because he seemed as a little boy full of delight when he said these words.

"Bear with me a moment then you will understand. We have spoken before of the duality and you all know that this is an inner teaching, not quite appropriate for the masses of yet, the masses whom we must gently bring back to the balance of the Divine. Each and every person and any other living, learning being is both masculine and feminine in essence, for to be otherwise one would not be able to experience life in any form. You then, according to your very soul's choice, decide which factor you will favor, thus you express your physicality in the feminine or the masculine with the other factor safely deep within your being to keep you from tilting too far into your energy."

"For instance, should you be only feminine essence, you mothers would not have the inner force necessary to protect your children and to organize your conscious minds, or to push forth into universal laws as structural grids. It is aggressive behavior that seeks to protect and to push forth you see, and when it is unbalanced it seeks only to control and to structure bars instead of grids to be used as guidelines. You men must likewise have a feminine part of yourself held safely within or you would lose your sense of feeling and intuitive *knowing* for the feminine is the part of yourself that moves beyond logic and organization into the pureness of understanding, without proof or reason to explain. This part identifies truth and cannot be contained behind limiting structures that restrict growth."

"This brings me to my topic, which is: there is always a counterpart to your soul, a being that reflects your other aspect in its perfection. This twin flame does not often appear to you when you live in physicality for it is part of the heavenly balancing factor, much like a guardian angel, and thereof assists your mission. Sometimes the mission is so great that it is necessary for both aspects of your being-ness, you and your counterpart, to choose to walk the path of physical life. This is a very difficult choice, for what one experiences, so, too, the other experiences, and this can be most joyful and most painful at the same time. It is my twin flame whom I have been reunited with this day."

"We are soon to solidify the inner group of the twelve plus the one, in its duality. The inner group will not be more important than the outer group of followers, just different in purpose and closer to the possibility of agony and suffering for the cause. If you become one of the twelve, know that you are beloved and appreciated for your great sacrifice. If you become one of the others, know that without you the mission would not move forth. The twelve direct the energy under the guidance of the one, but you carry it forth as a chariot of purest light spreading a trail of awareness as you travel forth. Know too, that there will be those who would attempt to stop you at all cost. The cost is high in this commitment, but the reward for All is immeasurable."

"The duality of this twelve plus one is this, friends, that I shall be as a true priest as I have been prepared for-to twelve masculine followers, for a true priest does not have supporters but rather has those who help him serve. There must also be an equally reflective group of twelve plus one made up of the feminine, you see, and I could not serve as a priest to this group for it needs a priestess to lead it forth. I give to you of myself then, even in that role, for I present my counterpart, my very feminine soul, *Mary of Magdalene*. He turned to me and beckoned me forth. "You know what to say and do," he said to me as he bowed and presented me by holding my hand high.

"The happiest day of my life was the day I looked once again into my beloved's eyes, for I had seen those eyes in my dreams before this very day of our meeting," I said to the crowd. "I have long known that my mission was the duality and I have come to serve Mother God, just as Jesus serves Father God and thus doing we serve the ONENESS OF GOD. It will be difficult for all of you women, as well as myself, for the need is great and the greed is tremendous. I will be proud to serve with you if you agree. We will be as One, as sisters who love and respect ourselves and the feminine within the heart and soul of everyone. We must, however, tread lightly and allow our beloved brothers here to open doorways ever so gently, so that fear does not stop this mission of balance. When your mission in this becomes apparent you will be defiled and called names that used to be names of honor, but now are spoken as the utmost in disrespect. Your sexuality will probably be smeared with accusations and assaults will surely come if we do not quietly move forth and they may come even with this discretion. Your names may be struck from the past record and your daughters forgotten but your willingness to offer of yourselves will be the key to the happiness of all women to follow, as well as for all men, and daughters and sons will rejoice. Those of you who are the supporters and the outer group, as with the men; your chariot of energy will take the message far and wide. You are critical to the cause and Mother God holds you all dear to her great heart, as the Father God does also. Shall we begin then?"

For a moment the women hesitated and looked at each other, then their eyes began to glisten and great tears of joy flooded their faces and they rushed forth and thanked Jesus for this great gift to them.

"Mary is the one to thank, for your counterpart is never less than your very self and both aspects must agree for such a mission." Jesus also said, "we will mingle our groups as one and keep only separated when the need is appropriate, but know that Mary is of the same essence as I and that we are ONE."

"Now let us plan our day in this small village," Jesus said, and the men and women sat down in the shade of some olive trees to plan and to gain more knowing.

"Each group is connected to the Whole" Jesus said, "and this small community is just as important as any of the larger communities. Just as each person's growth in awareness or biased ignorance affects the group, so, too, the groups affect each other. We begin with all of you. Now like a pebble thrown into the sea, your awareness will ripple and spread far and wide, first within this group, then within the greater community, then eventually to all creation. Let us plan the seeds we will plant today and then decide on our group approach."

"Shall we begin," he asked and I resounded, "We shall!"

Blessed Be,

THE SORTING OF THE CIRCLE

Within the circle we discussed the beginning of the mission in its duality quest. Jesus had not yet begun the three intensive years spoken of in the new testament of your bible story. I was in my eighteenth year at this time and he was twenty-seven, almost ten years older than I. I considered him older and wiser, but in time he would convince me that as counterparts, he was eighteen and I was twenty-seven as well, for we shared our experience. As twin flames, he was me and I was he.

We would be as directors to the group, he said, and would thus play the true role of the priest and priestess, which was to help the group focus on the issue or purpose at hand. This, he pointed out, was what our training prepared us for.

Each person present within the circle had an opportunity to introduce him or herself and to state their concerns and observation of the attitudinal mode of their community from their own perspective. The women, at first, found it difficult to open up. Jesus wisely asked me to comment on my perceptions and when the other sisters saw that my dissertation was respected and discussed by the brothers, they came forward with their observations, and those disclosures hit hard and true.

One woman said, "I am tired of being an object within my household only to reinforce my husband's sense of worth. While I have much help with the household chores, he tells me which robe to wear, which tapestry to hang and where, when to appear if his guests are in the house, what to say when they arrive, and so on. There are women who wish they lived in my circumstance, but I wish many times that I was one of my servants, for they are free to do their work and I hear them chatting to each other as they move from chore to chore. No one is telling them what to say to each other. Of course it is I who happen to be the overseer when they chat, for my husband is then about his business. When he is in the house the women are silent. I feel dead within and I want desperately to live!"

One of the brothers said to her, "What is your desire then, Miriam, would you rather be a servant than the lady of the house?"

"I just want to be free to be myself and be treated with the same love and respect I give to others. I want to offer an opinion once in awhile for I have listened as my husband made unwise investments, later to learn that what I knew could have contributed to the cause and ultimately was the solution. I want to feel great joy when a daughter emerges from my womb, as well as the son," she resounded. "I want to learn more for this world cries out to me to be understood and explored. I want to walk beside my beloved husband, not behind him, and I want to pick and choose my own clothing, as well as words. Most of all, I want my husband to know me, for he does not have a clue as to who I am. Our marriage was arranged, true, but I have much more to offer than being simply the one to bear his children, who are mine too, and to be his hostess."

A woman in robes obviously long worn and tattered spoke up, "May I speak, for I have never in my life had the opportunity to do so?"

Jesus smiled and nodded and she began. "I was born to a family with little wealth and my mother was the saddest woman I have ever known. But she loved me dearly and sought to protect me from the pain she suffered. My father regarded all of us as burdens that he did not deserve. He constantly told us that if it were not for our constant needs he would have more money and be better respected within the community. He was a digger of graves and also worked as the incendiary for those who were put to ashes at death. He felt his work lowly and his life unfair. We, his daughters, for there were no sons, and my dear mother, felt his wrath and frustration."

"I was sold to an old man when I was twelve years old. It was the same month of my first moon time but I am embarrassed to mention this to all of you for it seems so disrespectful to speak of such unworthy topics.

Jesus interjected, "to be able to bear children is not unworthy, so carry on, my sister."

She continued, "I was never officially married to this man. He delighted in acquiring young girls (he was wealthy enough to pay the required price) to break them into womanhood, as he said. He wanted to be the first to seed their unsoiled wombs. He ruined me, for I bled beyond my time and the wise woman had to come for me. She helped me recover but I was never to bear children for I was torn and defiled. I cried for days upon learning this for I thought my only worth was in being an instrument of childbearing. I was thrown into the streets. I have since lived at the mercy of those who offer assistance to the homeless. I have been raped, beaten and degraded. I had decided to go against the rule of God and take my own life and was at the point of jumping to my death along the cliff overlooking the ocean and the sharp rocks below. Just as I was going to jump I felt a hand upon my shoulder and a voice that touched my very soul, "You are beloved and the most beautiful being I have seen all this day, sister. Please do not go yet. Please walk with me awhile and let me enjoy your presence."

"I turned and first laid my tired eyes upon the one we call "master." I now want to learn of my own worth and that of all women and how we can be integrated into this world of men."

Some of the men looked stunned and remarked at how women could not deal with the day-to-day business that men could and should feel lucky to be looked after by the men. They had no answer for the discarded one, for she was invisible to them.

"We are not children, brother," I said, "We are your counterparts and we ask for no more than to be given the chance to use our talents and skills to the fullest and be respected for our individual contributions. We ask that you love us and stop judging us less worthy in your justification game of "she is not capable of thinking, thus she cannot reason." We ask also that you see us, for there are many who grace your life whom you ignore to the extent that we are totally invisible to you. You fear to look, do you not? For if you see such as this discarded woman you would have to think about what was done to her. Your reasoning destroys the divine balance of all creation, for it reduces all beings except the human man to objects for his use. All others can be discarded when not useful. Man is not the center of all things, as the Greeks and Romans mistakenly believed and taught. God is and God is our Father and our Mother, two in one. A duality."

The men who could not accept a mere woman explaining this concept to them looked to Jesus and asked, "Master, do you allow this woman to speak for you?" "Would you set her straight on this foolishness for she does not understand as you do?"

Jesus laughed a great belly laugh with his head thrown back until his smile graced the sky and when he brought his gaze back to the group he stared in silence, with a smile upon his face, at the questioner. Then to each man in the group he looked, finally, saying; "Were you birthed from an ignorant woman? When did your intellect out distance your mother's, my brothers? Was it when you found your voice, your words, or your attitude passed down from your male elders? Wake up! Would you discard your very mother? While you slept as a child your mother kept you alive and gave you opportunity to experience this life. When is she no longer useful in your life, for your reasoning points to this warped thinking? Wake up now for you sleep walk and cannot see but the lie that you accept as truth because you fear the power of knowing. I tell you now that the women come to *knowing* naturally and only lose it when they buy the lie of ignorance and lose their sight or are beaten to desperation. We, the masculine, must find knowing through a long journey of reason and thought within the moment. Our lovely sisters, mothers and daughters all find it by going within their very hearts and souls. When you negate their essence, their worth, you close the inner doorway to their hearts and they live in deep sorrow as our sister has just shown you."

"Some of you will come and quench your thirst with this group and then leave. Some of you will stay and become one of those willing to sacrifice their very lives to be of the twelve and the one. Some of you are ready to leave now because this truth is too much for you to bear or accept. This preparation for moving into villages to bring awareness will be a difficult mission. We must make sure we are ready. Before any of you leave, please let me say this: This masculine/feminine duality truth has been so long forgotten that we cannot force it upon the masses. Just as there are some among you who cannot accept this and want to leave, so, too, the masses will have many who would leave or stop the message. For that reason, with a pain deep in my heart, I must ask that we come quietly to this matter. Never let those we seek to enlighten see our group of women and men as separate, yet, also you must be so very careful how you interact. Mary will respect your leadership role, brothers, but you must respect that she is of me and mine, as I am of her. Upon this shock I expect to lose some of you and I send you on your way with greatest good will and blessings. One day we will meet again and take up this matter when you are ready, right here where we left off."

At that point more than half of the men arose and left the circle, but all of the women stayed.

"Now," Jesus said, "let us begin planning our first excursion into the mind and heart of the people. For the sake of reaching the ears and channeling into the minds and hearts, I will speak as director or master of this mission. I have been trained in techniques that will gain the attention and the amazement of those sleeping, thus I will find the doorway into many minds and hearts. I will need you, who have chosen to join me, to mingle among the crowd, never separate from this mass, and bring an equalization of energy therein, by just standing among the many. You will find that the level of your commitment and the depth of your heart's desire will radiate upon your being. You will effect those near you by your presence, not because you are more worthy, for we are never more worthy, but because you radiate the "knowing." My Father/Mother God, and yours as well, is *All Knowing* and as so beams brighter than imaginable at this stage of your development. Our mission is to integrate *knowing* into the being-ness of all we speak with. Some will shun this light; others will absorb it and move closer to the divinity of the LIGHT. We cannot beam a light unbalanced. We will seek to open hearts and bring this chaos back into alignment with enlightenment. Shall we move to the center of this little town now and begin?"

All arose and stood ready to move into the first teaching. They walked as a group, and there was a certain glow about this group, as there always was with Jesus. I would later learn I would emit this light also when I was not guarding my essence for the sake of the mission. We walked in silence.

Blessed be,

THE RELEASE OF PAIN

We moved along, a group of about twenty men and women with Jesus and myself at the front of the group, toward the little town close by our circle meeting. Those moving about the little villa noticed us because it was seldom that a group would walk together thusly, and the majority of those within our numbers were strangers to the townsfolk. Not only that was compelling in attention, but most of the animals within the community followed us as well. We had burros leaving their stanchions, cats and dogs following, birds, chickens and other foul also coming our way, all in great joy. A giant black raven flew down near Jesus and myself and did a back flip and flew on its merry way. My friend, no doubt, how this one could find me in so many places was still a wonder and reassurance.

Jesus walked right past the well in the middle of the village and as people gaped at the spectacle we presented, he swung his arms wide and high and said, "Come and rest a while and let us speak with you about the wonder of this life you live."

He had a mesmerizing way about him and most people just sat down their water jugs, or stopped their tasks and followed in wonder. We hardly slowed in pace as the villagers were invited to join us and followed along. We ended our journey upon a hillside along the edge of the village.

There were olive trees growing here and there upon this slope. Jesus invited all to sit in the shade of the trees and he stepped out into the sun. He seemed to glow out there in that light, and his hair appeared as quiet fire burning around his head and shoulders, where the hair fell long and twirling.

"There is an ache in your hearts, is there not?" he said to the crowd, "that sometimes can be ignored and other times cries for attention? Do you wonder of the source of that pain?"

Eyes stayed glued to his magnificent presence, for he commanded attention by his glow and confidence, even as his physical body stood tall and beautiful. And he was right, for all held a deep pain within the depths of their being, a place that seemed too deep to reach. Jesus was beaming brightly and was the first man ever that I saw the beauty therein as well as great strength. A reflection of the balance of the masculine and the feminine, I realized, and an example of how balance enlightens. The listeners noticed the glow of his soul as well.

"Have you ever wondered of your true worth?" he asked. "How would you measure such a thing? Is this *professed* worth of your being connected to your duty in this life you live? Or is it connected to who your parents are, or to whether you are a man or a woman? Can you raise this worthiness by being an extraordinary athlete or a courageous warrior? Is worth measured by physical beauty? What deems such beauty, dear ones?"

The questions just came like a mighty flood washing over the listeners, who by then began to realize that the deep pain within them was caused by a knife blade sinking into their hearts called *the measure of worthiness.* The handle was gripped by societal attitudes long engrained and tightly wrapped around this knife of judgment and control.

"I tell you there is not a blade of grass nor a bird on the wing nor a single being in all creation that is more worthy than another. All beings have something to offer in return to that which created and molded them. These are the true sacrificial offerings, to live life with gladness and glee. God does not want a life wasted in the mistaken idea that such a sacrifice would pleasure this Creator of All that Is. What kind of God would create only to destroy? Even as you waste precious beings in sacrificial rituals, you deem one sacrifice more worthy to die than another, do you not? How can you honor God by destroying what was a beautiful creation? You only take the life it was meant to live. I tell you this, my friends, a white dove on the wing is living its worth far more than the doves that the moneychangers sell within the temple to kill for an unholy cause. The innocent lamb that is offered upon the alter in bloody sacrifice is a tragedy to behold, for it can never give the gift of its life, the wool, or procreate or even provide meat to the hungry. Its blood is wasted and the offering is thus an unfit tribute to the Almighty One who created this being. This offering brings no joy to God, I tell you this day."

"You were born worthy of this opportunity of life and the challenges it provides. Those who measure your birthright are wrong, for God has measured you worthy of life. God does not create just to destroy or to degrade. Think about how you judge yourselves and then think about the perfection and the beauty of all creation. Some of you have come to serve and some of you have come to rule. Both are noble opportunities and the least shall be as the greatest in such a balance. Many souls will offer their very lives so that others can learn the value of this opportunity. But far too many, especially among our women, are never recognized for the precious, beloved beings they are. They are like flowers and fruit trees within a great garden; they will go unnoticed even as the gardener hungers for beauty and sustenance and dies unnourished and depressed. Without a mother you would not be, for it was the great plan that a Father would seed you into being, but a Mother would bring you forth. This plan is the Divine Plan of Creation and all Creation must move through the Father/Mother to manifest and experience life and learning. The spark of your soul is the seed and the light of your life is the nourishment of that seed into its full potential and seen as enlightenment. You cannot find light without the duality of Creation."

"The pain eases, my dear ones, when you remember that you are a Divine Creation and all that surrounds you are aspects of the Divine Creative effort as well. Bless the Olive Tree you sit within the shade of, for it has blessed you with food, oil for your skin, and its shadow to keep you comfortable, as well as beauty to behold. Would you rate it unworthy? Why rate it at all and thus bring pain of judgment to its being as other's judgment has caused you, likewise, deep pain. Ease the pain of the Olive Tree at this moment and touch it's leaves or trunk, or a portion of it, and thank it for just being."

At that point, many, almost unconsciously, reached forth to touch a tree. The trees trembled as if there were an earthquake and a look of surprise registered upon the face of each and every one in that crowd, for the ground did not shake but the trees swirled as if a great cyclone had touched them.

"The beings of the trees have acknowledged your appreciation and their pain is lessened." Jesus said, "Now, do this for yourself as well, for your shadow and your being and the fruit you bear are beloved by many, but most especially by That Which Created your very soul and deemed you a beauty to behold. Let the shudder of the releasing of this deep pain within you shake you as well and release the judgment of yourself and others. The shaking is the demon of the great lie leaving your being. Fill that dark hole with the light and love of truth. Let no one ever touch that place of your heart again with the untruth. Keep it sacred for this is the temple of your soul; you have the key to this doorway."

"My followers are learning to be leaders," he went on to say "and they will now move among you and look into your eyes and recognize the perfection and the beauty of you. My beloved co-partner, Mary, and I will follow them and balance the energy thus shaken into action."

The followers then went to the townsfolk, one by one, and looked deep within their eyes with a loving look of appreciation and recognition. The listeners, upon this gaze, most often began shaking violently, as the pain-demon moved out of their hearts. Myself, or Jesus, would then come to them and take their hands and they would quiet and the shake would leave and the pain would cease. We blessed them and kissed them on the forehead and said, "Go in peace, for you are free."

Thirty people were thus validated and freed that day, women, men and children and myself as well, for as I worked with Jesus I recognized him as master. I would be his mastress as well, he said, two in one, but because of the need, he would lead outward, forth into the mission and I would take the seekers into our heart place. Together we would send this offering to the Father/Mother God, offered in true love and appreciation for the sake of everyone we interacted with, and those they would later, themselves, touch. Like a mighty wave, we hoped this balancing energy would wash across the land.

Blessed be,

The Magical Night

After our experience in the little villa the followers knew that this mission affected everyone deeply and that it was of the utmost importance to continue. They were also impressed as to their power to equalize energy, as demonstrated when they helped those shaken by their pain to move through the agitation of the experience. Some were concerned for their families, however, and Jesus sent them back to their home, telling them that they would be as much a part of the cause there, within their families, as they would be walking with he and I. Some left other obligations in order to continue with us, but those obligations did not seem as important to them, and upon counsel with the master it was decided that they would carry on as followers in this mission for as long as they choose to do so.

The group dynamics, as you would call it nowadays, were complicated within this gathering. We were all one in purpose but the hierarchy struggle was threatening. There were those who claimed that Jesus was meant to be king and then there were those who saw me as a diversion for the master, taking him from his godly duties. The role of the women was a great concern because the attitudinal corruption of the society was deeply ingrained. My leadership threatened the power of the status quo, yet in all of this there was connection in that all knew that the established religious and governmental agencies were corrupt and self-serving. Their main purpose was to control the minds of the people through closing the doorway of knowing. According to them, God had chosen only a certain few to be allowed to *know*.

All manner of consideration was given to all that followed this cause, however, by those we visited. The magnetic master somehow acquired food and lodging for us everywhere we went. Whether or not he knew all of our generous hosts I was never sure, but they all seemed pleased and blessed to offer us food and shelter. There was something about him that opened doors to homes as well as minds.

The women were always separated from the men at the time of night rest, even one married couple split at this time. The wife went with me to the woman's quarters and he with the men. Jesus pointed out that such a couple, if they join the group, must support the structure of the group. "This marital coupling" he said, "was sacred and must not be defiled by judgment or jealousy of those not enjoying this divine union." The couple, and the little child they had with them, would often go, from time to time, to their home for family time. They were sent off in love and welcomed back with equal affection.

One evening we rested outside a humble home where our group was sheltered. The men occupied the stable area and the women were housed in the food preparation area. Jesus and I took a walk down a winding path through the vineyards of this unassuming place. We held hands as we walked and he told me the evening seemed enchanted. I could feel the same enchantment as I walked by his side.

"Do you love me from the depths of your great heart, Mary, as I so love you?" Jesus asked. I felt surprised because I, too, as did many of the followers, believed that this master could know all of what was in our hearts and souls.

"Do you not know, Beloved, how much my heart expands and beams as I look upon your being and feel your touch?" I said, with tears of joy in my eyes. He looked upon me in such a tender and concerned way and said, "I, too, have my moments of need to be reassured. These followers see me as a fully developed god when I am only, as they are, seeking one-ment with God and but a way-shower. The only difference between they and myself is that I know of the completeness of this ONE Who Created All That Is, and they only know of little aspects of this Great One. They are like the ant that thinks the mighty tree it climbs represents the entire universe, and when they climb out on a limb and are eaten by a bird they think that this tree-god created them to feed upon. My mission is yours as well, and now that you have arrived I feel more able to begin. I feel complete and whole. We must only take the first baby steps at this time, to measure the technique of accomplishing our mission of balance."

"The people will never accept me," I said, "walking with you as an equal. To act as your equal would outrage the listeners and thus we would not reach them."

He thought for a moment and then said, "That is a major concern for it may require that you make the greatest sacrifice of all, as all in the feminine have done for too long, and not show yourself to the masses in your true priestess role. It pains my heart to think that we cannot be open and forthcoming in our duality, but for your sake, and the sake of our women followers who may be persecuted, I will have to step forward and you will then be as my silent half, there in support and in confirmation. There is already dissent among our followers as to your position in this group. Some still think you a witch and me bewitched, and some think you are a temptation to the purity of my sexuality. I do, in truth, desire to merge with you as a man and woman joined in the passion of love and creation, within divine marriage. But we shall follow your ways when the time comes, for you are trained better than I in the sacredness of the sexual realms and the mergence of duality with marriage. I trust you in this and I keep your honor sacred. But these moments, as you well know, will be for us only, not moments to share, because there are those who would never understand such a union. However, if you are willing, in the next village we shall visit the temple and begin the process of marriage and enter the pre-marriage agreement and follow the precepts set forth for this place and time."

"I would be honored, my love, to offer myself to you in this duality of marriage and I willingly go through all steps set forth to begin the process of our merging."

We walked quietly then, hand in hand, through the vineyards. "Notice the grapes upon the vine," Jesus said, "they hang in groups, but after harvest they combine with other such groups of like fruit and become the wine. All must be in full growth, at the peak of their fullness to be harvested and enter into the wine vats to merge with the other grapes. The keeper of the vineyard selects only those grapes ready to become wine, leaving those not yet developed in fullness, and those far beyond their sweetness to other purpose. The ones not developed will be passed over and the birds and workers of the vineyard will enjoy their fruits as they come full bloom. Those past prime will drop from the vine and re-seed the vineyard. We are like vineyard keepers right now. We look for the clusters of grapes, however, which are slightly fuller, slightly sweeter, and slightly more ready to move beyond the limit of expectations of the old wine and form a more perfect wine. We will find a few within every group that have a glow of possibility. We will select them and ask them to join and group with other like ones for the sake of perfecting the wine that man does so thirst after."

"I will have to speak in such parables as this, my beloved, because to speak straight-forward, my words would be rejected in fear of truth. But to tell a story with an underlying message of truth then is to bring such awareness in through the sacred door of the heart instead of the guarded gates of the mind."

"Now, tell me of your childhood and your early training and I will tell you of mine." We sat down on a bench within view of the others who were also milling about and enjoying leisure before retiring for the night. We talked all evening until the birds chirped their morning welcome. Two vineyard cats had joined us and curled up upon our robes and purred and slept there as we talked on and on. Jesus was fascinated when I spoke of the Misty Isle and said he would love to have been a bird there watching the priestesses in training. When he spoke of the far off land he was sent as a child, deep in the mountains where the Tibetan one's dwelled, I found this place just as fascinating. After we had talked on and on about our childhood training, we fell into a light sleep, side by side, just as the birds were waking. A dream visited us that was the same for both. We walked hand in hand into a dark cloud and emerged on the other side separated and heart-broken, only touching each other by the very tips of our fingers from time to time, as we floated past a cloud that was dissipating somewhat, and not as solid now. We awoke with a start, at the same time, and looked at each other and knew of the challenge of this union. We would be the dark cloud busters, yet we would darken our days in doing so, for we would be torn apart in this task.

"The dreamtime warns us, my beloved," I said, and since we were both training in the language of the dreams, Jesus nodded, looked into my eyes and ever so gently touched my hand as he replied, "we have come to do this for the sake of all creation. Can you persist in this task and hold a broken heart together for the benefit of all women and men, and for all creation that reflects such?"

"I must as you must," I said in a whisper.

We arose and thanked the morning sun for its warming light and said our prayers for the day together and we moved forth to begin the day.

Blessed be,

Our Physicality and Other Questions

I find it odd that there is so much concern on the size, coloring and our overall physicality in the incarnations of Jesus and myself, and the mother Mary, who is remembered conveniently to fit the mode of exclusion. But this is understandably so since beings want to visualize in order to understand.

Jesus was approximately five foot six inches, which was a normal height for men in that space of time, and likewise, he was of normal weight for his height. He was a man of strong and solid build. Myself, I was about five feet five inches, nearly as tall as he, and close to one hundred pounds. Remember, we were not meant to stand out but to blend in with the norm, so that those individuals that were not, according to the standards of the day, spectacular in appearance, would be able to relate to us and to appreciate that true beauty is not an exterior appearance but an interior truth.

Actually, as all women of the day did, when in public I wrapped my chest tightly, for hygienic purposes; in a binding that helped keep me comfortable by absorbing the body sweat, for it was hot under all those robes. Within the temple I dressed quite differently and could even bare my chest if I so desired, with no embarrassment or shame, for the breasts of a woman are part of her glory. The idea that a woman should be covered in long robes emerged from the patriarchal attitude that a woman was a sexual object and that she must measure up to a man's expectations. Men did not trust other men, for this idea was a reduction of women to objects, you see, and men, deep within their very being, knew that this objectifying of the feminine would make them a desirable item to steal, fight over and compete for, even though they knew it was wrong. This valuable commodity then had to be keep under wraps, thus the excess clothing. Then, there is more to this concept, women being sensitive to men's evaluation of their physicality, did not want to be on constant display and subject to such judgment, thus they welcomed the long robes. At that period of time both genders used the long robes for protection from the sun as well. But the women, for the most part, were more covered, usually with their gloriously beautiful hair completely hidden.

Nothing is explained simply, yet everything is so simple! The simple fact is the attitudes of the controlling beings was the number one motivating factor in women's dress and wrapping of breasts, but it was also convenient for women in that everyday living was easier within this mode--so they accepted it.

In depicting the moment of our meeting by the well, I would be in my long robes with my breasts bound as they normally would be on a day of service, and Jesus would be in long robes also, but slightly shorter robes, allowing freedom of stepping forth, and his glorious hair would be long and flowing. He did not have a beard the day I met him. He grew the beard only after he changed his name to Jeshua. There is a slight difference, you see, in the name Jesus and Jeshua, even though you believe it is just a matter of pronunciation. I also changed my name to MiryAmah, both of us adding the syllable of *ah* when we felt we were joined completely in purpose and mission.

Now for some, here is more information that may answer some of the questions you feel taking shape as you read these words. Jesus' birth was when day was longer than night. You call it the summer solstice. He represents the masculine principle, which is light. My birth was when the night was longer than day and I represent the feminine principle. The two together equalize into the equinox, you see, so spring represents the duality, as does autumn. The light of the Sun and the dark of the night are due to cycles that equalize and then lean into the light, then lean back into the dark. It is part of experience and keeps it in a fluctuating rhythm, as the duality meets and then dances apart, taking turns in coming forth and pulling back.

Jeshua was born,

When there was more day than night,

He is the Sun,

He is the Light,

MiryAmah was born,

When there was more night than day,

She is the moon,

She shows the way,

75

The celebration of Christ's birth on the Winter Solstice is accurate, for the duality of Jesus was his merging into myself, as my duality was merging into him. In that we had two birthdays, since we both incarnated in this time and space. The celebration of Christmas, or *Christness*, as you know, was part of the plan to bring the ones called pagans into line as Christians, as they defined themselves. In actuality the Christians in power at that later time (after we had departed this life experience) were Roman in nature and part of the plan to control the masses through the practice of Religion. That was never the goal of Jesus and myself. Instead, we desired to integrate the balance of Masculine and Feminine into the attitudinal mind-set of all in physicality, or at least plant the seed of such, so that they would participate in the true spiritual nature of religion instead of the power and control mode into which it had eroded. This, of course, was woven in to bring sanity into insane practices. The miracles that Jesus is remembered for, and for which I have been forgotten, were due to our early training as priest and priestess within the divinity of truth as it was kept sacred in certain safe places upon Tara.

The idea of separating church and state, as you in your free-land have attempted to do, is a good idea, for when religion tells people what to think, or more accurately what *not to think,* and instead does the thinking for them, then individuals are no longer free to live a well balanced life and experience discovery. They have given up their gift of free will, a gift given by the Source. A church should be a place of reinforcement of discovery, not a place of demand or brainwashing. This idea will outrage those ingrained in religion, most assuredly, for they feel a God-given right to control the thinking of their congregations. God did not tell them that. Those in control, coupled with their own ego, convinced them of such. They are trained well to quote and mis-quote a source that has been only written from the point of view of the masculine and thus "his-story, not her-story or the truth of duality." The truth is there would be no opportunity for physicality without the feminine. She is more able to procreate alone than he, but to do so would be upsetting the great need to be balanced and in a dual effort with the counterpart, the masculine, and she knows this well in her heart and soul. This is the root source of the jealousy that has created the situation at hand. He (the masculine) thinks he must act superior in order to overcome this fear of not being vital to the creative effort.

The spirit groups that are working with many in the physical at this time are attempting to heal the wounded feminine and the wounded masculine as well, and bring back the sacred duality of these two counterparts to their true divinity. As you see in the energy known as *electricity,* there must be two sources, the positive and negative flow of energy, one working totally the opposite of the other, to carry the current to the goal. This is a universal law, that it takes this merging of two opposites to complete the whole.

Now you might think the opposite of good is bad, and thus a necessary experience. Again, you have a simple truth, but not so simple in manifestation. Evil is the stopping of growth or the negation of movement, which is evolution. Is evil then a duality of non-movement? No, it is the destruction of progress and thus cannot be an opposite for it destroys the movement. Without the duality there cannot be wholeness. Dualities then are related to growth and movement and cooperative energy that creates a balanced force that builds the light of experience. The only benefit of comparing good to bad is to know *what is not* in order to know *what is.*

Again, you might say, "Isn't night the duality of day?" The answer, of course, is "yes." Night does not stop growth but rather brings the attention to the inner realms as day focuses attention on the outer. See it like breathing, first in and then out. Remember always! Evil is not dark, it just hides there, just as it can hide in the light of day, especially within attitudes that judge the worth of God's creation.

While this is the base of all relational problems, including the relationship you beings have with the planet herself, it manifests in various ways. Governments that are unfair, depression and lack of self-esteem, lack of knowledge, suspicion of *knowing,* conditional attitudes pertaining to love, wars and power issues, fear-based thinking, and more and more are all due to the imbalance in energies and thinking due to attitudinal misalignment. That is why Jesus as Jeshua talked in parables, because the underlying message would bring attention to the imbalance and not directly confront those who felt safe in the prison of their own minds.

You were all meant to be free to think and learn and grow as your awareness expands. You were all meant to shine forth in your masculine glow and to create the beautiful music of the feminine intertwined with the light and part of it, as it is part of the song. I come to unite the light and the song, as my beloved has also returned to do.

Blessed be,

THE DUALITY BEGINS THROUGH CELEBRATION

One evening, after a long day of traveling and speaking to the people, Jesus and I decided the time was upon us for our pre-marriage. There would be the usual ceremony at the house of a follower who had offered to host this joyous occasion. This householder was a humble man of great wealth and owned a grand house. He intended to treat all guests as though they were royalty, but he missed the mark slightly, as Jesus pointed out. This was the house where the message of the wine was given by my beloved, for when the householder saw the great crowds of people who came to celebrate this occasion, he was not sure he had enough wine. He brought out his everyday wine to use first, saving the finer wine for the actual ceremony, to be shared only by certain guests as well as the guests of honor, as was the custom of the time.

This was a perfect opportunity for Jesus to offer the message of *judgment in worth* within the moment. He admonished the kind householder, in a respectful way, telling him that "the last shall be first and the first shall be last" in the kingdom of Heaven, so why would we not bring out our finest wine first? Too often those of lesser material wealth and position were treated as second-class citizens, he said. While all were grateful for the hospitality of the householder, there was still this overall attitude among the guests, house servants, and family, that there was a difference in what was expected in this hospitality, based on such measures. The good wine was brought out after this comment and when it was gone Jesus made even better wine from the well water and all quenched their thirst with the finest wine they had ever tasted.

This was seen as a miracle but was, in fact, due to the training he received as a child and fairly easy to accomplish. The ability to delve into alchemy and its associated skills, to change substances, is only taught to those who demonstrate the soul consciousness necessary to keep this feat sacred, for it could be used unwisely. It was a great honor to be offered this training and both Jesus and I were granted this opportunity. Jesus went on later to train some of the apostles in healing miracles that are also learned when the water lesson was offered, as did I my disciples. As women, we had to use those skills in secret because if we demonstrated such power, we would be considered a great danger to a society that would see us as a threat to their dictates. We could meet great pain or even death.

As we began the ceremony for which we had gathered, we began with the renaming, as was the custom. We would choose our merging names. "I shall be called *Jeshua*," Jesus said, "From this day forth, for now I have found my wholeness and the light of my life. Just as within every being created, there is a part of each soul's sacred energy reflected in masculine and feminine form in an inner sacred marriage." He continued, "So, too, should this sacred balance of God's essence be reflected in the outer realms, as two united in marriage. Whether it is an awareness of the inner or the outer reflection of such, one becomes a whole new person at such a moment of commitment; as such, I change my name to Jeshua."

In turn I said, "I, too, take a new name to honor this merging of my being with my beloved as the inner sacred marriage reflects in our intended union. I now will be known as *MiryAmah*, to honor and blend my energy, as reflected in our naming, with my beloved Jeshua." Jeshua then poured a cup of wine and sipped from it, saying "this wine represents the blood of life and in sipping this wine I pledge myself to you as husband and caretaker of you as a holy vessel of life-bringing." Then he offered the vessel to me and I also sipped of its sweet substance and said, "I share with you this wine which represents to me that my very blood is your life-force, as it is mine in this holy union, and I keep it ever sacred and honor your protection and your essence into my being."

Then Jeshua kissed the top of my head, also customary, and sealed this promise with purest love vibrating through my being and filling every hair on my head with a hum. I washed his feet with my energized hair, using the sacred oil to infuse the energy from the crown of my physicality, which he had just so sweetly kissed, sending his love to meet mine. By washing his feet thusly, this energy blended with mine, with the oil as a conduit, circled and cycled to our very souls and then brightened our beings to a brilliance that only such a love and commitment could charge.

We would wait three months for the final ceremony and at that time we would then enter the sacred sexuality phase of this union and circle the energy, literally, through this masculine and feminine union as the Source intended, to teach the awareness of and oneness of all creation. While we desired each other greatly, we were so aware of the sacredness of this gift of a man to a woman and a woman back to the man, in this natural beautiful moment, that we had no temptations to violate the pattern and looked forward to the process.

We also had to deal with the societal attitudes within this moment, which had eroded into the idea that sexuality was a weakness in humanity and that a man had to lower himself into such a union. It was, of course, strength, when viewed as sacred and a blessing, as the priestess and those few priests such as Jeshua knew well. It was this prevailing attitude that demanded that every woman offer her husband a child, preferably a son, which tipped the balance of creation as reflected in marriage. Women's pleasure was negated in this sacred sexual ritual, and it slowly lost its true meaning. She became just an incubator and housekeeper in this mind-set. This, as you see, was part of the problem facing all beings expressing upon this planet and was due to being misled by those who played at creation before they knew their own balance. But what had begun had to continue and find its way back to sanity and divinity.

The true fall mentioned in your Bible book was that the beings you term angels, who were not part of that group in reality, were part of the creation effort and actually beings you might see as *advanced* but not yet fully developed. They were not the Watchers, by the way, of which Enoch spoke and of whom he did not like, for they were not playing the game as Enoch felt they should. The Watchers were actually another group that were the gatekeepers of the planet and their memory has been twisted and turned inside out. This is a long story, however, and I will not go further for the Watchers will tell their own story. What I am saying is this, the seed of imbalance came early in this planet's ancient past, but it was not the plan of the Grand Creator to offer free will on this planet. The Grand Creator, The Great Mysterious One, allowed the free-will zone although it was the creation team, advanced scientists and experimenters are one way to categorize this team, which made the proposal. The idea behind the free-will zone was to test the ability of beings to ultimately evolve and return to the Source, The Grand Creator, no matter what circumstances they experienced. What a grand opportunity this is.

Now, back to the day of our pre-marriage. Jeshua was beginning to choose his twelve and I my twelve. They would act the part of our mission ambassadors, our inner team, as it were. He had the greater burden because he was constantly dealing with men who did not understand our relationship. They held the attitude that he was sidetracked from God's work should he give into the mystery of sexuality. They wanted to make him above such human needs, for they wanted God to manifest through him as they imagined the Unimaginable One to be. Jeshua told them that if he was a god, then he was a man too. He tried to tell them that all are what they emerge from, but in order to stay within the law of the day, he had to be very careful not to enter what the established leaders referred to as *blasphemy* and an offense that would have stopped the mission, should it be laid at our feet and judged harshly.

This relationship to God was kept secret by the few who understood it but the populace did not understand or accept and it is still not understood by many today. To know that you are god and human at the same time is to know your true worth. That was the controlling factor, you see, to convince people that some were more worthy than others. One feeling unworthy would then accept the crumbs society offered them, even though they deserved the *finest wine,* as Jeshua verbalized with "last shall be first and the first last and all shall be equal but different in gifts to share."

This was the official day of our name change and there were those who would not use my new name because of this pecking order, seeing me as unworthy to stand beside the one they called *Messiah.* Those who were the beginning of my twelve, however, afforded me great respect and used my new name in greatest joy. My blessed sisters understood fully. They were a blessing to me and to all women.

I can only tell you this story from my own point of view, for even as Jeshua is my counterpart, and I his, we can feel that which the other experiences, yes, but we cannot read each other's minds in perfection. This may seem strange to you who see that there are those mind readers among you who are always present in societies, but they, too, can only access a limited expanse of another's mind and only with the approval that the incarnated soul has granted. Of course Jeshua and I would welcome opening our minds, as we had our hearts, to each other, but the mission was to experience a reality as it would unfold for those experiencing the time and space and attitudinal circumstances we had entered. There needed to be a place of solitude and individuality within the duality to meet the challenge afforded. Thus, we had to be wholly man and woman of the time in order to show the way. I often wondered what Jeshua could be thinking when he spoke to people seeking awareness and courage to carry on, for I did not always understand his meaning. He would later explain it to me, if he chose to do so. His greatest pain was that his wife and his mother were not appreciated within the organized society as he felt we should be and that he could not change that misaligned attitude immediately and allow us to stand side-by-side with him. "My mother is blessed among women to me, because she brought me forth into this place, and my wife is blessed to my heart and soul for she walks with me through this opportunity and shares her life and merges her very soul with mine,"he said often. The memory of this statement would change over time to accommodate those who would not share the memory of Jeshua with the memory of me.

I only saw my beloved angry and uncontrolled once in that lifetime we shared and that was when I was first called *whore,* and oddly enough that came on our day of pre-marriage. One of the followers approached me with scorn written all over his face as he said, "You will regret the day you tempted the master, whore!"

Jeshua was not far away and heard this accusation. His face transformed immediately; he appeared red and frowning as I had never seen happen before, even scaring me, and he shouted, "What is this insult you lay at my feet by degrading a name that was once sacred, with which you label my beloved?" The offensive one looked truly frightened, never having seen this side of the master before. "As surely as I stand here I tell you that she is me and I am her and what you think of her you surely think of me! You disappoint me greatly," he said in a lower tone, "for I expected better of you than this; your jealousy has revealed your true nature and you do not love me or believe in the mission of balance and peace as you say. You are a whore, I say, for that corrupted label is referring to those who degrade sexuality and the sacredness of the union of man and woman. What you think you see in my beloved is the truth of your own heart and the truth of you. Be gone from this celebration!"

The follower gave one last resentful glare in my direction and it was obvious that he held hate in his heart for me, then he left, taking others with him, both men and women. The partygoers hung their heads and the gaiety mellowed. Jeshua said, "Make merry please, and honor my beloved and myself as I would honor you." And so the joy returned.

"Our work will be difficult" Jeshua said, as he looked at me in deepest pain. "I know," I replied, "but that is why we were sent, is it not?" I took his gentle hand in mine. He squeezed my hand and said, "For with all creation upon this free-will place tipped into imbalance, we have come and, no doubt, we will suffer failure as well as success in this great challenge," he whispered to me. "Without you I could not go on," and I answered with my heart as I looked into his sad eyes.

We walked away from the celebration then, leaving those party minded followers behind to enjoy the affair. We walked hand in hand to the homes we would spend the evening at, in our separate locations. We spoke not another word on our way to our temporary quarters, for our hearts were heavy, even as we were heartened with our pre-marriage now completed, we could not share our intention in the way that a man and woman should celebrate such. We had hoped that this moment would help others understand all male/female relationships, as well as gladden our hearts as we joined together in this mission. We still held such hope. We just knew it would be a far greater challenge than anyone could have imagined.

Blessed be,

THE RESCUE OF SARAH

The selection of the twelve was finally completed just a few weeks after the pre-marriage festivity and ceremony. Jeshua and I attempted to involve a variety of personalities within each group, for we did not desire all to be replicas but complementing, thinking aspects. I will not say much of the apostles for they were Jeshua's team and he knew them far better than I. We did, however, often mix the groups when learning and discussing the issues within which we wanted to be an instrument of change. Intimacy, as best friends exhibit though, was something that was reserved for the quiet evening times when we were separated, as the custom required. At those times we relaxed and spoke freely among our gender groups and came to know each other at a more personal, intimate level.

The evening of the completion of the twelve sister disciples, we all enjoyed what you would today call *girl talk* well into the night. We laughed, played jokes on each other, compared our pre-stories and experiences and just let our energies blend with the ease that develops between those bonded in passion and purpose.

While I loved all of my sisters equally, I loved them differently. Of the twelve, Sarah was the closest to me for she touched my heart, but each sister, Ruth, Salome, Annetha, Teresha, Marianna, Judith, Shema, Amielle, Elizabetha, little Tania, and another Mary all gave to myself and each other a special kind of friendship and support.

Sarah was thrown out of her family home because she refused the marital union her father had arranged. The prospective bridegroom was old and cruel; Sarah had a strong will and wanted to share her heart with someone who would appreciate such great love and devotion. She was dreadfully beaten, she told me, which left her face so disfigured it would leave her *unfit* for anyone else. For her disobedience, slash marks and a broken nose were inflicted upon her with a vengeance. When I first met her, before the twelve were all joined, she appeared as just a pile of dirty robes left against the well of a small community we were visiting. I could not imagine why anyone would leave there a pile of robes to be cleaned, instead of at the washing place. Then I saw the dirty material move slightly. I gently pulled back the top-most folds of the robe and revealed a swollen tear-streaked face caked with blood, the eyes quite vacant. I called to one of my followers who helped me carry Sarah back to the compound where we had arranged to stay that night. The other sisters, there were only six then in the inner group, all followed and we bathed and sang soothing songs to this poor woman and slowly her eyes began to see again. We do not know, nor does she remember, how many days she lay there, ignored and in pain, up against the well that all town folk often visited.

As Sarah began to see she looked into my eyes and said, "I have been waiting long for you." Somehow she knew that she would be taken into our fold. A woman just *knows* such things. "I know" I said, "and now I am here finally and you are free." Days passed before we knew of her story and she gave us her preferred name. We carried her from place to place as the missionaries moved. At first the men literally carried her in their arms. Once Jeshua asked to carry her and he held her like a precious child. Soon enough though, she asked to try her feet and she walked supported by the sisters and became stronger with every step.

As missionaries, our goal was not to change the religion of those who listened to us, but to change how they would view themselves within it. We meant to question and to hold the priests and rulers accountable for manipulation and twisting of the truths to meet their agendas. Those who joined us were not all castaways, for some had been waiting for us to arrive, *knowing* that they were part of this mission. Others thought they should join us, but upon meeting with the twelve disciples, the twelve apostles, Jeshua and myself, it was decided that they should stay and complete their present goals before moving into this mission. It was always a group consensus with Jeshua leading the group through the process as he was trained so well to do. I had my own training and gifts and I was the great listener for those who wanted to talk out problems, concerns, or just visit in an environment of non-judgment and openness.

Until Sarah grew strong, she had nightmares and I often slept sitting upright with her head in my lap, the only place she could find peace. I remember looking down on the scarred face and wondering why anyone would mar such beauty? What selfishness would destroy such a perfect image of femininity? I even asked

Jeshua's advice on whether I should use my healing talents upon this poor woman and we decided together that some experiences must play out for the benefit of all. This example of the wounded woman came to be a bonding factor within our group, for we all knew that this was why attitudes must change.

Sarah grew strong with the love of the sisters and she became the heart of the group. Jeshua loved her as I did and she finally became trustful around men again. She had lost that ability through the painful ordeal of being betrayed by one who should have loved her unconditionally and not as a piece of property. I came to learn that she was hated by her village people, for her father was a powerful presence among them and he had convinced them that she was deserving of being thrown away and discarded. According to him, she was an evil daughter that had sexual intercourse with demons. What lies he told! She had endured days of kicking, hair pulling and even biting, but worst of all she endured the betrayal of the women, whose only help was to call her vicious names. Within our group of missionaries she was treated with respect and love and blossomed into the sweet woman she always truly was. The scars faded from our notice and she ever seemed the true beauty to all of us, but especially to Andrew, one of Jeshua's apostles, who came to love her greatly.

On our travels we enjoyed the hospitality of many householders and sometimes we stayed out in the open under the careful watch of those who volunteered to keep us safe. On one such night my sisters asked of the relationship of Jeshua and myself and our great love.

"I recognized immediately the gift of such a union," I said to my friends. "I seemed to have known him before I met him and I saw total appreciation for me as a woman, as I saw the perfection of a man in him, all upon our first glance."

I told them of the compelling eyes in my vision of long ago and that Jeshua's eyes were one and the same. I discussed how our relationship was a model of what God had intended for men and women, the sacred duality, but had become lost in the hearts and minds of humanity, who fear such a powerful love union. I also told them, "Do not envy us, sisters, for we will surely suffer greatly for our deep love. A seed must die and be buried and give up its husk in order to sprout and grow and pierce through into the light from whence it came. Then, as it breaks out of the darkness into the light, it must have a chance to grow and become strong to bear its fruit. Our mission is to plant seeds."

One of those guarding us in the open this night called to me: "MiryAmah, may I come forth for I have a message for you?" "Come forth then," I replied, taking notice that he had used my sacred name. He came forward with the most beautiful white lily I had ever seen and said, "Jeshua asked the lily for a beautiful bloom for his beloved one and I am honored to deliver this sacred flower to you, MiryAmah."

He gently laid the pristine white lily in my hands and noticed the tears that ran trails down my checks. I understood that in this gesture Jeshua had somehow sensed the discussion the disciples and I had entered, of the seed and the emerging plant and the ultimate fruit it gave of itself. This Lily of white represented to me the perfection of all experience--suffering, unknowing, emerging, merging, bearing fruit, determination, and offering of self to others, and to me this all equated a perfect love. The Lily was always a sacred flower and our love was the same.

Blessed be,

MIRACLE OF THE CHILDREN

After the twelve and twelve had been chosen, the mission intensified. We moved from place to place and crowds grew to huge numbers. Little children were often present and they were greatly beloved by all of us, especially by Jeshua, for he loved their honest innocence and their ability to be in the moment. Jeshua began to grow a beard in preparation for our final marriage ceremony and the little ones would tease him endlessly on his sprouting stubble. He laughed and played like a child himself and I knew that he would be a wonderful parent for our children one day.

Some of the apostles held a different attitude though, for they often pointed out to me that *all children* were Jeshua's children and they hinted that to father other children would be unwise for he would then favor his own and his love would be divided. Jeshua tried to tell them that all children are everyone's children and that love could not be measured thusly but they did not hear him. I loved all the apostles and all followers to the depths of my heart, for we held a common purpose, just a different attitude as to how to arrive at this worthy goal. My greatest sorrow at such times was that they thought Jeshua above such basic human needs, which they felt were based in sin. How love could be expressed in the sacredness of marriage and child bringing could be a sin had never made any sense to me. They were beginning to elevate Jeshua to Godhood for that is what they envisioned him to be, and he was trying to tell them that they were all such Gods and sons and daughters.

"What I am you are also, and whatever I do, you could do as well if you but believe and see," he said often, but the group consciousness' desire to have a separate deity to worship was too strong to overcome. Jeshua could not and would not deny that he was the Son of God for that was true, but so was all creation the sons, daughters and aspects of the Great Mysterious One.

One day when Jeshua was literally rolling around on the ground playing with the children, one of his twelve came forward and admonished him! I remember wondering how they could see him as a deity and yet reproach him in such a way? The apostle wanted Jeshua to appear more serious for the crowds were forming for the daily message. "Please master," he said, "surely it is time to be serious about the work we must do this day." I was amazed at the patience Jeshua displayed as he responded to this remark.

Jeshua slowly picked himself up from the dusty ground. He then sat upon a nearby rock and a tiny child came to him immediately. The apostle reached out to stop the little one. Jeshua gently pushed the apostle's hand aside as he reached for the small one and said, as the child was lifted to his lap and as the other children were bid to join him: "These children are more wise than many of you, my friends. They find joy naturally and they totally give themselves up to this feeling often and lighten the burden of all who are nearby. They do the work you cannot or will not do. You adults with your minds thinking of what you need to do next or on what others may be thinking of you or any other such nonsense cannot enjoy the moment because you are so scattered in your thoughts and concerns. You miss the blessings that surround you everyday and the opportunities they afford. You have lost your innocence, your trust, and your joy. God's greatest joy is seeing you joyful. Why did you leave your ability to pretend, to laugh, to play, and to dance in the glee of joy behind you as you grew into your adult years? What happened to the joy of your work, for is it not joyful to be of service to all? Someone told you to be serious about life, no doubt. Or if they didn't tell you they demonstrated the role themselves as they separated the children from those grown into responsibility that they deemed so great and so stoic. I tell you this day; you will not understand God and you will not find your way home unless you find your true joy again. Find the child within yourself or find a child and follow that child's example and you will discover the most important emotion you were gifted to feel and experience, joy."

At that moment the tiny child on his lap reached up and put his tiny hand over the mouth of Jeshua, who smiled and stopped his dialog to bring his attention back to the small one. Many in the crowd thought this inappropriate, for surely the master had to have his voice active to deliver his message. To stop the message was not, in their minds, respectful. Jeshua didn't seem to mind though. This beautiful babe smiled back at Jeshua and hugged him sweetly while standing upon his lap so that he could look him in the eye, which he did with a long soulful look and a smile upon his baby face. He then wrapped his tiny arms around my beloved and pressed his cheek deep into Jeshua's. Jeshua closed his eyes in bliss and rocked back and forth with the babe in his arms. The other children then all silently, as if on cue, moved into the crowd and a great miracle seemed to unfold. All children spontaneously walked among the adults and one by one hugged each present in silence, but in earnest, and yet with such sweetness. A boy of about ten years of age came to me and I opened my arms to him and he held me long and tenderly. I felt this powerful but soothing energy move from his being into mine and then circle back to him, eventually swirling and enveloping us both. I knew I had been given a great gift and the joy I felt was beyond imagination. He, too, looked long and deep into my eyes. As I remember this I think: how often do we truly look into a child's eyes? Things have not much changed, I fear, as I remember all of this from so long ago. Children still have treasures and wonders yet unseen, for it is in the eyes that the gift is delivered.

As the children walked through the crowd those not yet hugged were mumbling, "what is this foolishness, what are those children doing, and who told them to do this thing?"

Great puzzlement and wonder was evident on the faces of all those to be hugged yet, but the opposite was quite true of those already blessed with the gift of the children. They, like myself, were so full of joy I thought we would burst. We began to laugh and notice everything around us. The clouds never looked so beautiful, the trees so alive nor the ground so sacred and earthy, and everyone glowed with a rainbow of hues, each and every soul like the most beautiful glow lamps ever imagined.

I am not sure how long it took to transform the entire group, for there were many and we were wonderfully lost in the blessing of the moment. Finally, I remember, that when all the hugging was done there was a great commotion as people were playing with children, doing all sorts of things funny and sweet. The very apostle that had demanded the children withdraw from the master was now down on his hands and knees giving two little ones a ride upon his back. I saw people dancing in a circle and holding hands with children of various ages. I saw men throwing giggling little children into the air and catching them in delight, not only pleasing the child, but as they laughed in glee, also themselves. There didn't seem to be enough children to go around, so some adults playfully interacted among themselves. I had never seen a crowd play such either before or since. This must have gone on for hours, or until the children began to tire and the others found the limit of their endurance. No one was noticing the time, that's for sure. As the little ones quieted, one by one, all sat upon the ground with the children by their sides and looked toward Jeshua, who was smiling in total delight himself.

When all were quiet he said, "You have given the greatest gift known to God, the Father and the Mother of all creation. You are beloved as always but at this moment you are blessed and you have blessed through the joy you have allowed to come forth. The children are your way showers and your true treasure. Keep this treasure safe, my brothers and sisters, and keep the children ever beloved and free. They are the keepers of divinity. They know how to live in the moment and they always know how to find the joy within that time and space they occupy. They are your sacred key."

The crowd milled around longer than usual that day, well into the evening, as most just sat with the children watching the sunset. Some sang to the babes and rocked them to sleep while they watched the wonder of the sun's slumber and the colors that blanketed the fading light. No one, I believe, ever saw a grander sight.

It was very late when we all started toward our sleeping places. Jeshua walked quietly with me, holding my hand. Sarah followed behind to offer us some privacy, for she always was devotedly near me. Jeshua looked back at her and said, "We will have a little girl one day and we shall name her Sarah, in honor of you, sweet one, if that is the wish of MiryAmah, my beloved."

He looked down at me and I replied, "Oh yes! A fitting name for the daughter to one day grace our lives." My beloved friend, Sarah, was pleased to hear this plan and said she would be as devoted to our children as she would have been to her own if she had been so blessed.

"Will they let us have such an opportunity?" I said. *They* being the society we faced each day. We both knew that the concern for our relationship was building and each time a miracle was forthcoming they elevated Jeshua further as God and separated us further as man and woman in love and marriage. This day's events would surely be seen as a miracle again, even though it was just

God coming through the children's hearts as naturally as always when allowed an open channel.

"Only time will tell," Jeshua said to me. "It is not prophesied thus, and the mind-set of the masses is on the outcome they collectively see, but as you and I know, we have come to redirect things into a more balanced un-foldment. Time will tell and my hope is great!"

"Mine as well," I replied as I looked deep into my beloved's lingering eyes. We then parted for the evening and bid each other to sleep well and stay safe.

Blessed be,

Casting Out the Seven Demons

There has been much misconstrued in the Bible book and the legends based upon the information therein. This segment of my story is in response to the many questions regarding the reference to Jeshua casting out of me seven demons.

This legend is not entirely remembered correctly; for it was a teaching that Jeshua and I demonstrated. The devils were attitudes. They were not cast out of me, as the story is told, but instead Jeshua attempted to teach the followers that all negation comes in cycles of seven in terms of attitude toward that being rejected. He asked me to speak for the women on an issue that was specific to women. I spoke of the issue that is the deepest pain to any woman, the issue of her self-worth and respectability.

I said, "I would then wish to speak of the demons of ignorance, my beloved, for within the realms of these demons there lies suffering for not just some, but all beings."

The first negating attitude or demon of ignorance is for any woman to believe that she is a sinful temptress and that merging sexually with her beloved means she has to choose to sin and she has somehow lost her purity in the eyes of God.

Jeshua said, "I stand before you women as evidence that in merging sexually on the sacred level, and even for those who know not the sacredness of the union, there is a result of good and creation, for my very physical being is evidence enough as is yours. Good is never the result of sin. Good can be chosen because of it, but it is never a reflection of sin. Even when a woman is defiled in rape, if she conceives and a child is born, she is not sinful to bring this child forth, even as its father was sinful, for he defiled a sacred vessel. This just shows that the vessel is always sacred, and men as well as women should know of this truth and respect it, for it is God's plan that beings shall emerge thusly."

"I then bring a light of blessing to any woman who offers herself to her beloved in purest affection and total giving, for she is sacred and the fruit of her womb is the evidence of such, for it is good, it is God manifest."

The second demon of ignorance manifests when a woman believes intimacy is not a good thing because she has been told that men and women are separate and should keep themselves insulated from one another. She is confused because this creates feelings of insecurity since the feminine, by design, must feel safe in an intimate relationship. The design was that the masculine would protect and the lack of intimacy leaves her feeling unprotected. <u>She becomes at odds with her needs and sees her needs and feelings as being less than worthy.</u>

To this Jeshua replied, "The seat of feeling (emotion) within us all is the measurement place of what is of God and what is Good, yet there are those who would negate this feeling place within their being until they feel no more, for they have closed that area off. To caste out this demon, this attitude of negation, one must respect one's own feelings and emotions, which should be used to guide one's actions. <u>Open the doorway and let yourself *feel the way, feel the truth* and *experience all of this through emotion!* These are your indicators of God Action.</u>"

The third demon of ignorance is when a woman is ashamed of her true beauty and she believes that to be only a child-woman or flower bud is desirable. When she comes to her full bloom she thinks the flower flawed, beyond its time, and does not see the brilliance and the magnificence of her self thus fully bloomed.

Jeshua explained that GOD is the gardener of all beings, and all beings are his true flowers. The feminine, the women, are special flowers to this Creator of ALL THAT IS. "Would you tell the gardener that the bud is more beautiful than the full bloom? The bud is but a promise of the beauty yet to come. When the bloom drops its lovely petals, even this stage is beautiful to the gardener, for how many of you keep such petals there present within your homes to future bless your everyday life. Why then would you not keep your own essence so preserved and so respected. <u>Do not place your self respect in the hands of another, know you that your value is beyond measure.</u>"

<u>THE BLOOM IS THE ESSENCE OF BEAUTY AND WISDOM TOTALLY UNFOLDED AND IT IS PERFECTION, NEVERMORE BEAUTIFUL BUT ALWAYS IN ALL STAGES PRECIOUS. SEE YOUR OWN BEAUTY IN YOUR TIME OF FULL BLOOM, FOR GOD DOES SO SEE.</u>

The fourth demon of ignorance manifests when the woman thinks that she is chaos and thus brings chaos as she has been told, and does not see the harmony her essence brings to her family, her community or ALL THAT IS. She does not think she is worthy of being loved.

Jeshua explained, "This demon is indeed a terror within a being for it is said that *you can only love another as you love yourself*. This not only negates a woman's sense of self, it limits her relationship with all others. I say to this demon, be gone, for you are not real. The reality is that God loves this one from the depths of the heart of all Creation, thus she is worthy and able to love deeply and be loved deeply. It is time to love her, for when you do, you bring harmony to your own life, which reflects then on All That Is and pleases that which Created All That Is."

The fifth demon of ignorance occurs when a woman feels that nothing she has to say has validity. She thinks that she is sick and cannot be healed due to her flawed state as a feminine being and has seen her life's blood as sickness instead of life's essence. She sees herself weaker than her counterpart because she is more complex physically. She cannot voice her concerns because she feels her voice has nothing to offer in terms of wisdom and understanding. She feels empty and without power.

Jeshua said, "This is the demon that takes the power of the communication away from the being. This demon makes truth hard to swallow and stops power from manifesting and keeps the individual in a weakened state because they are not heard. I cast this demon out of the throat energy vortex and I give back the power to speak to those unheard, for all beings have much to say. Truth is the power of such communication, and the blood is the truth manifest."

The sixth demon of ignorance is the belief that woman's intuition is an illusion and her feelings are a weakness and a negation of her innate wisdom. This concept is due to the non-acceptance of those who would stop this flow of natural goddess assistance by denying that there is wisdom within the woman at all, because, as they would have her believe, it is not built in but left out so that she should bow down to the masculine.

To this Jeshua countered, "Oh! Women, you *know* in your feminine essence, do you not, then why do you think you *do not know*? I would open the doorway of your heart and the channel it has to the mind within all of you, for there is a floodgate about to burst in each and every one of you. Your wisdom is a mighty force. This floodgate holds back wisdom and *KNOWING* and it is the force of this pent up truth that seems dangerous to those who would keep you closed off from it. <u>I cast this demon out by opening the gate of light there in each being, so that the vision and the *KNOWING* come together as one, and the Goddess and the God unite in all beings, for when this happens All are blessed by this sacred marriage within their very essence.</u>"

<u>"KNOW WHAT YOU KNOW! KNOW THAT YOU KNOW. KNOW BECAUSE YOU KNOW; KNOW!"</u>

Within the seventh demon of ignorance she thinks that he is complete and that she is not. She believes that he is worthy just because he is, but she thinks that she will never be worthy because she is she, thus she thinks that only he can talk to GOD.

And to this Jeshua's truth was simple, "This is perhaps the worst demon of all to cast out from anyone, for even when a man touches the feminine within his own being, in this attitude he thinks he has stepped down, become further away from God and thus cannot see the Glory of this one as clear and so dear. She and He must be united within the body, within the society, even within the universe, to ever approach God at the closest level, for if you cannot echo the energy of the Source, which is in totality feminine, masculine and the perfection of this perfect blend, then you cannot know this One. I cast this demon out and reveal the truth of each being. You are both the masculine and the feminine within your being as a reflection of that which sprang your very soul forth, so why would you negate half of your very essence? <u>KNOW YOUR TOTALITY, RESPECT YOUR FEMININITY AS WELL AS YOUR MASCULINITY, MERGE THE TWO TO BE TOTALLY ONE, THEN YOU WILL KNOW GOD!"</u>

This is the memory as coming from me, Mary of Magdalene. This was simply a teaching and it was hoped that the seekers present would understand this teaching and begin to move through it's many levels and change the unbalanced aspect of themselves and thus change the society. Those who remembered and wrote the Bible book originally remembered more of this lesson, but sought to simplify it so that more could understand. It was simplified to the point that many only remembered the seven demons and Mary of Magdalene. Too much was left out, but now we hope that at least some of you will know what a demon is. A demon is an attitude! One that grows in strength and is protected by ignorance and that hurts and harms those in its way and stops growth. Now some of you can cast out the demons that stop your growth, for you are all equally blessed and demons lie to you when they convince you that you are not!

Blessed Be,

MARRIAGE

THE SACRED DANCE Of DUALITY

You would think the most precious day of my life, my final marriage ceremony to my beloved, would be a day of great celebration; however, that was not the case. It was within the pre-marriage ceremony that I sealed my intentions to my beloved Jeshua. By cycling the energy sent from my beloved by way of a kiss to the top of my head, and by using my long hair to wipe his feet with precious oil, we thus bring the blessing through me and back to him to offer again and again. Three months after this ritual of dedication, we finally came together for the final day of commitment.

This was a controversial day for there were those bitterly opposed to our joining as man and wife and we had to keep the ceremony private, with only a few personal friends and family present. Of course, the ceremony was not done within the temple, for in the nation of Israel; the belief was that a man *fell* into such a union unless God chose him for priesthood, which many believed was true of Jeshua. Actually, they believed that he was even above this role, and was the most High Priest, the Son of God. As I stated before, Jeshua tried to mold this slightly erroneous thinking into truth but they seemed to hear only that which they wanted to hear.

The role of women, and especially that of priestess, was much different in this society, for many out-lying societies still held them holy, with women receiving legal rights and societal respect. Not so in the nation of Israel, there the priestess was the enemy to those who controlled the society. The patriarchal mood was spreading and long ingrained into the Hebrew people's minds and hearts. Even the Romans, who ruled overall, believed that a man was master of his family. A Roman male could arrange a daughter's marriage, demand she divorce her husband or even kill his wives or daughters should he deem it necessary. The attitude was one of ownership of the women and a woman raped, in Hebrew society, was required to marry her rapist. If she was already married she was put to death. This was the corruption of an unbalanced society that argued that this was *always so* and thus

99

the will of God. This concept originated, of course, with the creator gods, as a means of controlling the new species. This mistaken role of women rose and fell many times as the genders tried to find balance, but the power issue dominated the *divinity of duality truth* and many suffered for it. This attitude of that time long past still affects your time on many levels of thinking, as it still echoes in attitudes and power issues. Women, sad to say, often promote this twisted view as they have learned to survive by believing the oppressor.

Thus we had not many who would know of the sacred nature of our decision much less welcome the occasion. We brought Andrew and Sarah with us, to the place of our vows, as witnesses, and of course, Mother Mary and the brothers and sisters of Jeshua as well as my parents, to all share in the moment we pledged our commitment to each other. We looked upon each other with tears in our eyes and the truth upon our faces. No one could ever say that there was ever a more heart-felt dedication between two entering duality through sacred marriage.

We departed for one month after this rather brief but important ceremony. I took my beloved to the mountain temple to meet my sisters and then we entered the privacy chambers where we would languish in each other's presence and begin our union.

Jeshua was astonished when we entered the portals of the mountain temple. It was something he knew of but had never experienced. The crystal doorkeepers that opened the secret doors amazed him, and the women, dressed as they desired and involved in such happy activities, were a welcoming sight to he who felt so much sorrow for the state of all sisters in the outer.

"They are so beautiful in their freedom," he remarked, as he watched in amazement a dance in one courtyard where the sisters were learning how to combine song and dance to make a harmonious energy. The ancients called this *calling in the gods* because the harmony thus created attracted those beings no longer incarnated who served as guides and guardians and existed in a place of balance between dimensions. Thus the occasion would compliment the need of those in physicality no matter why the guides were summoned.

"Can men dance thusly?" Jeshua asked, with a look of mischievous delight upon his face. His joy wanted to express itself so I gently pulled him into the center of the circle and we danced there within the core of a purple mist that was created by the harmony. The moment was magical and the dance of the lovers was a sight to see, my sisters later told me, for I could not judge it while I was within this wondrous moment. It was the true dance of the masculine and the feminine expressed in perfection and my true joy of our marriage was finally expressed as we mingled our sound (song) and movement in this sacred dance. His voice was the most beautiful I had ever heard. He moved naturally and beautifully, with no awkwardness there present, as I did myself. The joy we gave to ALL THAT IS was immense and perfected as we sang and moved in perfect harmony and joy. If only we could teach those who had lost the way to dance this dance of creation and celebration, we both thought. We both knew the other thought the same thought during that dance. Some would rightfully call this a mating dance, for all dance is tied to sexuality in some form or manner. Even those beings in nature thus display their joy and celebrate their intention to merge.

Jeshua's movement and song, as he brought me near to his heart, was certainly the masculine calling forth to the feminine to merge and join into the wonder of all creation. This is the only intimate moment we shared with others, for we soon left for our chambers and our private courtyards within this complex and did not emerge until a moon had come full once again. I will not speak of the private time in which we blended our very souls into the One, for it is sacred and private and shall ever be the mystery and the memory of Jeshua and me. I will just say that this was the happiest time of all my lives in physicality and were it not for this time together I would not have had the strength to endure what would follow.

Blessed be,

THE VISION QUEST AND VISION TEST

We emerged from our blessed month of getting to know each other on an intimate level full of love and hope, as all newlyweds should. We wished that others could understand our union and that the sacredness of merging into a *marriage duality* was Divinely ordained, but we could plainly see that such a realization was a slim possibility at this point in time. Some understood, but most could not grasp the concept of equal, but different aspects, as reflected in masculine and feminine. The basis of our purpose in this life experience was to plant the seed of change, through example and stimulation of thought, and shift the unbalanced attitudes back to the divinity of the original plan. We knew well that eons of beliefs could not be changed in one single lifetime.

We had studied the legends of creation as children and we knew of the guardians, who were part of the genetic pool that we referred to as *the ancestral code.* We knew that there was a peace code, which you might call a *peace gene* there present and our hope was to activate this latent code and begin the change. Understand that there was no particular race that could claim this code for the gene had been passed to many diverse peoples to ensure that it would spread equally among those upon this Tara-land, Earth, as you call her. There was little to set those with the peace gene apart from others except a certain look in the eye, and one had to really look deeply into another's gaze to identify such a one. There was also a light purple glow about those with the gene, and for those sensitive enough, as Jeshua and I were, to perceive this aura, this was a true indication.

The mission moved on and into intensity as Jeshua performed the miracles spoken of in the Bible book. Lazarus was raised from a deep, deep coma, which was usually seen at that time as the death state. Many were given up at this stage, since the understanding of when life left the physical body was not complete enough to evaluate this moment accurately. My beloved knew how to stimulate the brain in such a condition but could not attribute or explain this to the others for it was a skill that could also take a life as easily as it brought one back.

Jeshua visited the temples and lost his temper, for he had great disrespect for those who would profit in the name of God and require that innocents such as the temple doves or goats and lambs and such, be killed and bled in the name of a pure offering to the Creator. "What blasphemy," Jeshua said, "to kill that which has not yet fulfilled its destiny as the Creator intended."

The stoning episode of the supposed prostitute was actually an event that took place a number of times with a number of women. Whenever a woman asserted herself and balked at the authority of any man, she could easily be labeled such and stoned to death. The oppressions were great for the feminine ones and she dare not even anger an unknown man upon the street.

Jeshua did not work within the structure and the religious laws set forth by the established priestly rule. He might be termed *a systems buster* these days, because he found examples that would bring attention to the insanity of many of the accepted practices of the time. The opposing sides to change lined up as hatred and fear grew, even as the crowds of followers grew in size.

Hate and fear are like a disease. They cast doubt into minds that have been otherwise enlightened, I am sad to say, for ignorance can be controlled but wisdom cannot. Jealousy grew among some of the followers also. They fought to sit near Jeshua, or walk closer to him. I was bumped out of my rightful place at his side so many times that I held bruises upon my body at the end of each mission day. Jeshua became more and more despondent with the uncertainty and confusion of those who knew the truth, to the point that he left the fold for a time of clearing his vision.

This is remembered as the forty-day retreat. His great temptation was to give up the cause, for he and I could clearly see that suffering and the perception of extreme injustice would be the only outcome that would be accepted into hearts and souls, where the seed of change must be planted.

At the time of Jeshua's retreat I was pregnant with our first child. Jeshua was greatly concerned for me and asked his mother to look after me while he sorted out his concerns and sought vision anew. She gladly came to me, and between her and Sarah, I was well served and loved.

I sobbed at the leaving of my beloved, but he assured me that this he must do because so many were confused and so many pulled at him for justification of their warped thinking. He promised to come back to his mother and I when he was cleansed of this depression. His energy was waning and his heart was in great pain, for he wished to have a balanced family time for us and for all and everyday that possibility was fading.

"Let your sorrow flow, dear child," Mother Mary said, as she held me and we watched Jeshua walk away. The tears seemed to have no end as a great dam of emotion broke loose within my heart, overflowing through my eyes.

"To be a woman is to have great sorrow right now, but to be one such as Jeshua is like a lingering death also," she said. "For he sees his beloveds suffer, as all creation does, because of misunderstandings supported by insanity and will-to-power." She held me long and compassionately until every last tear was shed and then we walked hand in hand and talked of our great love for Jeshua and his monumental sacrifice for the sake of others.

While Jeshua was gone there was great strife within the twelve apostles because their vision of the mission was not in agreement. Some questioned what the master really meant by the role of women in this time of change. I met with the twelve sister disciples too, and some of them were also beginning to lose the clarity of the mission. Jealousy was the greatest disease of all and there were apostles saying the disciples should know their place of service and not attempt to be a voice of decision in such serious matters. I reminded them that Jeshua and I often discussed major issues and that he had intended that the disciples would act in the same capacity for the apostles. Only Andrew held to this concept totally, with the others holding different degrees of agreement and opposition to the idea of this masculine/feminine balance and cooperation. Andrew stood by me that day but the apostles walked away from me in contempt when I pointed out this balancing intent. Jeshua was not there to intervene this time, and so quickly things fell apart without his voice of reason and Divine authority. Little by little the disciples retreated from the evening meetings because of the icy attitude towards them by the apostles. The meetings were held to plan the activity for the coming day. When we joined the group, the men would stop speaking and just sit in silence and refuse to even look at us. We had been poisoned with an attitude seeping into our midst like a thief in the night.

I tried to keep the sisters spirits up and told them to look for Jeshua to return and sanity to again balance our mission. We did not know how long Jeshua would be gone because he did not know himself. The forty long days and nights were miserable for all of us. We all reviewed our attitudes and our intentions in the mission, each in our own way. None really knew if Jeshua would return or if something had happened to him.

There were those who thought Father God (for they saw this God as masculine) had taken his son back to the heavens because he had lost his way in this mad idea of allowing the women such an important role. Justification of judgment is a powerful thought process and it consumed them and they molded it. I knew that Jeshua would return because he promised me so. I wondered how he would feel to see this lack of strength of purpose among his closest followers.

Just at sunset one evening, after a particularly long and harrowing day where the disciples and apostles had been bickering for hours, I saw him. He was a shadow with the sun behind him, walking slowly toward us. The closer he came the more we could see the toll the retreat had taken, for his face had aged much and his eyes were the saddest I had ever seen. He walked right up to me and his mother and together he hugged us and said, "My beloveds, I have missed your sweet presences greatly." Then he turned to the others who sat there staring in astonishment, and said, "What have you learned in my absence? Have you learned to keep the mission sacred? Have you seen who is strong in mind and heart and who has weakness therein? Have you discovered the strength of the disciples and the apostles as they stand strong and true in the duality of the group?"

He knew this was not true because as he approached us he took note that the women had been excluded from the men's group.

"What are you going to do when I am not here to remind you that to judge your women as lesser is to judge yourselves unworthy? Your mother's sacrifice of blood and life's energy brought you into this place of physicality. Your wife's sacrifice has brought you children to carry on after you can no longer serve. In sacrifice wisdom grows. Would you waste such a gift? You are all here to

105

serve and the least shall be first for they give the most. You have asked your women to give up their gift of wisdom to serve you blindly, so in your mind you have made them *least*. They are first, I remind you, for without them you would not have life or be able to continue such."

Jeshua looked at the dust upon the ground where he stood in sandals worn and almost falling from his feet. He stirred up some dust and said, "You leave your vision in the dust, my friends. When it floats thusly within the air it can find no place to seed and sprout. Only when it settles can it accomplish its goal, to be a place to nourish and to offer opportunity of growth. Your attitude of grasping for power instead of merging into a cooperative effort is making much dust. You are the dust, my fellow men. The women are the water that settles the dust and brings it ready for growth. How long will you keep the rain of the feminine from falling and settling you into your mission?"

"I have thought much during my retreat and I know that I must carry on in spite of the opposition to change that will surely attempt to stop this mission. I have processed great sorrow for I have had a glimpse into what will probably unfold in all of this, but my greatest sorrow was to see my own beloved followers moving away from the duality we had worked so hard to merge. Until all beings know the sacredness of the masculine and the feminine as it manifests within each being and as it is mirrored in the sisters and brothers, there will be no peace! My Father God sent me to bring peace. My Mother God sent me too, to bring back the respect of her children. Without Her you would not be. The Divine Duality brought you forth. Honor this Duality, which becomes a Divine Trinity when you realize that it is God the Father and Goddess the Mother and then we, their creation, that is the truth of ALL THAT IS. You are heading down the wrong path if you think otherwise."

Jeshua then leaned heavily upon Mary Mother and I and said, "take me home for I need some nourishment and much love that only you, my beloveds, can give."

Blessed Be,

THE LAW OF GOD IS NOT ALWAYS THE LAW OF MAN

After the return of Jeshua, the intensity of the mission increased. There were more and more present for the teachings but there were also those present who were acting as spies for high priests and government officials who were much worried about Jeshua, for he seemed to have too much power for someone unconnected to the status quo established rulers.

One Sabbath day a woman came to Jeshua from out of the crowd. She was so weak she could hardly stand and Jeshua immediately put his hand out to keep her from falling at his feet. She said, "forgive me, master, for I have come to you unclean."

"How is this so," Jeshua asked?

"I hemorrhage greatly and am losing all strength. I do not know why I am punished in this way and I ask that you help me," she replied in a gasping whisper.

Jeshua had to put his ear close to her mouth to hear her. He replied so that the crowd could hear well, "You have not sinned and your are not punished, dear one." He put his hand gently on her forehead and said, "I shall see what can be done for you."

Some in the crowd took exception and said to Jeshua, "Master, it is the Sabbath and to do any task upon that day is forbidden and she is unclean, for she is upon her moon-time and she should not be among us."

"These are rules made by man, not by God," Jeshua said. "Man has decided that the very blood that brings him life is unclean. How absurd. To God this substance is precious beyond measure and should not be wasted ever. This woman is almost gone from this life due to this bleeding, this sorrowful letting go of life's essence because it is not valued or properly understood by those who deem her unclean. She has given all she has to give. Would you have her give her very life so that a law that man made would over ride the intention of God?"

He then laid the woman out flat upon the ground and asked Sarah and I to come forward. He asked Sarah to hold one of the women's hands and I the other and he laid both his hands gently upon her abdomen. "When I close my eyes," he said to us, "begin transmitting your love energy into this poor woman's body. As you do this I will be taking the evil out of her. The evil is the lie of shame and it bleeds from her very soul."

At that he closed his eyes and we did as he requested. I had taught Sarah how to give of her energy and she was already very good in such situations. Jeshua's hands trembled as he absorbed the evil therein and then he broke his connection and threw his hands high and what looked like smoke poured forth as he screamed a sound I shall never forget. The crowd was mesmerized and shocked at the sound. They seemed almost in fear of the great sound that poured forth from Jeshua as he released the painful attitude of shame from within this poor soul.

The woman immediately began to improve. She could feel that the hemorrhage had stopped. She was helped to her feet by other followers and Jeshua told her, "Go now and forever more know that each moon-time you offer your very blood in love, you bless all mothers who need to learn to love their offerings. When the blood is withheld to nourish a new life, it is blessed, but when it is released because the child bearing time is not yet ripe, it is the sign that you are a holy vessel of God Almighty who desired you to bring life forth--as well as wisdom. Not every grape will seed a new vine. Most grapes will be made into wine. Your moon-blood is the wine of God. Never more bleed in shame."

She smiled and kissed Jeshua upon the cheek, another shocking event for the onlookers, and she walked away, stronger and more dignified than just moments before. She had a look of frail beauty that I knew would soon become a strong beauty and I silently blessed her and wished her well.

"You let an unclean woman come among us and even touch you with an unclean kiss, master, why?" This accusation came from an outraged man in the crowd with the harsh look of judgment upon his face.

"What is unclean is your minds," Jeshua said. "Someone has put dark, dirty thoughts therein and you cannot see the greatest gift of life known in the physical, which is such a woman as this. Her kiss is the sign of her commitment to life itself. Her wisdom and her blood are a treasure to God, and you who think otherwise are brainwashed and without your own free will to think clearly, as God intended you to. You were given a mind to think with. Use it. You were given a heart to pump life-giving blood throughout your being and to measure true love, which is signified by blood. How can you use half of your heart and negate the other half? Yes, your heart pumps your blood to all parts of your physical bodies, but the other half of your heart desires to express love. Every woman intended to sacrifice herself to love will bleed the truest love of all, the love of God. I tell you this day that the heart has authority over the mind but you have reversed this truth and even given away your God-given ability to think freely. You are empty. The blessed woman who just left here is full. She no long purges herself of the love blood of God but she will now keep it safe and holy. It is time to open your hearts and minds and fill yourself with the truth of love and life as presented to you by God in all of its manifestations. God created this opportunity of life for you to experience in the fullest. One can never experience anything in its *fullest* when they are empty."

Most in the crowd began talking among themselves upon this lesson and most began to see the light of awareness Jeshua had beamed. A few, however, walked away feeling good about something else. They now had proof that this alleged messiah blatantly broke the law in the healing of this woman on the Sabbath. They could only see a law broken. They could not discern the spirit of such a law as this, which only required keeping this day holy and appreciating life and the gift of such. Instead, they could not wait to bring the news to their superiors.

Jeshua watched them leave, as did I. We knew what was in their hearts for it was written upon their faces. "Trouble comes soon," Jeshua said.

"I fear for you, my beloved, as I fear for all the followers," I whispered.

"Fear not, faithful one," he said, "for there will be those who will betray me, and those who will deny me but you do not have it in your heart to ever turn away and I do love you beyond measure for your steadfast loving commitment to this cause and to me."

I looked deep into my love's eyes and saw the sadness of the truth of his statement, yet I saw no hate within those pools of deepest blue, the doorways to his soul. I looked long at my beloved. He had the bronzed skin of those common to this climate and place. His long hair was wavy in a softly repeating rhythmic way, with his hair nearly to his waist. It was the same length as my own, which was black. His was of the darkest brown with reddish highlights, however, and it was much longer than the normal fashion for men of the time. We both had the deep blue eyes, which were uncommon also, but not unheard of in our people. It is odd, but in this fleeting moment I was drinking in the beauty of his presence, as he was mine. In that brief period of time we memorized and appreciated every aspect of each other, for somehow we knew that we would need this memory soon.

Hand in hand we walked to our night quarters. It was wonderful to now spend the evening time with my beloved. We would talk into the night of our love for each other and of the child to come.

This little one had made herself known to us just previous to this healing day. She began to move about the preceding night and respond to both the voice of Jeshua and to my own. She had a different response to each voice and we even knew then that this would be our little girl, Sarah. We did not yet share this information with others, except Sarah, whom our child would be honoring with her name, and I think she confided in Andrew. Jeshua wanted to tell John, one of his favorite apostles, for John was a sweet soul and seemed so dedicated to the master, but Jeshua had a well-developed feminine side and followed his hunches and he felt that the knowledge was not yet to be offered to this one.

John was also one who utilized his feminine energy but he was not comfortable in it as Jeshua was. It was this balance of tenderness and intuition with strength and reasoning that made Jeshua so compelling, yet the men still fought to keep their tenderness secret within themselves.

Andrew was always there for Jeshua and never wavered in his loyalty and a better friend could not be found. Andrew's brother Peter was also one that Jeshua loved greatly for his strength, but Peter could be bull-headed about the role of women and he and Jeshua would often argue that point. John was always near Jeshua and he was so in love with Jeshua that he could be jealous at times, but there was never a soul more committed to the cause then he. His passion was unquestionable. The problem was that he was having a difficult time with the feminine/masculine issue and if he had seen this very issue described as I just did, with the *feminine* listed first, he would have been outraged. He had an inner battle going on inside himself but Jeshua believed that he would soon enough stop the war and merge himself and accept his personality as an integrated and balanced power within that was peaceful and whole and holy.

We fell into dreamtime together with sadness upon our souls as well as joy, for to be in each other's arms was joy, but what we knew was forthcoming was the greatest sadness of all. We slept peacefully together for the last time.

Blessed be,

SORROW IN THE GARDEN

As with all forward moment, when things begin to move in earnest there is an equally opposing force that seeks to stop the change. The status quo finds comfort and assurance in its boxed-in place, no matter how tattered and shattered it might be. So, too, this opposition presented itself with our mission, and the force grew in intensity. I will not retell the stories of your Bible of this time, for it would take away from the truth of it all in that it would disconnect from the underlying feeling of the time. Some Bible tales are true enough, some are combinations of situations, but much is left out and filtered to accommodate the mindset of those in power. The truth, as always, is held within the feeling of the events recorded.

To be in human form is to be hopeful, for that is one of humankind's greatest abilities, this ever-hopeful attitude with a vision of the future well connected to it. Hope is the power behind change and vision is the ability to change. Jeshua and I had hoped that somehow the mission of bringing balance through reconnecting the feminine with her rightful place of honor and respect, in duality with the masculine, would take hold during our life time. We greatly desired to stay until old age as living examples of how this sacred duality would work in marriage. There were the prophecies; however, those bits of information that are warnings and opportunities to change direction or face the consequences foretold. Too many believed that the future seen is the future set in action with no choice. That has never been the case and there have been many predictions that have not unfolded as seen due to conscious choice.

Jeshua, in the minds of many followers, was each day more and more molded to fit a prophecy, and there was a terrible blood sacrifice that this foreseen event would require. Jeshua and I often spoke to the followers of the waste of life a sacrifice required and how the Great One did not want life wasted, but rather wanted all life to complete its cycle and grow in awareness from the opportunity. How could cutting a beautiful life short by bleeding the very essence of life from it ever please God? God is the Creator, not the Destroyer.

Day by day, as we moved through towns and small villages the crowds grew and the momentum rose. The few that held loyal to the old ways of patriarchy made their presence known and grumbled and grimaced; yet the crowd as a whole absorbed the lessons. These learning times were often presented as examples or through opportunity as healing and as miracles.

The Roman rulers and the church High Priests were beginning to worry greatly because the masses were flocking to hear the words and witness the healings and miracles. Hope was building for the followers. The Priests actually had the most to lose and they held the greatest contempt for Jeshua. I was not a focus for I had remained in low profile since my pregnancy and conducted the disciple meetings in private. My sisters protected me for they knew that only Jeshua could go out there with the lessons and build hope and vision. I would be stoned to death should I say the things he said. Yet, even he would suffer for his words of truth, as you already know well.

You may think that we only taught duality, and in a way we did. At the root of all oppression is the lack of balance in thinking and feeling. Thought without the measurement of feeling is empty and ruthless since it has no conscience. While both women and men think and feel, because both masculine and feminine energy are present within each, the negating of all that was female kept people from assigning importance to their feeling natures. For instance--the Roman ruler of the area was fascinated with Jeshua. His thinking however, told him that this man could be a threat, but his heart, the center of this feeling, told him that Jeshua was a humble and loving soul. The inner conflict could not equal sanity because he gave only one part of himself credence, his thought. He negated his feeling and the truth it held in this great moment. He could not balance his masculine energy in thinking and reasoning with his feminine energy as feeling and intuition, so he just gave the entire matter over to the Priests. He thought that would absolve him of blame. How wrong he was.

To control another's mind is a great misuse of power, and through religion this can be accomplished when such an organization misuses its position in the lives of the congregation. When religion, in any form, loses its sense of feeling, it cannot see its own imbalance and it negates hope and vision in the people. A religion that makes marriage a fall from grace is certainly off-balance, for it negates life itself in all its holiness. Many purported spiritual centers have required sacrifice to the gods or to God, and that is the direct effect of the imbalance. The sacrificial ones are always the innocents, the oppressed, the prisoners, and often the women and children. If *feeling and intuition* were present to balance this warped rationale -- that to please the gods one must kill and bleed something -- then it simply would not happen. The Mother One is protective of all creation. It is the Mother part of God that nurtures creation, and yes, she can rage and be a most terrible force when She is in anger, just as the Father God can also be.

Anger is an emotion that is directly tied to feeling. One does not think, "now I will be angry;" one simply feels that emotion. When the priests threaten you with the wrath of God, such intimidations are triggered by their inability to see the Wholeness of this God. The only thing that angers God is the needless destruction and negation of all creation. All aspects of creation are dependent upon each other and all should be respected as part of the plan. All aspects have two dual forces or energies, so that they can experience in the fullest--the masculine and the feminine, which is sometimes called the positive and the negative. Whatever you choose to call them, there should always be complimenting and balancing factors in equal measure.

I tell you this because the time came when the ultimate sacrifice was offered, not by the faithful in the name of love, but by the priests for the sake of power. We were all in a garden place when the madness began. We had entered the city with crowds blessing us and laying a carpet of palm boughs before us to walk upon, a loving welcome in support of us. Someone brought a little white donkey for Jeshua to ride into the gates of the city. This sweet animal loved Jeshua on sight and connected its spirit to his immediately. The result was that he simply had to think where he desired to go and the little white one would know the desire and would act accordingly. How proud this little white one was, stepping in almost a prance as he carried my beloved into the city. We all enjoyed such a wonderful reception this day, especially my beloved, who had such great hope in his heart.

After a long day of teaching and demonstrating the miraculous by bringing balance back to situations, we retired to the garden of a wealthy follower. The apostles had been arguing for days as to

114

what Jeshua should do now because his popularity was at an all-time high. There were those who wanted him to take a position as *King,* such as Judas, and then there were others who wanted Jeshua to take position as High Priest and throw the corrupt ones from the temple. Jeshua tried to tell the followers many times that the only temple he could be high priest in was within the mind and heart of God, which, he said, "occupies space within each and every one of you. You can only rule your own heart and soul. You can do it wisely by honoring the duality within, or you can be unwise and try to rule such from only half of your being."

The sisters were among the apostles and they sought to help the situation by gently urging the men to hold their faith in love and to listen, to truly listen to the master, for he was not getting through to them. Since the women's opinions were seen as inferior, not many listened; they became more and more agitated.

Jeshua said nothing. He just watched the agitation and then he finally said, "Leave me to myself. I must speak through my heart to my Father, for I know not what to do with you who have visions that serve some other god, certainly not the God of my Father."

He walked away with tears streaming down his checks. I went to him and he asked me to stay with the group just in case they finally moved through their wall of confusion.

"I need to pray alone, right now," he said. He walked to a secluded section of the garden and knelt down and leaned upon a great rock. A light bathed him as he wept. I could not tell if the light emanated from him or from another source, but I knew that he was not alone in this sorrow. I could feel the presence of the Almighty, who felt the sorrow from deep within the heart of Jeshua.

I went back to the others as I was asked to do and tried to calm the deluge of worries since the group could not agree upon the next stage of this mission. I saw Judas leave and return. I wondered how this group could be so torn for just that evening we had all dined together and they seemed so committed and quite in agreement with the master.

I often wonder why the images of this last meal do not include the women, for we were there and I was right next to my beloved. I heard him say to those present, "one of you will betray me before this night is over."

All were aghast and reacted with various emotional outbursts; most saying they would never do such a thing. Jeshua went on to say that one he loved greatly would deny him and that his words would one day be twisted to the point that they would fit the mold of the priesthood and his true message would lie hidden until his spirit would once again try to unlock the hearts and minds of the people.

Just hours before, during our last meal together, the entire group was astounded that Jeshua could believe such things and now here they were, arguing about whether Jeshua would be a king or a priest to the people. They saw only the opportunity to take the literal *seat of power* in this moment preceded by the great welcome to this city of temples. They did not see the opportunity to bring the established government or religion into balance through attitude. It was this attitude that needed to be changed, not the seats of power. If those within the seats of power could balance within their own inner duality then all would change. That inner place was the true temple.

Some of the followers saw the light upon Jeshua as he cried and prayed. They could see him nodding his head in agreement to what he was being told. "See," John said, "God tells him to listen to us and to take his rightful place as leader." I asked John, "shall he be Emperor or shall he be High Priest? How much killing would be sufficient to put him in those positions of power? How many would have to sacrifice their lives and spill their blood for this dethroning to happen? Why can't you see that he cannot be what you want him to be, for he must be what God wants him to be."

"What would that be, lady Mary," asked Thaddeus as he emerged from the group. I answered, "God is the true king and my beloved is the Prince of Peace."

"He has, indeed brought peace to my heart," Thaddeus said, "I only pray that he can open the heart of all people and bring peace therein."

"Thank you, Thaddeus," I said. "To know that the message was received by you and others from the giver of peace brings joy to my soul at this time of trouble. To see you and your beloved wife, Mary, so devoted to each other and changed by the teachings is of great comfort. I do not know what will happen. This should be a time of celebration because the number of people coming to hear the master is vast and the moment is near when the balance could shift, but if you followers, the closest ones to my beloved, do not understand after all this time together, how will those listeners in the crowd integrate these truths into their lives? I feel that a great sorrow hangs over us all right now. The need for sacrifice is a strong opposing force that does not want awareness to cut off its victims."

"I wish with all my heart," the wife of Thaddeus said, "that they would listen to you, my sister, MiryAmah, for your wisdom is great and your heart true. You know the master as no one else and he has said that "he is you" and "you are he," but those in confusion will not see."

I replied, "we can only open the door, we cannot make anyone enter the sanctuary of the soul, my friend."

I left them to do my own praying, not far from my beloved, where the little white donkey was tied. I leaned upon its back and wept in greatest sorrow. I could feel this little white one merge with my being and offer me his strength. We both lay down then, the little white one first and then myself draped across his soft warm body. I know he felt the same sorrow that I felt. I would not take all his strength but he was willing to give me all he had to give. These blessed little ones are so committed to the human's cause and duty. I asked this one to save himself and to live a long life as a gift to me, whom this one would have given all to. I knew he would honor that wish.

Blessed Be,

JESHUA IS TAKEN AWAY

It breaks my heart to remember this time but, after all, this is my story as well as his and the journey is not always an easy road to take and his memory is just as painful. After Jeshua finished talking to Our Father in Prayer, he arose and walked back to the followers. He looked at Peter and John and asked if Judas had left yet and returned.

"Why, yes, master. What is your concern?" "It has begun, this destiny that I had hoped with all my heart would not be necessary," Jeshua replied. "Now the legend will be tied to the sacrifice and not the example of perfection. My heart is indeed heavy."

John stood near Jeshua and said, "We are concerned for your Mary, for she seems to be in a trance along with the little white donkey. They are over there, not far from where you prayed. She does not respond to our nudging but she still breaths, so we know she is not gone."

"Leave her be for now. What is about to happen would be too much for her to bear and she needs to keep our child safe."

"John, do you love me with all your heart," Jeshua asked. "Surely you know of my great love for thee, master," John answered, "There is nothing I would deny you. Do you want my life? It is yours."

Jeshua looked deep into John's eyes and said, "You are beloved to me as well and I trust you. And so I ask you to keep my beloveds safe for their entire life upon this place and in this time. My mother, Mary, and my wife, MiryAmah, these two are beloved to me, for one brought me into this life and one gave me strength to live this life. Promise me, my beloved friend, for there are many I love, but those I call beloved are the closest to my heart. Promise me that they will be safe in your keeping."

"I so promise," pledged John, as the tears coursed down his cheeks, for he knew then that Jeshua would be leaving soon.

Peter looked both worried and afraid upon witnessing this conversation with John. Jeshua said to him, "fear not, my friend, for you will be the strength of my mission if you so choose and you will have to use your greatest strength to forgive yourself, for your mind is stubborn, but your heart is just as strongly tied to your love for me and your commitment to the cause."

"I will do anything you ask, Jeshua, my master," he said, with great pain in his heart as realization began to sink in as to why this would be asked.

"I ask that you remember the balance and you keep the faith within the truth."

Next Andrew approached when he saw the devastated looks upon John and Peter's faces. He looked deeply into the master's eyes and said, "Who should hurt you so, master? Tell me and I will slay them if need be, for no one shall touch you with sorrow if I can but help."

"Always you are my protector, Andrew, are you not? I know that I can always count on you to be there by my side. My Father has shown me that there will be a duality in this mission. The seed that I and my beloved, and all of you, have tenderly planted will grow two stalks from the place of seeding and become two towers from one cause. One stalk will be under the guardianship of Peter because it will need the greatest strength to be not bent to conform to a false doctrine and serve a false purpose. This stalk will grow in the west. The other stalk, in the east, will be under your guardianship because it will need a committed, loyal guardian to keep it from forgetting the balance. Andrew, hear me. Just as I know of your great love for our Sarah, whom history will rename because she will go into exile and change her name for safety, remember how she keeps your thinking balanced by her passion and her intuition. Keep the mission, as symbolized in this second stalk. leaning eastward, sacredly balanced. Do not forget that without the women, we, none of us, would be here in this life experience to discover how to become whole and enlightened."

Andrew answered, "You know, master, that I will forever be in your service and while I am alive in this life experience I will keep the eastern stalk of the mission on the path."

Peter had become distracted for there came to the garden at that moment soldiers with swords, and there was much clatter and much shouting and screaming.

I know of this conversation and this time because Jeshua told me of it later. I still lay sleeping with the white one through all of this commotion.

The followers were pushed about and some slashed as the soldiers barged through. They shouted at Peter, "Where is this blasphemer, this one who calls himself messiah, for his lies have brought his doom!"

Peter, as strong as he was, experienced great fear for his hope was great and he had believed they were on the verge of victory in this mission, at least the victory that he envisioned. Soldiers threatening the followers and slashing through the crowd was not what he expected. He told them, "I do not know who you mean. There is no one here that has claimed to be the messiah."

"Don't lie, Peter! We know that you are his right hand in this treachery."

"I know no messiah," Peter said, with the sudden realization that Jeshua had known that he would deny him and if that was true then one of the twelve had also betrayed him. Peter's great heart almost stopped at that moment and he ran, believing himself a coward.

I will always believe that to see this one weak area manifested in his being was a great shame and a great sorrow for Peter, this great fisher of men, as Jeshua often called him. It was his presence, his demeanor of the masculine in all its strength that would be the bait to attract those men who needed to understand how the feminine would equalize them and compliment them. That type of man was the dominant type and the very ones that Jeshua knew had to be enlightened and brought into feeling, for their minds ruled their hearts and their thinking had no feeling to direct their actions. Peter was his rock of hope, his plan to bring feeling back to the masculine.

Because of the screams of the women, I began to awaken. I roused to see the last of the men run away and Jeshua standing there alone. The women ran to him and I immediately ran forward because I knew that something terrible was about to happen. Jeshua said, with a look of pleading upon his face, "Stop, my beloved one, and think of our child to come, for I must do what I must do and you are left to carry on. I love you with all my heart. Remember that and take comfort within this truth."

Two of the sisters, I cannot remember which ones, held me back because the soldiers were upon my beloved Jeshua all too soon. They knocked him to the ground as they stabbed him with profanities. They seemed delighted to see him bleed from their blows and I remember one of them saying, "see, he bleeds like any man and that is all he is, just a man. A mad man!" Then they drug him away as they cheered and laughed and took turns beating him with such tremendous force that I believed my heart to be crumbling to the ground as I stood there.

My sisters held me so tight I could not move and they rocked me back and forth until my rage subsided and until the great wailing ended, for the sounds that came from me were sounds that I knew not that I had within my being. I believe those sounds were coming through me from She, the feminine side of God, for the mission would now take the long road instead of the short road. If only Jeshua and I could have lived a full life and offered the example of perfection in the balance as we so desired to do. The opposition to changing the imbalance to the divine duality was so strongly engrained that now it would be a long, long time for the balance to come.

I cried myself unconscious and in this state I dreamed a vision. I saw in this vision that the men would split into two factions, each with their own vision of how they must continue. I saw my child and myself left out of this development and in danger. I saw a brother of Jeshua, who had been devoted to him, yet not a follower from town to town, come forward and take me into his protection. Josephus, who would become known as Joseph of Arimathea, was a kind soul and he was the only one, besides his beloved mother, who really understood Jeshua. In my vision he took me away, back to the land of my long ago people. My vision then took me to the Great Mother who told me to stand true and to not believe all that I see, for there was a great plan that could take root and there was much unseen power for the cause yet to manifest. She asked me to follow my intuition and to remember my great love for Jeshua and honor that divinity in each moment, with each breath, and beyond breath forever. "I now give you my strength and my greatest intuitional power, for you will need it, my dearest daughter."

I then slept deeply and without dream to rest my body, which was full of child. I awoke knowing what the term "Christ" really meant. It meant to be totally balanced and totally aware. It was a blessing and a huge sorrow to be such, for I could feel Jeshua's sorrow and read his thoughts perfectly upon this awakening. I knew of his concern for me and I could transmit my thoughts to him and assure him I would take care of our child and myself as he wished and as the Great Mother told me to do.

"I love you, my beloved," I sent through the divine channel of our duality "hold our love strong for nothing can touch it and whatever happens it will survive and it will keep your soul safely guarded. It is the essence of this Divinity of We."

Blessed be,

Our Mothers and the Priestess Arrive

Watching Jeshua dragged from the garden was horrific, to say the least, for my heart wanted to stop but my soul knew it must not. My sisters held me long and rocked and soothed me. We agreed to stay with the cause no matter what, and we would stand by Jeshua to the bitter end if things should get worse. We feared, we almost knew, they would.

I was literally carried to our quarters where a kind woman householder gave us refuge. We all cried and cried and some left the compound to go for news. When they returned they told me what I already knew, things were not good for Jeshua. The men had scattered and seemed afraid to make themselves known. A crowd of people had gathered around the place of Jeshua's detainment and some of the very same people that claimed to have understood the message of peace and unity now were taking the side of those they found most powerful.

This is a survival tactic often used by those who live in fear and it did not surprise me. What surprised me was the news that some of the apostles were in the audience and saying nothing! It was the women followers who spoke up for the master and of course they were shouted down by angry voices of men.

"He has been convicted of blasphemy, MiryAmah," they told me. "How can that be? He has not broken God's law of love, only man's perception of God's law of obedience." I said.

"What will become of him?" I sobbed through tears of anguish.

"We fear they will put him to the cross" the messengers told me.

"No!" I screamed, "How would they waste a true gift of God such? They are truly blind men, who are not of God, who do this thing. I must go to him," I pleaded.

"But the babe, MiryAmah, would you put his child in danger?"

At that moment a beautiful elder-woman walked through the doorway of the house complex, followed by my dearest mother.

"We have come in your time of need," my mother said. The elder-woman was none other than the high priestess of the mountain temple. She came to me and touched my stomach gently with her old wrinkled hand, which gave the impression of being fleshed of the finest silk.

"She is still strong within you, MiryAmah." I bring you a potion that will keep you calm, yet not keep you from the emotions you will need to process this event that unfolds. It will keep the child from suffering your anguish and rejecting life. You will not lose this one, my dear, and you will not lose your beloved in the way that you fear."

My mother came to me and washed my face and asked for clean robes for me. My own were soaking wet from tears, as were the sisters who tended me. Mother asked of the householder, "do you have robes of red?"

These would be kept hidden for the men hated women to wear red, the color of their life bearing blood, and the color of feminine power. Not many would have the sacred robes still, since to be found with them was to be in dire peril.

"Yes," the householder, replied, "I shall be glad to give them to MiryAmah, for I will no longer need the red robe. My days come to a close soon." She was an elder widow herself and had lived a long and full life. The brightest red robes were brought forth and I was bathed and dressed and readied to go to the prison place that held my beloved captive.

I was noticed from the moment I left the compound. I walked with my mother and the high priestess, who were now in street robes, and the sisters, of course, dressed appropriately. I was the only one wearing red, the color of my grief, the color of my sorrow, the color of my sacrifice and the color of the power of the feminine. I walked proudly, yet the grief was evident upon my face. Women from households along the way walked from their residences to join me, some in spite of husbands threatening and shouting in their wake. My mother was on one side of me and the priestess was on the other, holding my hands as we walked. Then the priestess gently let my hand go and another hand took its place. I looked to my right side, drawn to the moment, only to see a tearful Mother Mary gently take my hand. We walked together, my mother on one side, my mother-in-law on the other, and Sarah and the others close behind, until we reached our destination.

Already word had spread that the women cometh and that one wore red robes. We approached the steps of the temple where the high priest resided, which was close to the prison cell that kept Jeshua, only to see my beloved already dragged from that cell and held there for us to see in his agony. My mothers held me tight as I began to faint, for my beloved was beaten with his flesh ripped until the bone was exposed and caked with blood. He looked at me and I could see his greatest pain was for me to see him this way. The high priest stood with his arms crossed, in a defiant stance.

"See what happens to those who violate the word of God?" I found strength and rejoined, "you are the violator, you imposter of a priest, for you have taken God's greatest gift and defiled this precious offering that was to help you to truly know the word and law of God."

"I could kill you at once for your impertinence, harlot, for your insolent words and for your display of sin by wearing red here at this holy place. But I will not, for I will enjoy watching you suffer for your sins as your lover dies slowly upon the cross of justice."

I looked the priest right in the eyes with my soul blazing through and said, "You may kill his body but you will never kill his soul and you will be dammed for eternity for what you do. As long as a woman lives and breathes he will be remembered and his message will be spread. Would you then kill every woman in existence? Then you would kill yourself and all mankind."

"Be gone, foolish one, and take all of your dim-witted sisters with you, for you could not hope to comprehend that of which you so boldly speak. You do not have the capacity to see beyond your desires of the flesh. Soon you will see what happens to those who give into such desires, for the flesh will hang upon the cross and it will rot and fall from the bones. You women are like the flesh. You serve your purpose for a time, then you rot away and slip from a man's soul, thus cleansing him finally of your evil presence."

Mother Mary said to me, speaking into my ear for only me to hear, "let us only speak to Jeshua and then depart, less he suffer even more for this mad man's fury."

I knew she was right, for no one could pierce the heart of this evil high priest. I doubted if he had a real heart within his wretched body. His mind could only seek power and control through any means. I looked at my beloved and said, "I love you, dear one, with all my heart. I will follow wherever they take you and I will keep your treasure safe within me, of this you can be sure." I could not openly tell them of my pregnancy for only a few knew of this and it would be dangerous to reveal this truth.

Mother Mary said, "My son, I will likewise stay by your side through this ordeal and I promise to keep your treasure and your beloved safe in my keeping as long as I am able."

My mother told me that help was on the way and that I should trust that this terrible event would ultimately be a force for good.

They took Jeshua away then and we moved on to the garden to meet with other women who wanted to know what could be done. "I wonder what the men are doing," I said to my mothers. "No doubt they will do the same -- regroup." They will find us in the garden, for that was where we were split and that is where we will unite."

When we reached the garden I sat upon a lonely bench for I could stand no longer. I asked to have a moment and I cried my grief alone for a time. My sisters and mothers were not afar, but they knew that I needed some time alone in this sorrow and they kept a short distance away.

My child within was sleeping as the priestess said she would. I feared that she might have died therein for she was an active child already in my 7th moon month. All my fears flooded my mind and heart at that moment and if I was to lose this child it would have been at that very time, for my body convulsed in sorrowful pain. The high priestess came forward then and wrapped her robes around me. No one could see that she was holding her right hand upon my stomach and she was sending life energy to my child, our child, Jeshua's and mine. I could feel my body stop its convulsion and I could feel the babe move slightly.

"Release the grief but do not release the child," the priestess said to me, and then breathed directly into my nose and mouth because I had lost my ability to breathe once the convulsions stopped. She sent life giving breaths into my lungs and I watched from slightly above my body where my consciousness floated. I am not sure how long she gave me the breath of life but when I again could breathe on my own I was also wrapped in the robes of the Mother Mary and my own mother. They had made a tent of their garments around me so that the process, an ancient ritual of life giving, could be private and its miracle would be secret. At this time to openly reveal such a thing would bring the enemy upon us, for they had every intention of stopping any such happenings.

It must have been a sight for the sisters to see, this tent of robes comprised of the mothers and the priestess, with the red robes I wore centered within. But, I think it was a pleasure for them to see me emerge from this tent of the feminine, whole and strong again and ready to be a pillar of strength for Jeshua, to help him go through this time of terror and pain.

We arose; my mothers, my priestess, myself, and we walked with our heads held high and went back to the temple cell to hold our vigilance there, close by our beloved one. The sisters walked closely behind us, with Sarah in the lead of that group. I looked back once and my heart was over-joyed during these moments of sorrow, for every single woman there, and I know we were at least one hundred strong, had tears running freely down their sweet faces as they openly showed the sorrow they held in their hearts. I could feel their strength expressed in their open emotions pouring into me and I knew that the sorrow of the feminine would come through us all and be funneled through me to assist my beloved in this event he must endure. I also knew that forever more this sorrow would be held deep within every woman's heart until the duality manifested, as my love and I had shown it could.

We walked on in silence.

Blessed be,

THE GIFT OF GOD IS REJECTED

I don't know how long we stayed at the temple cell because I lost all sense of time. The women brought me water but I could not eat. I prayed with all my heart for my love's life and to keep him from suffering so for his goodness. Finally, after some sort of court hearing, he was brought forth. There was much commotion from the public there present but most were frantic with the desire for blood sacrifice.

He emerged bleeding and weak. Jeshua descended the steps of the temple alone, unsupported and abandoned. He looked at me in the crowd and his eyes held a look so sorrowful I could not bear it. He knew that I would suffer along with him, for our hearts were as one. He looked from me to his mother with much that same dread. He said, "my beloveds." We could not hear the words over the sound of the crowd but we could read his lips and his face quite clearly.

He stumbled and fell several steps. I started to go to him but soldiers cruelly pushed me back. I knew then that I could never get closer and still keep our treasure, our child, safe. I then just followed as they forced my beloved Jeshua down the winding street through the city, toward the place of death. The crowd parted and through it came the heavy cross, carried by several strong soldiers. The priest called to them that the messiah did not need their help and would carry his own cross. They threw the dreadful thing toward Jeshua, who fell under its great weight. He tried to lift it but it was too heavy. One of his guards had a horrifying whip with stones tied to the ends of the straps, snaking off the end of the whip like terrible demons with eyes and teeth. He lashed out at Jeshua, ordering him to pick up the cross. My emotion came so grievously that I could not see through my own tears and the entire world seemed but a blur and a cruel nightmare to me. I did see a shape, a person had come from within the crowd and helped the master pick up this final burden and through the blur I could see them progressing down the street. There were those in the crowd who were excited and shouting obscenities; many of the faces were the same that had come to hear the teachings. How soon they forget, I thought. I saw a woman, again in my blurry vision, who offered Jeshua a cloth to wipe the blood, tears and sweat from his face. I heard the Mother Mary, who was helping to hold me up, say "bless that woman for her kindness, may she forever more be remembered for this one moment of mercy."

I could not walk as fast as the crowd and could not understand how Jeshua could move so fast. I later learned that more came forward from the crowd to help him bear the dreadful burden he carried that fateful day. I could hear the sobbing of those in deep sorrow. At first I only heard those bellowing for blood and punishment, but now the sobbing sounds grew stronger and the weepers were there all the time, just behind those who sought blood and vengeance. I had heard myself wail great moans when this all started and thought there was no way anyone could ever create such a mournful sound, but I heard the same wailing again and again that day, from the women who knew.

I did not know how far we had come and I still could not see very well but the procession seemed to stop. I knew my mothers were there with me and I will always love them dearly for their concern and their help. The crowd stilled, finally. Not even a whisper could be heard. Then I heard hammering.

"What is this noise, I asked my mother."

"I fear they have decided not to tie Jeshua, instead they may be nailing him to the cross."

"Oooohhhh," my heart bled, "is there no end to the torture that they will inflict on one who is the messenger and the hope of God? How can they claim to love God and kill his son, for Jeshua is the perfect example of what God's son is. God's sons and daughters are One! That is simple Divine truth, yet feared to the point that what God has sent, what God has made, what God does desire, is being destroyed by those who claim to be his priests. My God, my God, help us, for we know not what to do."

The crowd parted and we walked through, for our right to be there was recognized at that moment. My eyes cleared and I saw the cross being raised with my beloved nailed to it in agony. He looked at his Mother and I and then toward the crowd. He then looked toward the heavens and requested nearly the same prayer I had, but more directly. He pleaded, "My God, My God, help them, for they know not what they do."

In his last moments he loved all humanity so much that he prayed for them, his oppressors. I think I truly realized the scope of this being, this one I loved so much, at that moment. I knew that his love was immeasurable and that his suffering would somehow be a force of good. I dropped at the foot of this cross he bore. Mother Mary collapsed also and we wept for what seemed like hours, draped around the base of this pillar of horrors. I felt the pain of the tree that had given its life, only to be used in this impious way, to stop God's love, for the tree was newly cut and its essence was still within the wood. I prayed now that Jeshua would not suffer long. I prayed now for his death and an end to this nightmare of pain he endured.

A soldier came forward and pierced Jeshua's chest with his sword and said, "I give you relief from your pain, son of God," and he left. I could not decide if this was an act of compassion or an act of hatred. I would never know. Jeshua moaned in agonizing pain while blood and a substance that looked like water poured forth from this wound. Another soldier, one I had not seen before, came forward. There was something about this one that seemed quite different. He was so tall and he emitted a glow that was mesmerizing. The crowd seemed to go almost into a trance as he came forth. He had a sponge upon a long stick and he said, "Jeshua, you thirst, drink of this cool water and your thirst will be quenched and your pain will be gone."

Jeshua opened his eyes and looked at the shining one and nodded, as if he knew him, and sucked the moisture out of the sponge presented. The agony upon his face seemed to wane almost immediately. The shining one disappeared into the crowd, which was coming back to full fury and noise once again. The weepers were there now, near the front, and the taunters were beginning to leave, thinking that it would be morning before this blasphemer died. This day two other crosses were beside Jeshua and occupied by those who were also condemned for their deeds, much different deeds, however. I saw my love talking to one of those also crucified. I heard this man say that to be honored to accompany a man such as Jeshua in his final journey was his greatest joy. "Your joy shall free you and you and I shall meet again one day at the throne of glory of my Father," Jeshua said to him and then he looked toward his mother and myself and said, "farewell, my beloveds. John will keep you safe and I will always watch over you."

Then the clear evening sky suddenly produced rolling clouds that seemed to explode and move as a serpent to the place we now stood, with the master there upon that honorable tree, now transformed into a horrifying death chamber. The colors of the sky were red, dark blue and black and the light behind the clouds was dramatically alive as the skies filled completely, blocking out the setting sun. A great lightning bolt cracked through the sky and everyone reacted to this jolt, but we could not see where it struck. We could smell the sulfur and the resulting thunder shook the ground we occupied. Those still there, the weepers and the guards, thought that Tara was quaking and about to swallow them. I know that she was aware and angry and I would not have been surprised if we had all fallen into her hot lava chambers. The earth, you see, was shaken to her core and the heavens were cracking open as well. It was the effect of the sorrow of All That Is, whose great gift was rejected.

I looked toward my beloved to see how he faired this event and I knew that he had passed from this body and was not suffering anymore, for he hung limp now, his body empty. Mother Mary and I, and some of the others, lay in heaps of robes and bodies upon the ground and cried until there was no strength left in us. The guards notified the priests and the rulers and they came in the early hours of the morning because now they feared the dark. They knew of their sin. They brought down the cross in the early morning light and removed the nails from Jeshua's body. They laid him down in the laps of his mother and myself for a moment. It was a moment of kindness for our grief was so vast it must have affected these men who hours before were so insufferably cruel.

We held our beloved Jeshua and we rocked him like a baby, his body lifeless there between us. Then the followers came forward and asked if they might take him to a tomb donated by Lazarus, ever-faithful follower of the master. Mother Mary and I were so weak from grief that we handed the lifeless Jeshua over by just releasing our hold upon his beautiful physical body, so tortured and torn. There was a crown of thorns that someone had put upon his head and we did not notice it until that moment. His Mother gently took this thorny crown from her son's head, not even realizing that the thorns were piercing her very heart as she held him in death and rocked him in sorrow. Her robes were red with both his and her blood upon her chest where her heart had continued to beat through her pain. She fainted as she let him go. John picked her up in his arms and I believed I had followed him as he carried her back to our quarters with the elder woman. I was so far beyond coherence at that point that my memories are not clear. Many of the sisters followed also and assisted me and they were the ones to bathe and prepare us to rest, for we needed to regain some strength to survive. Mary's thorn wounds were many upon her mother's breast but none were deep enough to pierce her heart. Her heart could not have been wounded more, even if a thorn had found its depth.

I felt my own mother and the priestess take me aside and listen to my chest and my babe's heart within my womb. They told me that my little one was safe and then I asked of my beloved, "did you see where they took him and who took him away?" I said. My mother answered, "I think they were followers but there were two that I have never before seen. They were quite tall and very strong and they seemed to glow as they carried the body of Jeshua away. We will find him tomorrow. I promise you. Now sleep, sleep as surely Jeshua now sleeps in heaven for we all need to finish this ordeal."

I remember no more until morning. I slept so sound that I did not even dream and I only remember that my mother and the high priestess were chanting over me as I slumbered off. They were smudging me with a sweet smelling herb and rubbing oil of the same scent. Oddly, I felt finally at peace.

Blessed be,

JESHUA DIES YET HE LIVES

So in agony and full of grief was I that my memories of this time had become confused. The time of the crucifixion is still a horrifying blur for me and I know of the major moments, but the moments in-between can be foggy. I remembered arriving back at the women's quarters after the crucifixion, assuming the sisters had brought me there. Yet the next morning, early, before anyone else was up, I arose and went back to the cross, which was now being taken down. Jeshua was gone from this heinous place. Some of my sisters heard me leave and followed me back to the cross location where I thanked them for taking me to the quarters the previous night. They told me it was Josephus, the brother of Jeshua, who had brought me there. They told me that when they approached me, after John had picked up Mother Mary and carried her away, I had asked for a few more moments alone with my beloved. They said Josephus found me there alone, a short time later, and he had promised his brother, Jeshua, that he would see to my safety. It was the back-up plan, as you might term it, for near the end Jeshua was not certain that John would keep his promise to keep both *beloveds* safe from all harm.

I bring this up because it is important to know that the family of Jeshua, including his brothers and sisters, however perplexed with Jeshua's mission, were nonetheless devoted to him. Even his brother, Judea-James, came to support us and eventually, for the cause of Jeshua, he died for his dedication.

I felt stronger this morning, possibly because the state of shock kept me in a semi-conscious mode or maybe because, within my being, I knew that I could not be truly separated from my true love, my twin flame.

As I stared at the place of my beloved's death, it began to sink in that he had been moved to a tomb arranged by Lazarus, for the cross was down and the body gone. I began to look for this place of rest. Two of my sisters came with me to search for the burial tomb. Someone told me, I cannot remember whom, which tomb to seek and that a huge stone had been rolled into place to seal it, as last they had heard. I continued in spite of the knowledge that I could not enter, for I felt the need to be near the body, even if a giant stone prevented me from the closeness I desired.

We came down the tomb path, as directed, and low and behold, the rock was not blocking the opening. "Oh my, we can say our farewell to my beloved without a rock between us," I said to my companions. And I rushed into the tomb. There was nothing there but the burial cloth, lying upon the floor with blood and dirt caked upon it.

"Someone has stolen Jeshua's body," I cried. "Will the anguish and torture never end," for there seemed to be no end to my tears. My sisters helped me from the tomb when I saw a man near by. He spoke to the sisters and me, but bid me come closer because he had an important message for me. I felt compelled to go to him and hear this communication that he felt was so important.

"Do you not recognize me, MiryAmah, my beloved?" he asked.

At that point the man transformed into my beloved Jeshua.

"Listen carefully." he said, "for my energy and my time is short. First, do not touch me for my spirit transforms over this one I use; my energy is not yet reorganized from the ordeal, and should you touch this physical body it will throw off my opportunity to use it. I am not dead, for I live. My life as Jeshua is dead, however, and for the sake of the mission I am dead and arisen to go be with our Father. I will never be dead to you, my love, so take heart. I will come to you again and to the apostles. I need to reassure them, for they are over-taken by fear. I shall attempt to bring them back into the alignment of the mission. Go and rejoice, my beloved, for you shall see me again soon."

I just stood, listening and wondering of the sanity of my own being, for I just saw my beloved transpose over another man and become again a man in flesh. The transposition ended and the original soul returned and promptly left after seeing the dumb-founded expression upon my face. Reality set in and I ran back to my sisters and said, "Did you see that?"

"What, dear MiryAmah," they said?

"Did you see that man transform into Jeshua?"

"We saw you approach him and we saw him leave but that is all we saw," they replied. "But if you say this is so, then we believe you as always, for we trust you fully."

"I know not what has truly happened, my sisters, but I do know this; my beloved has risen from the dead and he lives. I am not sure of how this has come to be or how it will play out, for he told me he is dead and risen to our Father in Heaven, but yet alive to me and will speak again further."

My joy was written all over my face. I said, "I must go to the followers and tell them of this thing I have seen. He worries rightfully about the followers, especially the apostles. He told me he would be visiting them as well." I ran off with the energy of joy lifting my feet as I made great speed to the garden where I knew the followers would be assembling again.

My sisters could not keep up with me. I ran into the garden crying in elation, "He lives! He lives and is not dead, for he has arisen!" I threw my arms around Andrew, who looked at me astonished. "I have seen Jeshua near the tomb which now lies empty. He says he will visit some of you soon and to keep heart and stay focused on the mission."

"You have had too much to bear, dear lady," Andrew said, "for I fear you talk nonsense. You should go back to your quarters and rest. We are about important business now and should not be distracted."

I looked at Peter and said, "How is it you can be about important business without me present, for am I not one of you and the closest to Jeshua and do I not know his heart and mind like no other? How then could you make decisions not knowing all that I know? He will come to you and I will talk further when you know that I do not speak nonsense."

I left the group of men to their important and exclusive meeting and walked away. I heard Andrew, of all people, say, "She is but a woman and she does not understand the scope of the master's mission." Sarah, as always, was close by. She looked at Andrew and he looked back at her for a long moment. She held such disappointment in her gaze as he revealed something that we both did not know about this apostle, this friend of the master, that he had not understood the message after all. His loyalty to Jeshua was great, but he did not really understand the basis of the mission. He held disrespect and distrust of the feminine.

I shall never want to see that look of instant extinguishment of love and hope again, for the color left Sarah's sweet and scarred face and she left with me, knowing that she would never follow Andrew into his world of exclusion.

"We have both lost our true love," she said, "But God has given yours back to you. I wonder if He will give me mine as well, but I fear not, for I did not see the man I love within the eyes I just looked into. I must have loved an illusionary man, for I know this man not!"

We walked away hand in hand, not knowing what would happen now but knowing that surely something was about to unfold.

"We will somehow go on, my friend," I said to Sarah, and she nodded in agreement.

Blessed be,

BETRAYAL AND ESCAPE

Jeshua did appear to the apostles, but he appeared without transposing over another being in the physical as he did in my presence at the tomb. Instead, he used a technique to project his spirit. This was something we had learned of in our early training but it was a technique that involved a being in the physical leaving the body and appearing in a different location in the ethereal sense. I had no experience with those who had died coming back in such a way but the high priestess often spoke of such a thing. She said that it was possible if the need was great or the soul, upon transition to the spirit realm, was still unsettled.

The last time I saw my beloved in this ethereal state he told me to go to the apostles because he had instructed them to respect me as the apostle in authority, for to I alone would he entrust this leadership, since I knew him best.

"Am I now an apostle, my love?" He said, "You have always been such, just as I am one of the disciples. The terms are just the masculine and the feminine form of the same thing, meaning dedicated followers to the cause." I will not tell you of all that transpired in this visitation, for there are tender moments that should be private between soul mates.

After this brief visit I went to the apostles, as directed and agreed upon, for I was never really told what I must do but always shared in the decision. I found the apostles, not meeting in the garden anymore because of the danger, but this time at the home of another householder who sympathized with the cause. They were grouped in the interior courtyard and as I came to the home I was greeted by the householders with all due love and respect and shown to the meeting place.

I embraced all there present, for not all had found the courage to carry on as of yet. Peter asked me to share any secret teachings that the master may have shared with me, for as he said, I knew him best and I would know of the direction needed to carry on. I thought I would test them so I gave them some information on the levels of consciousness, as the duality parable unfolded to both Jeshua and I in twin dreams.

The lesson therein was that one must stay at certain stages of experience and process seven levels of each before one advanced to the next level of awareness. Awareness was *enlightenment* since it made the mind, body and soul more in tune with the Creator, the brightest light imaginable. In our dreams it was known that some stages had definite pitfalls and that if one did not really understand the totality of a previous stage, they would surely fall back once they stumbled into such a gap in understanding. This falling back in awareness and consciousness doesn't mean that one has lost anything, just that one must re-experience something so that they can be prepared when next they encounter this same pitfall.

"The greatest drawback for human kind is that the genders judge themselves using different sets of standards to measure self-worth and worth of others. Half of all creation is deemed less worthy because of gender measurements. Is an apple better than an orange? Both are fruit. Both nourish and reseed their kind. Both have a core center, made of seeds and a peeling to protect itself and the flesh of fruit between. Both are God's gift and divine creation with specific purpose. If you would not think of measuring these two fruits because you know that they are wonderful in their differences, their flavors, their gifts, then why do you continue to separate God's equally wonderful creation of humanity?"

Andrew said, "Surely, MiryAmah, you do not compare yourself to an orange or an apple? A woman is much more complicated than such a thing."

"We carry the seed within us, do we not? We depend on pollination from an outside source to bring us from blossom so the fruit can be set. All creation has purpose and all purpose intermingles and merges, as was God's plan. We are all stewards of each other and just as the bee does not tell the blossom it is unfit to bloom and present itself for pollination, so, too, should man not tell his counterpart, the woman, that she is less than he and that he owns the fruit of her womb. He may plant the seed but it is she that brings it forth. They are one in this purpose, physically, mentally and spiritually," was my reply.

Peter listened carefully and seemed to be acceptive of the teaching I offered as I shared our twin dreams. Jeshua and I often talked long and discussed the meaning of such dreams but I wanted to see what the apostles would think of this one, which I found quite uncomplicated. They would need to work many things out on their own to carry on in the mission and this would be a perfect opportunity to see them in action, for Jeshua and I had planned that they should go out as beacons of light to the masses, scattering the sparks of *knowing*.

The action that was forthcoming from Peter's own brother, Andrew, was not what I expected. He looked at me with disregard and said to Peter, not even being gracious enough to address me in a straightforward manner, "Personally, Peter, I do not believe a word this woman says." Levi, another apostle, said, "This woman is the master's closest companion, whom he loved like no other. Would she not know him best? What purpose would it serve for her to lie?"

Andrew answered Levi by saying, "I am sure she thinks she is correct in what she says, but being a woman, she does not have the capacity to understand the deepest purpose of Jeshua's mission, as we do."

I am a patient woman by nature, but this was too much. "Oh, my financial support is accepted but what I know in my heart and my mind and soul is of no use to you then, you say, Andrew. You, who claimed to be the guardian of Jeshua, now would reject his mission? The mission is Jeshua as it is I and all of you. We are all one with this cause."

At that point I just walked away, for I could see the minds and hearts of the majority present were closed and that Peter was tilting toward the prevailing attitude of exclusion of my leadership.

I returned to the place where I had been staying. As I entered the woman's compound, James, the brother of Jeshua was there waiting for me. He was not always certain of Jeshua's mission but he had heard of the visitation and he was anxious to speak with me on this matter.

"Is it true, MiryAmah, (I took notice that he used my chosen name out of respect for me) that you have seen my brother since the crucifixion?"

"Yes, true, James, he has come to me a number of times and has so, too, spoken with the apostles to ensure that the mission continues to bring balance and sanity back to the people."

"You know, MiryAmah, I believe I finally understand the importance of the work of my brother and it is too late to give him that gift of love. My heart is heavy. May I be of assistance to you in honor of my beloved brother and in respect to you and your part of this task? I offer you all that I have to give," James told me.

"Jeshua and I are pleased and we appreciate your dedication, not only to the family but as a man of wisdom, for I can see it in your eyes as I saw it in your brothers also."

Josephus then came to the compound and he looked full of distress. "MiryAmah," he said, "and James, I am glad to see you here, for it has become known that MiryAmah is with child and the soldiers come to take her away. We must flee now!"

He grabbed my hand and began to run so fast I could hardly keep up with him with my stomach so full of child. Eventually, he just swept me off my feet and ran like the wind, James with us, ducking in and out of doorways. I feared we would all fall and be injured. We came to a doorway and Josephus said to the occupant, "The soldiers want MiryAmah. They want to end her life and the lineage of Jeshua. We need help. I know you have loved the master. Can you assist?"

We were immediately ushered into the residence and taken to a large meeting room with a tapestry hanging upon the wall. I shall never forget this tapestry for it had the tree of life upon it and it bore the blessed emblems of the sacred duality, masculine and feminine. One image I have always loved is the image of the black and white swan circled together. To visualize this image think of the eastern image of the yin and yang with the swirling, but equal white and dark areas, with a little white in the dark and a little dark in the light. It is odd that in a split second one can take notice of such a thing. I knew that this was indeed a person of wealth who owned this home for common folk could not afford such luxury.

The householder's wife indicated that we should follow her. She heaved the tapestry aside and pushed on a block of stone that pivoted, revealing a secret doorway. So perfectly balanced was this portal on a single swiveling point that it swung without noise or resistance. There within was a tunnel with torches already lit, and we entered in great haste. I felt the air change as the doorway quickly closed behind us.

"Follow me, lady of the master, for I pledge thee my support. You are the hope of us all." I was able to walk now at this much slower pace and Josephus set me to my feet and he and James walked on either side of me, making sure my step found its footing.

We wound and turned and seemed to be going deeper and deeper into the earth, through what appeared to me as solid rock. We finally came to a vast chamber that held magnificent images of the feminine and masculine in the dance of duality as I often remembered from my childhood days in the emergence temples. Within a great room there were twelve rocks carved as comfortable seats with a thirteenth place slightly higher for the sake, as I knew from my own days in councils, of the leader getting the attention of those present, should the need arise. This was a feminine meeting place, much the same as my aunt's center.

I looked at this householder woman once again and she threw back her head covering and allowed her beautiful, long, wavy hair to escape its captive place as she smiled sweetly. She was none other than the woman who wandered, so long ago it seemed, too far to gather herbs and had been caught in her priestess garb and stoned. Her sincerity was evident as she said, "we meet again, my friend. It is the feminine that Jeshua has come to protect and bring back into balance and it will be we who will safe guard his treasure and his own feminine counterpart. Welcome to safety for the moment. We will begin the work of finding a safe haven for you and the child I sense you will soon bring forth."

We came then to more chambers beyond the meeting area and there were sisters there waiting whom I had not previously met. To greet my arrival there was also the high priestess and my mother. Quarters were ready and safety was assured for the moment. My heart felt warmed. So much was happening beyond my imagination, with Jeshua visiting and now this mad escape from those that would harm his loved ones.

As I embraced my mother and the priestess I asked, "How is it that you are already here when the brothers and I did not know where we would find refuge until but moments ago?"

The priestess explained, "Your steps were guided using the powers of olde, my dear. Your love tie to your mother was all we needed to bring you to this place of safety, for we brought her here first. She is trained well in finding her own as well. It is time now for you to rest. We will stay by your side and when you are ready we will conduct a meeting of the twelve plus the one, but this time we will have your disciples here for you to lead through the next phase of this rescue mission, or at least those of whose loyalty we are certain. But first you must rest and while you do, we shall build the ritual fire and bring the elements and ingredients to this sacred flaming light for the purpose of this planning moment and to enhance the vision and the wisdom.

James and Josephus then bid me farewell and said they must go to their mother to insure her safety as well. The Priestess and householder woman both assured them that she could be brought to this place should they believe her safety threatened.

"Thank you for your assurance and hospitality," James said, "Now how do we depart this place, surely not the way we came in, for the house could be full of soldiers by now."

I later learned it was. They had even pulled back the tapestry and the door fit so perfectly that they did not suspect the secret of it. The householder woman led them down another pathway to one of the many escape portals. James told me later that they came out in a market place from behind a curtain where rugs to be sold had been stored. This shop belonged to those same householders; tapestries and rugs were their trade.

Upon the prepared bedchamber I fell into a deep sleep for I was exhausted from the events of the last few days. I saw my beloved in my dream but he seemed to be still in pain, which puzzled me even as I slept. Someone was washing his body and giving him potions and talking to him in a strange tongue. They were saying, "stay with us, Jeshua, for there is still much for you to do, only now you will move in a secret, invisible way, through your work."

I saw great concern upon the faces of the men and women in his presence and something happened that frightened them. An elder-woman leaned down upon him and gave him the breath of life as the priestess did for me when my breath stopped. I saw my love twitching and shaking and then suddenly open his eyes in amazement. "He is back," I heard the woman say. "Rejoice!"

Blessed Be,

EXILE IN THE NIGHT

I stayed in the sanctuary for a few weeks, I think, for I actually forgot the time of day and the days of weeks as I met with the sisters and grew larger with the babe within. Sarah came to me shortly after my arrival and insisted that she have a floor mat placed near my bedchamber so that she could be there should she be needed. The householders brought in much straw and made her a quite comfortable place to rest but worried about the quality of her accommodations. She assured them that she had seen much worse and that to her this was extreme luxury and she was grateful beyond measure.

She worried over me constantly, and gladdened my heart with her enthusiasm and optimism that always overcame her worry episodes. I felt totally blessed by her loving friendship and commitment to my safety and happiness.

At our first meeting within the secret chambers we found that only one of the disciples had strayed and we replaced her with Mother Mary for this brief span of time that the twelve plus one would convene. We knew that we would soon disband physically and go our separate ways to spread the teachings as the apostles were supposed to do. We wanted to be in unison however, not with different visions of purpose and intent muddling our minds. We knew the need to plan the course of action accordingly. I felt odd sitting upon the higher seat with Mother Mary there slightly below me but she assured me she was honored to be there at my side and to just do the work as I knew it must be done.

We decided that we would have to work in a very subtle way. For us to boldly bring the teachings forth as women would be to open ourselves to danger and compromise the desired seeds we wanted to plant. The madness was wide spread, according to my sisters. The followers were fighting and in need of direction but had rejected the one sent by Jeshua, myself, to keep unity. I sought no glory or power but they could not see that truth. I simply took the responsibility requested of me for I was the one most in line with the concept of divine duality as it manifested within my beloved and myself. Times were hard as the fight for power ensued within the society that killed my beloved and those who claimed to

143

support the cause for which he died. Soldiers went door-to-door trying to shake out the followers and bring them to what they considered to be justice.

It seemed odd in a way, that I could feel so safe here, below the turmoil above ground. I rested often and continued to dream of Jeshua and in my dreams I could visualize him going from weak to strong. He had many elders there present in these dream visions. They worked attentively to bring him to full wellness. I could feel his great heart reach out to mine and his sweet voice often said to me, "I miss you, my beloved, yet I visit you often as I travel between our heart-tied beings that no distance can separate. I will myself to live for your sake, for the sake of our great love, for the sake of our child, and those I hope are yet to come. I also will myself to live for the sake of all duality." Then he would smile and seem to penetrate me with his piercing, loving gaze and the dream vision would fade.

These visions energized me in the most calming and soothing way. I did not feel a vibration of urgency, instead I felt the harmony of love within my being, and the strength returned to me as well. I should say the strength returned to us, for our daughter actively made her presence known as I found my rest.

I could tell when it was morning by the cooking smells from above. One particular morning, as I arose, Sarah appeared and brightly announced, "Be up and about, my friend, for this morning you have a special guest to join you for your awakening meal."

I could not imagine who this could be and hurried about my dressing, which was becoming more and more difficult since I was now so heavy with child. As I came into the place of dining, I saw my attending sisters in a circle, talking as if to a child to someone there within their group.

"You look much better now, little one," Mary Margaret said, "so much stronger and so healthy."

Mary Margaret had a child-like quality to her presence and had I not known better, I would have guessed her to be about ten years old. She actually was closer to twenty-five years of age. Another sister, imitating the way Mary Margaret spoke, said in a similar child-talk voice, "You are the sweetest little one I have ever known and I love your softness and your charming little face."

Then I saw her lift the face of the little white donkey and kiss its soft muzzle. I was astounded. It was the same little white burro that had served Jeshua so well upon his entry into Jerusalem, and who had given me all of his energy that day of great sorrow within the garden. I thought that the poor creature had died giving its life to me on that fateful day. I moved through the group in delightful amazement and embraced my friend gratefully.

"I rejoice in your safety and your good health, my dear one," I said as I held him to my body and felt our heartbeats merge. I swear that I could read the thoughts of this little one. He told me he had been sent to serve me and was honored to be of assistance. He stayed with me throughout the meal and became like a pet to the sisters in the following days. He played and brayed great noisy sounds when we played tricks upon him. I would hide from his eyes and he would always seek me out. What fun this was. It was almost easy to forget the madness then happening within the community.

The householders came to see me each day and one day they even brought a nice riding rug for the little one. I said, "that is so nice of you but surely no one will ever ride upon his back again after the master's sacred journey."

Josephus and James there upon entered the chamber just in time to hear this prediction and James said, "The danger grows and to raise a child within the deep darkness of these caverns is not what my brother would have wanted, MiryAmah. The little one was sent to you to take you to safety. He will gladly bear your weight, which will not be a burden to him. He lives and breathes to do this for you and for our dear brother. Upon bringing him back to health the animal priestess learned that he needed a mission to remain in the physical. We have granted his wish and hope that you will, also. We must leave at the end of this day."

We prepared to leave that very night, which I only learned was night as we departed from our safe haven that evening. My precious burro was blackened with ashes to dull his pure white color. He was truly a shining one, with his pureness of white, and would be easily seen in the dark. He was fitted with the riding rug and I was positioned upon his back in a side-riding saddle that would support my back as I sat with both my legs upon one side. I told my protectors that I could walk quite well and they just patted my protruding belly and said, "sure you can, but you will not."

James would move ahead and whistle, emulating a particular night bird, but with a repetition that was recognizable as his signal, to give us clearance to continue at each step of the way. Josephus and Sarah would accompany me, one walking on each side of my white one who carried me easily upon his strong little back.

The tunnel that took us to the outside seemed ever long and winding. We eventually emerged, upon hearing the night bird message from James, into an area outside the city under a starry night sky. We would follow a path pre-planned by the brothers toward the place of my birth, Egypt, the place of the pharaohs. I would be safe there. Every so often we would stop and wait for the all-clear signal and then continue on. By day we took refuge in secret caves and the safe habitats of faithful followers. We traveled for close to a month. I grew heavier and heavier with child. I hoped to find a suitable place to birth our child and Josephus assured me that we would and that there was no need for worry. Sarah did not say much; I knew her heart was heavy too, but with a heartbreaking burden as she remembered Andrew. She just held my hand and walked in silence.

Blessed be,

THE SACRED EMERGENCE OF SARAH

I arrived in Egypt after a long hard journey, mostly by night, and sometimes through the cave passages of the underworld. My little white burro friend, now back to his whiteness of coat, bore my weight with the greatest strength and dedication. I still consider him one of my dearest and most faithful friends.

Upon arrival, since James was always ahead of us for safety reasons, I was taken into a temple of Isis. There was no formality to my entering for I was still to be kept secret to the outside world until safety was assured. There waiting for me was a mid-wife priestess from an emergence temple. I was amazed that there was still such a place within the chambers of this mysterious and great sanctuary I had come for refuge. It was held in secrecy here too, since the feminine was also threatened in this place of old ways. The climate was somewhat better, however, and open hostility towards women and girls was not yet to the degree of that in the holy land area.

I found this sanctuary for the parents, the emergence place, especially the mothering and birthing place, quite fascinating. We were led through many secret passages while still upon the back of my white friend, whom I could not think of leaving in anyone else's care. We finally arrived at a place deep within Tara. The term *going underground* is connected to such times as these, when safety could only be found within Tara's underground sanctuaries, where darkness and inner vision still hold to truth, even without the light of day.

The inner temple was huge with columns that were shaped like the feminine human form, some long and sleek and some bulging as ready to bring forth life. There were also animal forms gracefully holding the safety of the chamber in place, running from floor to ceiling, which must have been twenty feet high in some places. All figures were gracefully elongated to accommodate the span. Many cats roamed this area and many statues of Ma'at were present. The feminine and the feline are very compatible in energy and intuitive ability. Those of this Egyptian place knew well this similarity and used the energies to the utmost. In the first rooms there were beautiful women in graceful garb and of bronze skin similar to my own. Some were on task and some lounging about but all appeared happy and content.

"Welcome home, MiryAmah," the high priestess said, as she met us coming through the last portal, "for a temple of the feminine is always home to our sisters. We give you our blessings and our pledge to keep you safe." She then laid her hands upon my abdomen, after asking my permission, and closed her eyes. The expressions upon her beautifully aged face were those of one in deep conversation without words, simply within feeling. Her head nodded, as if in agreement, then shook from side to side as if understanding some point of concern or sorrow. She smiled as a tear rolled down her well-lined cheek and dripped there from her face, splashing upon my garments. Then she opened her eyes and looked at me in such a concerned, knowing way and gently said, "Your child tells me of what you have experienced." I replied, "I had hoped she would not be aware of the pain and anguish of recent times. She knows well, but I feel no spiritual damage for she knew upon the decision to come through you and Jeshua that this could be a truly terrible time to emerge, yet a time of great need. She also knew that she could bring joy and hope back to your life, my faithful sister. She has been through many life times with you and Jeshua already and she has never once regretted any pain or sorrow that she experienced due to her decisions to incarnate. She told me of times of great joy, and she hopes to again experience such with you."

"Mother-One," I said, "how is it that a babe can remember and know all of this and tell you of so much knowledge and knowing?" The high priestess smiled, for she loved being called *Mother-One* and the term of endearment came quite naturally to me since she radiated this essence.

"Ah, sweet MiryAmah, the emerging child remembers far more than mothers can often believe, for they have not yet come through the channel of forgetting." They must, during the pregnancy, sort out their final commitment in this entry opportunity so they must be totally aware. Do not think they are not sweet children still, but they are so aware that they are, in fact, the sweetest example of knowing-innocence. What I mean is that they are totally aware of all experience and all connections to this opportunity but they cannot test their knowing or expand such unless they forget, for a time, the particulars of all previous experience as they emerge into the light of day. So, as they move through the birth channel and emerge into the physical world they become little beings of feeling and need for a time, yet are still so vitally aware within these modes of understanding. This assures the bonding of love and commitment between the child and parents, especially the mother, and also begins the soul growth process."

"How is it then, Mother-One, that I can remember glimpses of past lives? Did I not forget sufficiently?" I asked. She explained that the veil between this memory is thin, yet strongly in place. Once you have gained the ability to see through it you can remember glimpses, but never the totality, because that would be a burden that would pull away from the sacred moment of "now." I thought about this for a few seconds and then asked if that was why my teachers on the Misty Isle screened us so well, to see how far we had come in awareness and wisdom, even as children?

"My dear," she said, "You would not have come as far as the Misty Isle were you not already screened as determined and ready. You learned much there, but also there were moments of ritual that activated the ability to remember key connections so that your mission would stay strong and on its path."

As I pondered this, trying to remember the rituals, a great pain gripped my womb. The effects were clearly seen and the Mother-One called to those present to help her immediately, announcing that the child had made her decision to come forth.

James and Josephus, who were still there, were amazed at this emergence place for they had never dreamed that such a place existed. They watched with eyes wide in wonderment. They soon realized this was not some evil, female hellhole of which the priests warned, but a sacred, feminine temple. They watched the commotion from the sidelines, looking somewhat helpless.

Even in my pain I heard Josephus say to James, "did you ever dream of such a place, my brother?" He replied, "Never! Would our mother know of such as this?" "If she does she has kept the secret well hidden, and wisely so, for surely those in control of the laws and the people of our time and place would not permit such a wonder as this," Josephus answered with conviction.

Two priestesses approached the brothers and advised that they say their farewells, for I had woman's work to do. Both lightly kissed me upon each cheek and assured me that they would keep me informed of the mission and should I need them they would be at my side in the shortest possible time.

By then great pains were upon me. Mother-One insisted we make haste to the emerging room, for this child would not be born in pain. I was whisked away and even as the women carried me in slings made of their joined hands, another poured a sweet wine potion into my mouth as she explained that it would begin the easing from the inside of my body so that I could participate in this event while in pleasure. I could feel the effect even as the potion was on my lips. Wherever it touched it warmed and relaxed me. I entered the emerging room ready to welcome my child into physicality.

The room was glowing in red with all surfaces as different shades of such. Paintings adorned the walls in many forms, but all were happy images to welcome the small ones upon their entry. A slanted, cushioned birthing chair was present and also in a shade of red.

"Since this is your first child, you may wonder why all is red," Mother-One said. "The child emerges from a red place within you. Your very red blood prepared this place and nourished this tiny one's new body, readying it to begin this journey. Red is the color of the feminine power of creation as granted by Sophia, Mother God. It is her offering to all life and yours as this child's earthly mother, in that she gives her life's blood to the cause through you. When the babe comes into this red room it does not have such shock, for it finds comfort therein."

Then she looked at the silent sisters and said, "It is time, bring Sarah forward." My dear friend came into view. "I understand that this girl child has already been named," Mother-One said. "Yes," Sarah responded, "she has been offered my name."

"Do you agree with this plan," Mother-One asked? "For if you do, you must give of this name fully and take another."

Sarah looked as if in deep thought. I could feel my babe preparing to emerge and taking the birthing position, but I felt no pain. My attention then went back to my beloved friend, Sarah, who finally said, after long thought, "Yes, I would be honored to give my name to this babe, as is my choice, for Jeshua, my dear friend, desired this and I do as well. But, Mother-One, I would request that this name be cleansed of sorrow, for my life has held much pain and suffering. I would like this babe to take only the loving vibration of this calling sound, not the pain it has absorbed."

"Well thought out, dear one," the high priestess said. "It shall be so." She looked toward me and put her hand upon my belly full of anxious baby. "Child," she said, "wait just a little longer while we prepare your sacred name."

There was much hustle and bustle in the chambers as sisters brought forth various objects. One object was a beautiful, clear crystal skull that looked like it was carved of purest ice. It was placed on a small alter within the room, close to me. Sarah was asked to put both her hands upon the skull as she stood behind it. This was necessary for there was to be no space occupied between the babe and myself and the cleansing skull.

Upon the proper positioning for the name cleansing, the Mother-One asked those present to sing the name into the skull. A forceful but beautiful sound filled the room immediately with all voices in unison singing "Sarah, Sarah, Sarah," over and over.

I could see the color of yellow first as it pulsed through Sarah's arms and hands, followed by pink, red and then blues all traveling down into the icy skull. As the colors entered the skull of crystal, my dear friend's face, which had been so serene, suddenly grimaced into a face of pain and utmost sorrow and the most unpleasant murky colors ran through her arms and hands. Every blood vein stood out as if to burst and I feared that some evil had taken over the process. The murk entered the skull and the other colors absorbed it immediately. My friend's face eased once again and then another great wave of pain over came her and she let more murk come through as she shook and trembled, while still holding tight to the crystal skull there on the alter. Finally a great release seemed to happen and she let go of the last of the pain and sorrow. The singing changed tempo at this point and it became less forceful and more serene in tone and rhythm. Certainly I had never heard the name Sarah so beautifully voiced.

All watched the skull and when all the colors had cleansed the murk and the skull had returned to the previous clarity, Mother-One sang to the group and myself in a beautiful, elderly, feminine voice,

"Sarah, Sarah, Sarah, cleaned now pure and true,

Seeks her namesake place deep within the blue,

Of this emerging soul so dedicated and true,

To be one upon the babe now coming through,

This mother MiryAmah and father, Jeshua too,

In all due honor freely given to you,

Sarah, Sarah, Sarah, child that shall see,

All that is of love and sweet Divinity.

My friend looked so relieved as she gave up her name. The temple priestesses continued to sing "Sarah, Sarah, Sarah," but added, "bless us with your presence, dear one, for your time has come." I felt then the babe moving through the channel of birth, and I had no pain. Instead I felt a similar feeling as I had felt at the most intimate of times with my lover, my beloved Jeshua, my husband, as we merged in sacred sexuality. It was the feeling of pleasure building and building into a huge explosion of release, that I felt now again reminding me of the moments leading to conception of this child within. Then Sarah made herself known to the physical world and emerged to song, incense and love. As she peeked into the soft red light of the room I felt the most extreme climax of pleasure imaginable. Sarah seemed to cry in unison with the song of her name.

As I found my breath again, now having brought forth my child while sitting in a semi upward position, I remarked that I never knew that birthing a babe could be such an experience. I had been confused between the first teachings which did allude to such and to that of the women in the outer world who talked of pain and sorrow because of the sin of Eve, whose actions tainted all women and deemed that they would suffer to atone to God for such an act.

Mother-One smiled and even laughed out loud. "Those jealous old men that want birthing to be painful to take a woman's greatest moment of pleasure are pathetic. Overtime a woman lies with the love of her life, her masculine counterpart, and the sexual merging is completed in the totality of love and respect. This coupling feeds the universe, the very Source of all life, with the greatest joy of creation. It does not matter if actual conception takes place at that moment, or if it follows later. What matters is that the merging is sacred and complete and divine because of the masculine and the feminine becoming one in love and wholeness. Thus when the babe does decide to emerge, it celebrates the perfection of duality through creation as the parents have demonstrated. Those old fools living in fear keep the greatest of pleasure ever from even themselves, for they have reduced this sacred merging to a duty, a sinful fall from their idea of grace."

While we spoke I was aware of my now nameless friend, who gave her name to my child, cleaning and preparing the babe, my sweet Sarah, whom she had helped into this world. The high priestess had positioned my friend there between my knees, sitting cross-legged on a cushion upon the floor with a small basket of absorbent blankets, ready for the child. When little Sarah came through, she was gently caught and held for a moment, then wrapped in the blankets and then handed directly to me to bring to breast. My bared chest was smeared with the blood of my child and myself and the water of my womb, as well as the leaking milk my body could not wait to offer to little Sarah. All these substances were part of the sacredness of creation and life. It was a luscious feeling to be aware of these sacred liquids of life and to smell the aroma of birthing upon my babe and myself. In sacred birthing, as done in this temple and all such places, the cleaning up of the liquids was not an immediate priority because it was part of the experience.

Little Sarah opened her tiny eyes and looked into mine and took the nipple immediately and in delight. She had no trauma or fear in her. She had emerged in love and honor. We both fell asleep and upon awakening I felt the sacred substance of birthing being carefully coaxed from my body with an ivory birthing scraper. A smaller version was used on little Sarah, and all of the sacred liquid was saved in beautifully crafted jars. All were shades of red with patterns depicting the divine feminine upon them.

The after-birth was kept within a large vase for later use as well, and the mother-child cord was carefully preserved and laid full length upon the alter where the crystal skull had been. The skull had been removed at some point while I was busy in the pleasure of this emerging child. All of these holy substances would be used for healing and for potions of good when needed. Some would be preserved and dried and kept safe for use should the babe ever need a great healing due to disease as it manifested through the body due to contamination of others. It could then be utilized as a re-balancing agent.

My now nameless friend was still at my side. "I love you, MiryAmah," she said. As she looked at me I saw that every scar upon her radiant face had faded away. Even her nose was not twisted and broken anymore, but straight and true. She was restored to her full and true beauty.

"You have come back to your true beauty, dear friend!" I gasped. Her hands went to her face and she realized that a great restoration had occurred with her unaware of the transformation. She looked toward the high priestess for explanation.

"You have released your pain and sorrow and you are without the stain of such negation now," she explained. At that point my friend buried her face in my circled arms and cried tears of rejoicing, as I did as well with my face in her lovely, sweet smelling, soft hair. Never could I bond so closely with a friend as I had with this one. I treasure the day I found that heap of dirty robes there by the well so many years ago, when I saw the ever so slight movement there under that captured my curiosity. It was then that I discovered a better friend than ever I could have wished for.

I arose then, with my babe, Sarah, in my arms, and my best friend and I walking inseparably close. We entered the new babe chambers with the same wish; "I would that Jeshua could have been here," I said, "but somehow I know he was."

Blessed be,

MY FRIEND FINDS A NEW NAME

It is a tad disconcerting to have a friend without a name. As I walked away from the emerging room with my closest friend and my new babe, Sarah, cuddled within my arms, I wondered how I would identify my friend now that she had given her name to my child. Her restored beauty was an incredible sight and should have to be coupled with an appropriate identity. She walked as if lighter, almost gliding, and I noticed a brighter glow from her being. The deep sorrow had been lifted as well as all the traces of abuse, for she had released them completely.

The chambers that had been designed for my little family there within the emergence temple were beautifully adequate. They were usually intended to accommodate a man and woman for a yearlong personal time with the newborn. In my case, our little family would consist of my nameless friend, my sweet baby, Sarah, and myself.

I found a precious cradle near my sleeping shelf. It was made of a light colored wood that had captivating swirls in the wood grain. The swirls showed the true essence and past experience of the wood as it grew to the tree state. Soft sheepskin padding lined the rocking bed. The priestesses made the blankets and embroidered them with little lambs, kittens, babies and all manner of new life images. The colors for my Sarah babe were of soft pastel blue with the animals embroidered in their natural colors, dancing among red and pink roses.

My own sleeping shelf, which was built within the wall as a snug alcove, had an equally comfortable mattress covered in sheepskin. The blankets were woven from soft angora fibers that were deep rose in color with blue roses there embroidered by the hands of the priestesses. My friend's sleeping shelf was nearby and she was similarly treated with the softness of sheepskin to sleep upon and blankets of angora as well. Her colors were pale yellow, with the flowers of the sun upon them. The sleeping places had beautiful scenes painted on all surfaces, even walls and ceiling, which reminded one of the wonder of childhood and this precious time. I would often light my sleeping place candle and watch the scene above me come to life as the candle flickered and caused the picture to dance.

One of the priestess sisters met us and helped us orient ourselves to this new home. The fireplace was already lit as we entered and was graced by two chairs that rock, made of the same light wood as the cradle. A rug of the orient in burgundy colors was there before the fireplace and was large enough to fit under the rocking chairs too. A special smaller rug caught my eye. It lay near the chairs. It was woven with the unicorn design prominent and it was white and red in color with splashes of clearest blue here and there, especially in the eyes of the white unicorns.

The sister saw me look and wonder of the purpose of this beautiful spot, for it seemed that every stunning object within this chamber had a purpose. "I see, new mother, that you like the unicorn rug and wonder of its purpose," she said. "We have a surprise for you, shall we bring it to you now?"

"Of course, I love such moments of surprise," I said. Then I heard the great-carved doors open and several sisters came through the opening with a graceful and long cord trailing them. I wondered of what this could be and then I saw they were leading my little white donkey friend into my chambers. He was quite spoiled with attention I could tell, for his gait was quick and his head held high. He must have been basking in quality priestess care for his coat was shiny and clean and he had the riding rug upon his back as gifted from the householders back in the holy land.

He brayed a soft greeting when he saw me and moved immediately to investigate the new babe. His soft muzzle checked baby Sarah out from head to toe with his lips lightly tickling the child as his attention went to such areas as tiny fingers and face and tiny feet. I knew this tiny burro was a gentle being and posed no danger to my precious babe. I was delighted and I am sure this reaction was evident upon my face. I said, "Thank you, my sisters, this surprise is perfect for I had wondered of the welfare of my faithful burro friend. He has carried both the father and the mother of little Sarah and I am glad that she will have the pleasure of his company also."

"Watch this," one sister said. Then, talking to the burro she said, "Little white one, where do you like to rest?" The burro looked at her as if taking every word she said in complete understanding (which I *know* to be true) and looked about until he noticed the unicorn rug where he laid himself down. We all laughed in delight and knew this little one would be a great amusement and friend for many years to come.

We were left to rest at that point and spent many days there in front of the fire rocking the babe, Sarah, and laughing at the antics of the White One, who was quite the clown. We could take our meals where we pleased, in the great dining hall with the other priestesses, or here in the chambers. We usually stayed in the chambers where we felt safe and secure and where we bonded as a family as we were meant to do.

One day my friend asked me to help her with her new name. "It is time, MiryAmah," she said, "for me to identify myself with a proper name." When I asked my dear friend what name she would have, she said, "I have given my name to your babe, now I would ask to have your old name, Mary. Would that be in agreement with you? Would you give this up to me? For I admire you endlessly and that day when you found me, a wandering lost soul, it was you as Mary that brought me back to seeing once again through my battered and bruised eyes. It was you as Mary who touched my soul and transformed it to the point that it again desired to live. Should you honor me with giving me this name, I would always be connected to your essence, as your little babe is connected to mine, through the name I gave to her." Then she looked at me apprehensively, for she thought that possibly she had asked for more than she deserved.

"My dearest, loyal friend," I replied. "There are many Mary's but none will be so sweet as you and I would be honored to give you this name. We shall consult the high priestess of this temple and begin the process in all due haste." When the attending sister came to check on our needs we sent a message to the Mother-One that we would like to speak with her on an important matter and she promptly replied by showing up at our door.

"May I enter this sanctuary?" she asked, as she stood there in her elder beauty, dressed in soft flowing robes of royal blue with red accents upon the hem and the ends of the sleeves. "Please, Mother-One," I said, "Do enter, for we would be honored to speak with you on a very important matter."

"I have expected this call, for it is time to do the naming ceremony, is it not?" she said.

"How did you know, Mother-One," I asked.

"So soon you have forgotten the abilities a high priestess must possess to hold this position, MiryAmah. You, who full well have the same abilities." she said.

"I have been in the outer so long now that I forget the feminine powers, Mother-One. Yet I know that the question was answered before it was given. Forgive me for my lapse of knowing, Mother-One." I said.

"Your feminine powers have been temporarily put in a safe place, my dear, and now the safe sanctuary of this knowing can be opened and again activated. "Shall we begin?" When we nodded agreement, another priestess, as if on cue, immediately walked through the doorway with the crystal skull upon a black velvet pillow, followed by yet another priestess with an ornately carved, tall table with a round surface that was approximately the size of the skull pillow. She placed it in the middle of our chambers and the skull and pillow were set forth there upon. The carving upon the table caught my eyes, for there were cat feet splayed on the ends of the legs yet the connecting top of the legs to the roundness of the table were woman's faces. The legs again, as the columns had in the big hall, took the shape of the feminine body. There were three sets of two legs holding the table stable. Each elongated body held the shape of the feminine, one in her little girl body, one in her pregnant mother body, and one in the body of the elder, all nude and beautifully carved in a dark, richly colored wood. What a fitting place for the skull, I thought.

"Are you two ready?" the high priestess asked, "for I already know that your dearest friend, MiryAmah, she with no name because she has given hers to your child, has desired to bring your given name into her being?"

Mother-One knew much I thought, as I nodded to indicate my agreement and that we should begin. This time I stood behind the skull, as directed, with my hands upon it while my friend stood before the skull with its face in front of hers. She placed her hands upon the side of the skull where the ears would have connected.

Someone brought a robe of golden threads to the Mother-One and draped her in this sparkling garment.

"We shall then begin," she said. "We have a soul in this place in time without identity" she sang in her sacred voice. "This soul knows well the vibration she does desire and she does desire to merge with the vibration of her beloved friend MiryAmah, who herself took another name at the proper time for such a change. MiryAmah, who was known as Mary of Magdalene, and who is now known as MiryAmah, (she who has merged with her counterpart in wholeness and divine duality,) your dear friend desires the name you no longer use, do you agree?" "Oh yes!" I replied, looking into my dear friend's eyes, "for this one is as a sister in blood and soul to me and I would be honored to be thus tied to her being by giving with greatest love this name to serve such as she." Mother-One said, "visualize then your name of Mary, that you have kept safely there within your being since you needed it no more. See it move through your heart center and down your arms, then into your hands and give it freely to the skull to prepare for transference."

As I followed instructions I could see an aqua blue light travel through the pathways suggested and finally reaching the awaiting skull. Then, a pulsing brilliant blood red light began to move through the same route, scaring me somewhat, and mixed with the aqua within the skull. I looked puzzled, as my friend did also.

"Ease your mind sisters, for along with the grace comes the sorrow and the sacrifice. It shall mingle and merge before the transference."

The colors swirled in an incredibly beautiful aqua and red light, as if a light show performed within the skull, finally blending into a beautiful warm violet. At that point the color did not travel as I had envisioned, through my friend's hands, for she was a balancing factor, I later learned, and was hearing the name transform, but instead, the light poured out through the eyes of the skull and beamed rigidly, much as what you term a laser beam. This beam went into the eyes of my friend, which seemed to drink in the color. Even more astonishing, the color miraculously split just before entering, with the aqua going in one eye and the red in the other. Her eyes glowed of these two colors in the most amazingly radiant fashion. Then the color must have merged within and the area between the eyes began to glow the sacred violet again, mixed and merged, as her spiritual eye opened and gave us a glimpse of her very soul.

The attending sisters told me that baby Sarah awoke at this time and watched this process in amazement herself. They said she showed incredible awareness for such a young one.

Eventually the glowing on Mary's forehead gently began to recede back within her being and it was finished. Mother-One said, "I introduce Mary of the Violet Light to you all. Rejoice with her and forever more call her Mary, the little bright one, reserving the full title for sacred ceremonies, for with so many of this name it will be confusing to separate the others so named." We took our hands from the now crystal clear skull and smiled at each other. We were now closer than sisters of the same womb. We were much pleased.

Food and drink was brought at this time and we all made merry and played with little Sarah, setting her upon the white ones soft back when she presented us with her first giggle. Much later we all went to our sleeping places, Little Sarah still slept with me, with her cradle nearby should I decide to place her there, yet still I loved her closeness and could nurse as she so felt the need. We slept sound and had pleasant dreams.

Blessed be,

THE HIDDEN OASIS

Mary and I spent little Sarah's first year privately within our chambers in the new babe area of the temple. We needed time to process our grief and confusion for we were well aware of our separation from Jeshua, but we did not yet comprehend the details of this ill-fated event. Most of all, we needed to bond as a family.

James and Josephus visited about every three months and they delighted in the growth and progress of the babe. They brought us news of the mission. James was taking a leadership role now and had much trouble with Andrew and Peter, who both wanted to run the mission their way. They reminded James that he could have been of support to his brother during his lifetime but since he had chosen not to, there was nothing that gave him the right to lead the mission at this time. James held many of the same qualities as Jeshua, so he patiently listened and carried on with what he knew he must do.

Neither of the brothers could believe that Mary, Sarah before she gave her name to my new babe, was one and the same person. Her beauty was a vision to behold. She still held her memories of Andrew and the great love between them, but the sorrow of the parting as Andrew's heart and mind closed down toward the feminine, especially towards me, was not as painful as previously. She had the wonderful babe Sarah and myself to entertain her and we laughed and played often. It was an almost perfect first year. The only thing that would have made it more perfect would have been the presence of Jeshua himself. Little did I know that he was ever-present.

I often dreamed of him and he told me that he was in a safe place healing and learning. I could see men and women in robes similar to what I had known during the three-year seeding mission, the time Jeshua took the new ideas to the people, but the robes were draped differently and the people had a slightly different way of speaking and moving. I could sense that they were of God, however, and quite connected to the Source. I awakened always in peace.

At Sarah's first year birthday we moved to our new quarters outside, in the fresh air of Tara. The celebration was the leaving of the Emergence Temple and each priestess gave all of us a heart-felt kiss and blessing. We were moved to a complex within the desert area, but it contained a wonderful oasis.

I remember well the moving day. Camels and horses pulling chariots arrived to take us forth. Our little family, along with many protectors and other families also ready for the move, left the inner chambers in great celebration. Upon leaving the underground, for several days we had to shade our eyes with veils of blue because the light of the torches was of the yellow light, a subdued tungsten type as you would know it now, while the sun of the desert was a much different light in intensity. The sunlight could have harmed us if we had not been prepared. The blue veil was only part of the protection for we had been rubbed down in special oil made to filter the harmful rays of the mighty sun.

The smell of the sand, the rocks, and the air, once outside, were wonderful. If you ever forget how sensational this creation is, this being called Earth to many of you but Tara to the feminine, just take yourself away from some aspect of her for awhile and re-emerge. It is truly amazing what you overlook each day.

I especially enjoyed the camels that served us. They, I discovered, held conversations among themselves as we moved along. My feminine powers had returned to full force during that year of bonding and healing, and the little white one, my burro friend, had been helping me perfect my ability to converse with all creation. The camels would talk about us in amusing ways. They all wanted little Sarah upon their backs since they found her to be quite charming and funny. They actually laughed often and were quite the good-natured lot.

Oftentimes accidents cropped up, like a pack falling off a chariot or someone stumbling to the ground. In these clumsy instances the camels would find such delight. They knew full well that humans thought them to be quite awkward with their big feet and funny faces. They found us equally hilarious. The little white one seldom carried a burden these days. He just romped and enjoyed life and entertained little Sarah, who called this one her *BeeBa*.

To this day I am not sure what that means. I, who can understand the language of the animals, had not yet mastered the language of my own child. It is such a joy to see a child name things as it chooses, but we come along and say, "No, you must call this thing by its proper name." Well, BeeBa's name was never changed by anyone and did indeed fit this playful donkey quite nicely.

There were chariot horses with us too, but their conversation was centered on their great desire to run like the wind, for they discussed who was fastest among themselves. They were free spirits who dreamed of being totally free. They also lived fearfully and were always on the lookout for danger. Several dogs and one cat accompanied us as well. The cat felt herself superior to the dogs. The dogs told her that if she was so superior she should come down off her high place upon her camel friend and walk the ground with them and then see just how superior she really was. She informed them that she was above such demonstrations and that they should go find a sand hill to pee upon and relieve themselves of their frustrations. I laughed to myself at the way their personalities playfully interacted.

The journey took a mere two days and then, upon coming to an enormous hill of sand, we saw the oasis. As we reached its apex I stood amazed. There were ribbons the colors of the rainbow hanging from the trees, and lying upon the entry path to the oasis were flower petals of all colors. A congregation of people, men, women and children, came to meet us and they were all dressed in white. They reminded me of the Essenes, a group of which both Jeshua and I were connected, and in fact they were of that group, only with slight differences in practice, I would later learn.

Mary said to me, "Oh, MiryAmah, let little Sarah ride into this place as her father did into the city of Jerusalem, upon BeeBa. She already sits in stability upon the little white one's back."

I worried as I explained that that was a good day, for sure, but what happened after frightened me in this decision. Even while I made that statement, Sarah, who was riding a camel, began to call her BeeBa and reach out for him. She, as I had also at one year of age, had already begun to talk.

"Me need my BeeBa," she kept saying so I just shrugged my shoulders and asked the camel to kneel and allow me to take my child from its back. As I did so, the little white one immediately presented himself for the task that he knew belonged to him.

OK, I thought, and looked at my friend, Little Mary, who was giggling into her hands and looking so satisfied, here goes. I then set baby Sarah upon BeeBa's back and she grabbed little handfuls of his white mane, there ready for her stabilizing needs, and quite independently moved on toward her goal. BeeBa proceeded with head held high and proud, taking careful steps, fully aware of his little rider and his sacred task. Sarah moved to the front of the caravan with all there present watching in wonder and amazement at her courage and her ability to lead at such a young age. She looked back at us and smiled sweetly and then moved forward and went directly to meet those in the white robes.

She approached the white robes, while sitting proudly upon her BeeBa, and went straight to the elder of the group, who welcomed her and asked me to come forth now also. The elder placed her hand upon little Sarah's head and then directed her to follow the flower-strewn path. I walked forward then too, followed by Little Mary and then the entire caravan. We were all welcomed with the blessing of the elder, the hand upon our heads. The silent look of knowing I received from this elder made it known to me that she completely understood this journey I had traveled in my life to this point and was grateful for my effort.

We entered the oasis feeling perfection in love and gratitude as we merged with those waiting for us. We would spend, if all went well, the next five years here, as Sarah grew ready for her training. It did my heart good to know that little places in the outer could be so balanced and so complete.

I watched my little babe so confidently directing her friend, BeeBa, at such a young age. She had my skin color, my little girl, yet her hair was the color and texture of her father's, falling in soft reddish curls down her back. This child of perfect love was a blessing to all she graced her presence upon. No mother could love her child more than I did she. I knew that she would be an important soul in this mission. I felt honored to be the vessel of her choice and the first temple she visited, as my womb housed her physicality. How life could contain such deepest pain and sorrow and then bring such joy was truly the miracle of this experience we live. To be grateful is an understatement, but I know no word for how I felt that day following my beloved, my love child, into the oasis in the desert.

Blessed be,

EXPLORATION AND A WELCOMING MEAL

We followed little Sarah into the Oasis. What a site that was, the entire caravan of about thirty-five people and numerous animals following a little white donkey with a one-year-old girl atop, sitting like the queen she was destined to be. The flower strewn pathway led to an interior place shaded with many trees of various shapes and sizes, providing much in the way of welcome coolness and relief from the dry arid place we had come through. There within a rocky area was a natural waterfall, spilling fresh water about fourteen feet down into a deep aqua pool. We stopped at the falls, for there was an inviting area to sit there present. The elder caught up with little Sarah, who just sat and smiled as she watched us approach her. What pleasure she took in this moment of being leader.

The elder advised us to quench our thirst, for the animals also, so that the brothers and sisters could then show the way to animal quarters. We languished by the pool for a long time, enjoying the sound and the coolness after our long hot journey. I remember the smell of the place so vividly; it was cool, fresh and fragrant for there were flowers of many kinds there about, growing among ferns and natural green plants. This was, no doubt, the source of our welcoming trail of colored flower petals in this surprising oasis. Little Mary said, "This must be a dream. I thought the Emergence Temple the most beautiful of wonders and now this!"

"Oh," I replied, "you haven't seen the Misty Isles yet, my friend. When you do, your imagination will take another giant leap!"

"To think," she said with a dreamy, remembering look upon her face, "that I used to think that the holy land was the way the entire world was, dry, dusty, and unfriendly to such as me."

"Yes, my friend, I could see how you would think that, but even the supposed *holy land* is not really holy if you think about it. That is the sorrow and the tragedy of it all."

After the animals had found their quarters, we were led to our own. We entered from behind the falls on a hidden pathway that no one would have suspected existed. We were again moving into underground places along natural corridors of stone. The walls had artwork I had never before seen and later learned were of the ancients. The depictions were fairly realistic, mostly of animals I did not recognize, some were human forms and some were half human-half animal.

I was later to learn that these thus portrayed were of the experimentation in creation, when animals and humans were intermingled by creators in training. As it turned out, the elder informed me, it did not work, for animals live in the moment entirely and humans live in the past, present and future, within their minds. It created a very confused being and thus was discontinued. But the memory lives on, the elder said, and the beginning of discrimination began with such beings. They were found inferior because of their differences and for their lack of planning. Sad, because they simply were what they were, as you are you and I am myself also. They, for the most part, had some good and some bad actors within the group, but their condition was not of their making, but still an opportunity to experience for the souls that chose to do so. Their flaw was their sense of only the present moment and lack of vision as far as affects of their actions. Just as humans have problems living in the present, those in the animal kingdom have a problem with all that future planning. They do learn from the past however, the elder explained.

We wound our way to the inner chambers and found the most pleasant and gigantic chamber with a giant crystal carved into exactly calculated facets, much like a jewel. It hung in the middle of the inner ceiling while gleaming and illuminating the great hall. It seemed to have no source of light, yet it glowed in rainbow colors one minute and the next it integrated into pure white light.

Little Mary was fascinated; her eyes held wide in child-like wonderment. The other families were equally impressed and little Sarah was pointing to the pretty light. She was still astride her beloved BeeBa, for she would not allow separation between the two of them so they had to allow this beloved little one access to the inner chambers. I saw some cats and dogs and even monkeys and birds in presence there too, so this was not unheard of.

This room had carpets woven from reeds upon the floor. The woven carpets were painted in brightly colored, geometric shapes. The shapes, I noticed, varied from circular and oval shapes to squares and elongated linear forms. I learned eventually that this was the masculine and the feminine as depicted in forms, dancing and entwining in duality. There were many white robes there about, as well as some in robes of pastel colors of blues, light aqua and sky tones, as well as pinks, and coral colors, with even yellows on some people. If I would say what delighted me in temples the most, it would be the color I found therein. The outer was a place of subdued color, for the most part, which I believed tantamount to quieting the joy.

Off the busy inner chamber were many corridors leading to various quarters and family-by-family we were led to our new dwelling spaces. Mary, little Sarah, with her beloved BeeBa, and I were soon entering our new home. Within this place was a channel that allowed the light of day to flood in through the ceiling. It was accomplished with mirrors, the elder told me, who was our guide to this sacred place we would call home.

I immediately noticed that each sleeping shelf, positioned along the walls, was painted as before (ceilings and walls in murals) but with different scenes. There was a night scene with sparkling stars that twinkled through tiny holes. "Another channeling of light effect," the elder pointed out. It showed the heavens (the universe as you would term it) in a most striking way. Little Sarah made a beeline (yes, this saying was well known even in this time) for this spot and said, "Me sleep here, Mam?" She called me Mam, which was her version of Mother and MiryAmah combined. She always named everything as she so chose. I selected a chamber that was simply swirls of pinks and blues and Little Mary selected one that was full of yellow flowers, her favorite.

There was a central round table that reminded me of my days in pre-training in that it was low to the floor and had a perfectly clear and round crystal there in the middle glowing brilliantly. I knew then that Sarah would begin training even as a toddler, just as I had with my parents long ago.

BeeBa's rug was quickly unpacked and put next to Sarah's sleeping shelf. There was a fireplace as before, with chairs made of twisted reeds that were suspended from the ceiling, (lower in the chambers) so as to easily swing. Each of the three chairs, two of normal size and one very small, held cushions of bright colors and soft fabrics. "Is this not too much luxury, MiryAmah," Mary asked in concern. "Surely we will be spoiled."

"Enjoy while you can for all too soon we will be back to living like Roman Spartans," I said.

The elder then said, "Do not feel guilty for experiencing comfort and joy for to know such a thing is to know the opposite of which I understand, Mary, you have already experienced—such great sorrow." The elder went on to tell Little Mary that after you know the extremes then you will find your balance.

We were left to settle ourselves into this new home and explore our new world. We did not travel with much baggage and quickly put things away and headed out to see this new place. Sarah no longer wanted to be carried by Little Mary or myself; she wanted to ride her mighty steed everywhere she went. We looked quite the sight with Mary, myself, and this beautiful child astride her white BeeBa.

We ran into other families also exploring with their child or children (one family had identical twins). Each child was a toddler, for we had been directed to the walking babe wing of this place, made especially for those in that sacred stage of experience. We found several fountains fed by natural springs along the way, some cool and some quite hot. We found the baths and thought them quite interesting, especially Little Mary, who could not imagine taking a community bath, however charming, she said. We then found our way out through several of the exits to the oasis. There were stables for the animals that were the cleanest I had ever seen and made of living trees bent to form living shelters. The camels, that were communicating so much on the way to this place, were now just lying about in a grassy place, sighing delight and chewing their cuds. The horses were munching sweet smelling hay, and some were rolling over and over again in a sort of contest. I knew they were somehow keeping count of how many times each rolled over with each trying to out-do the others.

We then found the gardens, what a sight. Never have I seen so much color in the world of nature. The white robes were everywhere tending plants and talking softly to them when we approached.

One gentle woman introduced herself as Tarlina, the garden keeper. She said she had been experimenting of late and was singing to some plants and not to others. That explained the beautiful song we heard as we found her. She showed me the two groups that had been separated by a sound barrier, so only those elected could hear the songs. There was a path through some rocks that lead to the silent garden. I must say, there was a marked difference in size and brilliance of flowers. "The ones who hear the songs mature twice as fast, too," she said as she noticed our reaction. "If plants react to sound this way, just think how important it is to this sweet child with you and also to her friend here nibbling my flowers," she said, nodding toward BeeBa.

"Oh, BeeBa," I said, "don't eat the flowers, please." Sarah was trying one delightful looking morsel herself. "Sorry Tarlina," I said, "they did not know."

"Please do not give it concern," she said as she smiled at them, "because at the evening meal some of those very same flowers will be served. They are edible and quite tasty. A good selection, my friends," she said to Sarah and BeeBa.

We continued to wander the garden then returned to prepare to join the others at the first evening meal in this new place. There would be a special banquet for the new arrivals to be served in the hall of the great crystal.

Upon re-entering this huge place, when the meal bells were played, we could see that low tables were there now present. Cushions were splayed along the floor for those who desired them at the round tables. Round tables were something seen mainly in the temples, seldom in the outer. We were invited to sit anywhere we pleased, for there was no hierarchy here. Soon food was brought in and we feasted. People ate and then got up and relieved those serving and they joined us. The atmosphere was joyful with songs breaking out here and there in spontaneity. The toddlers were giggling and reaching for their hearts desire on the food tables, without reprimand. Their little faces were smudged with food remnants and those at the table with them laughed and gently cleaned their little faces over and over again. The animals in attendance were also invited to partake and it was quite the sight with BeeBa enjoying a taste of this and that but preferring the red flower petals in honey.

During the meal we were welcomed officially by the elder who met us earlier and showed us to our new quarters. After the meal, a thanks was given to Father/Mother God for the abundance, the good company, and the safety and the joy of this group.

"Father/Mother God," the elder said in a singsong voice, "we love thee as no other and we thank thee for all that you bestow upon us. Know that all present honor your Presence among us as you manifest in all here and all the plants, animals and other life forms that have gifted us with their beings as food for our bodies. We wish to give back to you the utmost that we can give. We will always attempt to find the joy behind all the sorrow; there waiting to be rediscovered, and we will present you our joy at each meal we partake of and throughout our day. So, upon this day of gladness and welcoming, we offer you our true Joy for your Divine Feast and nourishment. Peace be ever possible on our journey home to you. We are ever gratefully your creation." Nodding toward us, the elder dismissed us to go to our quarters and to rest from our journey and first day at the Oasis.

Blessed be,

JOSEPHUS VISITS AND BRINGS NEWS

The years spent at the oasis and within the inner chambers were both peaceful and pleasant. We spent one year within the Egyptian sanctuary, but we did not mingle with those in the outer near this community for there was always danger, as my beloved brothers-in-marriage told me whenever they visited. Because of trade and the migration of people, there were always those willing to carry news to others. The news could be a blessing or a curse, depending on who received such.

James and Josephus were loyal protectors who often visited together if opportunity presented itself. Our first visit from Josephus was a great pleasure for my little family and I but the news he brought to the oasis was not good.

"They have forgotten who my brother was, MiryAmah, and they are twisting the teachings to fit their own limited vision. Unrest grows and questions pertaining to you are ever there on the minds of those most threatened by the truth," Josephus explained. Will it ever balance, I thought, for I am a threat to no one who loves life and wants to live this experience to the fullest.

"I fear for you and Sarah and anyone closely connected to you," he went on to say, "for now they say you were never married to my brother, just a woman loose with her sexual favors of temptation, and they say you caused the master to stray."

My heartrending look caused Josephus to venture closer to me and to hold me in a great hug of protection and love. "My sister, I love you like no other brother could, as a true sister, and I bless the day you found my dear brother, your soul mate. Fear not, for I will keep you safe. This I promise you and Sarah."

With that he picked up Sarah, who was almost two by this time, and he lifted her high as her giggles delighted him. As he raised her high again and again, in order to amuse her, he casually said, "How can they say you do not exist, my beautiful niece, for here you are in all your glory?"

That was the first time I realized that even the faithful followers were now confused to the point that the few we trusted with the news of our child now doubted the manifestation resulting from the great love within our divine union.

Josephus was quite fascinated with Sarah and BeeBa as they interacted in ways he had never seen between animal and child. "Do you not fear that the donkey will harm the child, MiryAmah?" he said with an apprehensive and yet puzzled look upon his face.

"No, my brother," I answered, "for this child of Jeshua did ride this faithful animal into the oasis much like her father did also into the city of Jerusalem. There is a bond that only the two fully understand. It is as if the little white one has taken the safekeeping of Sarah upon himself, and believe me, this animal has never harmed so much as a hair upon little Sarah's head. I could not ask for a better nanny. When Sarah moves toward a dangerous situation, for instance the hot pools, the little one she calls BeeBa steps between her and the danger and distracts her. He then leads her away without her realizing she has been in any danger.

"If I had not seen these two in action I would find that story hard to believe. It reminds me of a tale made up to amuse children," Josephus replied.

"Oh yes, I often wonder of how much is actuality within such tales and how much is self-styled imagination." As I said that I wondered what this loving brother would think of the Misty Isle or those of the middle-earth, who guard the sacred tunnels. Yes indeed, I thought, life can be fantastic and more surreal than imaginable for many.

Josephus asked of Little Mary, for she was usually within a heartbeat of me. "She is doing some catch-up training within the temple, and leaves each morning to return at the evening meal. If you stay long enough you will see her, and I know that she will love the reunion as well."

I had been privileged to have extensive training almost from the day of my birth but Little Mary was raised much differently. For her it was her extreme beauty that was a source of pride and possible riches to her family. They prized her looks and only cultivated that aspect of her being. When she was sold to the highest bidder to be one of his many wives and to make this wealthy nobleman look even grander because of her beauty there upon his arm, she made her stand. Who would know this beauty had strength and courage too, but then, that was not cultivated in such as she. When she repeatedly refused to consummate this marriage, and would not even enter into the giving ritual planned to transfer the funds, she was destroyed by her father's own hand. She was beaten senseless by him and by her family, and eventually even some of the people of the village joined the carnage. To take her beauty in such a way was to them, who held that as her only worth, to render her worthless. The villagers who joined in the torture were jealous. In their eyes she had beauty and riches but did not appreciate either, so they felt justified in helping her find her humility. Little did they know of her restored physical beauty; beauty that matched the loveliness she held within her heart. Such a complete and lovely feminine one she represented, and now she was literally drinking in the knowledge her heart and soul did thirst for, each day, without fail, in her oracle training.

Josephus said he would not miss a meal with the likes of us for anything; he even stayed two days. The mealtime that evening fascinated him, especially the great crystal in the meeting chamber. "I have never seen a stone such as this, so carefully carved and gleaming," he said as he watched it shimmer and spin high above the tables. "What is it then, MiryAmah?"

"I cannot give you all the secrets, for that would keep you too long in this place and they would send out those to rescue you, but I will tell you that there is a mighty energy that has both masculine and feminine aspects that converge when God desires to make light known. This is the essence of God and each aspect of all creation. You have seen it manifest as light upon occasion in the outer, where you call it lightning, always followed by a mighty roar which some say is God talking to us. The basis of this stone is that it stores such energy and the facets thus carved represent the different ways this energy can split light into the colors of the spectrum and then back again to merge into pure clear white light. There is a channeling of the light of day into this place, I have learned, and they have a way of containing it and redirecting it into the crystal stone. At that point there are specialists who control the turn and the vibration of the saved energy and they are responsible for the light show you perceive here."

"Amazing!" he said, again and again as he watched in wonder. "But" I continued, "There is much more that this stone can do and

I am not expert enough to begin to tell you of all its amazing qualities."

Then little Mary came forth. She walked toward us wearing a beautiful light yellow robe, which flowed gently behind her. Her hair of gold flowed as the robe did, in soft ripples, trailing her striking presence as she walked with head held high and a smile upon her lovely face. That was how she always presented herself these days, confident and gentle with the look of wisdom intensifying each day.

I had not realized that Josephus had not really looked upon her of late and had not seen the complete transformation since the crystal skull ceremony. Whenever we had visitors, she covered herself in old, dark robes and hooded her hair and face. I never questioned for I knew she did not trust anyone and wanted to keep her truth private.

"This is the most beautiful lady I have seen in a long time," Josephus almost whispered. "Would you know of her and introduce her to me so that I can say I have spoken with such a one?" he asked as she approached.

"Why yes, Josephus," I said swinging my arms and hands in grand presentation, "I introduce you to Little Mary, formerly known as Sarah until she gave that name to the child of myself and Jeshua, (Sarah giggled at that point and it was clear that she understood most of this conversation and was delighted to be part of the explanation) at which time I transferred my old name to she, my most beloved friend."

His brow wrinkled in great thought, then recognition dawned. "My God, My Goddess," he exclaimed, (as he said that I thought, finally I hear him giving some credit to the Divine Feminine) could this be the little abused one of so long ago? What matter of miracle happened to bring you into such beauty?"

Little Mary, usually one of few words replied, "I have given up the pain and the sorrow, my friend, as my name was cleansed and transferred to the babe. This is always so in true giving of the heart for in giving you also receive. The result is restoration to my former physical condition which I have had some problem trusting. For it was this thing you see as beauty that caused all of my pain and sorrow in my early life. I am free from that now with the help of many temple priests and priestesses who support the mission of MiryAmah, my dearest friend, and her Jeshua, who is the same dear friend in his duality to her, to me and to all creation." She nodded and leaned down to where Josephus was sitting upon a floor cushion by the table and lightly kissed each cheek of this amazed friend. We then dined in laughter and the pleasure of each other's company.

"How is the Mother Mary?" I eventually asked. "She sends her love," he replied, "but she still mourns my brother greatly, I must admit. She is having many dreams of him in a faraway land with strange robed ones who heal him. She wants to believe such visions but those around her who claim to be her safe-keepers confuse her and tell her this is not reality, just the wish of a mother's heart."

"I too, am having such dreams on a regular basis, and in fact, I can see some of the rituals and the techniques used to heal my beloved. He now begins to walk again, as I see it in my visions. It has been over two years now and his injuries, according to my dreams, were extensive."

Josephus said then, "I wonder of all of this. You know they say that Jeshua went to the depths of hell and then arose again after three days and now is in heaven with the Father God."

"Yes, I have heard this too," I said. "The three days of hell, according to my dreams, had to do with the first stages of the great damage done to his body. However the pain of that was not as bad as the pain of the betrayal, at least that is what he has indicated to me in my dreamtime. I think, as I try to understand the unfolding of this time, his spirit left his body and came to us for assurance that he would be OK and somehow resolve this and get back to the mission. I believe that the resurrection is even still now in process and he lives physically as well as in spirit, as my and his mother's dreams indicate. Do you believe that this is just the wishful thinking of a grieving wife, Josephus?" He answered, "No, MiryAmah, I believe you well for he pays night visits to myself and James as well."

"They will not let him be a mortal man, MiryAmah," he said with anxiety and sadness, "much less allow him to live a physical existence now, for they need something beyond life to cling to and to worship. If they found him alive I truly believe those who claim to love and honor him most would kill him to fulfill their dreams of prophesy."

The weariness was evident in Josephus' voice. I sighed as I said, "he never wanted that. He always said to worship life itself as lived in love and respect, not to pay homage to a God that mere man has molded to fit his needs. Now they would mold even Jeshua and make him into a false God! Did they not hear him say that what he was, all could be? That since he was the true Son of God, so too were all men and all women the true daughters! Where were their ears? What should I do, Josephus, to save our mission of love and duality?"

I cried for the first time in years, great sobs of sorrow revisiting and causing painful memories to flood my mind and haunt my heart, "I fear," he replied, "that you will one day have to emerge and take your place leading the church they would build to carry on this mission."

"A church! What is this place you speak of?" I said.

"Like a temple, MiryAmah, but with rules and a rigid structure dictated by those who think they know the truth." I stood there shaking my head in dread for I knew well what would happen.

"Who begins this idea of church now, in my absence?"

"Andrew and his brother Peter are at odds with each other, both claiming divine direction to rule such a place. Each wants to lead the new church and each believes that Jeshua gave them specific orders to do so and build an institution that would guide the followers to the kingdom of heaven."

"Kingdom!" I said in disgust. "What about Queendom? Why must they always demand authority over that which cannot be ruled but must be merged? Must I lower myself to fight them on their own ground and take the leadership of the new church into my own hands?"

"I fear they would have you killed and the child also, for they are jealous of the sacred union of you and Jeshua and wish to wipe the memory of such a human need from all record. They see sexuality as a weakness, not a sacred strength of creation. You, they tell everyone, are just an harlot, and Jeshua was tempted by you, but instead of his fall, he saved you from your weak feminine self."

"Such lies," I cried, and the others dining with us looked up in alarm, for only peace and joy were usually evident within this sacred place.

Tears ran down my cheeks and my face flushed from the emotion of this excruciating news. "Forgive me, MiryAmah, for I have brought you bad news and hurt your heart," Josephus said.

I held my face firm and stood tall and said so all could hear, "I will die and live again and again and I will enter into every incarnated wise woman's heart and soul and live there forever after I leave this place of hell, until the respect of the feminine is restored and the sacredness of my union with my beloved is known and understood. I will make sure that through Sarah, and any other children, should the Lord Father/Mother God allow Jeshua and I more opportunities to bring, that they be the seeds for peace on this earth place, for Tara deserves that for her great sacrifice to such stupid beings as we!"

I then ran to my chambers. My declaration affected the great crystal, which sent out flashing and sparkling red lights that made the entire colossal chamber flicker brilliantly. Then the sound of wailing emerged and those present knew that the Divine Feminine cried at that moment for all her daughters. Josephus called for me but did not come forth, for the elder took the lead then and asked that he stay with the astonished Little Mary and babe, Sarah, while she assisted me.

I rushed to my chamber and fell upon the floor crying as never before. The elder reached me and took my hand and lay over my trembling body. I whispered in muffled sobs, "How can they, elder one, make the creation of life through the divine union of man and woman a sinful thing? Jeshua and I were supposed to bring light to that old lie and see it die once and for all, but now they make it live stronger through a twisted memory of my Jeshua, my love, and they negate me and our child as if we were mere bugs that they must squash to find their comfort!"

She held me, and as she did I finally realized this bald elder was actually a woman. I never knew until I felt the softness of her breast crushing closely into my body as she rocked me and held me tight, singing the song of comfort and recognition of pain.

"That is what we are here for, is it not?" she finally said, "to bring all God's creation in line with the original intent of Divinity through Duality. Just as God is our true Father and our True Mother, so, too, is all creation a reflection of this Divinity, dear one. You know it. I know it. Jeshua, wherever he is, knows, and so do enough people now that you two have reseeded this truth once again, and it shall emerge one day and be accepted by the masses who will finally see that without both he and she, they could never be WE. And WE are part of God the Source. WE will never give up!"

Blessed be,

DEPARTURE TO SAFETY

Life continued at the Oasis as Little Mary made great progress in her oracle classes. The elder saw her destined role as an oracle the moment she entered the complex, she told me one day, and she rejoiced for she not only received the Priestess of the Divine Feminine (as she called me) and the Queen Child, (little Sarah) but the oracle that had been promised in prophesy. She saw this a great part of her mission and lovingly served us all well, as we served her too.

We sometimes went into the villages of Egypt for trade with the merchants. We grew some herbs within this oasis that were rare and they could bring us much in bartered goods for the compound. We always dressed as the natives of the villages to keep attention at a minimum. Traders can be jealous beings and we always attempted to seek out those who traded honestly but eventually we came to one who did not think we gave him the good deal he deserved. He wanted to practically steal the sacred herb from us, for on this day of the trading it was two women and myself who were dealing. In such a trader's mind, to offer a fair deal to women is a waste of opportunity, for we were not worth such honor. This attitude was the poison that Jeshua and I hoped to transform into the divine duality where the feminine and the masculine live in total respect.

The herb that we alone grew in abundance was one that reduced fever and was restorative to damaged body tissue. Its healing qualities were life-saving and dramatic. It could be made into a tea or a paste to apply to a wound that would thus heal with no scarring. That would have been a great help in healing Little Mary, as she was Sarah, back when I found her. We used other herbs but I must admit that this one was superior to any I have ever known. It could also be used for fertility, boosting opportunity of child bearing and preparing the feminine to carry a child successfully. Men bought this herb, for the most part, thinking that the number of children, especially sons, was a true mark of wealth.

Just as often the women came to us later for another herb that prevented conception. It wasn't that they didn't love children. It was the reluctance to be just another brood body to enhance a man's wealth. The loss of emergence temples, which had been driven underground, resulted in there being no allotted time to enjoy and bond with the new child before another was brought forth. The emergence temples encouraged at least five years between children and considered daughters as precious as boys. Twins were never to be separated; even in adulthood, and the bonding time was of great developmental importance to the child and parents. The trends had moved into bringing forth a child every year and having slaves as the caregivers for those of wealth. For those of the hard-working classes, the care would go to the mother and older children. But always of late, there was no time to enjoy childhood as it was meant to be experienced, in total joy by parents and child. The inner sorrow ran deep for many women. They would visit the wise women for the herbal tea to stop the constant flow of child bearing, which often took their life and left their children motherless.

Getting back to the merchant, however, as I previously mentioned, he did not want to barter fairly with we, who were in his mind, *low status women,* and I was the one who said, "another day then, we shall trade, for you are not of fair mind this day, sir," and we left, with myself setting the pace as I held my head high and walked in dignity. He was a Hebrew merchant and had only set up shop there in the land of Egypt in the last year or so. He watched me closely as I left with my sisters, to find a fair trade for our precious herbs.

There must have been something about my walk that reminded him of a few years back when the one called *Messiah* taught the masses, with his lady by his side. He remembered that there were those who attempted to locate her after the crucifixion, to silence her, no doubt. He knew that the ideas these two presented would certainly upset the system of power in place. In his selfish mind, he probably quickly calculated the bartering worth of news such as this and thought of nothing but the profit; for this reason, my life changed yet again.

Josephus came within the week. "Word has reached those who would harm you, my dear sister," he said, "that you are in this region. We must take you and your child and friend to safety now." The oasis was quickly prepared for intrusion, for that would surely come as there were Roman soldiers combing the dry land trying to locate the compound of those herb growers who harbored me.

People moved in a very fast and purposeful manner, as if they had prepared for such a day as this. The inner portals were prepared to be sealed. The animals were taken to the safety of various locations. The beautiful gardens were harvested and the plants literally pulled from the ground, for should the soldiers feel that this was the place they sought, due to the evidence of gardening, they would certainly torture and kill those present to get at me.

It pained me to see the beautiful flowers up-rooted, for I loved them so. They were taken to the inner chambers to replant later, I was told. The tied down trees were coaxed back into natural, straight palms once again. The gardener who I had met earlier did this. She held conversations with the trees and asked them to unwind and find their upright positions once again. The vines that made the rooftops of our animal shelters were also spoken with in this manner and they looked like many snakes as they unwound themselves and eventually circled and twined again around the now upright trees. They also grew great thorns, even as I watched, and it was impossible for anyone to explore the previously beautiful stable area, for they would be ripped to shreds should they enter there. The gardener also asked the grass to pull back into the ground and allow the sand to blow in so that the lush meadow became arid and dry as the outer landscape appeared. To see the grass *ungrow* as it looked, as it shortened and receded, was truly a sight to behold.

Finally, within three hours, all was ready. My spirit was low, for I felt that I had disturbed this little oasis of wonder and security for so many, which had to disappear because my presence had become known. The elder said, "Fret not, MiryAmah, for we are dedicated to the Divine Mother and it is an honor to serve Her through serving you, or any one of those in training here, for Her cause."

She smiled at me and I hoped that one day I would be so beautiful in my wisdom years. She then said, "We will be fine. Go in peace. The soldiers will find no one, so wipe the tears from your eyes, but you must take little Sarah now and go into exile, for you were not meant to live your lives underground. Your child must see the light of day to find her destiny. And, my sweet MiryAmah, I see that you have a great surprise there awaiting your arrival in your own destiny."

Then everyone bid us farewell, myself, Sarah, now five years of age, and Little Mary, who would not leave my side. BeeBa came too, as was Sarah's demand, for she would not leave her friend to live underground either. She would take him to where the grass was always green, she said, and the desert sands did not blow. I stood and watched every last person enter the portal behind the falls, and then the falls began to ebb its flow until, within a minute or two, there was no more water flowing over this beautiful rock, as before. The portal doorway could not be seen. I watched in wonder as the very rock face seemed to shift itself and the pathway was no longer passable. The magic of life always amazed me.

Josephus had readied the camels that would take us to the river Nile. We climbed upon their backs so that travel could be in haste. Even BeeBa was taken upon the back of one of the camels, who thought that was rather funny, a burro upon his back, for they often discussed and compared their strength and their abilities, the burro and the camel. The humor of the camels was always a blessing to me, for they never ceased to amuse themselves or me. I could not imagine how others could not notice how much they enjoyed life, almost as court jesters in far-away lands.

We set off just before sunset, when the colors of the sun were at their most intense and beautiful. I loved this time of day, for it left me realizing how incredible this opportunity to live in the light was. The night was a pleasant resting time to prepare to move back into the light of experience the next day, announced by an equally spectacular sunrise. I looked back and saw a sandy oasis where there were lush gardens and water in abundance, not that many hours ago, now with no signs of life therein, seeming dusty and desolate except for the presence of the trees.

I knew my friends and companions were safely in the inner chambers. Those chambers were connected to the underground tunnels that wound into the midst of Tara, who would lend them shelter and security. I had traveled and visited such chambers before and knew that there were wonders to behold that those not aware enough to be so privileged, would ever discover. Tara's secret places are many.

"It seems I am always leaving someplace, Josephus," I said. "Will I ever have a home to grow old within?" "I pray you do for you deserve such a sanctuary in which your great courage and dedication would be honored and not held as a danger to you, the beloved love of my dear brother," he answered. "I shall pray that it is so," I whispered.

We were taken into a long riverboat that held a cabin at one end. There within the cabin was a false floor and under it was a secret room. Into this room I was ushered, along with my child and my friend, Little Mary. Mary could have stayed above-board but insisted that where I go there she shall be. What a comfort she was to me. The secret hold was comfortable when readied for us, but not grand on any scale, nor did we desire such grandeur. Warm blankets upon sleeping shelves were there for us with tiny window openings for fresh air to enter this musty place. There were lanterns for light and many bags of grain and rolls of straw and hay there, so we had to be quite careful with our lights of fire. The plan was that should the hold be discovered, those peering within would see it as a cargo hold with the grain and straw and not know of our presence therein.

We traveled all night upon the great river and well into the next day, eventually coming to the great inland sea. At that point, in the darkness of night, we transferred to a ship and again took our place within the hold of this much bigger vessel. Josephus assured me that it would just be for a week or so and then we would be free of this security measure that kept us so confined.

I so wanted to stand upon the decks and breath the sea air. Josephus must have realized this, for one evening he took me to the now almost deserted deck. He had me dress as if a man to ensure safety, and we went to the front of the mighty vessel where the ship pierced the water as it moved forth. "I wanted you to see this," he said. There out to my left I could see the Misty Isle, for it had a certain green glow that I remembered well and often longed for when within my dreams.

"Are we heading to this place of my youth," I said. "No, MiryAmah, and I apologize for being so secretive about our destination. I could not even mention it to you for fear that someone might compromise your security. We move to the shores of the main land where there awaits many of your followers. Your beloved isle just opens the mists to welcome you." Then I watched as the beloved home of my childhood simply faded into the mist.

183

I heard a lone sailor say, "Island ahoy!" to alert others on night duty. Then, as the island disappeared, he yelled, "Sorry mates, it must be the wine that is making me see things, for no island is there as I thought I saw. (I translate as well as I can but sailor talk is pretty much the same everywhere because of their coming and going to distant ports constantly.)

I then went back to the safety of my quarters to prepare for landing. Sarah and Little Mary were already in preparation. They were both quite intuitive, with Little Mary just opening those centers since her oracle training and Sarah always able to see the unseen and in the *know*. Sarah was loading her precious things onto BeeBa's backpack. She had some stones and dolls made for her by the sisters at the Oasis, who spoiled her constantly with gifts. She was always so thankful and full of gratitude that the gifts just rolled forth from everyone. Sarah picked out just a few favorites and then carefully offered her other treasure to other children and people before she left, who accepted them in the same loving spirit they were given. BeeBa, as usual, patiently stood by and from time to time nibbled gently upon Sarah's surprisingly light colored hair. Sarah had the bronze skin of myself, but the light hair and blue eyes of her father; however, her hair was light reddish instead of the dark reddish of Jeshua.

We would depart the ship in the night along with a load of grain that was to be delivered to this seaside village. We were loaded into long boats that were lowered into the sea. We sat between the piles of grain bags huddled in silence, our presence only known to Josephus. BeeBa was there with us and as quiet as we. Josephus was directing the oarsmen, as a traveling merchant would do, for that is what they believed him to be. At a certain point, Josephus said to the oarsmen, "I understand that you are weary mates, just relax for a moment and catch your breath, I am no slave driver."

The men seemed suddenly so very tired and yawned and stretched, appreciating this moment to relax. Little Mary then looked into my eyes since we were almost nose-to-nose in the darkness and tightly within the midst of the cargo. She whispered, "Do not watch me or let Little Sarah watch me, for I have work to do." She then gently closed both our eyes with her tiny, child-like hands and blew her breath upon us. We went limp but were totally aware of what was happening about us. We had no desire to open our eyes, even as we heard the sounds of snoring and relaxation from the oarsmen. I could hear her singing unfamiliar words and moving about slightly. I thought I smelled a familiar scent too, that of the sleep flower. Then she said, "It is safe now. Open your eyes, my friends, and as we did so, Josephus had moved some grain bags and was bidding us to follow him. Sarah was the first to notice. "The oarsmen sleep, my mother," she remarked. "So peacefully, too," Little Mary said, as she winked to Josephus.

We were very close to shore, but not at the cargo docks. We could see some people there in the dark, waiting quietly for us upon the shore. We jumped into the water and waded to the group who welcomed us with quiet smiles and gentle hugs. Not a word was said. I remember seeing Josephus carrying BeeBa through the water and thinking how lamb-like this little burro was. Even BeeBa knew to be totally quiet. Sarah followed Josephus in the shallow water, holding onto BeeBa's tail to guide her. She would not go with me when I beckoned. She was the most independent child, for sure.

Once ashore we moved into the landscape quickly and Josephus bid us farewell, for just a while, he said, for he would come to us to ensure we were well safe within our new quarters. At that time, he told me, we would begin again, if I chose to do so, with our plans for the future.

"Is it not time," he asked, for me to take my rightful place as leader of the mission. I agreed, "Yes, Josephus. I feel that Jeshua urges me to follow the mission through. How I do not know but this I know: It shall be done!"

Blessed be,

A NEW LAND, A NEW BEGINNING

We moved from the shore of the land you now call France, where we landed in the night, inland through trails that were seldom used. These trails seemed hidden and were difficult to follow. Had it not been for our leader, Hellenica, (I do not remember her telling me her name, I just *knew* it) we would never have found our way. She was another wise elder and she walked with her hair flowing free like long wavy ribbons. From my vantage point of walking behind her, I would judge that her long white hair fell nearly to the ground. Sarah, riding BeeBa, was ahead of me in this winding line of night travelers, with Little Mary following closely behind me. We had to trust that this leader was on the right trail for she walked confidently in this near moonless night, without hesitation or doubt. Silence was total, as it was on the beachfront.

We finally arrived at a segment of the forest that had great towering trees. We stopped to rest among them, and as I touched one of these majestic ones, it spoke to me in the silent mind-to-mind manner. "Welcome to the forest, my dear friend," the tree communicated to me, and I remembered thinking how nice to have a tree refer to me as "my dear friend!" "I am honored that you should rest under my arms," the giant one continued, "for I have some spare discarded branches that lie about and should you desire fire to warm yourself, feel free to use these parts of me to warm and comfort thee."

At that point Hellenica said to me "I see the ancient one has offered you some twigs and dried branches for a fire." This was the first time I was close enough to see her face. Her eyes were white where the color would normally be. You could only determine the iris of her eyes by a defining dark line around the perimeter, separating it from the normal white area. "You find my eyes unusual, sister?" she said. "I can not see much during the day unless I look through a veil, for my eyes are made for night vision and extremely sensitive to light. I have communicated part of my name to you telepathically but as you were once known as *Mary of Magdalene* and now *MiryAmah*, I am known by most as *Hellenica, the Night-walker.*

She and the others then made a small fire below the tree, which seemed pleased to offer some part of itself to assist us. "It will be morning soon and we will move on then." Hellenica said, "but this is the coolest part of the day, just before the sun rises, and you are weary and the child needs rest so we shall stay until the sun comes forth."

The fire was pleasant and did indeed offer us great comfort. The ground was covered by soft forest undergrowth and a clearing had been made for the building of the fire, but the softness and the forest smells beckoned us to stay and rest. Sarah sat on my lap within my circling arms and I was pleased that BeeBa had made of himself a resting place for our weary heads. I sat upon the ground and leaned upon this faithful friend, soon joined by Mary, and we slept soundly with Hellenica and several others on watch. I could never tell how many there were there with us, for the group seemed to change constantly with some coming and some going. I later learned that sentries were sent out and then reported back, and others took their turns to insure safe passage, but the Nightwalker was always with us to lead the way.

I awoke rested and rejuvenated, just before the sun presented the first light. As the light emerged from the horizon I could not imagine a more beautiful sight, even though I have often thought the same thing time and time again upon many sunrises in many places. The colors were intense and unique and the warmth immediately penetrated any vestiges of the evening chill. Everyone awakened refreshed, and I really believe this majestic ancient tree energized us as we slept there under its protection. We all gathered some berries, as directed by Nightwalker, who was now totally veiled in a sheer purple head covering. Some berries, she said, are not for us to eat, but for medicinal purposes only, "but these" she said as she showed us some medium sized berries of red that glistened in blue, "are most nutritious and beneficial for energizing in the morning." The abundance of berries was tremendous; especially the red/blue ones Nightwalker suggested, and soon enough we were full and ready to proceed.

We did not have much with us, so the traveling was at a good pace. We eventually came to more open land and followed a well-worn path to a castle-like compound, the first of such places I can remember ever seeing. It was not a huge building complex, but it was fortified with a protective natural stream that encircled it.

There was a bridge presently folded up, and I thought we would enter that way, but Nightwalker led us to a rocky area about one hundred feet away, near a small grove of ancient trees. We actually entered the largest tree through the base, after some vines pulled back.

"These vines are poisonous," Nightwalker warned, (for I remember her most by this preferred part of her name) "so whenever you enter this passage you must ask the vine to allow entry."

She did just that, but in a language not familiar to me. The vine, reminding me of the oasis vines over the stables, untwined, and there appeared an entry down into a tunnel. As we entered the dark, Nightwalker pulled back her day-veil and handed the rest of us a small torch from a torch holder upon the wall of the tunnel, which she lit just by touching it lightly as she handed each of us our light. I had wondered how our fire under the ancient tree had been lit so quickly, now I knew.

"I will lead because I do not need the light," she said. "Follow with your torches and watch your step. There are many traps for those who would find this entrance by accident or by treachery."

She walked forward and we followed as directed. I did notice that there were great holes that seemed bottomless, hidden behind floor stones in many places. There were also pointed knives protruding here and there that could have easily slashed anyone unaware of their locations. I sensed other dangers but knew that Nightwalker would not let us stray from safe passage.

After a short time we emerged inside the castle complex, exiting into a deep inner chamber. It was here that I met the most wonderful couple I have ever known. They awaited our emergence hand in hand.

The system of rule was much the same as what I had experienced in the Holy Land in that there were governors over areas that answered to the rule of Rome and the Emperor. This area, as in most places boarding this inland sea you call the Mediterranean, had all been affected by various empires, including that of the Romans, Egyptians, Aegean's and so on, but the area regents were often called *kings* and in some cases their counterparts, the *Queens,* ruled as regents also, as was the rule in the days of old.

The lack of communication and distance to the main authorities caused there to be much difference in opinion on how to rule and these *kingdoms* often clashed. This couple was what might be termed a *minor* ruler but their influence was *major* and their example was the perfect compliment to the mission of duality.

They saw themselves as leaders instead of rulers and made no decisions unless they both met with the counsel of equality, which consisted of equal numbers of men and women, chosen for wisdom, and from all segments of this tiny kingdom.

Bridgett, the Queen, was a beautiful woman and quite round and healthy of stature and again with child when I met her. She had many children and loved each one totally and recognized each one's talents almost immediately upon emergence. Rainald, the King, was the strongest and gentlest man, next to my own dear Jeshua, that I had ever met. He insisted, Bridgett once told me, that at each emergence of his children, his hands be the first to take them from her womb.

"Out of the sacred temple of Bridgett and into my hands, has God delivered this child to my care," he would say as Bridgett remembered his pledge at each birth. "And I promise to honor this child's mission to journey through discovery and to reunite with you, God our Father and Mother, as you have brought us into existence to also do." Bridgett said Rainald would then tenderly wipe the child himself, kiss the newborn, cut and tie the umbilical cord, and offer the after birth and the cord to the attending priestess as an offering of life to be used in sacred rituals, medicines, and for the good of all.

After the child was clean and snugly wrapped in a cape that Rainald wore before the emergence, during the preparation period, he would take the child to her and say, "Behold, our beautiful child, my love. I wrap this sweet one in my protection forever more." The child was placed at her breast then to find its nourishment and divine connection to its mother. The cape would be kept always with the child until the child was ready to give it up as a blanket, but kept always as a symbol of the love and promise of the father.

Sarah's birth had been quite wonderful too and slightly different in my memory, but the ritual aspect was similar in spirit. She, too, had a favorite swaddling blanket that she still slept with. It was gifted by her name sake, my dearest friend Little Mary, now, for Jeshua had nothing to leave me except the most important gift of all, his love and his message of hope. I still saw him often within my dreams and now he was telling me that soon I would be united with him, as I have ever dreamed. I often wondered if that meant I would soon die and go to the heaven that so many speak of. I knew I had seen him after the resurrection, but was not sure how he continued on, if in spirit, or just a memory.

Our new quarters were beautiful and more than adequate. Even BeeBa was allowed to climb the steps to our residence within one of the towers, and join us at his usual fireside place of honor. There was a great study with books and a large table for reading and writing. I was well trained for both. There sitting at the table when I first entered this room within our new home sat James.

"How did you know of my arrival?" I asked in total pleasure at this surpass, giving him a kiss of greeting.

"We have our sources," he said with a sly smile and then found Sarah and picked her up and threw her high, as he did when she was just a small one. She still giggled and loved her uncle, especially James, whom she found to be as mischievous as she.

"Welcome home, beloveds," James said. "It is time for you to live a full life out in the open light of the day."

My gratitude was in my smile and in a very matter of fact manner I said, without planning to make such a statement, "It begins again. Will they let the mission unfold, for it is for them, even those who would stop all of this, that this mission is of most importance."

Blessed be,

THE HOMECOMING

I found the people of this new place of familiar spirit to my own. They reminded me, as I experienced their overall energy and demeanor, of those upon the Misty Isle of my youth. Of course this place we now called home was not so very far from that lovely island. The legends of other Misty Islands are many, since there is a certain dimensional place that these islands occupy. When they are seen in the physical, third dimension, they appear as *in the mists*. Their security lies in being able to retreat to that in-between dimensional place.

I had wondered how to proceed now in the mission, for I knew the time was ready, but was I? I was experiencing a melancholy type day and asked Little Mary and Sarah to give me some time alone. I just wanted peace and quiet within our private chambers. I went to my sleeping shelf and lay down for a moment to shut my eyes. I felt lucky to be in this place of openness, for I had suffered exile and hiding long enough. I missed my beloved though, as always, but this day the sorrow was especially evident and my heart was heavy.

I thought I was within a dream again for I often heard Jeshua speak to me in dreamland. "MiryAmah, my beloved one, I have come to be with you finally."

I smiled with my eyes still closed, afraid to stop this most pleasant dream for the voice was soothing to my sorrowful heart. When I felt a gentle kiss upon my cheek, my eyebrows wrinkled, yet I kept my eyes closed and tried to determine how this dream could seem so sweet and real. I felt another gentle kiss, but this time upon my wrinkled brow. I heard the voice again say, "What is this worried look I see upon my beloved's face? Do you not want me to enter your dream and emerge from it?"

I finally opened my eyes and I cannot begin to describe the feeling of this moment adequately, for it was the greatest joy I have ever known. There, looking down upon me was the sweet and strong face of my beloved, Jeshua.

"Either I am having the best dream in imagination or I have just received the best gift known to any woman," I whispered. "How can this be?"

Jeshua's tender face seemed to drink me in with his eyes and his entire expression. He seemed to be looking deeply into my soul, but not missing any physical detail either as he gathered the vision, then he said, "I have prepared you for this telepathically, in your dream time. Did you not understand?"

I answered to this vision, for I still could not believe he was real, "It was too much to hope for, so I could not find my faith, my love," then I glanced away from his gaze, ashamed of what I had just said. He pulled my chin back ever so gently and whispered, "Do not feel guilt for guarding your heart thus, for how could you know that which we blocked from you?"

I was troubled by this statement and asked, "Why would you exclude me, my love, for anything that involves you or us, for I thought we shared all things?"

I could see that his heart hurt for this decision and then he explained, "It was done to keep you and our child safe, for should you know, even intuitively, for certain, you would surely have become a sacrifice also. And, my love, they would not have glorified your memory. That is a pain that I could not suffer.

"You mean as they glorify yours?" I questioned, knowing that his life had been remembered conveniently to accommodate the agenda of others.

"I hate the lies as much as you do, but the only hope of the mission as it relates to the Holy Land is to see if, in memory, they can finally understand the message of love we have tried to bring through. It has brought me great sorrow that the very ones I carefully trained to be those message bearers now fight over what I mean, instead of what *we* meant, and whether I am the son of God."

He looked almost angry as he raised his voice, however slightly, and I jumped as he spoke, "For God's sake, I am the Son of God as are they, and their wives are the Daughters of God, will they never get it?" Then he sobbed into my shoulder and I just held him there and joined him in this heart-breaking sorrow.

We cried our tears, holding each other, and spent the afternoon catching up on the intimacy that a man and wife enjoy. We desperately needed this time to rejoin and merge ourselves physically as we were soulfully. We were not disturbed. Having intuitive friends and such a sensitive daughter comes in handy at such times. We found our joy beyond our sorrow.

We found moments for conversation and I naturally wanted to know of what happened. Jeshua told me of the plan to save him from the cross. He had not known if he was abandoned in this endeavor, for the pain was great and it did not seem to go as planned. When the soldier stabbed him, he said he thought he was to die after all and that all was lost. He did not know then of the heavenly beings present, planning to intercede if need be. These angels could see that his lungs were filling with bodily liquids that flowed to overcome his wounds and were about to drown him. Jeshua only saw a Roman soldier with a spear and felt the pain of being stabbed. He did not know that the purpose was to give a channel for the excess blood and fluids to flow freely out of his lungs. He did feel the warmth of the blood exit the wound and told me that he felt immediate relief after the pain of the pierce. He wondered at that, he said. He also said he could remember hearing his mother, Little Mary, myself and others crying in agony there. He remarked on how the women did not leave him in his time of pain and suffering. He remembered the soldier with the vinegar on the sponge, but that was another angel, he told me. The sponge held a powerful potion that caused coma. This angel laughed and told the other soldiers that he had offered vinegar to this blasphemous retch.

"I didn't remember much after that but dreamed that I left my body and came to you through a gardener. I remember your pale face, wet from tears, and I thought then that I had offered you nothing but sorrow. I also dreamed that I talked to the apostles and disciples and urged them to keep true to the mission," he continued as he probed his memory of that dreadful time.

"I learned later that the angels took my body from the tomb Lazarus had arranged for my use, for only they of great strength could have rolled back the huge stone that had been placed there. They took me to a secret location where the healing began. I am told that many times they had to perform the *kiss of life* and breathe air into my lungs to revive me, for my body wanted to give up."

As I watched him tell his sad tale, garbed only in the blanket we shared, I said, "They say that you died and went to hell. They say that on the third day you arose again, my love, supernaturally."

He thought for a moment and said, "If the pain and suffering I experienced was not hell, I know not what that place could be. I died to the life as Jeshua, in the land they claim to be holy. I did arise again, in that my spirit did walk out of my body for a time and visit those I loved and whom I trusted."

He seemed then to be in deep thought and said in almost a whisper, "There are those who still have the vision. I pray that they will not lose the sight they have gained for the sake of us all and those yet to be born."

"Did you then talk with the angels, my love?" I said. "Not really," he replied, "they came to do what they must, then left me in safe hands."

"Where have you hidden all this time, for it has been nearly five years?"

"I have been in the far land where there live the people of the White Mountains, named for the snow that falls frequently thereon. This place was high and remote and not many knew of its existence. The leader of this country in these high lands is reincarnated again and again and the people find him and bring him back to the position of Holy One. These gentle people had me for the healing time and then I traveled to the land of the East to learn from the wise ones there who were so willing to support our effort and on the same mission. I have missed you and our daughter so much, whom I would love to meet soon, for my heart has been full of her as well as you, my dear wife."

I realized then that I had been hoarding all this attention for myself and had not yet introduced Jeshua to our little girl.

"I have heard that you honored my wish and gave her Sarah's name," he said. "I wish I could say it was just me, my love, but Sarah gave her name freely, as was her own desire, after cleansing the sorrow from it. She then asked for my old name *Mary* for she gave her name completely."

Jeshua smiled and said, "I had heard of this and I am amazed at the wisdom you women constantly tap into so readily and completely."

"Shall we then prepare to reunite our family?" I asked. We dressed and went to the great hall within the complex where we found Bridgett and Rainald there waiting with our beautiful daughter, readied in the finest dress a little girl could possibly desire. This dress was a welcome home gift for her from Bridgett and Rainald, so that she would see her father in her true glory. There, at her side was BeeBa, of course. All those who live within this complex, at least two hundred individuals, were there also, quietly waiting for our entrance.

We entered hand in hand. Jeshua saw Sarah immediately, so beautiful with her hair much like his but a bit lighter in that glowing reddish tint, and with skin and features similar to mine. The combination was striking and she was truly her own little beauty. She stood there with an irresistible smile upon her face and when she could stand still no longer, she ran to Jeshua and cried, "Father, father I have seen you in my dreams, and now you have finally come to me as you promised me in the night visions!"

The embrace of these two had everyone in the hall crying great tears of joy. Jeshua cried and kept saying to her, "I love you, I love you, my sweet little one," over and over again. "How did they know?" I asked looking at Little Mary. "Sarah told them," she said.

She knew that her father had come and she went to Queen Bridgett and King Rainald and very matter of factly stated, "prepare a feast and reception, please, for my father has come."

They did not hesitate but did exactly as she instructed. I was told that her demeanor was of absolute confidence and her word was not for a moment doubted, even though no one knew how this could be. She is truly a leader even at this tender age.

After the heartwarming hugs and tears were finished, Jeshua looked at BeeBa and said, "Do I not know this little one?"

"You should, he carried you in glory through the gates of Jerusalem and he has served both myself and your child since."

BeeBa, as if on cue, came to Jeshua immediately and brayed a welcome to his old friend. "This is my best friend, father," Sarah said. "He keeps all my secrets and he makes me laugh. I love to laugh, don't you?" Jeshua said as he touched little Sarah's head and looked at everyone in the room, "the little children shall lead us to true joy."

He continued by saying to Sarah and I, "We are now united as we should be. I cannot say I will not leave again, but I can promise that I will always come back."

We both realized our hunger, for a great feast had been prepared and it smelled wonderful. We had long been isolated in our reunion and forgot our physical hunger, instead fulfilling our spiritual hunger. All were invited to partake, as was the custom in this place I had come to love. There was no table of honor or no head table here. All helped in one way or another and all dined together. Laughter mixed with the sounds of dishes being passed and food being shared filled the room. We sat, for the most part, upon cushions on the floor with small raised tables for our food. The King and Queen offered the feast in honor of the sacred family. All families, they said, which love each other as this family demonstrates, enter into sacredness and thus please God Almighty, the All Loving who created the family through Divine Marriage of ONENESS.

"This is perfection in relationship," Jeshua said. "We have come to live it, my MiryAmah and my Sarah and I, and hopefully more children, but unfortunately we cannot share it with the world as we hoped. There are those from our homeland and other such places who are lost in fear of duality. We shall keep trying to plant the seeds of change. Do you agree, Sarah and MiryAmah, that we should continue in our mission?" he said to us.

Little Sarah said to her father, "Is our mission then to give love a chance to grow big?" "Yes! Little one," Jeshua said. "Given the chance, love will grow big!"

Blessed be,

GOOD-BYE IS NOT FOREVER

This idyllic place, this king/queendom I lived within, was the perfect place for Jeshua and I to reunite. We discussed the mission but knew the work would not be easy even here, for patriarchy, as it separates itself by negating the feminine, was on the move all over the land, much like a spreading disease. For the most part this was due to trading, which is ironic, because trading is a practice directed out of feminine energy. But the journeys were hard and long and men separated from their families were the principle laborers on these excursions. The temptation for riches and power, by the financiers of these expeditions, proved a thirst too strong to hold their vision in line with Divine Mind's plan. This distorted mindset went so far as to declare that a woman on board a ship was bad luck! Such nonsense, the only danger of a woman's presence was that she would see through their transparent logic and make them feel guilty for the stupidity of their thinking.

"They plan to build churches instead of temples," Jeshua said one morning as we arose for our break of day ceremony.

"What is the difference?" I wondered out loud.

"Not much," he said, "Except that the feminine was the original maker of temples and they represented the womb of the feminine. All the deities there worshiped were but aspects of the Source, symbolized in memory by many actual beings that were part of the beginning of this type of experience. The church then is God's house in his masculine aspect, but I do not think they can rename such a place for *She* will always be present therein, for certainly God does not want to live in a bachelors quarters without the presence of the feminine."

"They can bring the Mother Mary in for that part," I mused.

"I understand they are already cleansing her of the priestess taint of sexuality, and they now say that Father Joseph is not my real father but a step father." I was amazed at how people would bend the truth to negate the most beautiful gift man and woman had to offer each other, their sexuality, their passion and need to be merged in a sacred union.

"How do they explain your existence then?" I asked. "It is sad," he replied, "for they do not want to acknowledge my brothers and sisters. My sisters have had the priestess training and thus they have become invisible to the memory of me, as they would mold it. True, my mother was a virgin at my birth, for virgins are young ones, male or female, who are in preparation and ready to bring forth life, but they have now decided that to be a virgin means that one has not tasted the purported *sin of sexuality*."

"Oh, then they think that all children are born in sin!" I exclaimed with a look of total disgust. I continued my diatribe in aggravation: "is it a sin for the farmer to plant his seed? Or is the sin the fertile earth that beckons the seed to come within and rest for a while in order to sprout and grow? Where does this stupid thinking come from, my love?"

"Fear, MiryAmah, fear used unwisely corrupts the mind and closes the heart."

"If the people need a church then shall we abide?" I asked.

"This will be a delicate situation," Jeshua said, "for Peter and Andrew, brothers apart, argue over which one of them will lead the mission now and both want to head such a church. And you know that they have rejected the feminine within their own hearts, for they knew well that I left you with the leadership."

This was always a sad thing for me to think of, for all women suffer greatly from this attitude of superiority and exclusion. Jeshua told me that he had to remain dead and risen in their minds for any good to come of this. "If they find that I have survived they will surely move into chaos and murder and mayhem will follow for they want a God, not a man."

"All I can do," he went on to say, is hope that the memory finds its true path. They cannot acknowledge my humanity, it seems, for they hate their own humanity and I regret that they do not see and recognize their own divinity." He then wrapped his arms around me and pulled me close and whispered to me as his face felt my soft black hair and his mouth spoke words only for me, "they will not let the Feminine Goddess live in their hearts, MiryAmah, for they fear her greatly. They know of their great sin and they do not want to face that which they have rejected. That sin is the true fall of man. Not the fall of woman, unless she buys into this lie. And certainly not the ancients some called the fallen angels, for they loved our women more than our men did. For we all are feminine and masculine, as they tried to tell us, but our genders chose one dominant energy to manifest, and unless we can love ourselves completely, we are destined to chaos of unbalance. Growth cannot know its full measure in such a garden, where the seed is held holy and the soil is disrespected and neglected."

I listened, held there in total love and respect within his strong arms. I remember such seemingly little details as I reflect upon this time. For instance, I remember the smell of his body and hair, which was so compelling and so sweet to my senses. When energies mingle such as this, in sacred love unconditionally expressed, there is total bliss, even as there are issues of sorrow to surmount, we still rejoiced in the closeness and moment. I felt a great power rise within my being as I enjoyed this embrace. I had never felt such a surging of energy before in my life. I felt as though the Great Mother had entered my being, making me strong, determined and glad of my feminine essence. I looked at my love, eye to eye and said, "Then I shall build a church of MiryAmah, in your memory, and to keep the mission pure. If the people require a structure of the masculine, then I shall give this structure the name and essence of the feminine to bring Divine Balance. So shall it be."

"Yes, MiryAmah, my determined and strong beloved, this, I believe, is good. I will be departing soon for I must do my work of balance now in a much different manner. My survival shall not be known, for I am better left dead and deified to those lost in such imbalance. I travel now to many places where there is a hope-light there burning. Some will know my true name and some will give me many other names. The moment of need will determine how I am called. I go to learn of how such wise ones know of enlightenment, and then I blend my own light, and yours also, since you are me and I am thee, and hopefully these beacons will gain enough brilliance to bring a change for the good of all."

After our day-break ceremony and our first feast of the day with Sarah, Little Mary and myself, since the others deemed not to join us this morning, (Sarah at work again, for she knew and she asked for family time) he left. We had a great morning feast and laughed and fondly remembered sweet moments of long ago. Then the feast was over. Jeshua kissed Mary on the cheek and she cried softly. He then approached Sarah and told her how proud he was of her and that she should always know that her father loved her greatly. She threw herself into his arms and told him that she would wait for him in her dreams and then she left too. How these friends and family could just sense the needs of our parting is a mystery, but yet a reality.

Finally he turned to me and held me close and said nothing, for what we communicated with our heart could not be translated. He walked away by himself after that divine communication, as he had come, quietly and alone. My heart tie stayed firmly connected to him as he moved away from me, but my arms ached for his physical presence to stay and it took great strength to not run to him and throw myself at his feet and beg him to stay. I knew he could not, and to do so would bring him even more pain then I myself felt at this parting. He glanced back over his shoulder at me and stopped for a moment, with his long reddish, wavy hair falling down his back, and there seemed to be a glow about him.

He said, "In the dreamtime we will be together, my love, yet you will walk with me as always in my heart, for I am you and you are me and we are but one divine entity. I shall return often." Then he walked away into the nearby forest of Ancient Trees and disappeared from my view.

Even as he disappeared a miracle happened, for it was at that moment that I knew he had left me a parting gift, I knew that another one was beginning the journey into the physical within my body temple, and I rejoiced that Sarah would have a sibling to love as I would have yet another beloved child conceived in perfect love.

I embraced myself in recognition of this true gift of love and held my own belly with grateful hands in thankfulness. Surely, there were none so blessed as me.

Blessed be,

I LEAVE TO BEGIN

Even as I watched my beloved walk away to do the work he must, I knew that I would begin immediately to do the work that I knew was now my destiny, to build the Church of MiryAmah, in honor of him, thus keeping Divine Duality alive and well in our mission.

I returned to my quarters to speak with Sarah and Little Mary, for we needed to express our sorrow at Jeshua's leaving and also to reaffirm our intention to stay focused on our mission and remain joyful. We had much to be grateful for, with Jeshua surviving the terrible ordeal and now healed and heading into another aspect of the same work. We were safe here in this new place, at least for a while, and we had each other.

Soon enough we were about our separate tasks so I asked to see Bridgett and Rainald. They received me as a friend, in their private chambers, and we sat upon their floor cushions around a small round table that held hot drinks and fruit for our pleasure.

"He has departed, then?" Bridgett asked, yet knowing the answer and only asking in polite concern for me. "Yes, but he will be back, I know not when, but I know he will,"

Rainald said, "You know, MiryAmah, that when there is a coupling in truest love and honor, in the true spirit of divinity in duality, as with you and Jeshua, as I believe is even true with myself and my beloved, to part as such is an enormous sorrow for the leaver, for they must be the one to let go and string out the tie that forever will bind."

"I know, my friend," I lamented, "for I could feel his heart grow heavy as he walked away. He did tell me that because we are one, as he is me and I him, we would always be together because of this tie and I take comfort in those words of truth, just as he does."

"Now," I said, "The Great Mother has given me strength and direction to carry on. If it is a church they want to deify my beloved then let me offer them such a structure of the masculine. But I will fill it with the feminine love of the counterpart as instructed by the Divine Mother. I shall call the first church, *The Church of MiryAmah,* not to celebrate myself, but to marry the church to my beloved, as our true marriage reflects such divinity.

Yet even as I do this task I know that Peter and Andrew, with the influence of others in controlling positions, are about to build empty churches that they will insist are full of God's wisdom and love." I felt a great pain as I uttered these last words, "how can they bring God into this building and call it His home when he cannot have His Beloved Feminine Self therein to be honored also?"

As I tell you this story I think on this issue. Just as there are parts of each of us that are energized in the masculine and feminine mode, we must deny that which is tender and intuitive within our very beings to enter into such a patriarchal place, for She will always be unwelcome in this divided place. As I remember these times and see what is upon your plates of experience right now, in your so-called modern times, I see not much difference. I still see women as second-class citizens (even though they often do not know it or seem to consciously care,) and held as objects to glorify men instead of compliment them as equals. They are still in bondage and the bonds are tied with their own attitude of buying into such a system. I also see still that churches say they are God's place and yet they have different standards for men and women therein. That is why I have come again and again, and especially now, to reveal the truth, for it is time that the truth should see the light of day finally, once and for all. But I have jumped ahead in time and it is my life as Mary of Magdalene and my memories of that time in experience that I am telling now, so I return to my visit with my friends, who were very supportive of me and still are.

Bridgett and Rainald said, "We will assist you, MiryAmah, in any way we can, but we must warn you that our position of influence in this land is dwindling, for our very existence is a threat to those in control, whose main wish is to control."

I looked at my friends and thought of this wonderful place to be, where servant and lord shared all burdens and men and women stood side by side in equality. "Why, oh why," I asked, "do they hate us women so? If it were not for our love and commitment to the very ones who hate us, they would not have physical life. They hate and despise the very breast that nursed them. They call it lurid and require that we keep our bodies hidden lest we tempt a man to sin, yet every man wants to hold and to fondle our bodies for their own gratification, and return himself to the suckling days. The

Great Mother weeps at this insanity," I said. "Father God, her counterpart, grieves also, for this lie denies God as a totally Divine Being and negates the wonder and good of all creation divinely manifested through duality."

Rainald answered, "It is my shame as a man to see what such corruption of mind and heart can do to soul. This division is the true downfall of humankind. I will assist you until I can no longer breathe air into my body, and then I shall assist you from the place of spirit." Bridgett looked at him in great love and said, "and I shall be right there also, for we know that divine duality is truth, and that exclusion and judgment is not."

We held each other's hands then and vowed our promise to carry on. "I shall begin, then," I said, and left the presence of my friends.

I began to pack my things from my own chambers soon after. I knew I had to move into the village and I had made arrangements with a family whose daughter served me well here in this perfect place, to take me in. I would leave Sarah in the hands of Little Mary for a time, until I was sure it was safe for her to come. Mary, with the help of my friends, had been continuing her Oracle education and was *seeing* for those needing vision within the complex. She could not carry on that mission from within the humble village, for they would fear her role as oracle, since not yet proven. They still believed in the powers of such a one as she, but they did not yet know her well enough to keep her safely within their midst.

Sarah put up quite a fuss when I departed, although I assured her that she could come and see me whenever she wanted, but that she had to come humbly, for if I was to lead a congregation of followers, they must see us as one of them and not privileged ones dripping in finery. She assured me that she understood, and she helped me pack my old street robes and some precious items I would use for my task. I really did not have much to take. Soon enough, I told her, I would come for her things and take her to be with me, for I would need her to assist me in preparation for her new baby brother. Upon hearing this her eyes lit up and she jumped and squealed with glee. "A brother for me!" she said over and over again. "Yes, my little one," I said smiling though tears of joy of my own, "for your father has left us a great gift to await his return."

I then walked away too, even though it was a short distance of only about ten miles, to this place I went. I had to let go, just as Jeshua did not so long before. It was indeed difficult to leave Sarah and Little Mary behind. The people I would live with had come for me and we walked away following a two-wheel wagon with large wheels pulled by oxen that carried supplies given to the family by Bridgett and Rainald. They would know no hunger for a while, of that I was sure. It took us the better part of the day to reach the humble home. It was beautiful to me because it was a house of love.

Blessed be,

I BEGIN AGAIN

The work continued but took a new direction. The past five or six years were transitional in that the emotion of the tragedy of Jeshua's crucifixion had to settle down so that direction could be chosen. It was obvious, as Jeshua and I had discussed, that to be an instrument of change he had to play the role of God instead of man. After all, we all play parts in the dramas of our lifetime, do we not? Each emergence into this place of physical experience, we make progress upon our journey home again to that wonder of wonders that sent us out in the first place, The Source, the Grand Creator of ALL THAT IS. Each lifetime we learn differently and fulfill different needs for those we interact with.

I know that I casually allude to the concept of reincarnation as I tell this story, and for some of you who read these words, that is but one of the many areas that can upset your perception of *what is.* It is difficult to change a preconceived ideology into a *what is not,* I know. I just want you to know that the memories have been molded conveniently and the ancient books often altered, even as also the temples had images chiseled from their surfaces so that minds could be held in rein. In the beginning, you see, the concept of reincarnation was totally accepted as the truth of experience and never questioned. It was simply *known.* But in those days dreams and visions were also accepted, as were supernatural forces, for in days of old there were those beings thought to be Gods who played creation upon this Tara-place. They left ultimately, for the most part due to the effect they were exacting upon the new physical vehicles (humans). Those in the experience herein kept the memory and the knowledge of the cycles of life within their knowing. The problem with this type of *knowing,* however, is that it can be mis-used easily by those who would lie to meet their own agenda. So it was by some of those who claimed to *know* but who really wanted to *control.* As humans, the new species became more technologically advanced; they were more able to qualify this inner *knowing* scientifically. Again I move ahead of my story. I wish to speak of the beginning of the church now, at this point in my life, not of the many developments that preceded this lifetime and this need of equalizing the essence of God. You are all the essence of God, you know, in masculine or feminine form and expressing in both energies within your physicality even as you prioritize one or the other as gender, while you move through this experience.

Returning to my memory story, soon after moving into the village I began my work. The first concern upon my agenda was to again form the twelve plus one. I asked my new family if there were still those priestesses practicing the old ways in this place and was assured that this was true, but the practice of such was becoming more and more secret due to influences of fear. This was due mainly to the influence of the Romans. Their controlling doctrine had spread all over the lands near the inland sea, the Mediterranean. Their practice of crucifying those in opposition to their beliefs, lining them up along popular roadways for all to see the suffering, was enough to plant the seed of fear into anyone. The men of these places and times, who had always been family protectors, began to feel that to be on the side of such controllers was the best defense they could afford those that they sheltered. Then the attitudinal change crept in as they sought to justify the insane thinking and behavior of that which they had become a part of. This is the corruption that created and supported the fear. It is fear that separates the masculine and the feminine.

I was welcomed into a sacred priestess meeting within the week of my inquiry and arrival. The meeting was held in the forest at the home of a wise-woman that was the local mid-wife and herbalist. She had expected to see me soon, for she could sense the women who would require her support to bring the new souls into emergence. My Pregnancy was already *known* to her. She reminded me of Nightwalker, except she was not one with the night-vision, with eyes that had to be veiled during the day. This wise one, known simply as *Crow Woman* to the local people, because of the bird's attraction to her, was similar to myself in that she could speak mentally to birds. An interesting facet of her personality included speaking the verbal language of many animals also. She was fluent in wolf, horse, dog and cat, but especially bird languages.

As I approached her humble home she conversed with crows in their language, cawing and making curious cackling noises. I could read their minds myself so I knew that they were excited about my coming and were announcing my progress through the forest paths. Crow Woman paused in her conversation and greeted me by announcing, "Welcome, my sister, for I have waited with great joy for your arrival."

"I did not know myself, wise one, that I would arrive at your doorstep until this day, so you must be a seer of tomorrow."

She smiled as a crow landed upon her shoulder and she said to the bird, "As you said, my friend, she is beautiful to look upon, her heart beams bright and she is full of questions." The crow flipped itself onto my shoulder in a familiar sort of way.

"Could this be my friend from long ago?" I said in astonishment. "Surely no bird could live such a long time but you remind me of a bird from long ago in my childhood days." In my own language the bird replied, "but you know I am no ordinary bird, my dear friend. As a child you did not try to reason your way through all such observations, if I remember correctly."

At that moment the crow lifted off my shoulder and in front of my eyes he transformed into what you might call a wizard, but what I know of as a *Sage*. Standing in front of me was an elder, a man with long white hair and a beard that was nearly as long as his hair, which nearly touched the ground. He stood not quite as tall as myself and his smile was one of mischievous humor.

"Do you like me in my crow garb better than my human form, my friend?" he asked with a smirk upon his wise old face. "I do find aerial flips more fun to do but I can always find a way to flip into your presence," he said so matter of factly. He then did acrobatic flips, spinning like a top at the apex of each flip, circling around me, and landed once again at my side, quite unaffected by this physical effort. Crow Woman laughed and remarked that he always affected her so. How many eons of time have you been shape shifting and flipping in and out of the lives of those you watch over?" "A long, long time, you old crone, or should I say, "you old crow," he responded playfully.

He then told me we would catch up on old memories when the priestess meeting was done. I entered the dwelling and was ushered into a large room, for the home was built into the side of a cliff and the interior was much larger than one might expect.

I found a gathering going on, and was welcomed at this meeting with open arms by a group of mostly women, but there were some men there as well. Crow Woman had previously screened those present as candidates for my council of twelve. Crow Woman, who could be called high priestess, elder or leader--already knew that I would need my council soon. It was near universal that groups of twelve plus one worked together, at least it was where there was awareness of the essence of balance within groups of like mind. As I met with these sisters I was convinced that they were pure of heart and determined. I reminded them that this mission that I had devoted my existence to would take much time and energy and total dedication just to begin again. I could see in their eyes that all had the heart required for this project. We excused ourselves and went outside the home into a nearby meadow where sun streamed down through the trees upon soft, tall grass.

This pleasant place was a small clearing that appeared enchanted. This illusion resulted from light trails created by the sun as they filtered through the forest and fell upon the ground. I began to speak of this thing called a church and to explain the meaning of this building I wished to have constructed.

"The men will build it," I said, "a building for the purpose of keeping the Divine connection, and they will consider this place a source of pride, for in its structure, as well as the rules they will no doubt establish, they will put their divine masculine energy into full force therein. It is up to us to bring the feminine within this structure and into the heart of this organization to assure that it is balanced and reflective of the sacred duality. We will have to do this privately, secretly even, right under the noses of most of those involved, to the point that we shall have to take oaths to keep the full scope of this work safe from negation and corruption." The sisters understood completely, for they were all aware of how the feminine, and all ways of such as reflected in everyday life, was being negated and pushed back of late because of the changing attitudes.

"See that wonderful light as it streams through the trees?" I said. Within the structure of this building to be called *church* we will open portals for the light of knowing. The masculine will be the foundation and the feminine will be the presence of light therein, streaming through the heart of God." The building to be constructed will be called *MiryAmah's* church because I will be the one this time to initiate it, but the men will build it and they will take ownership of the physicality of it, not by my wishes, or yours, but because that is what men do. They build and construct, and then they say, "I have done this so this is mine and it is good." This ownership has always been different for men and for women. Women inhabit a place, or utilize a place, while men must think in terms of protection and reckon to own it ultimately. That is the difference between the temples of old and the new temples, now to evolve into churches. When the High Priestess, with the help of the High Priest, served within the old temples, they were not a place of ownership, not even for the Gods or the Source, but instead, simply holy ground, or a holy place for use as needed for holy business. When the High Priestess was forced to step down a rung lower than the High Priest, and eventually down further and further, he began to hold *reign* instead of holding *service* in such places. He, out of balance with his counterpart, began to believe that God had given him authority. That is always the effect of the imbalance of God's gift of essence, this separation into what is mine and what is yours. The essential aspect that looks down then begins to feel in authority over all it perceives below and regards itself owner of all that it perceives, or at the very least, God's authority over such. The idea of worthiness then enters into the equation, and cooperation, consideration, total respect and equality of experience suffer for this lack of divine balance. It works the same no matter what part of this essence (the masculine and the feminine) holds the upper position, but of late it is patriarchy that is losing vision and balance. It is like a house falling down with one wall dominant and constantly leaning upon the other wall. Eventually it all falls down.

What I am asking you, my sisters, is to get up off your knees and take your positions, rightfully, alongside the priests, but to do so with caution, for it is the mind that sets you upon your knees. It is the mind that builds the temples, churches and homes, you see. The heart will always stand tall. A home without an equally strong heart is not stable. Churches will come and go, I assure you, for the need for such a place will also come and go and change over time. Some churches will be named and dedicated to women, some reincarnations of goddesses of times of old, and some to men, some of which were also gods. But always it will be the feminine filling the inner spaces created by the masculine and seen as streams of light in the physical space as well as in the mind, for God is Light and darkness is simply that from which light emerges. These streams then symbolize how the Divine Masculine emerges through the Divine Feminine into perfection. A church perfectly built and filled is then well balanced with the essence of God. Light can be shut out in many ways, dear sisters. Let us keep the windows open. Let the men build, as they must do and as they do so well, and we will fill the space with light, as we must.

This was the beginning of my teachings to those who had joined me. They would be the disciples of this new place and they would learn the inner teachings as well as the secret teachings, through myself, and as directed and requested and agreed upon with my beloved, a beloved they would only know of as a conceptualization, for that was the only way now.

Blessed be,

THIS CHURCH SHALL HAVE
HEART AND SOUL

I left the meeting meadow with a feeling of accomplishment and gratitude because finally I knew the mission was still alive. I met Flip, who had taken the form of a rabbit for this meeting. I suspected that he had joined our meadow meeting as the ever-flipping crow, hanging out in a nearby tree. I had earlier noticed him out of the corner of my eye. I knew him not to be a spy, but a guardian, as always. I was grateful for his presence in any form. The rabbit joining us gained our attention by performing a couple back flips, which indicated to me that my friend, the shape-shifter, was having his fun again.

"You seek to amaze me again, my friend, Flip?" I inquired. Then he became the sage that I knew and loved so well, changing form there in front of my eyes. We walked and talked, remembering the journey of my childhood and our previous interactions together.

"You are still as beautiful as ever, MiryAmah," the Sage said, "and your new name suits you perfectly." I answered by saying; "I took this name when my mission began, when I connected to my beloved Jeshua, who was then called Jesus. But it seems that most will simply know or remember me as Mary from Magdalene," I said, "since they cannot grasp the importance of taking our names to another level." I opened up to Flip then and said, "I have known great joy and sorrow since you last flipped into my life, dear friend."

He looked at me as we walked then looked ahead and seemed to be thinking hard on this statement. He finally said, "I know, dear one. I can read it in your heart and see it in your eyes. There lies great hope there and yet painful memories. I come to bring you joy and to assist in this project should there be the need. I shall in all ways try to bring the joy that is ever present, behind all circumstances, to your attention, as I did on that long journey when you were a child so young, leaving your home and family."

"What I need, my sage-friend, is to find the right builders of the church that I would have constructed. I shall not build a temple, for the time of the temples is gone for me. Can you help me with building a church place?" I asked.

"Oh yes!" he laughed, "for I work closely with a society of masons which had their origins in the long ago past time and are the ones responsible for most grand monumental structures. Pyramids and temples owe their majesty to those of this group. They can be trusted for they have pledged their very souls to the divine masculine. Those of the Masonic Order would, I believe, be quite interested in this project you propose, for your dedication to the divine feminine is the equal and the counterpart of their own mission."

"I am very interested in this possibility Flip, my beloved friend", I said. "When can we begin this communication?"

He gently took my hand and said, "Follow me, then, for now is not too soon." He led me down a nearly invisible path that branched off the main trail. But for following him, as when I followed Night Walker, I would not have known where to step, for the way was not well trodden. In a short time we arrived at a small cottage within the towering ancient trees. Sitting upon a chair made of tree twigs, on a porch across the front of the dwelling, sat another elder one. He noticed our approach and yelled out a greeting, "Welcome to my home, Flip, and welcome to your lovely friend, too. What brings you to my little house in the woods?"

"My friend is Mary of Magdalene, now known as MiryAmah, and we come to speak of a great building project she must carry out," Flip said cheerfully.

"This is a first, friend Flip," he remarked with a smile, "that you have not flipped into my presence as a creature doing great acrobatics. This must be a serious project for certain, and if so, we should talk," the woodsman said.

He ushered us to a place beneath the trees, where more chairs were at hand. They were made of living vines and small trees trained to grow in a seating shape. I had never sat in a more comfortable chair when Flip remarked that the chairs were guided by a master builder who knew the spirit of the building materials and worked with them rather than against them.

"Forgive me, MiryAmah, for I have failed to introduce myself," said the woodsman. "I am Ranulf, builder of places divine, for all structures are creations and thus divine in nature. That is at least until their divinity is soiled from corruption of mind and heart," he qualified.

"How so?" I asked, not really sure of what he meant.

"To build a temple, to make connection to the Divinity of the gods, or the Master Creator (Builder of ALL THAT IS) is a privilege and a sacred task, as you well know. It must be accomplished from a true heart for what exists in the heart is reflected in the building, you see. I cannot tell you how many structures fall to the ground, not because of faulty construction, but because of faulty hearts." He seemed to reflect for a moment. "When they bring blood sacrifice to the temples, they bring imperfect offerings. This practice," he said with obvious aversion, "stems from the fact that they drove the priestesses out of the temples, and she was the source of donated blood offerings, of which I am sure, MiryAmah, you know well. This sacred blood of life itself is a substance of life in many potions and the men could not recreate it so they sought to substitute it. They somehow managed to rationalize to justification this practice of killing an animal or captive human. That is the corruption of which I speak. God does not want needless death as a gift. This abhorrence negates the gift of life our Creator has given us. All creation must die and be born again and again, but all in its own time and purpose, never as a sacrifice!"

"You are a wise man, Ranulf, and now I know that you are the one I seek, not to build a temple, for they have been built, defiled and destroyed too often. I want a church built, a place to celebrate life. A building made by the physicality of humanity in its most masculine form, so that the feminine can fill it with her energy as well and form a perfect place to honor God and all creation.

"I might be interested," he replied, "as overseer to this work, of course, but I must ask, what god do you honor, for there are many gods it would seem, but one true Source?"

"I honor the Source in the totality of Divine Essence, both as Father and Mother, as Husband and Wife, as Son and Daughter, always balanced and complimented in perfection. It is my hope that in honoring the perfection of this Divine Duality, we can begin to see how we reflect that which created us."

He nodded his head as if positively considering the option. I knew I had to be completely open with this one, should he choose to take on this task, so I told him quite frankly: "They, the people seeking a way out of corruption, these people who need to find balance, would need a Son God, it seems. They do not want a Moon Daughter for they fear the dark and the moon is of that mysterious element."

"My beloved Jeshua was crucified for the cause of balancing attitudes and essence in physical experience. He is now dead as a man but alive in many hearts as the Son God, so for him I must begin this church. This church shall hold the blueprint for the change, for there are those, even now, who are changing the pattern of his memory and mission to suit their agendas of control and power. I need to turn this project of the sacred structure over to one such as you, for I have the *knowing* that you are true in heart and I want that heart essence to be the foundation of this sacred place."

"Then consider it done, MiryAmah, for I will be glad to oversee the construction of such a holy place. It is my honor to be chosen. I would recommend that our mutual friend, Flip, take you back to the wise woman, the midwife of the woods, for it is she who will help you locate the best site for such a place as this. And, unless my imagination is lying to me, and it seldom does, you would have need of her services sometime soon, for surely one who beams such a light as you do, MiryAmah, surely prepares another soul for emergence soon."

"I have not yet announced this, Ranulf, yet this is true and I tell you the *Son God* shall have yet another blessed child to love and honor. And this child, as all children are, shall be the child of God."

Blessed be,

THE ORACLE ANSWERS THREE QUESTIONS

The construction of this first church building began soon after my meeting with Ranulf, The Mason of the Wood, as he was known. His specialty was the wood itself and how the energies of the building ritual merged with the living substance. As it turned out, he was the Grand Worshipful Master of the group of Freemasons in this place, a society that has kept its teachings secretly guarded for the sake of keeping the truth. They were among those, as I said before, who have been involved in all grand scale building projects upon this and other planets. They were all bound to an oath of alliance to balance the duality within Divinity.

Ranulf soon brought together the brothers of Masonry and they worked closely with myself as designer of the structure. The design and the purpose would be inter-married, just as is the masculine and feminine so too within each enlightened individual and within each sacred marriage as Jeshua and I have enjoyed.

I wanted this building to be tall and as full of light as possible. I wanted echoes to sing from the walls of this church to remind everyone present that all things echo endlessly into other realms, just as a ripple echoes its shape endlessly within the sea, at first strong and direct, then later with the subtlety of the wings of an angel. I knew the building would have to reflect the human body, for the animal kingdom and the elementals and element beings need not such a place to worship. They celebrate in life itself.

The structure would reflect the energy path within the physicality of the human body as one entered at the root vortex (root chakra) and moved through a long nave energizing each vortex along the route to the apex vortex at the alter, which represented the crown vortex (chakra) where all energy would merge and the divine marriage of duality would find perfection. It is the human being that believes that a house of God is necessary and since the human body is the true house of God, I wanted this structure to reflect such a truth.

The temples of old were sacred places also, but meeting places and learning places not seen as entering a body but as entering the environment of a god or goddess. They were places to meet them, yes, but not in the same mode as a church would be seen, for the church would become a body more than a place. The idea of building churches actually upset me when I first heard of this as an attempt to continue the mission because Jeshua found everyplace to be the Holy Temple of God.

He actually did not like the way the temple structures had manifested after the priestesses were lost, for the environment had changed and now only a few were deemed worthy to enter. The requirement that the faithful offer of their meager wealth, even the very food needed for survival for those deemed worthy of entry, so that the organization could thrive, angered both Jeshua and myself. The priests who required this sacrifice enjoyed the result, not God. It was a motherless place and lacked her compassionate heart energy, this temple, as it drained the resources of the poor and struggling it was meant to serve.

Still the direction of the mission had to be determined and yet be flexible enough to survive. Just as Jeshua, the followers and I had to change our focus when they crucified my beloved; I too knew I must see how I could use the prevailing trend as yet another pathway to the goal of Divine Duality. This church was the beginning even as my child was beginning to feel restless within my womb.

Visiting often, Little Mary still held close to me because of the soon emerging child. She only left at night for her oracle duties and she became one of the leading sibyls of the region. She would return in the late morning after arising at the complex and seeing to Sarah's needs. Seeing my dear friend serving my Sarah or me so humbly during the daytime, there was never a hint of the wisdom and power that emerged from her when she sat as *SHE WHO SEES* at the full moon of each month and whenever summoned. I requested such a session before we started the actual building phase of the church, for I felt great anxiety as to the undertaking of this task. It was then that I more fully understood the scope of Little Mary's nightly duties.

She came to me at midnight that evening, her usual time of oracle visitation as she had informed me upon my request. She came dressed in a soft white cape that covered her entire body. The material looked so like velvet that if her face and demeanor had not distracted me, I would have asked to touch this soft material.

She looked like someone from another world. Pale as the finest porcelain vase she was, with eyes not really seeing the outer because her being was so focused on a different dimensional place. She looked as though she would be easily broken should anyone bump her and she was indeed fragile, for she had sisters there to keep her safe.

Carrying an ornately carved chair, her sisters preceded her entry into the chamber. They placed the throne-like seat before the hearth. The chair faced the fire and as the fire's light reflected upon it, I noticed its mysterious design.

One side of the chair was carved of ivory and in the shape of a centaur, half horse and half man. The other side was also carved into a centaur; only this side was of ebony and was half horse and half woman. The rumps of the centaurs formed the arms of the chair with the human faces turned outward looking away from the chair and forming the back rising components. The male figure looked up and away and was on the left side as you stood before this great seat. The female figure looked downward, beyond the base of the chair. The seat of the chair was covered in lambskin and calfskin, representing (I later learned) the innocents. The back of the chair was upholstered in fabrics made from flax and natural reeds that were intricately woven into flower patterns. Silk threads of many colors adorned this astonishing chair, some in the form of symbols that I cannot, to this day, reveal. The white lily, however, was prominent with its shadow areas embroidered in rare purple silk threads. It represented the purity of life as God, the Creator, intended all experience to resolve itself. The entire cycle of the flower, from seed to bud to full flower, and then even to death and rebirth, was part of the pattern of the chair. It fascinated me until I almost forgot its purpose. I describe this chair for it was the seat of psychic power as channeled through the oracle and part of the ritual of her advice and service as I requested.

My friend then entered the chamber behind her assisting sisters. I did not see my familiar friend therein, for she had transformed into a presence unknown to me. She had become *SHE,* the oracle that *SEES.*

SHE sat upon this great chair of authority with her eyes appearing glazed and distant. I was not sure she even knew where she was or recognized me as her faithful friend. SHE simply said, "I have come to answer your questions. I will answer three. Present them in order of importance." Then she waited.

I pondered these requirements a moment then said: "First I wish to know if the mission will ever come to completion? Will the masculine and the feminine ever manifest within physicality as the Great One envisioned?"

SHE fell into a deeper trance and the sisters had to hold her in the chair, for she seemed to be mobilized in agonizing energy. I noticed then, as she was thrashing around within the chair, that she wore nothing under her great soft white robe, for she moved about within the chair as if feeling her answer come through her in the most powerful way. Her sisters had to do all they could to keep her seated and safe in this state. Eventually she gained her composure and her face returned to the distanced porcelain stillness that I had perceived when she first entered my chambers. Sweat poured from her lovely forehead though, and her hair looked as if someone had just poured water over her. Finally SHE answered:

"You ask the most painful question first, MiryAmah, for the Source finds great sorrow in this aspect of the creation experience. There runs hatred and jealousy between these two reflections of this Divine One and the pain of the Mother God is as great as that of the Father One. All creation must resolve and find itself within love, unconditionally and totally. That is the challenge in physicality and once this resolution takes place, then the spark has returned to the Divine Light, the child has returned home, the creation has reached perfection, the Divine Parent rejoices. It sounds so simple but it is not, for there have been many moments of experience when beings have learned that certain actions will bring certain results."

"This, then, was the origin of expectation and conditional manipulation, which in and of itself is a good tool for movement through evolution and a force for positive change. Yet it can be just as effective as a tool to stop movement and evolution. This journey takes two energies, different but equal in importance, to the cause to complete itself. These energies must merge equally to create light at its purest level. Only pure light can reunite with Divine Light, which desires beyond your ability to imagine, that all sparks come back home once again. To stop the flow of one of the energies then means the other energy cannot manifest this level of light in its purest form. What is manifested then is chaos or incompleteness, which always seeks to find that which it knows is missing. It cannot return and reunite with the Source. The homecoming is delayed. This causes great Divine Sorrow. Not anger."

"When human beings, or beings of like nature, negate one of the genders representing priority of experience (your terms would be male or female) then they stop that which they need for completeness. Since all creation in the dimensional realm of physicality is dually manifested in primary masculine or feminine modes, it is evident that this is an important stage of evolution. Each stage of evolution has a major aspect to arrive at the *knowing* and for you in the physical, the merging of the masculine and feminine is the paramount knowing. This must take place within the individual as they come to recognize that they have a dominant gender, but also have the opposite force as inner strength to balance the experience. They must accept and rejoice in their totality of beingness. This is reflected in all relationships or experiences with others. Once learned, the being is ready for the next step of evolution, which is the name for the journey back to the Source, the grandest of homecomings. Your answer, then, MiryAmah, is *yes* it will happen and you will be part of this accomplishment."

My second question was this: "Will this church be a force of good for the cause, or a force against the cause?"

SHE answered: "Within the heart and soul of the church the spirit of the feminine will keep the hope burning, but the organizational component of the institution and branches of it yet to come will keep trying to douse this fire. You must place this sacred fire therein the building and the hearts of those who would enter such a place, MiryAmah. And it will be your task to keep the sacred fire burning forever. The Mother-One and the Divine Wife will merge to become keepers of the light within the churches, but the road will be long and the way dark, at times. The main purpose of the church, as it is manifesting as a need for place of focus, is that this tiny spark of divinity is there burning and connecting to everyone who knows how to enter the sacred chambers, even as they enter the building. It will be the secret treasure of truth. Not every king is a true king. Not every queen is true either. It is at the core of their being where the truth lies, that this is so or is not so. This is the place that keeps the flame of truth, and without a proper balance within the being, it cannot burn therein. By building your church in honor of the duality mission, and by honoring your beloved, you have lighted the inner flame. It takes perfection in duality to light such a fire. The passion of the feminine is the fire itself, and the complimenting protection and devotion of the masculine is the wind that feeds the flame. To answer your question directly: Yes, the church will be a force toward the goal, for it will be there that the imbalance will manifest, upon the holy ground, because the intention for the structure and the organization was sacred, at its deepest level, even though on the surface the intent was corrupted into control and power. Will it then be a force for the good of the cause? <u>Yes, for it will be an instrument of change in hearts and reexamination of intents.</u>

My third question was: "What will happen to my children, the children born in love divine to Jeshua and myself?"

SHE spoke: "They will thrive and become leaders throughout eons of time where their physicality code will bring about peace, for you and your beloved are of those who resulted from the early experimental marriages of those beings deemed more peaceful and more likely to seek such a state. Sarah shall rule one day, but her name shall be forgotten in time and then remembered again. James, the child about to emerge, shall also move into a leadership role as will Josephus and Tamara, but due to the highly possible manipulation of past experience, the true influence of your children shall be known to those beings who oversee physicality more than those within this experience. Fame and fortune is not happiness when sought for the sake of security. Your children shall be among those who demonstrate that leaders who serve are far more precious and offer more divine security than rulers that sit in judgment for the sake of power. The entire planet, the beloved Tara, shall have points of brilliant lights within the darkest of her experiencing places, but because of your children, who will always find their way to light up the darkness of stagnation and ignorance, the darkness shall be pierced. <u>Yes, they will suffer and they will find joy, but they will always pursue peace.</u>"

Upon this statement SHE simply stood up and left, just walked away, back to where ever she prepares for these moments. Soon she would find her way to my chambers and the sleeping shelf prepared for her use this night. I found her soundly sleeping in the morning and I thought of how child-like and innocent she seemed as she slept there. I wondered if she would be one of the ones called *eternal children* yet I had seen another side of this jewel of a friend, that of Powerful Oracle. How complex our lives are, I thought. We could play so many roles all at once in this tiny span of time and place.

She awoke as I sat watching her quietly. She seemed surprised for she had expected to go back to the complex to our chambers there, but I had insisted the sisters bring her back to me. I knew that the time was ready for her and Sarah to join me, and I wanted to speak with her on this matter before she left. She looked quite spent but insisted upon arising immediately. I brought her some morning tea and she said, "What happened upon my visit as the oracle, for I never remember a thing and this is a rare opportunity for me to know what was said and what was understood." I wrapped her in a soft blanket as she sat in her chair by the fireplace. There we took our morning tea and I settled down to answer her.

"To answer your question," I said, "The duality will be accomplished because the Source, that which created All That Is, believes it to be possible. To *believe*, my Little Mary, is to *Know*, is it not?" She smiled and waited for she knew that there would be more things to speak of during this meeting. I continued, "You are called SHE, of which I am sure you know. You are most beautiful and powerful, but in your oracle mode you seem to go through great pain and agony and lose almost all strength as you reach for the answers. SHE gave me three questions and I have spoken already of the first.

The second answer assured me that the church would ultimately be a force of good for the mission because those within, not those who control it, but those who come there to quench spiritual thirst, will deem it so and demand the end of corruption and the beginning of divine direction toward perfection.

"And the third question?" she eagerly inquired. "Yes, it was told to me that my children would bring light to dark places of experience because they held a special code within their physicality, planted there long ago by beings of peace and love." "This is good, MiryAmah, for I love your children as I love myself." I answered by explaining that they would suffer and they would find joy but they, and their children and their children, would persist and bring peace." She sighed and wrapped herself even more tightly within the blanket and sipped on the warm tea.

"Now can we come home to you, MiryAmah, for Sarah and I miss you greatly?" I realized then that Little Mary looked like a long lost child herself. "Yes," I said, "it is time."

I put my hand upon my now bulging tummy and felt my little boy move there inside my body, eager to join us out in the light of day. Now I knew his name to be James, after his uncle who had been so faithful to me and now continued his brother's work even as he protected his brother's family.

"The time is right!" Go and bring Sarah this very day, as soon as you feel able to travel. Make haste for baby James comes soon to our arms," I said. "Oh," Little Mary said, "you have chosen a name for this child?" "No," I answered, "the child has chosen his own name and you have made it known to me as SHE. Now go and return quickly for this little one is impatient."

Blessed be,

THE EMERGENCE OF JAMES, THE SON OF JESHUA

The flow of the mission was again in movement and traveling in the right direction of Divine Duality. My masons were gathering the material for the actual building of this first church. Each stone and piece of wood would be carefully selected. The proper communication would take place to gain permission from the elemental being within the substance for the purpose of this project. The twelve disciples were among those preparing them for their part in the mission and I could finally relax and tend to other concerns. My new babe was impatient to emerge. I knew I must go to the mid-wife in the woods, for my time was near.

Little Mary and Sarah came the same day that I summoned them and it was the next morning that we departed for Crow Woman's home. The message of *all due haste* was heeded and my family was almost complete and ready. I wished my beloved could be here for this second miracle, this second treasure he had bestowed upon me, our first-born son. My labor began to make itself known and I hoped that this child would wait until all was in readiness for him. I tried to walk when we left the village house, but soon upon entering the woods it was evident that I could not walk much further. Sarah brought BeeBa forward and beckoned me to sit upon his back. I did so without hesitation, for I needed to rest. I was and still am truly grateful for this little white donkey's constant dedication to our family. Little Mary walked beside me to hold me steady and Sarah led BeeBa along the path. Some of the male followers preceded for the sake of protection as well as followed us for the same purpose. We must have looked much like Mother Mary with Joseph when she left for the census so near the birth of Jeshua. I thought about how much this little donkey had given to my dear ones and myself. The animal beings were such a blessing to humanity. In spite of the suffering I have experienced, my life was a gift, for there was deep love therein, manifested again and again in so many ways. I was full of love and appreciation for this time of joy.

I found Crow Woman already prepared for me. Most women now were staying within their own homes to birth, and she would go to them, but occasionally one such as I would need the old emergence practice and she would take me to the secret temple deep within Mother Earth, Tara. It was not a far distance from her home. The entrance was cleverly concealed in the face of a rock formation within the deepest and most dense area of the forest.

By now moving into such places seemed quite natural and the torch-lit tunnel was familiar and welcoming. I could see many passage ways along our journey through the tunnels, but we finally arrived at a giant double door which had a crystal imbedded within each door. The doors were carved in images that represented fertility and birth. The wise woman placed each hand upon the crystals; they glowed at her touch and the doorways opened. We entered a large, warm room. There were people within this room already. There were those preparing the birthing chair and fires as well as busily making sure all sacred items were ready for this occasion.

I saw several men there also. Crow Woman said, "You have those who would wish you well in this glorious time of birthing. They wish to speak with you, and then they will await word within the waiting chamber. James was first to come forth. He helped me down from BeeBa, who had carried me constantly from that point upon entering the woods trail where I lost my strength.

"MiryAmah, my beloved sister," he said, "I have come to be close to this miracle, for I am told that my brother has indeed resurrected and visits his beloved family."

I smiled and felt great joy for I loved James as a blood brother would be honored. I told him that this child that would emerge was the proof of what he had been told, and that I was honored that he was there, for this tiny son of Jeshua and myself, conceived in purest love, would be named in his honor. I could see that he was much moved by this news, for tears rolled down his cheeks. He kissed me lightly and said, "we will speak more when you are on the other side of this moment of emergence. I love you, my sister." He then stepped back and Josephus came forward.

This protector of mine, this one I, too, loved as a sister loves a blood brother, said simply, "I bring you a gift, for I knew your time was near and it seems that my timing was perfect, for I have just arrived." He then stepped back and Mother Mary came forward. Her eyes were sparkling even as the tears trickled down her beautiful face. "How can I serve you, my daughter?" she said.

"Stay with me please, Mother."

She explained to me that my parents could not be there, but that they sent a message. She handed me a beautiful pink quartz stone that I remembered well from my childhood. The message was simple, that their hearts lived in this stone. "My mother used to give me this stone when she and my father had to go away. They told me long, long ago that they had put their love within this circular stone to keep me warm and safe." Now I cried freely, for I missed them greatly. I was indeed blessed to have such wonderful, loving parents.

My child demanded entrance, so the men were rushed out of the chambers. Mother Mary held my hand and Little Mary wiped my forehead, for I began to show the signs of last labor as the sweat poured out of me. Little Sarah stayed by the cradle that little James would lie within. Her job was to keep it protected through prayer until her brother came. She prayed sweetly in her musical-child voice.

I was ushered into the birthing chair. Usually the husband would be the one to catch the baby. At Sarah's birth, Little Mary held that honor, but this time I wanted the Mother Mary to be the first to physically hold her grandson. She had lost so much when Jeshua was taken from her life. Such sorrow she has known that I wanted her to feel the joy I now felt. She moved to the position and the child orgasm began. The great floating and flooding of passion entered my body. Just when I looked to make sure Mother Mary was ready, I thought I was within an hallucination, for there instead of the Mother Mary sat Jeshua, with his own mother behind him, her hands upon his shoulders. He was smiling at me.

"No, you are not dreaming, my love," he said, his voice echoing notes of tender love and adoration. "I am here to catch this child as he emerges into the physical, for to do so is an honor and privilege that no father should miss. I was too ill at the birth of Sarah, who I know forgives me, but for this one I am here and I am ready."

At that point James emerged, slippery and perfectly formed, into the waiting hands of his father. Jeshua's smile was the unmistakable sign of his joy. He patiently waited for the mid wife to cut and tie the cord between mother and child. Then he gently kissed his newborn son and held him high as he said, "Dear God Almighty, how can I ever thank thee for the joy you bestow upon

me. A perfect wife and perfect children, all perfected by love!"
Then he wrapped James in swaddling blankets and brought him to
my breast. Sarah asked if she could leave the cradle to be with the
family. The wise one nodded and she came to my side. I lay there
with my newborn suckling his first milk, my husband holding me
tenderly, my little girl holding the hand of her brother, and Mother
Mary too, with her arms around her own son as she watched him
glory in his own child. Little Mary had stepped back and was
holding the hands of Josephus and James, who were brought into
the chambers for this moment. The wise one began the song of
birth and we all joined in. We knew the words, even though each
birth song was slightly different. We just *knew* them. This moment
I will always treasure as I do this family of love.

Blessed be,

FAREWELLS TO MY BELOVEDS

Every family should have moments such as that experienced by Jeshua and I with our little family on that birthing day, complete with Mother Mary and the brothers. Jeshua also had sisters, but to leave their homes for this journey was not a possibility. Especially when the reason would have been simply a *feeling* that their presence would be timely.

After the emergence, as I rested I could see and hear Jeshua and his mother across the new-babe room catching up on their lives. The babe was done with the first important suckling and now laid to rest within his cradle and we had been bathed and moved. Sarah rocked James gently and sang him a little lullaby. I did not want to eavesdrop upon Jeshua and his mother's conversation but I did hear her tell him that she had been notified that he survived but did not know how she was to believe it. She thought it meant what everyone was saying, which was that he ascended into heaven and was now a god, and God. I then heard Jeshua say, "They must have a demon or a god, and now they call me THE GOD!" "My God!" he exclaimed, "what will they do with me next?" I then fell asleep and their conversation was their own private communication.

When I awoke I was in the new babe chamber. Jeshua sat next to me with a big smile to greet my awakening. As I opened my eyes he said, "So, my little mother awakens." I felt a warm glow for his presence was usually just a dream, and I was beginning to understand that this was not so, not this time.

"How did you know my time was upon us?"

His reply was somewhat surprising, for he said, "I always know of your condition and your heart voice, for I study with the Lamas of the high mountains and they have taught me well. They have also taught me to be in two or more places at once." I know I looked at him strangely for he laughed a great belly laugh, the one that I love to see, and he touched my face gently with his hand, brushing my hair from my cheek as he explained.

"I am here just as physically as you are, my dear beloved, but I am also deep within a meditation cave with a high Lama, my teacher, there to monitor my progress in this journey."

I looked at him, puzzling, and asked, "Are you telling me that you are in two places at once, in full physical body?"

"That is so, MiryAmah," he whispered, "but my physical vehicle back in the high mountains is limited in ability to function, for I am still training in this technique, so my teacher keeps watch. I will eventually be able to transmigrate to several locations all at once and still be fully functional."

"Oh!" I exclaimed, "This should reinforce your Godhood even more should your appearances be overlapping and recorded."

"We are all Gods, MiryAmah, as you well know, and anyone could do these things if they but believed and if they moved beyond the road blocks of greed, power and negation of their own being as duality souls. I will teach you this technique when you are ready."

I pondered this option then finally proclaimed "If this means I can be with you in the high mountains, then let it be so and in all due haste."

He would stay with me for the first month of our new babe's physical journey. The new babe chambers opened into the forest and Sarah and BeeBa played among the trees with the little people. They were so child-like and free, such humorous little beings. Sometimes Sarah would go to the Crow Woman for her teaching. She would soon go to the Misty Isle to begin her training, but after all we had been through as a family, I was reluctant to let her go. She was far past the usual beginning age of five, well into her seventh year. Crow Woman was catching her up on her first training, with my permission of course, and I could not have found a better teacher for this bright child.

The family members, who also stayed with us, held little James constantly, but they also had their own accommodations within the underground temple. James and Josephus often came to cuddle and rock the new babe. Uncle James vowed to always protect his little namesake. Jeshua was touched by this announcement, for he and James were not always in agreement when he walked the holy land as master teacher. They were typical brothers, friends one day and fighting the next. When James said to Jeshua, "I live to complete your mission where you began it, my brother," I thought Jeshua would collapse in tears, and my concern was great. James was greatly concerned also at this reaction and asked what he had said to bring such sorrow to his beloved brother. "I cry not for sorrow, my brother, but for joy, for I have always loved you greatly and now you honor me with this dedication. How is it that I am so blessed?" he asked.

"When I saw you upon that cross, suffering and defiled for bringing the voice of God, I knew then that you were indeed all that you said you were and more," James said.

Jeshua replied "But I am only as you, my brother, and every other being who is simply a child of God seeking to reunite with this Divine Father/Mother Source."

James looked concerned and replied, "I know, beloved brother, but they will only see you as divine at the moment. We will have to be very skillful in bringing your humanity into their minds and hearts, for they believe that the flesh is weak and the spirit is strong. They see you as spirit only, with no desires of the flesh, which they equate with weakness."

"If only they knew of the many times I have doubted, stumbled, followed the wrong path, and even cursed that which sent me to this mission, then they would see the humanity in me. I am far from perfection, but that journey is why we all came, is it not?"

Josephus joined the conversation then and said, "They see this seeking for experience as weakness, my brother, and they cannot allow you that truth." Jeshua dropped his head and said in the most sorrowful voice, "They cannot allow me a wife, a family or a great passionate, physically manifested love for my beloved MiryAmah either it seems, for they are now saying I was born without the sacred sexual merging of man and woman, and I know that they call MiryAmah a prostitute repented and only a friend to me. What will they do next to kill the feminine in all of us? Where is my beloved friend John, who assured me he would carry on with the mission and protect my beloved wife and mother?"

He seemed to begin to anger as he continued, almost yelling, "Now they would build churches that would enslave the followers, control their minds and make the woman feel guilty for their natural ability to bring passion to life. What fools that will not see!"

James said, "I am working on this issue, my brother. I assure you as long as I live and breathe, your work shall continue. I need your guidance; however, and I am thrilled to see you once again in the flesh. How can you direct me in this?"

Jeshua said, "I dare not come to you in the flesh, as you see me now, so I will come to you in your dreams, brother. But I warn you; you may indeed die for this cause. Are you ready for that possibility?"

James thought a moment and replied, "You died for this mission and I can only know that if this mission is that important to you, then it is equally important to me."

"Do not qualify your dedication upon my back, brother. Do this for yourself, for our mother and sisters, for our brothers and fathers, for our daughters and sons, our grandchildren, and nieces and nephews, for all who would live a better life if they only loved and respected the duality of creation."

"So be it then," James said, "and now, brother, I take my leave, for I am needed in this work I now know that I must carry upon my own back." Jeshua kissed his brother good-bye and Josephus came forth.

As Josephus walked forward he was holding the hand of Little Mary. He said to Jeshua and myself, "as you know, my wife has passed from this life years ago and I an now a widower. I know that she was done with this life experience and my children are well cared for, and some already grown and on their own paths. I never believed that I would feel a great love for another woman, one that I would wish to be my beloved, but I do, much to my own surprise," he said as he looked lovingly at Little Mary. "I do not know how this beautiful lady has hidden for so long, for I have seen her often in your service and presence, MiryAmah, but she was always covered completely in her robes. At this blessed birth-time of little James, however, she was not so robed and her face struck me like a lightning bolt. I have known that face in my dreams for a long, long time. I often spoke of this face to my beloved wife before she passed and she was so sweet about it; she simply said that there were many loves in one's life, and that somehow this face would show up and comfort me one day, for she felt not betrayed, but blessed by this presence. Because I loved her greatly I would always tell her that I could not love but her.

231

She would then just look at me, knowing that this was not true, even if I did not yet understand. The women know these things. Now, here I am, wanting to be a husband once again, wondering if I am truly worthy of such an honor, and holding the hand of the dream woman of my vision."

Little Mary then said, "I did not believe that I could ever trust or love a man in my life, for all I had ever known from my experiences was that of pain and sorrow. The only man I have known whom I truly trust and totally love is Jeshua, and my love for him is that of a sister, not a lover or wife. Then, upon the birth of James, I chanced to look into the eyes of this sweet man, Josephus, standing there so close, waiting for the arrival, and low and behold, there were equally kind eyes, and there, too, was the sparkle of one I recognized as one I would love to merge with in totality. I have been in the presence of this one before, but I have hidden from his eyes. Instantly this time, as I finally looked at him by chance, I *knew*, but feared that I was presumptuous in this *knowing*. When Jeshua held his hands out to catch his son, therein upon his first breath, as if not thinking, we, Josephus and myself, reached out to each other and connected by holding hands. The energy surged between us. It was as if we *knew* at that moment that this we would do also."

She then looked sadly at me and said; "Yet I have vowed to serve you, MiryAmah, and I am in deep concern, for my desires pull me in two different directions. My heart will surely break into two halves in this matter."

I could see the sorrow and heartache written all over her face. "Concern yourself not, my friend, for to be my sister-in-law is the greatest joy you could ever bring me. Follow your heart, for you shall always be in mine, there close to my very soul, no matter where you go or what you do." Jeshua said too, "this is so true for myself as well. I could not wish for a better match then the two of you, for my beloved brother. Go in peace and love, and may God protect you always." They then left, hand in hand. I knew my life would change, as would that of my dear friend, Little Mary. To carry the name of Mary is never easy. Mary's give the most from their hearts, and suffer the most for their generosity. I hoped that this Mary would be more protected from sorrow and pain.

Mother Mary came close to me then, and put her arm around me and comforted me as only a mother's total love could do. As my friend disappeared I began to sob. Mother Mary held me close and without saying a word, took me into her heart. She knew how difficult it was to free those we love so much, especially when it meant that they would not be there present in our everyday lives. She had given up so much in her lifetime. She knew. She had to leave soon also, for it was the brothers who brought her and they who would take her home again.

Jeshua came close to me, also, and wrapped his arms around both of us saying, "I must bid my brothers farewell, and you too mother, but I will return, MiryAmah, so do not let your heart mourn my leave yet." He followed them out then. I felt the absence of them all and went to my children. "Sarah," I said, "Bid your uncles and grandmother farewell," and she hastened that way, with BeeBa following. He was like a family member now and always nearby and usually with little Sarah. The two of them made quite the pleasant sight as they walked together in the path their father, uncles and grandmother had taken. I took the newborn babe to my breast and rocked and sang him his song.

Blessed be,

THE DIVINE PASSION

Jeshua stayed for a month as he promised, which other family members did as well. He left soon after his mother and brothers, however, for there was work for him to do in his new experience now unfolding in the land of the east. I still found it hard to believe he could be there, even as he was here with me, for his embrace and his physicality was fully present to all my senses. It seemed like the most fantastic miracle to be with him and have our little family together, for so much of our family life had been shattered and spread to the far reaches of Tara-land.

I was very lonely for little Mary right from the moment of her departure with Josephus. She knew our parting would not be easy and she did not come back to my chambers to re-experience the parting again. Jeshua told me that he believed that Josephus would one day move to this land of the Gaul's, for he said his brother felt that his work neared an end in the holy land. I hoped it would be some time soon, for I could not envision life without my dearest little Mary nearby to laugh, cry and work with.

We kept to the underground chambers and the deep forest trails near them, for the most part, while Jeshua and I bonded to our newborn. The paths hidden from the outer world led into the forest, and Little Sarah spent much time out on these secret trails riding BeeBa and discovering nature. The little people of the forest kept watch upon her coming and going, for they knew she was innocent of possible danger and they could feel her connection to them as they perceived her actions and her interaction with all nature. I will always have a tender part of my heart reserved for these little ones, for they watched out for me as well in my own youth. I knew once placed under their protection that safety was insured.

James was a contented baby, emerging into his father's hands from my sacred womb. All women's wombs are sacred, and all fathers should experience this "catching of the child." This was a perfect beginning for this child and his nature reflected this practice of old, for he was delighted with his new life experience and smiled from the moment he opened his eyes. Jeshua and I used some of our time together to catch up on the unfoldment of events since last we were together.

"The followers want to make this church, MiryAmah," he said, "but the Romans want their skins first, for they have their temple gods and they are jealous gods, for certes. They would make of the followers lion food, for they go against the governmental religion of the warrior rulers. If the followers did not argue and fight so much among themselves as to what I am, a man or a god, they might be able to unite and move forward in spite of the Roman oppression," he continued.

I answered with a heavy heart, "is it all a waste, my dear husband, this work and this effort we have been through?"

Jeshua thought for a moment before he said, "The Great God sends all beings to experience something that the source cannot since *All Knowing and All Seeing* prevents this type of discovery. So all beings have a mission, from the tiniest insect to the greatest animal, a mission of discovery for the pleasure and sake of the Divine. We fall in there some place, MiryAmah, but as human beings we have the ability to integrate our memory of the past with our now, and to even envision the future. This is a great gift and a heavy burden at the same time. Since the animal, plant and even mineral kingdoms all live in the now, they are not constantly judging who is better and who is lesser among themselves. They simply live for the moment and react to the energies that surge through their beings. They do not separate those feelings of the moment, for they trust their intuition."

"The mother deer does not hide her nipples when she nurses the fawn or feel inferior for so doing. She does not envy the stag for his great horns either, I assure you. She simply does what she knows she must and accepts that she is fulfilling her purpose. So, my love, you wonder what this has to do with our mission? It is this. All things have a purpose. Our purpose was, and ever is, to bring balance to the human experience through equalizing the energies of masculine and feminine as reflected within and without God the Creator. This task we are given because we are best suited for such enlightenment action. We have not wasted our time because we have been working toward our goal and fulfilling our purpose. We will always find a way to do our work, just as that graceful doe will always find a way to nurse her fawn, without apology or guilt. If we fail, we shall try again and again and again, and so shall she, for she sometimes fails in motherhood and mourns her loss as we would, but a new day will bring a new way to the same goal and she will continue. That is the way of it. We waste nothing, but those we assist waste the opportunity to bring their experience into joy when they stop the flow of truth. We are only the messengers and cannot take responsibility for those who distort or destroy the message. This message will come again and again until they face its truth because God desires so."

Having stated this, he announced that it was time for him to take his leave. My eyes filled with tears and he dried them with his own hair and told me that he would return to me soon and teach me the transmigration technique.

"Do not touch me when I step back from you, but you may watch this process, for soon you will have use of it," he said. He then kissed me passionately, exciting every fiber of my being, and stepped two steps backward and began to vibrantly glow. The brilliance of this light should have been blinding to me, but it was not. I watched Jeshua's form merge with the light until it had totally absorbed him. Then the light circled me and shot straight upward and out through the ceiling of my chamber. I stood in amazement then collapsed in great tears.

I felt someone rubbing my back as I lay there upon the floor sobbing. I looked up to see Crow Woman, and I knew that she fully understood this grieving I must endure and somehow felt my need of her tenderness as she came to me now when I needed her strength and wisdom.

"Let this grief flow," she said, "For there is always such a reaction when two souls such as you and Jeshua must part."

I felt miserable and engulfed in my anguish as I said, "Why can't I have a normal marriage and a normal family life!" My tears flowed like great rivers down my cheeks and soaked my long hair. Patiently and compassionately Crow Woman reminded me that it was because that was exactly what I had come to change. "Normal would imprison your beautiful soul, MiryAmah, as it does so many women now, as you know well, and your beloved would have to hide his respect and his honoring of you."

I knew the truth of this but felt angry just the same. She continued by explaining, "Normal is not necessarily right. You came to make things right, not to experience the norm." I knew she was correct in her response, and I also knew she understood my need to speak utter nonsense from time to time when in great frustration. Feelings just had to flow through words, whether making sense or not.

My babe began to cry then and I could feel my breast full of the mother's milk for his nourishment. I arose with my wise elder's assistance and went to the cradle and put my James babe to suckling. I could see his father in him already, for his hair was of the same hue and his expressions already echoed that of his father, especially his smile. What a treasure this child is. What a gift given to me by my beloved. How would anyone understand that the Jeshua they thought was dead and risen to heaven was still able to father a child such as this, and our sweet Sarah, too? I knew that should that secret become known in places ruled by fear, that my children would be targets for the enemies of truth.

The truth that everyone feared was that they were part of God and thus had a responsibility as a God Child. They were more comfortable fearing something separate from themselves. The God that they thought they knew fed on fear. They did not want change in their belief system. The greatest belief system of all is love, however, and I was part of a great love, manifested and maintained in a complicated manner according to the traditions of the time, but nevertheless, this love lived strong and true, and I would always believe that the truth of love would ultimately overcome the fear and the lie.

As I nursed my babe, Crow Woman stayed to visit with me and told me that little Sarah was ready for her training now. "I cannot bear to send her away too," I said. "Then do not do so," she instructed. "I was once one of the teachers upon the Misty Isle," she said. "I could begin her training and I assure you that there are those near by, unseen for the most part, that are friends true and who would be able to help in this task. Allow me to be Sarah's teacher, but please allow Sarah the final decision," she said. "I would be greatly pleased to make this arrangement, my dear wise friend," I told her.

At that moment, in came my little forest discoverer and her buddy BeeBa. She was excited because the little ones were now making themselves known to her and teaching her about the tree people.

"The trees talk to each other, mother," she exclaimed excitedly, "and they love their children. They call them *seedlings* and they like us for the most part, but they do not like to be forgotten when we use their bodies to build houses. They still live on in the houses and we forget," she said. She continued, almost out of breath from the excitement of this discovery, "And the little people live under these trees, mother, and sometimes within them, in secret little houses, and they have children too, mother, and they love them also."

As I watched her report to me her grand discovery for the day, I knew that, indeed, she was ready to begin her priestess training.

Not wanting to miss the opportunity, I asked her, "Would you like to begin your priestess training, my little one?"

"No!" she said flatly. "I will not be a priestess, I will be a queen!"

The wise one then said to her, "Would you not like to be a high priestess and queen, my child? For to be so would be beneficial for the service you would be called to give to your people and your Queendom. It would make you the best queen ever," Crow Woman said to the child that stood so confidant there as she pondered the idea.

Sarah thought for a moment and replied, "OK, but only if I can stay close to my brother and my mother. They need me."

We laughed at her monumental sense of responsibility even at the tender age of seven, but in those days a girl child was often given in marriage by the age of ten, and sometimes even rushed into motherhood by the age of twelve or thirteen years. The old priestess ways would not cheat a child of their budding years thus shortened and leaving her then weakened. Those in the care of the priestess were not deemed ready for such merging until at least eighteen years of age and after training in the ways of the feminine. I hoped she would consent to priestess training for many reasons, but mostly to allow her to be a child until she was ready to be a woman in full bloom.

Crow Woman and I explained our plan to Sarah and she was delighted, for she had made some friends among the little ones in the wood, as she just voiced, and she did not want to leave anytime soon. She agreed then that she would train to be a Priestess-Queen and that she would be the best one ever. She would make sure the little people were rewarded, she said, for all the good they do in the forest and for keeping her and her mother safe as children. Sarah was such a serious seven-year-old.

I was given a beautiful house on the edge of the wood for my family and myself by some of the new followers my disciples were bringing to the cause. They wanted to see me more often and they wanted to keep the children and I safe. According to my disciples, who were now visiting me and preparing my new quarters, there was no doubt that Jeshua was both god and man, and the fruit of my womb was proof of his humanity. To them it was comforting for they were beginning to understand that they too were of God, created by God and children of God, all sons and daughters of that which they emerged from.

They were not far removed in their understanding of the concept of the Mother God birthing the universe, for their pagan understanding was still strong within their minds and hearts. It was the belief of the Roman rulers that held that god was many beings and the most powerful were the male gods. It was the occupying Roman people who felt that gods could be jealous, angry and controlling and who sought favor of such beings by being just as mean and controlling.

The ancients called these beings Annunaki, the creator gods, and they believe they fed on blood in order to stay immortal. Some thought them to be angels and some saw them as demons. This fear of those deemed more powerful than oneself was the controlling factor in many nations. So it was that religions seemed to follow the path of fear rather than the path of love, and the fear always required blood and sacrifice and pain. There was much to overcome in the equalizing effort we and many others sought to bring to this experience upon Tara.

I moved into a new home where my disciples tried to keep me in total comfort, much to my embarrassment, for I loved to keep my own house and do my own water gathering. It took me a while to understand that the sisters loved to have the opportunity to carry my water or prepare a meal for my family. I finally relented, but not totally, for I would not be one to be waited on hand and foot and grow weak and lazy. Little Sarah soon began her priestess lessons and rode upon the back of BeeBa to the wise woman's home in the deep wood each morning. Disciples took over the task of keeping her safe on this daily journey as they walked with her through the secret trails, using a different one each day to keep the trail from appearing frequently used. The little people were always there too, following along secretly off the path, watching and playing great funny tricks upon the sisters to the delight of Sarah. My beloved little Mary was with her new husband, and happy, I hoped, in this new love and life and now a sister truly tied within the law of the land to me, as tightly as she was heart tied and now totally my beloved sister. Life was good to us.

Jeshua, true to his word, showed up shortly after our move and inspected the entire household as any husband would. "Where is my sleeping shelf?" he inquired. "With me, of course," I said, "for I would not waste even one night that you were home being anywhere but in your arms."

"Oh woman," he replied, "you would cause such a scandal back in the holy land for the practice of separate sleeping quarters is their preference there, remember?"

I replied quite frankly, "Maybe for them it works, but not for me." I was beginning to get used to the idea of him appearing out of the light from time to time. I was not sure how it worked but I was extremely glad it did work and I was very glad to see him physically in my presence once again. When a husband so loved must often go away, the homecoming is sweet.

"Shall we rest then, after your long journey?" I said, knowing well it took him but seconds to arrive here at our new home. His answer was evident as he simply took my hand and we closed the door to my chamber.

We found much comfort in each other there upon that sleeping shelf we gladly shared. He would come often, monthly at least for the first year, and then disappear for many months at a time, *upon a mission* he would say. I always had a vision of his place in time and space, for my dreams were vivid and controllable now and I could seek him out easily. I could often see him speaking with people who looked different but were familiar to me at the same time, and he was teaching now, and studying also. There seemed to be less danger in these places I saw in my dreamtime and I was thankful for that. But now he was not in my vision, he was in my arms. He told me that he would train me to do as he could do, this flashing in and out of time, as soon as little James was weaned.

The vibrational level, he explained, would be too high for a suckling child to handle, for, as Jeshua clarified, "one must bring every cell in their being into this high vibrational mode before one can partake of the transmigration of energy. The part of you that you would leave behind would be just as tangible but the energy that would course through you in both modes would not be compatible for the child, whose delicate system could not tolerate such a high degree of light vibrations. Your very milk would be super-charged and harm this child, curdling within your breast before suckled, I fear. So be patient a little while longer, my love," he said, "and soon enough you will visit me as I do you, and not just in a vision, either."

"Before I leave this time, for I can only stay a day and a forth night, I would like to meet Ranulf of the wood, the master mason." Jeshua said as we lay talking. "Would you chance that he know of your presence then?" I questioned.

"He is of the brotherhood and I have learned that he is a sage," Jeshua said. "Just as there are those wise sagas, those of the feminine force, he is of the masculine force and a wise sage and an ally in this mission. I believe that there must be some attunement within the building he prepares to supervise and I have learned of a technique used by the Lamas in the high mountains which I believe should be utilized. I must confer with him on this, even as you and your sisters discuss how to bring the sacred feminine energy therein also. We both have our work to do together and with our sisters and brothers specifically."

"I like the work we do, just you and me alone, best," I said, changing the subject to suit my desire, as I looked at my beloved with the fire of my passion in my eyes, no doubt.

"If you can light the fire within this church place the way you burn that passion within your being, surely the feminine will be alive and well within the walls of such a place." With that statement he took me in a great embrace and rolled on top of my body in closeness that lovers crave. For this, I thought, I live and breathe, for my passion and my heart had taken control of my great physical need to be merged with my love, my sweet and strong masculine husband. My heart pounded shamelessly within my chest, as his did also. His kisses and his touch drove me wild and I knew no control of my responses once he joined with me, which was soon, for neither of us could wait a moment longer to be thus united. Our passion surely must have fed the universe with its great exploding energy. Surely God would experience a wondrous discovery as we let our physical needs take control of our physicality. This was the power of the masculine and the feminine in divine action. This was the expansion of Love. Jeshua and I gave into this expansion, as we always did, totally and completely, but this time there seemed to be a more brilliant exploding light, a louder hum, a Divine moan of pleasure that was joined with our own moans. To be in this one moment was worth any effort it took to arrive at this place of totality. Our souls merged. Our bodies reflecting this oneness, our hearts beating in unison, our breath hot upon the others face, warming and blessing the union. Our mouths, hungry for the taste of the other, nibbled and touched tongues to the utter delight of each of us. We kissed each other's eyes and whispered longings into each other's ears. Our hands were running wild over the surfaces of the beautiful bodies we offered each other. How could there be fear of this passionate union of man and woman? How could anyone fear such ecstasy as Divinely created with two energies merging like this? I will always know that Jeshua and I are the perfect lovers, who loved perfectly and completely.

Blessed be,

Reflections and a Third Pregnancy

As I remember my lifetime as Mary of Magdalene, or MiryAmah, I will always remember best the passionate love that Jeshua and I shared. While it is not my purpose to amaze you with such memories, it is important for you to know the scope and nature of our relationship, for your history has left much out in the name of the cause as seen by those who think they know what is best. I have never before spoken of such intimate times during this life experience, and I shall not bring them up again unless the truth of such moments helps to bring an understanding of how beautiful a well balanced relationship can be, even in adversity.

I regret to say that the crucifixion of my beloved did not end the pain and terror for those who would dare to think differently or question the status quo of the times. Even so, Jeshua and I agreed, before our emergence into this time period, to work toward the balance of the masculine and feminine energies as reflected in attitudes and societies in experience. We knew we could not bring the simplicity of the mission out into the light in a straightforward manner. We could not just simply say, "She is as good and worthy as He, and if you would understand this concept and reflect it in your living experience, your journey would be more blessed and your distance from the Divine Source much less."

It is the distance from the Divine Source that brings true sorrow. The real mission of all in physicality is to constantly move closer to this grand homecoming.

Ignorance is a dangerous foe nevertheless, for it will do anything to stop growth and knowing, and thus movement closer to the Divine Source that sent all out to find their way home again. If we had just laid out this truth in it's celestial simplicity, those who wished to control through stagnation would have stoned us to death, for it is really their fear that allows such negating attitudes to become appealing. Consequently we had to be subtle and endeavor to display the truth in our own relationship and the way that we interacted with others as prime examples. We knew well that the major task would be to bring the feminine up to the equal of her counterpart, the masculine. It is well known that Jeshua held no bias against the women, for he loved us all as we did, and always will, him. The women followers grasped this concept readily, but many of the men could not open the doors of their minds, long closed and sealed by societies that ingrained such lies. Lies only live in ignorance, and to dissolve a lie then, was a threat to the security of those supported by it.

When the mission became side-tracked because of the decisions of those in powerful positions within the government and religious factions, (the crucifixion) to salvage the effort it was necessary for Jeshua to allow the followers a chance to build upon his death and the sorrow of it. As I have said before, he did die to that life, for he could nevermore be the same man walking among his family, friends and followers. He couldn't be a man at all to those followers, for they wanted a God. It is a sad fact that the most precious aspects of your life you often have to lose to appreciate. This is also true of the group, as well as of the individual, and the followers did not truly understand or appreciate Jeshua, and certainly not myself, as the messengers sent to them from the Divine. They believed that change was necessary, they were in total accordance with that, but they did not believe that women were a part of this change as leaders or equals. When they lost Jeshua they remembered that he had said he was a Son of God, but they forgot that he told them they were also.

As you can see then, the most basic truth that could have saved everyone was rejected. Even so, those apostles left behind, once they had regrouped after scattering far and wide when the danger and terror manifested, did move into what they felt was the mission after the crucifixion, and they suffered terribly for their efforts. All the horrifying scenarios you've heard about -- they suffered. They were stoned, crucified, murdered, tortured and degraded, and all but John died gruesome deaths as they held to the cause as they construed it. Peter was so chauvinistic, as you would term it now; he truly believed that no woman had the brains to make her own decisions, much less decisions that impacted anyone else. He soon forgot that Jeshua did not hold that attitude and his memory became dominant. Andrew was just as ignorant in many ways and his memory of the mission was shaped by his attitudinal mode as well. I say this now as I have said so many times before, *ignorance resists change.* Even though Andrew loved my beloved friend, Sarah, (Little Mary) he would not listen to her, or ever believe her capable of blooming into the magnificent oracle that she became. It would have been impossible for him in his entrenched attitudinal prison, to allow her as his wife to hold a position of such wisdom, for he felt that only men were true channels. This stubbornness and unwillingness to see what Jeshua had demonstrated and taught to them, that the women deserved the same respect and opportunities as the men, was the root cause for much of the pain endured by all the apostles and by all who would buy into this line of thinking down through the ages. The masculine just could not, and still cannot, elevate itself into enlightenment by leaving the feminine on a lower level of esteem.

Even with this daunting reality before us we knew that we must carry on with the mission, even if it had to be at a level of subtlety that would go unnoticed and build slowly until it would present itself strong and no longer a truth that could be hidden from the masses of people, one day. (Hopefully that day is soon to dawn.) So I moved forward with the building of the church and with the council of twelve disciples plus me, in the land you now know as France but then called the land of the Gaul's. I worried about the building project and my disciples spread the teachings. I was amazed at how the Gauls were more likely to accept this truth. The Roman rulers were not able to stop their open minds from listening and learning of the life of Jeshua and myself and all those involved as this mission manifested in this time period. We felt we had a chance here.

Not long after my beloved left once more for the high mountains of the east, I knew that I was again with child. Our passionate reunion was very productive, if short in duration, for Jeshua's visit was brief. I was happy, of course, to yet another time be privileged to see the results of Jeshua's and my perfect love, yet I knew that this would mean developing time for this babe within my body temple and then suckling time. So the lessons in transmigration of the body would have to wait even longer. I would not be able to go to my beloved as he could come to me because of the frequency of the body energy when involved in being in two or more places at once in physicality. Having the children so close to me proved to be a great blessing, for I was plainly too busy to feel sorry for myself. Yet, my heart felt heavy and I missed every second of our separation.

Little James was only about a year old when I became expectant with our third child. The Emergence Temples of old would have suggested waiting at least five years between children so that each child could be properly enjoyed and developed before another came to the family. The priestesses would have given me a tea so that I would not have conceived. They would advise the young parents to wait, yet those times were now gone for the most part, with only pockets of places still connected to the Divine Feminine through such temples. Jeshua and I did not live a normal life, though we reflected what should *be normal* as far as love and attitudes between a man and woman in love and within a sacred union. His popping in when I least expected it kept me from planning our lives as I had been instructed to do when attending the priestess schooling. There would be no expected pattern to follow for us, you see, and when I was with my beloved I could not resist sexually merging with him in full passion at every possible opportunity. I could never risk taking the tea of decision to delay the emergence of a child that might desire to come through us, for I did not know if I would ever again see my love and could not chance missing such an opportunity. As a result, little Josephus was born just nine moon cycles after Jeshua had come to inspect our new lodgings.

Again, Mother Mary, who I was closer to than ever before, came to my side. It was she that told me that my parents had both died, and it was she that held me as I cried. I remember her words so well. She said, "It breaks my heart to be the one to bear such bad news, and with you so close to birthing, but your mother had requested that I be the one to tell you of their passing. Your father has been ill for some time and he knew his time was close. Your mother loved him so much, as you well know, and she wanted to stay at his side throughout this journey and on into the next. She held him when he took his last breath and then she just said to her friends and family present, "it is done," and she died there with him in her arms. Before she left she said, "Tell my beloved MiryAmah that she should never give up this divine mission she and her own beloved have embarked upon, and that I will work with her from the realms of the heavens, for I will enlist every angel I can find to be at her side. This child, my MiryAmah, is the hope of the feminine and a Divine gift to the masculine. I leave her in your hands, Mary, Mother-One."

Blessed be,

JOY IS ON THE OTHER SIDE OF SORROW, WAITING PATIENTLY TO BE DISCOVERED

I really wish I could tell you, the readers of this memory, that somehow my relationship with my beloved was always perfect. Relationships are meant to bring you closer to perfection, (that is ever the goal) yet you would not have a perfect relationship in physicality for there would be nothing to learn from it. In other words, do not evaluate your relationships on perfection, rather on how you move through all aspects of such a union. This is true for any relationship. I know that now, but like you, for I am no different, I assure you, I have moments when I forget this truth also.

Mother Mary came just before the birth of little Josephus, as I have already said, but I jumped ahead of my memory for I had no name prepared for this child yet. I awaited my beloved Jeshua's return to make such a choice. For someone who has the ability to be in two or more places at once, I felt that he would check in from time to time so that I could tell him of this glorious event, but he did not. This memory I relate to you is my own, and I cannot speak for my beloved, for his memory is his. As you may have noticed, within relationships there are always slight differences of memory, for each one involved in such experience remembers moments from their own perspective. So it is with us as well.

It is important to understand that Jeshua and I were no different than you are. Even so said, as I remember this time it seemed that Jeshua did not walk through my dreams as he had previously. I wondered how we could have such a passionate encounter and then be so parted. I grieved this separation greatly and feared he would not be present for this birthing.

Now also, after Mother Mary's message from my mother, I grieved my parents passing as well. I knew that they could only be happy together, and I was sure they were still blissfully together, yet I would miss them as well, even as I missed my beloved and my heart-tied friend, Little Mary. I often wondered why I must be so separated from those I loved so much. Mother Mary has always been so tender and patient with me, and having her near me as the time approached for the birth of our third child was a gift that touched my heart as none other could.

I remember well her elegant hand softly rubbing my protruding tummy as she talked to this child yet to emerge. She said tenderly, "Your father loves you, child, and your mother does as well, and you come through love into this world that needs your presence. You shall bring great joy to those in sorrow." As she said this the babe totally flipped over within my womb, in readiness for emerging. It was a sight to see, this flipping of this child within, for my abdomen could not hide the deliberate decision of this tiny one. His time was near. "I see that this one does hear me well," Mother Mary said.

"Oh yes, Mother Mary, for this child often comforts me when I cry great tears of sorrow and longing for Jeshua. I find much comfort from such a tiny soul there knowing and caring of me so tenderly."

I then dissolved into tears and asked, "What has happened to my beloved, mother? I have not seen or heard from him since the day of this child's conception, and I fear that he is gone from the children and me forever. I am not sure I can go on without him."

"You know that this is not true, for Jeshua and you are part of the same duality, the same over-soul. No matter what happens, that connection can never be severed," she said. "I know this in my head, mother, but in my heart the knowing is not there, and I fear such a great loss," I sobbed.

"No," she corrected me, "it is your <u>head</u> that does not know and your heart that <u>does</u> know of this Divine connection that is forever. Now let us work on this task and move past the mind that struggles and into that great heart that has so much strength and so much love there within."

Mother Mary said this with the conviction of one who knew well that other affairs demanded my immediate attention. At that moment I was taken by sudden contraction and great pain was upon me. I screamed! I felt as though a great hatchet had buried itself into my belly and laid me wide open in pain. I had never before heard Mother Mary's voice so loud and commanding as she called for assistance.

"Come at once" she announced in a voice not of terror but of urgency, "the time for this child's emergence is now and this child will not wait a moment longer." My sisters came to me forthwith and they prepared me to move to the emergence temple but it was soon evident that this child would not wait for such a journey. I remember well the pain of this one, for with the others I experienced discomfort but not such searing pain.

My private room was made ready in all due haste, and I was carried there by the strong arms of someone that seemed so familiar to me, yet through the physical reactions of the moment I could not focus upon him. I actually remember wondering, between the painful contractions, if my beloved had returned to me? Yet I knew the vibration was only similar in frequency and not he whom I wanted so greatly to be present and to comfort me.

The room was barely readied before this child came forth. A birthing chair was improvised by tilting a chair to the proper angle. The sisters rushed around with clean towels and bandages and any other supplies needed for this time. As for me, I just didn't care, my heart was heavy with sorrow and the physical pain was great. Mother Mary held my hand and I remember her saying to me, "let go of the pain, my sweet daughter, the sorrow you hold deep within you is the cause for this discomfort you feel and is a danger to yourself as well as your child. Remember your love for this child and especially for Jeshua, and allow this one to emerge in total love, not sorrow."

"Why can't Jeshua make a miracle now?" I cried, as I convulsed in a painful contraction. "He is so good at such things for others and now when I need him, where is he?" At that moment, in the birthing-catch position I heard a familiar voice say, "he sent me, MiryAmah, and he wants you to know that he would be here if he could make it so." I looked down and saw the beloved brother of Jeshua, Josephus, waiting to do the honors of catching this child. I then realized that my beloved friend, Little Mary, held my other hand.

"Peace be, my friend, for this child has come to continue the cause of peace and must come forth in peace." At Little Mary's words, I felt my body relax and the babe move through the channel of emergence, slowly and perfectly.

As I felt the relief orgasm of the emerging babe, I could see on the face of Josephus that he was delighted to stand in for his brother. His smile was broad until suddenly he stopped smiling and the look upon his face I shall never want to see again. Great tears formed and coursed down his face as he cried, "Why, oh why, this?" Mother Mary and Little Mary both looked immediately at Josephus and paled also.

My concern brought back the pain I had let go only moments before and great rivers of blood flowed from me and I lost consciousness. I saw Josephus performing the life-kiss upon my babe. When I awoke I was frantic. I had been unconscious for about a quarter of an hour, I was later told. There was much concern for my survival as well as the babe's. I was weak from loss of blood and continued to hemorrhage, yet the placenta would not expel itself. The wise woman was summoned and again I lost consciousness. Finally I awoke to a quiet room and the wise woman was there with me, using herbal treatments to stop the flow of the life's blood.

"You gave us a scare, MiryAmah," she said, "but you will survive, I assure you, for you have great work to do yet, do you not?"

"Your placenta did not want to give up the womb, for your sorrow kept it attached there," she explained, "but we have brought it forth and now it will continue its purpose within the temple and merge with other sacred substances for use in healing." My first thought was for the babe, this child of passion and the one so comforting to me in my grieving time. "My child, how goes it with this babe?" I asked anxiously.

"Someone did a great job of teaching your brother-in-law the kiss of life, MiryAmah, for he knew just the right amount of breath to give to this child to bring it into the physical and now the child does better than Josephus."

"What do you mean?" I felt such panic to hear this news.

"This child has a power not yet developed and as the kiss of life was given to the babe, the energy surge to the kisser of this one took its toll." I could see the scope of the matter upon her wise old face. "Josephus is in good hands, my child, and he improves even as we speak," she reassured me, yet I could read the uncertainty of that statement in her eyes. "This has been a most difficult expectancy," I said, "how could so much trouble ever bring good?"

The Wise One smoothed my hair back from my forehead with her soft, silky, old hand and said, "trouble is the affect of doubt and both these are but aspects of the journey called life, where you learn that out of such moments come blessings and spiritual growth. It is a growth toward the Divine, as you well know, my sweet child-mother." She then whispered softly into my ear, "are you going to grow from this trouble or are you going to stagnate in sorrow and deprive your child his chance to find his way in this life experience. You are the way-shower for the light of this child. Would you dim such a beacon?"

It was then that I learned that I had another son. I asked to see him and Sarah brought him to me, his sister, my beloved first born. She was beaming and as she approached she said, "Thank you for the brother, mother. This one is as sweet as the other but he seems to glow more brilliantly, almost as if he were super-charged. Sarah always could see the life glow around all beings. Do you think he is a baby sage?" she asked. "Can I be his special guardian, mother, for I think I must watch over this babe carefully, 'cause he needs me?"

For being just between eight and nine years old she seemed so grown up and so wise to me. She seemed always to be well beyond her years in wisdom and dedication. She then laid the babe in my arms, and as with every child and mother, it was love at first sight. When I looked back at Sarah her brows were wrinkled with a look of concern, the unanswered question still upon her mind. She repeated herself, "Well, mother, can I be the guardian of this child 'cause he needs me?"

"Yes, my dear, you are from now on the special guardian of this little boy, even into his manhood. You better prepare yourself for a big job, for I can feel his great energy already and he shall be a handful." She smiled and hugged us both. "Don't worry mother. BeeBa and I shall keep this one busy and out of harm's way, I assure you." I then fell into a peaceful sleep while my little son suckled and my daughter held watch.

Within this peaceful sleep I saw my beloved Jeshua as clearly as if in my conscious presence. He looked stressed and a bit ragged in appearance. "I love you to the depth of my soul, MiryAmah," he said. "Please forgive my absence these last months, for I have been in great need to others. I knew you could carry on in this love emergence, yet I knew of your great sorrow as well and it pains my heart to see you so."

In this vivid dream I remember saying, "Did you even know that a son was forthcoming?" He simply nodded his head and a great tear ran down his cheek. "I knew," he said. "Did you know that your brother suffers from the trauma of giving this child the life kiss as well," I retorted.

My beloved just looked at me, his patience even forgiving my irritation with him. More tears found their way down his face so dear to me in this vivid dream vision. He finally said, "My brother has given much to you and I out of pure love and devotion and for this I will be forever grateful as I am sure you are too, my beloved one."

"How can it be?" I remember asking him in this dream, "that he must give his very life for this devotion?"

"He shall not lose his life," Jeshua assured me. "I will move heaven and hell to see him restored to health if I must." His words seemed so full of conviction that they frightened me. "My mother shall not lose another son in this life experience, not yet!" He then kissed me gently upon the head and asked what name we would call this new son of ours. I told him that we had named our first son for James, the brother to Jeshua, shall we call this one Josephus for this brother who has done so much for my safekeeping and for this new son? Jeshua smiled and looked deeply into my eyes as he said, "This would please me, beloved. Let it be so." And so it was.

I awoke then to the soft cry of my tiny new son who was trying to gain my attention. I have never seen so much light around a child and I thought to myself, what an impact you will make upon this world, little one. "Welcome to our lives, Josephus."

Sarah was still there, the ever-faithful guardian as she had promised and she echoed my sentiments when she said, "Welcome, little brother. We shall have much fun, you and I and little James and BeeBa too." Then I noticed that she had James with her now. He was wiggling and squirming about and wanting to reach for his new brother and taste his tiny hands for at his age everything went into his mouth first, for the sake of taste, discovery and for comfort with his teeth coming through.

"Oh no you don't," little Sarah said, as she saved the tiny hand of Josephus from being taste-tested. "You will have to wait a little while longer before we let you and this new brother have a go at each other," she wisely said to James.

He clung to her with the familiarity that illustrates how great bonds are made in life experience, for he felt as safe with her as he did with me. I kissed his little cheek and he gave me a very wet baby kiss. I wondered how I could ever be a good mother to two babies? The usual waiting time was not taken with these two. Somehow I knew Sarah would be a great help and that comforted me.

"James must be changed, mother," Sarah announced, "so we will leave you for now, but we will be back soon," she said, as if to reassure me that all was in good hands. Her reassurance was a great comfort for I knew this to be truth. Then she left with James tottering behind her. I thought to myself, "when did that child learn to walk?" Sarah turned and looked back at me and threw me a huge smile and said, "This is your birthing day surprise, mother. We have been working on this surprise for over a month now." Children are such blessings.

Little Mary came into my chambers then and I remember saying "Little Mary, I am so glad to see you, and I am concerned for Josephus." She kissed both baby Josephus and I and asked if I had chosen a name of yet and then bid me not to worry about Josephus, for he was in God's hands and she was sure he would recover. When I told her of my vision and the name chosen for this new babe she smiled, cried and kissed me again upon each eye.

"You have had the wisdom and the vision to give the greatest gift a soul can give to another, that of the divine name in honor of one so loved. For this you have saved the one so honored, for I could not request such a gift, but knew if you named this child thusly and from the depths of your great heart, that my own beloved would be totally healed, and now it is so."

I looked at her in amazement and said, "How is this so, my friend?" completely forgetting her oracle training and practice.

Little Mary explained, "When Josephus performed the kiss of life he asked this babe to stay and to live a full life for the sake of his brother and you, who loved him unending, as well as for all needing his presence in this opportunity of life. When he made this request he then poured his own divine soul essence into the child to sustain him until his own energy could take over, for my beloved knew that it would take such purity of energy to sustain this one. This type of energy exchange is highly connected to the vibration of the name one holds and comes from the depth of the being in physicality at that point within."

"When you gave this child the name Josephus then, without being requested to do so, you gave back the energy in equal measure to the source, my own beloved, in this case. You gave back pure love and devotion, the only source of replenishing such essence. Thus in this you gave as much to me as well as to he, whom I love greatly, for you gave us our lives back as a duality also." The tears that ensued were of pure emotion and gratitude. "You have already given me so much, including your name, of which I will always be grateful and keep sacred as well, but," she continued, "I must tell you that I have resolved the Sarah experience and I must now ask to share that name once again, for I cannot disconnect from it as I thought I could.

"You want to be known as Sarah once again?" I questioned. "It seems that the vibration of that name is connected to my soul as well, just as you will always be known as Mary of Magdalene, I too know that I will always be known as Sarah, but I feel the need to change the sound just slightly to better fit my energy as it now expresses."

"What would that be, then?" I inquired again, seeing how important this was to her. She looked long out into what seemed space and said, "I guess I will always be a Sarah, thus I wish the name *Asara* to be restored to my being." I thought about the many times I had to think twice before I addressed her as Mary, for she always seemed as a *Sarah* to me too.

"Perfect name, my friend," I said, "and I feel that this vibrational coded name has always been yours to keep, so shall you be to me always, Asara Mary, my beloved friend. We knew as only two friends this close could that this was the perfect time to make this pronouncement and the perfection of the naming in completion.

At that moment Mother Mary rushed in, all out of breath. She was smiling happily and even as she was running toward us she was saying, "A miracle to behold, my beloved daughters, for Josephus has come awake and is asking to be given food, for he is famished, he says. Shall we join him and watch the wonder of my son coming back to his full energy together?" Asara ran from the room in joyful tears, and I knew where she was heading. I said to Mother Mary, "let us prepare and present a feast and rejoice this day!"

Blessed be,

FORGIVENESS IS THE KEY TO CHANGE

The great feast was enjoyed by all, even with those who served us finally settling down within our midst to partake of the celebration. We celebrated the joys of this new babe and the restored health of Josephus, I remember well. Asara and little Sarah, now not so little, took turns holding the sweet glowing babe that had just emerged through me and into his uncle's hands. I knew that this uncle would play an important part in this newborn's life, yet I still worried about my own beloved. Where was he, and was he safe, and when would he come home?

Sometimes a home is a place too seldom graced with the presence of all of its members, but it is still a beloved home, nevertheless. That was the case for Jeshua, as he told me many times. It was usual for family members to remain within the household of the new babe for about a month. When Josephus was about two months old the family present at his birthing were still there with me. It was then that Jeshua finally returned. He looked much the same as he had in my dream visions, those visions that worried me so. He was indeed stressed and in deep sorrow and his clothes were tattered and torn.

He seemed to be cheered, however, as he held his newborn son and asked, "Did you name him as we agreed in our shared dream vision, MiryAmah?"

Why I doubt my own dreams I do not know, for this statement validated the truth of such meetings in the realm of the dream and I answered, "Yes, little Josephus has been named in honor of your much-loved brother, and now you have a son for each of those brothers you hold so dear."

At that he broke down and wept great tears and such moans of sorrow came forth from him that I knew not what to think. I ran immediately to my beloved, this strong man there holding his tiny son, a man now crumpled and weeping desperately. I embraced both he and our tiny child in his arms, our child born of the purest love and passion, and my heart seemed to break also, for I could not know how to stop his tears, much less the cause of them.

"What shall I tell my cherished mother?" Jeshua cried, as he looked at me with eyes in deepest pain.

"Of what do you speak?" My alarm was great but I had no idea of the reason for this emotional outburst.

"How can I even remember what I have witnessed without my heart breaking once again?" he said, as he seemed to pull his grief-stricken voice from behind a large obstruction within his throat.

"Just tell me as best you can, my beloved, for your sorrow is my sorrow and together perhaps we can bear this great pain," I assured him.

"It is James," he said. "After the crucifixion he especially realized the scope of our work and he could see that the other apostles were moving into the attitude of old, the attitude that only men are worthy in God's eyes. This was the very thing we have incarnated to correct and we have shown a perfect example."

"James was determined to minister, as an apostle and as my brother, to this situation and to correct the misdirection. Why could they not see?" Jeshua cried. "What fear keeps a man from loving a woman, for it was she that was the channel for his very physicality and the love between them is the seed of life itself in this physical world." Jeshua still cried, but now with silent tears, for the sobs now were channeled into the telling of this story and I knew it was a bad situation to take such a toll upon my beloved.

"James held true to our mission, which was his as well, and every man and woman's task to do. The followers are being unspeakably persecuted by the Romans," he said. The concern and compassion upon his face spoke volumes. He continued, saying, "The absolute cruelty to these we left changed is astounding, for they are a threat to the ways of old and to the false concepts of the gods as the Romans see them."

He stopped for a moment to reflect and then said, "James came upon Peter preaching one day and Peter had twisted the role of the feminine to suit his own conception, and though his heart was pure his mind was twisted in this attitude, one we had spoken of so many times and now I see he still held to his own exclusive view. James argued with him and Peter stalked off in anger. Before he left he told James that I had given him authority to lead the followers and that the brother of Jesus was not more important than he, the rightful leader now. Those listening to him evidently were forming a firm bond with Peter and they were angered that his authority would be questioned so."

"How could you know this moment?" I asked him.

Jeshua explained that he was practicing the transmigration technique and was disguised as a follower within the crowd. He witnessed this confrontation first hand. He was so angry he said he wanted to attack Peter, but realized that his masculine energy unleashed in such anger would do more harm than good since it would reveal his existence. To keep his death illusion sacred and his life now secret was the only means of hope at this point. Should he reveal himself he knew that all his loved ones would be destroyed by the madness that grew. The need to shape this new theology into a power was mounting, and power struggles always resulted in pain and suffering followed by death. That is why the Romans were so brutal, for they could sense a power in this memory of our mission, be the memory conveniently shaped and more and more resembling that which it was opposed to, but nevertheless, a power worth their concern.

"When Peter stomped off, even as my stomach was about to wretch, James called the followers attention to him. He said, "Listen dear ones. I know my brother well, and I knew of his teaching and he did not want women excluded or defiled for he loved women, as they did he, and he wanted you all to love and honor your mothers, sisters, aunts, daughters and friends as equals of same worth and same capabilities."

The crowd, especially the men, became agitated and loud. They refused to allow James to continue.

"You fool," one said, "would you trust your life to a mere woman?" James answered, "I did upon my emergence from our Mother Mary, did I not?"

The angry man retorted, "The only good thing that woman ever did was to have one child without the stain of sin, but that wasn't good enough for her. She fornicated and bore more children because she was greedy for glory."

This statement wounded James, for all of us love and honor our mother as no other and there is not a part of her that is stained or corrupted. Our mother is surely without sin.

"I am not sure what you mean." James yelled back at this man, "but I know that you dishonor my mother and I tell you that no child is born in sin and that the sacredness of childbearing is not stained, as some would have you believe, for it was designed by God, who would not devise a plan of such flaw. Her purity at the birth of my brother was the same pure state she was in, and every woman is in, at the birth of any child," he said with the conviction of one who spoke total truth.

"Some followers began to argue with the women, who took the side of James, even knowing the truth of his words, but their husbands took the other view, that of women being sinful and tempters of men. Husbands were hitting their wives and shouting profanities at them. Eventually they cast them out of the area and James was appalled, as I was also. He had not noticed me yet, for his attention was on trying to stop the angry men from abusing their wives and daughters."

"Stop!" he shouted, over and over again. "See what happens when you buy into such a lie, for now you are hurting that which loves you the most, that which brought you into this life, that which brings you your beloved children. You dishonor yourselves in this unspeakable treatment you give."

"When he finally got their attention, the unruly crowd turned their anger upon James. They accused him of causing the problems in their families by filling their wives' heads with nonsense, and now they would have much sorrow within their families because he had caused them to forget their place."

Jeshua said, "I can't remember who actually hurled that first rock toward my beloved brother, but it hit him in the heart physically and emotionally. He fell to his knees with a look of astonishment written all over his face, for these were those who claimed to love me, his brother, acting in such heinous manner. I ran to protect him and even tried to use some techniques I had learned in the high mountain place, but knew instantly if they discovered me that my entire family would die to suit their agenda."

"An old man, crying as I was, held me back even though I struggled to be free to protect James. Rocks flew from every angle for there was a project nearby to build a well and a convenient pile of hand-sized rocks had been stored there. The entire scene seemed to play out in slow motion. Every stone flew as if floating on time and found its target, with blood splattering well out into the angry crowd. James was stoned to the point that every inch of him was a bloody mess. The old man that held me back yelled to the angry mob, "how could you say you love Jesus and then stone his beloved brother?"

"The leader of those in revolt shouted, "we cleanse the memory of Jesus by separating the clean from the unclean."

At that point the old man was stoned also. I ran to his side and he said, "They know not what they do. Forgive them." I remember saying those same words myself as I hung upon that dreadful cross. The old man died in my arms.

I went to James nearby and tried to cover his body with my own. Some rocks found their way to my body as well, hitting my back and my hip, but the pain was nothing compared to my inner emotional feelings for my bloodied brother lying there about to die. And why? Because he understood me, and what you and I came to do, MiryAmah."

"As I lay there upon him, trying to shield him from further injury, he recognized me. "Forgive me," he said, "for I have failed.""

"I kissed his torn face and whispered, "There is nothing to forgive, my sweet brother, but can you forgive me for not being able to stop this madness?" He smiled and said, "let us forgive each other for not having the strength to stop such an ignorant and corrupt power that it hates the very essence of itself. I shall have to go now and join our father, Joseph, for I can see him here now. Can you see him too?" he asked."

"I looked up and there was my father, the one that so many deny was actually my beloved parent. He was smiling and said to me, "Fear not, Jeshua, I will take James with me now.""

"As I watched him speak to me I saw a rock fly right through him. I knew then that he was in spirit, and I was not hallucinating, and that the best man I knew would escort my beloved brother to a better place. Then I saw James leave with him, even as I still lay there upon his bloodied body. I sobbed and sobbed there upon the evidence of our mission being twisted and merged with the old corrupted attitude."

As I listened to my beloved tell this tale I struggled for breath between the sobbing and tears that threatened to drown my very being. Jeshua continued. "I was suddenly grabbed harshly as someone shouted, "do not touch this tainted one, old man, for he would bring the master down should he live."

I must have looked aged in my sorrow, for this one who uttered such nonsense looked me right in the eyes and did not recognize the master he proclaimed to serve so faithfully. I said, "Do you really think that your master would want you to kill his brother, who tried only to continue his work?"

The man standing over me seemingly transformed into a monster as his face contorted and he spat, "He would certainly want us to cleanse his family of this vile lowlife that is a dishonor to his memory, you idiot!"

"I cried out, "This man has not dishonored his brother, he has honored him and your sister and your mother as well!"

That was the last I remembered for upon this statement I was beaten until I lost consciousness. When my consciousness returned I found myself lying in the street with the elder man there dead beside me. The body of my brother was gone and so were the followers. The silence was deafening. I thought in my mind, "followers of what are you that would do such a thing?" Then I answered myself, saying out loud, "Madness! That is what you follow-and you call me the idiot."

The look upon Jeshua's face as he told this story was that of great despair. In a voice strained from crying he said, "I looked toward the heavens and I cried in great sorrow and asked, "Dear God, what will become of the mission you entrusted to me and my beloved MiryAmah?"

As he said this I knew that my depression in this pregnancy was more than just the absence of my beloved. I was feeling his sorrow as well, for we are as one truly and we are in this mission equally.

"How long did you lie there in that forsaken place of betrayal?" I asked.

Jeshua seemed to look through me as he still snuggled our tiny son close to his chest and said, "I know not, woman, but I do remember that after darkness had fallen that it was the women that finally came to me and took me to a safe place where I was again in need of much healing. I believe I was within the temple of old there near the city, but in the mountains. I remember not much for I was too injured by the stones thus thrown, but I remember an elder wise woman giving me herbal drinks, and other women putting salves upon my injuries."

"Oh my beloved," I said, "But could I have been there in your time of need, for I would surely have healed you with my tears."

"You were there," he said, "for you are always in my heart where I need you the most."

"How long did you stay with the healer?" I asked. His reply was somewhat surprising to me, "Until I rescued myself," he said simply.

I just looked at him and thought, "How could that be so?" when he smiled brightly for the first time in this meeting and explained. "I can see your puzzlement, my dear. You have not yet had the transmigration training. It takes tremendous energy to do this thing, to be in more than one place physically at the same time. My teachers of the high mountains have taught me well, and they have cautioned me on the perils of physical damage to one of the bodies in action. They did not however, at the time of this occurrence, teach me how to deal with such a thing, for what one body feels, so too does the other, and there are definite techniques to separate the experiences on a physical level."

"I cannot imagine how you could deal with such a problem," I said.

"Well, as it were," he continued, "my master teacher knew immediately of my peril, for he is soul tied to me, and you knew also, my dear, and he began the necessary rescuing of the physical body there with him. He knew that the rescuing of the other presence with the healers was happening. In haste he had to teach me to go physically through time and space and gather myself to my essence in order to merge and return. But I was weak from the effects of this tragedy, and the going was difficult at best. It is hard to explain, but at some level, you see, my beloved MiryAmah, we all rescue ourselves," and this was key to my strength returning enough to accomplish this merging of myself once again."

"Then what happened, tell me it all for I must know of your welfare," I pleaded.

"Then I ended up back in the cave dwelling of my master teacher, and my emotions could not be controlled, for greater than ever I missed you, my mother, my children, my brothers and sisters, and those dear friends who remember the true mission. I knew of the child's readiness to emerge. I hoped my brother had received the message I sent him, to be at your side should I not make it, and for him to honor my son and catch him into this world. I just could not be consoled in my grief so my master teacher transported me, even in my weakened state, through the heavens and to this place here with you now. Before I came, however, I remember meeting you in the dream and the naming decision, but I was not sure if this was a reality until I confirmed such with you and held this little babe, my second son, in my arms." Then he dissolved into tears again, but this time the cries were softer. I cried also. Our little family had to cleanse our sorrow.

I am not sure how long we cried, but when we were finally spent from this washing away of sorrow, we noticed that we were not alone. There with us in a circle was Mother Mary, sobbing as if spent herself from the grievous emotion. I knew she had heard about her beloved James. Josephus was holding her as she cried, "My poor James, how could they do this thing to my beloved child, one so giving and so loving?" Mother Mary said over and over. Next to James sat Asara and she too was face-wet from tears, and she held the hand of little Sarah, who had her head buried into her name-sake's chest and who was obviously crying in deep sorrow herself. The healer, the wise woman known as Crow Woman, was present, as was Flip, who always shows up when his energy is needed, and they stood behind the family with their hands upon the shoulders of those in deepest pain of sorrow. I knew that they were giving needed energy to the mourning ones. All had come in unnoticed and heard the story of James. Who summoned them I do not know. I never asked.

When Jeshua looked up and saw the group, he handed the babe to me and went to his mother. "Mother, do not sorrow so much, for father has James safely with him now." Then he embraced her and they wept together. I could not see how any more tears could fall, but somehow I knew that we needed this time to release. I cried then again, for my parents, for James, for all women whom I knew would continue to suffer, for Mother Mary who would lose her sons because they loved and honored women, I cried for my beloved who felt he had somehow failed in this Divine Mission, and I cried for this child in my arms who had entered such a world as this.

Jeshua finally turned his attention to his brother Josephus and Asara. He embraced them both and thanked them for all they did for the children and me and thusly for him as well, in keeping us safe. "Brother," Jeshua said, "you did get my message to be present for this emerging, and I am gladdened that you brought our mother to assist in my son's birthing."

"It is my honor, Jeshua," Josephus replied. "But you have your work to do in your merchant business," Jeshua said, "and I know that you sacrifice much to honor me so." Josephus said, "My sacrifice as compared to yours is but nothing. I have sent word to my son of my first wife, whom I hope is with James now in heaven, to take my affairs to himself, for I shall not return to a place that kills my brothers." He then looked hard and long into the eyes of Jeshua and asked, "with your permission I would like to stay here in this place with MiryAmah, where there is some memory and honor to the divine mission, for Asara and I would like to bring our child up in such a place."

Jeshua and I both forgot our tears then and looked at Asara and it was evident that she was indeed, with child. We both answered at once saying exactly the same words, "Oh! How wonderful and what a pleasure it would be for our children to grow up together."

Little Sarah lifted her face from the bosom of Asara and looked up at her and said, "I will help you with this child, I promise, for I am getting good at keeping the children. You can count on me, my beloved friend, friend of my mother's and my friend as well."

Asara smiled and hugged little Sarah close and simply said, "I shall need all the help I can get, for I never dreamed that I would be blessed with such a gift as a child. I thought my father had taken that from me long ago."

I remember looking at her in such compassion and saying; "in an odd, terrible sort of way it was your father who brought you to us and to this life, Asara." She simply nodded. "Can you forgive him his ignorance and realize that the early experience was part of your preparation to be the compassionate one that you are now?" She simply said, "I shall try, my friend."

Mother Mary then said to us all. "The greatest honor you can pay to all those who suffer and to myself as well is to forgive those that hurt you in ignorance, and even those who know better, for it is only in forgiveness that change can happen. This mission we are all vitally a part of depends on change."

Then she stood up and asked to take the babe now held in Asara's arms, for somehow, unconsciously, upon learning of her expectancy I had handed her little Josephus, the namesake of her beloved husband. "May I hold my grandson?" Mother Mary asked. Asara handed her the tiny babe and she quietly walked away with him, leaving us all to wonder where she was going and what was on her mind.

Blessed be,

Life Goes On

As is probably most evident, my memory of this time and place with my beloved is wrapped around my experiences and what is most prominent in my memory vision. There will be those who will scrutinize historical documents, especially the Bible book, to look for validity, but I tell you that your very lives are remembered differently by those you have shared them with as well as those who were simply onlookers, and yet each truth is nevertheless valid. Each being has their own perspective and perception of events that mold them, and of which they in turn mold once again. It is true that each individual's contribution to this project of physicality changes the entire totality of it, yet each person perceives their part differently than those who perceive them, and this is the confusion of the memories.

So it is with this story of my life, a *her-story*, not a *history*. The blessings and the challenges are ever many in any journey and the journey of physical life is no different. As I return to my memory I shall never forget how Jeshua suffered as he witnessed over and over again how his loved ones were tormented for their love and support of him and the truth we beheld and offered to share, as was our mission. He saw his very life and the memory of it taken away from him and remolded to suit the agenda of those who thought that they understood, but they did not, as I saw my own identity smeared with mud. The mission of bringing the masculine and feminine back to equality was, and still is, the most critical adjustment needed to bring the Divine Goal back into vision. That goal is, of course, PEACE. You all came to find this true treasure and to bring it as a gift of purest LOVE back to that which loved you enough to send you out in the first place, as a parent would send a child out of love out into the world to experience, when their heart really would rather keep them safely at home.

Jeshua stayed for a while with us, his family now of two sons and a first-born daughter and me, his devoted wife. He was just as devoted to me as well, for in duality no one takes the priority in sense of worth or devotion over the other. But the truth was evident. Rumors that I was reunited with my love were finding their way back to Rome, the center of control of this part of the world at the time of my memory. The Emperor was afraid of losing control, yet knew that the empire was almost too vast to keep under such constrictions, and thus had reasoned that to control the people he must control the spiritual leaders of those within his jurisdiction. This group of Jesus' followers, outside of the controlled thinkers, was certainly a threat, for the Emperor had just gained a slight control over the Hebrews and now this.

So, as it were, you see, not only did the followers lose vision, but they were persecuted as well. Should it become known that Jeshua survived the crucifixion, much less have a family complete with sons and daughters to carry on the line of Jeshua, the children of the god they themselves created, then there would be some question as to who should be in charge and why they were wrong. Should it be James, the brother that they stoned and took away, never to be found again even though legend has twisted this tale? Should it be Peter or Andrew, brothers who felt that they knew what the master *really* meant when he said all those things about women, or about anything? Or should they realize that Jeshua survived, would he come back to take the reign again and correct the corruption of his memory? Then, the worst possibility of all was, what of Mary of Magdalene? Jesus had trusted her the most and had made it plain that she was his co-leader, not his follower. What if she took the leadership and allowed the women again to believe that they were in equality with the men? Would that not upset society as it was known? Would that not be a threat to every man, since, they all reasoned, Adam was so tempted by Eve when they knew equality in the garden and look what she had done? As you can see, the stakes were high for those who felt that control and power were the way.

The whole affair was a very complicated one, for certain, and it was soon evident that Jeshua had to disappear once again for rumors were spreading. There was the problem of the children, for we would not plead immaculate conception as so many have decided was the case for the birth of Mary and her son Jesus. Much later that concept would be more accepted, but in this time it was the mere seed of an idea. So Jeshua and I began a plan in cooperation with Josephus and Asara. They would become the *Parents in God* to our children, or Godparents, as you would now term such an arrangement. When the Roman soldiers came, and we knew they would, our children would be known as their children, for the sake of their safety.

Asara, my beloved friend, who believed that due to torture by her father for not following his command to marry a wealthy but cruel merchant, would never know motherhood, was now with child and the honorary mother of three more children.

I will never forget our meeting when Jeshua and I asked this favor of our sister and brother. Asara, now becoming large with her own child, stood abruptly at our request and looked as if one in shock when we proposed this plan. "You would trust me with your children, whom I know you would lay your very lives down to protect?"

Jeshua answered her; "we have already trusted you time and again with our children and our very lives, my dear friend. What makes you think that we would stop such faith in you now?"

She looked mystified as he continued. "We must devise a plan to protect these children of ours for in their very beings, in the codes of their physicality, is the key to peace and it must be preserved. We do not ask you to do this just for us, Asara and Josephus, we ask you to protect that which God has sent to change this world gone so far off balance that it hates part of itself."

He looked long and hard at Asara and Josephus, as I did as well, for their faces did not give us an answer and they seemed as if in shock. Then they both came back to full consciousness and total awareness, and they both answered at the same time, "your children are our children and we shall tell all that this has always been so and always will be so, for in truth, your children are the children of all who live and breathe, are they not?"

To hear such sentiment, in its entirety, uttered in unison and in total devotion by these two was the sign we needed to know that this was indeed the blessing we sought. From then on, in public, I was Aunt MiryAmah and Asara was mother. Unfortunately, Jeshua was a family friend from long ago. It had to be so, as I said.

Jeshua stayed a long time it seemed, but in reality it was a mere six months. He departed after this request however, and was gone for such a long time, longer than I would foresee. He still had not taught me the transmigration technique but again I was suckling a babe so again it was not possible.

Asara's babe came soon after the emergence of our own Josephus and a son graced the life of these two so happy for his arrival. Of course he came into his father's hands, as he should, and he was named Braun, a Gaelic name honoring the new country of which we had adopted.

Asara often had both her son and mine with her and eventually suckled both for my pregnancy was difficult and my milk was not plentiful for this child. The boys were three months apart but looked like twins and the townspeople believe they were twins, one named for the father and one named for the land. I am grateful that Jeshua was able to see this nephew before his departure, and he held both babes often, as well as took much time in playing with the other children as well. He always believed that children were the closest to God because they did not believe they were not. He loved them totally, all of them, and often played with the children where ever he was.

The growing threat to the safety of those who were followers of Jeshua and myself began to spread toward us, and we knew that the big house on the edge of the wood would not be sufficient. The masons who had devised an entire compound for this church place I would have built had not yet started the actual building, for they were in location of the materials still. A place had been chosen, but they decided to move that location to the top of a hill where one could see approaching danger more easily, so thus a new town began. This place had the meeting hall in the middle, we called it the Church, with many houses and stables and other such needed buildings surrounding it and fanning out in the shape of a rose. The rose's petals were the model and the symbol of the project, and within two years of the birth of my little son Josephus, the compound was finished. We then all moved to the new community, as did many of the new followers that my disciples had gathered. One secret follower was the overseer of this segment of Gaul, and he did his part to ensure the safety of my family and our mission and appointed a new regent for this area, one who would reside within the castle complex protected by the Order of the Rose.

I always missed Jeshua when he left, and I had asked often of what he did on his times of absence. He told me that he was working at a universal level now and would one day depart to work even more effectively at this inner-dimensional place. I began to cry at this statement, for I could not bear to be in physicality without him some where in the physical then too.

"Do not sadden, my love, for if I do depart I will be even more close to you than I am now, and one day I will come to get you and we will both work at this universal level toward the success of this mission."

At that I allowed the pain within my chest to lessen its hold, and I accepted that in accepting this mission we would not have a life of ease and happiness, for the challenge was great and the need massive in proportion. I did not lose my dreams this time, and I often enjoyed passionate encounters with my beloved within the dreamscape.

I was, one day, called to the Roman Overseer's home for conference, but it was a secret meeting and I was disguised as a wise-woman bringing herbal remedies. Upon entering this one's private chambers he asked all to leave us so that this wise woman could administer her medicine.

His bodyguard frowned and asked of the wisdom of this, saying that surely someone had to make sure the medicines were not made of poison. "This time," the overseer said, "I shall give my wife the honor of that duty, so bring her forth."

The guard, who had put his own life on the line countless times, not because of loyalty, but because he had no other choice, was greatly relieved, for he feared he would have certainly found his death in drinking a potion by a woman. He brought the wife immediately, as instructed, and departed. When I saw this wife enter the chambers I smiled, for I knew her well. She was one of those faithful to the cause, as was her husband, who was the half brother of the original couple who had kept me so safe and secure upon my exile not so very long ago, when I first put foot upon this land.

We all smiled and then the Overseer, who I shall not name, for even now the safety of his family is an issue, said, "shall we begin our plan? I have thought hard on this Regent we must appoint to keep the complex from suspicion, and my wife and I believe we have a perfect candidate and wish your approval before I make it official."

"We know that you must have a regent that would never betray you, for the mission must move on. This regent must be of the utmost wisdom and hold the heart of a compassionate one. She must hold the Eck energy, he said, making me lift my eyebrows, for it was evident he was considering a woman for the position. He then went on to say, "For she will be the one to keep the lineage line chaining on into the future."

I had not heard the *Eck* energy mentioned for a long, long time for it was of the old Goddess ways and had to do with the power used for the benefit of all, not just for the glory of the position or the individual within the position. You might term it thus, "The Divine Power that holds authority for the good of ALL." I was now in rapt attention, even more so than before.

My wife and I have discussed this extensively and it is time, MiryAmah, for little Sarah to grow up and become the person she has been trained and destined to be.

"But she is only just past ten years!" I protested, not wanting my little girl to be grown so quickly. And what could she do in service to this Regent at such a young age?" I worried.

The answer jolted me. The overseer said, "She is the Eck, and in honor of queen *Nor*, for I am a descendant of hers and I bid her all due honor, with the authority given to me by Rome, I appoint your Sarah, Queen Eck-Nor-eial. And you, my dear MiryAmah, shall be her advisor and Asara shall be the mother attendant, for we know of the arrangement you have constructed and believe it a sound one.

"But, your Excellency, there are many who know of her true lineage. How shall we pull this off?"

"We shall confuse and confound those not trusted to keep the truth, for only those with the purest of hearts and the most honorable intentions shall realize the connection of this Queen, be she ever so young, to you and your beloved Jeshua," he assured me.

So thus it was. On the day of moving into the complex, which by then had been carefully constructed with the proper reverence for all the energies of those who donated body and substance to the cause, (the wood, the stone, the very earth, as well as that of the workers) we traveled in great celebration to our new home. Little Sarah led us, the new Queen of this complex, riding her magnificent steed. No, not a huge white stallion, but instead, her little white BeeBa. He was good enough to carry her father into

Jerusalem, she said, and her mother into Egypt, so he was good enough to carry her into this new queendom, as she called it.

I thought to myself, "look out world, here she comes!"

The years passed and the work continued. I could tell you many other stories but this is the story of what it was like to be in experience as the beloved of Jeshua. Josephus was invaluable as protector and as overseer of the trade the community did with other so-called principalities, yet this was more of a *Queendom,* as our newly crowned Ecknoreial had so named it.

We did not always have an easy time in our new quarters, for there were many times the Roman soldiers came to check on us. Asara and Josephus kept the children safely with them during such times. They were amazed at the beauty and wisdom of the Queen in residence, for she charmed them greatly and openly attributed her wisdom to her selectors. Plainly, most overseers would have chosen a young man for this new position. They had no idea how young she really was, for she was in her stride in this position and her wisdom often told her to counsel with her advisors for more information, thus her decisions were always remarkably accurate. I considered that her best attribute, for she knew when to ask for help and whom, and where to seek it.

When Queen Ecknoreial was in her fifth year of reign, so loved and honored was she that there was a celebration planned. It was then that Jeshua found us once again and this time he stayed for nearly six months. He was disguised as a trader friend of Josephus, and only in private did our family call him father or husband. He brought news of the other followers saying, "MiryAmah, the apostles suffer so much for this cause, even as they get it mixed up with the ways that brought the need forth for this mission. And I fear," he went on to say, "that the women suffer still, and even more than before. I regret that most of the faithful shall die terribly for their role in trying to change society."

I looked at him with total sympathy, for I had known for a long time that suffering was the order of the day in such societies of control, and those societies were the normal mode now. "We have all suffered, my beloved, but cannot we remember the times of blessings too, for surely there have been many," I said as I pulled our two sons close, thinking of how much I loved these children of ours.

"You are such a wonder, my beloved," Jeshua said, "for you can find a moment to pay gratitude even in the most terrible anguish. How is it that I was so blessed with such as you?"

"You are blessed with me because I am you, as you have said so many times, just as I am blessed with you, for you are me and we are one, is this not so, my beloved?"

Just then Sarah entered our chambers and said, "Oh no! Here we go again. You two, when together, are so crazed with each other," she said in mock impatience. "How is it that you can be so old and still be so hotly desiring of one another?"

"Oh, my child, you may be a queen but you are still thinking like a child in many ways." Jeshua said. "Bring your wisdom child," I said. "You are called Eck now so tell us why this should be so?" I commanded as only a mother could.

She thought and thought and finally said, "Oh! I see the need of this now, for certes, for the masculine must see the feminine as part of him as she also sees him as part of her."

She looked so smug in this revelation, allowing us to know that our example was understood, and she continued. "This is the law of the universe, so that the energies will be attracted to each other and integrate again and again so that all life will grow and evolve into a ONENESS!"

Jeshua looked at her with such pride and said, "You are a wise Queen, most assuredly, my lovely little Sarah, and I shall forever honor your new name, Ecknoreial, for you represent the truth that youth and adult are not so very far apart and that truth unites them thusly."

Then Sarah dissolved back into the little girl she must hide from the populace, and she ran to her father's arms and kissed his face over and over in fondest welcome and snuggled comfortably within his lap.

The next six months are mine to keep sacred. But when my beloved left I was again with child, not so surprisingly. Jeshua laughed at this situation upon his leaving day saying, "it is a good thing I am not always present, my dear wife, or you would be the mother of many more."

"It is my love for you that manifests a child each time we meet, and the missing of you so greatly that insures the conception, I believe with all my heart, and I hope that this missing of you will not continue forever."

We had to keep this expected child somewhat secret, at least when I was in public. Asara was to stuff her clothes to the point that she seemed with child so that when this babe came she could be the mother to those not in need of the truth of it. Josephus again held the honor of catching the child, for Jeshua did not make this birth either, nor later, nor ever did I see him in this physical life again. But I move ahead of myself, for this time we were graced with another little girl. We named her Tamara, in honor of the goddess of love and devotion, long since forgotten, but related to the name of Tara, the Goddess of the very earth. And she became closely aligned with the earth; for she loved Tara with all her heart from the moment she put her foot upon the sacred soil.

I waited day in and day out for the return of Jeshua so that he could see the beauty of this babe, for she was like no other, patient, healthy and of an exquisite beauty, yet constantly wanting to play outside upon the ground that she loved to eat.

Asara's own beauty became the confirmation for those who would see her as this child's mother, for she was a beauty too, especially after her face was restored now so long ago. I wished I could take that mother honor out in the public, for I was proud of our children, but the Romans were still there watching, and we could not take the chance for the safety was more important.

Year after year passed and still I saw my beloved only in my dreams. He kept telling me that soon I would join him, for he was in a new dimension now, having passed into it shortly after the birth of Tamara. I would not let myself believe this, for I was in the physical and my heart and mind were tied to physicality in many ways, as others in this realm are also, as was the plan, and I could not accept this crossing concept.

The disciples continued to oversee the cause with Martha, who came from the original group there and was of such a blessing to me, especially in my later years, for our bond grew close as we aged. We knew that soon we would have to pass the cause along to others. We felt blessed that our little Queendom had not been overthrown or destroyed, but we can thank Ecknoreial's husband-consort for that, for she took to her heart and her soul a half Roman, half Gaul husband, who was as sentimental and compassionate as she. His name was an odd name for one of this heritage, for it was Erick Aurelius, but we simply called him "Erick." He told us that in the family of his mother, way back was one she revered called *Erick,* and that the rest of the name was of his father's family. He came to know our secrets and he kept them honored and all of us protected, even as his dear wife officially ruled.

But I grew old, as I said before, which is the plan for those in physicality, and one day while visiting Martha, my old friend, I saw my Jeshua there standing behind her smiling at me. He had not changed a bit and still made the blood run hot in my veins though I was elderly now, without a doubt. I smiled at him and Martha looked behind herself to see as to who entered that pleased me so. She saw nothing.

"Who or what does my lady see?" Martha asked.

"I see my beloved here to take me home." I remember my great joy as I reached for his hand. I remember quite clearly that as I looked down at our hands joined so sweetly, it was not the hand of an elder there grasping the ever-young Jeshua, for the hands were equally perfect. I wondered of this thing when Jeshua bid me look into the reflection in a bowl holding the roses that my sweet daughters brought to Martha and I daily. Our sweet Tamara was such a wonderful gardener and she showered the entire complex with her wonderful flowers and her extraordinary vegetables. There in the water of the vase I could see many things reflected. I saw myself young again. Not as a maiden, but as a woman in my prime, and behind this image I could see Martha holding my old body there, rocking quietly with this heavy burden in her arms and tears streaming down her face. I knew I was finally free of this journey. I knew that I was to join my beloved at last, and nevermore to be separated from him. I knew also that my friend Asara, now a widow herself, would take my place as she had already done for many years, as mother to our children and keep the watch that only a mother could. I knew that our children would live on and experience full and challenging, but equally wonderful lives and bring the lineage of Mary of Magdalene and Jesus of Nazareth, or MiryAmah and Jeshua, as we called ourselves, down through the ages so that the desire for peace would ever be present within the physical codes of all that sprung from our children through us. I knew that it would take eons of time to reach this goal, but it would be reached nonetheless. And finally, I knew that no one dedicated to this project, and given this challenge by the Divine Creator, would ever give up. We would all continue until all creation loved itself in totality, so that it could Love Itself home once again.

Blessed be,